*Praise for*

# THE SURVIVALISTS

"A great and engrossing read, Cauley humanizes a way of life that is often made fun of and makes the reader understand why someone would go to such great lengths to prepare for the future, so much so she almost sold me on those Life Preserver soy bars!"

—TREVOR NOAH

"Kashana Cauley's novel, *The Survivalists*, is beautifully written. With language that is smart, economical, and clear, she renders a story that is about relationships and our culture. I love this character Aretha, her observations, her arguments, her irony. This is a nice piece of work."

—PERCIVAL EVERETT, author of *The Trees*

"*The Survivalists* is a hilarious, deeply satisfying novel. Through crisp storytelling and an irresistible main character, Kashana Cauley offers us her sharp and inventive take on our deteriorating present condition. Doomsday reading never felt so good!"

—DEESHA PHILYAW, author of *The Secret Lives of Church Ladies*

"This is a banger of a book."     —SAMANTHA IRBY, *New York Times* bestselling author of *Wow, No Thank You*

"The brilliant and outrageously funny Kashana Cauley shines her laser on all the things that make our country suck, but her wit and calm intelligence make *The Survivalists* such a warm hot toddy of a novel."

—GARY SHTEYNGART, author of *Our Country Friends*

"Kashana Cauley understands all the possible ways in which our lives—relationships, roommates, jobs—can go suddenly, absurdly, inexorably, almost thrillingly wrong. If there was such a thing as required reading for living through the twenty-first century in the United States, I'd put *The Survivalists* near the top of the list. I loved it."

—KELLY LINK, author of *Get in Trouble*

"Kashana Cauley's sharply observed take on the American Experiment is dark and funny and deliciously unexpected—the perfect companion for our chaotic times." —JADE CHANG, author of *The Wangs vs. the World*

"*The Survivalists* is an edgy, darkly funny look at a group of gun-running doomsday preppers hiding in plain sight in the middle of hipster Brooklyn. Kashana Cauley follows her protagonist—a Black corporate lawyer—down a rabbit hole of paranoia and alienation. In the process, Cauley reveals some surprising truths about race, work, friendship, and love." —TOM PERROTTA, author of *The Leftovers*

"*The Survivalists* is a gun blast of a book. With enough power to keep a whole city running, Kashana Cauley questions what it means to live in fear, or through it, and how much of ourselves we sometimes have to lose in order to reveal our most brilliant parts. Even more impressive is her masterful precision in capturing something we've all felt: the need for escape from everyday monotony. This is a delightfully irreverent novel that will leave you feeling alive, prepared for anything, and, most important, understood." —MATEO ASKARIPOUR, author of *Black Buck*

# THE

# SURVIVALISTS

# THE
# SURVIVALISTS

## A NOVEL

## KASHANA CAULEY

**SOFT SKULL**
**NEW YORK**

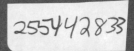

This is a work of fiction. All of the characters, organizations, and events portrayed in this novel are either products of the author's imagination or are used fictitiously.

First Soft Skull edition: 2023

ISBN: 978-1-59376-727-3

Library of Congress Cataloging-in-Publication Data
Names: Cauley, Kashana, author.
Title: The survivalists : a novel / Kashana Cauley.
Description: First Soft Skull edition. | New York : Soft Skull, 2023.
Identifiers: LCCN 2022023060 | ISBN 9781593767273 (hardcover) | ISBN
    9781593767280 (ebook)
Subjects: LCGFT: Novels.
Classification: LCC PS3603.A89875 S87 2023 | DDC 813/.6—dc23/eng/20220516
LC record available at https://lccn.loc.gov/2022023060

*Jacket design by Nicole Caputo*
*Book design by tracy danes*

Published by Soft Skull Press
New York, NY
www.softskull.com

Printed in the United States of America
10 9 8 7 6 5 4 3 2 1

To everyone who's ever fired me

I see people as the nucleus of a great idea
that hasn't come to be yet.

—RICHARD PRYOR

# THE

# SURVIVALISTS

**A**RETHA STOOD IN FRONT OF HER dresser, waiting for something in her wardrobe to declare itself up to the existential challenge of her third first date in a week. The first guy scratched his neck too much and filled conversational holes by obsessing over taxes. He rattled off deductions with the excitement of a six-year-old listing their favorite types of candy, while Aretha wondered if she was already dead. The second guy called himself a "visual storyteller" instead of admitting he was a guy who made abstract, plotless movies only his mother was willing to watch.

Tonight's guy would get gray yoga pants and the closest bar to her apartment. The second he failed to pan out, she'd ditch him, put on real clothes at home, and head out partying with her best friend. Doomed dates deserved athleisure. She was sick of meeting guys who, after they learned she was a lawyer, spent the rest of the date mentally calculating how much less money they made. Or the freaks who thought a first date was the perfect place to showcase how much they loved ferrets or cosplay. No more dresses for guys who didn't have the decency to not suck. Because she spent eleven-hour days glued to her email and phone and searching for the case law that kept companies from imploding, she shouldn't have to spend her precious nights on the apps, attempting to avoid dying alone. The thing about Brooklyn was that you could get whatever you wanted delivered to you in half an hour, no questions asked, from food to live bees. So someone should have invented a service that dropped the right guy off at your door.

If this next guy didn't work out, she was going to suck it up and get a series of dogs, because one of them would outlive her. If she had to live with something that shat, at least a dog wouldn't say anything dumb. Or maybe she'd just die alone. She briefly pondered the perfection of a world in which she'd never have to compromise on a single decision for another seventy years and somehow couldn't paint that world rose-colored enough to stop getting dressed for a third fucking date.

Loneliness had a noise to it. A hum like a running refrigerator had settled down right inside her head that intensified when she saw happy couples on the street or in restaurants, looking at each other with something she'd never felt for anyone. Fourteen years of eyeing guys at clubs who didn't outrank their dance moves flashed before her eyes, a slow death suffered in jumpsuits and under makeup while watching her college and law school friends let their own inability and unwillingness to pay exorbitant rents lead them out of the city to cheaper apartments and the occasional cheaper house full of dogs and partners she sometimes remembered and sometimes didn't. But her own plan had always been to get a partner she'd remember. She could see the corner-office, happily married, property-owning version of herself, even if that other person couldn't quite see her.

She rifled through her bottom dresser drawer and went with her fanciest pair of gray yoga pants, which had horizontal lines across the thighs and calves that made her look fast. They were comfortable to wear and stretchy enough to let her escape at a decidedly medium speed in case the guy sucked. The guy she was supposed to meet in fifteen minutes didn't look sucky in the face. Warm and open, even. But so many guys looked promising until they opened their mouths.

And once she had had to ditch a bad date by crawling out a bar bathroom window, back in college, in her Wisconsin hometown, after she'd made the mistake of making out with a guy who thought no meant yes if he pushed her down a little harder. Ever since then, she did dates on her turf, on her terms. In her neighborhood if she could swing it, in a place she chose, staffed with the kind of bartender who'd run interference for her if the guy truly sucked and she needed to leave in a hurry. That night she'd picked the only bar she knew that had a layout she could draw while passed out. Wooden front door, booths to the right, bar to the left, a back door that opened into a backyard patio with heat lamps in winter and flowers in summer. The bathroom had a window that pushed up easily in case of trouble and would drop her right back onto the street where she started, sans man.

She put on her fanciest sweatshirt to match her fanciest pair of stretch pants, and went outside into the warm late-September air to walk the four blocks down the street to her bar. Her neighborhood was a tiny triangle behind a basketball arena in Central Brooklyn with enough friendly older Black neighbors who believed in nodding at her from their stoops in good weather that walking up the street gave her the same sense of warmth she imagined newly crowned Miss Americas felt the second they learned they'd won.

Her bar, Blaine's, sat darkly on an otherwise well-lit street. Inside, its vibe lay halfway between brothel and family restaurant: the red light, the TV shooting sports into all corners, the tables of adults with kids downing burnt burgers the menu called chargrilled. But the burgers were cheap, and the sports something to look at if Aretha forgot to bring a book or a shitty date. The general vibe was a welcome vacation from all the bars whose TVs kicked out 24/7 political analysis to satisfy the bottomless demand for news about the new president. Aretha's favorite Black bartender had been there every time she showed up. He was good at throwing out asshole guys for her and making her signature drink, a limeade, which had lime juice, vodka, and sugar. She'd created it because she was sick of menus advertising shitty drinks at bars, so she made up one that always tasted good. One limeade wasn't quite enough. Three was too many. She spent most nights in the glow that set in if she had two.

She ordered her first. The bartender, young enough to have dyed his hair gray for kicks, slid it across the bar, liquid and alive. Her date rolled in, looking much better than his already excellent profile picture. He was a crisp and clean Black man in a red-and-black plaid fleece shirt and the kind of trucker hat she thought everyone had stopped wearing in 2005. He looked like he chopped wood for a living right there in the middle of Brooklyn and looked damn good doing it. He also wore a pair of cowboy boots, as if he'd tried to get to the bar a little early and gotten lost two thousand miles west. His trucker hat said "Tactical Coffee." His profile had said something about coffee, but not that it could sub for a crossbow in a pinch. Probably just that he liked to drink it. She thought she'd googled everything about him, but apparently not. He recognized her immediately among the families and the single people seated at the bar, all of whom looked determined, like they considered their nightly drink to be a key part of their superhero origin story.

"Aaron," he said, holding out his hand for a shake.

"Aretha," she said, returning it.

He sat down across from her in the booth. Blaine's had two-seater booths to make dates feel like they were taking place in their own private cave. Aretha liked them because their high walls hid bad dates from most of the other people in the bar. So far, based on one word, Aaron seemed OK, though she still wondered if she'd have the patience and interest to make it through an entire date. At work she'd been put on a new case about trying to avoid government payouts for Hurricane Sandy–related house damage, and a good half of her just wanted to go home and google background info on the hurricane, which she'd missed. Sandy hadn't bothered with her section of the sloping hills of Central Brooklyn, where her freshly minted lawyer self rose the minute the rain cleared and went out to get a bagel along with everyone else in her neighborhood, as if nothing had happened.

"This is one hell of a bar," Aaron said.

"Why?"

"I can't figure out the vibe. Usually bars are kinda goin' for a particular feel."

"I think they're going for all things to all people."

"And achieving a lot of 'em," he said, which shocked her. She thought he'd say something cynical, because six years of practicing law had left her thinking roughly 98 percent of people were born cynics. There was something oddly sunny about Aaron that he enhanced by stepping over to the bar and ordering soda water instead of something that would kill him faster.

Even though she'd heard him order soda water, Aretha stared at it as if an alien had plopped itself down in the middle of their booth.

"You pregnant?" she said.

"What?" he said.

"You're not drinking."

"I don't."

"Why not?" she said, bracing herself for the churchy reply that would send her right back to her apartment and into that future with a dog. He must have taken a long walk in the woods, where the Lord appeared to him in the shape of a tree telling him not to drink anymore, and led him here to take down soda water and wreck the point of being in a bar.

"Sandy caught me drunk, so I don't bother anymore."

Aaron told her a story of a former East Village apartment of his, with stuck doors and swirling hurricane water and an absent rich roommate. "Can you believe he was skiing in Aspen," he said, with a sense of wonder that he might have used to talk about a roommate who'd invented the car. Even she, as someone who made decent money as a mid-level lawyer at a white-shoe law firm, couldn't believe people waited out hurricanes by skiing in resort towns where breathing cost a couple thousand dollars a minute. She took a brief detour from the date to remember the party she was at that night, in a Park Slope dive bar where her reward for escaping a guy who refused to stop talking about zoning laws was getting to sling a drunken arm over her best friend's shoulders while the two of them wailed out "Bad Romance" only sort of in time with the jukebox in the corner. Aaron told her about the bar he used to work at, and the hundred-dollar tip his fellow bartender had stolen from him that night, which he might have used to escape the hurricane. He left with six tequila shots as the chaser, his halfhearted attempt to party with everyone hurricane-partying down in the bar. They'd both stumbled home drunk and alone, but Aretha woke up and greeted the pot of coffee she'd set to brew at nine a.m., and Aaron said hello to the water that seeped through his apartment walls until he'd finally passed out on top of his roommate's dresser, cold and wet and exhausted from being afraid for hours.

"How much water?" she asked.

"Inch after inch of it. It was freezin' my ankles and threatenin' to lick my calves."

"You had cold ankles."

"The coldest."

"That's as far as the water went up," she said, unimpressed.

"You tellin' me you wouldn'ta freaked out?"

"I don't really freak out," she said. "But that does sound terrible," she added, going for the save, because she liked him.

What threw her off about what he'd said was that at work she'd spent the week looking at photos of people who'd lost it all in Hurricane Sandy. Their houses, their heirloom Christmas ornaments, their framed pictures of grandparents and children. Everything they'd ever accumulated, now in wet piles on buckled floors. But at work all that destruction took on the detachedness of evidence. Aretha mechanically scanned pictures of destroyed houses for a sense of scale, and a vaguely itemized sense of what was gone. She looked at ruined belongings with the same amount of emotion she dedicated to dust or lukewarm tap water. It was her job to defeat the wrecked clothing and the broken coffee makers and the people to whom they belonged. But Aaron was a real person, just like all the other people who didn't suffer the misfortune of being pitted against her at work. A full tenth of her heart melted at the cosmic injustice of taking a shallow bath in your own apartment.

If only she could get over the soda water. Aretha looked down at their drinks. The cool green punch of hers and the nothing of his, duking it out on a stretch of brown wooden booth table. Another three of hers would get her to the same place as her last really terrible hangover. A year ago, she and her best friend, Nia, had gone out to celebrate their best friendship and toast Aretha's escape from a guy who couldn't stop talking about the scarves he knitted.

"Fucking scarf guy," Nia said through rum, whiskey, scotch.

"I should have guessed he had a fake British accent," Aretha had said, three drinks in.

"Real friends secretly record those fucking assholes who might be faking their accents so their friends can text them back and tell them," Nia said, tossing an imaginary hand-knit scarf over her shoulder in solidarity.

Aretha had gone to sleep and woken up to a beam of sunlight that sliced right through her forehead to a spot behind her eyes. Maybe Aaron had a point about drinking. She went up to the bar and ordered a glass of soda water and survived the bartender's skeptical look to take it back to the table. Maybe this was the first minute of the rest of her sober life.

She sipped. Salty, bubbly nothing. How the fuck did he do this? He told her about growing up in Texas, which she enjoyed because it always felt comforting when people confirmed at length the stuff you'd already googled about them. Once a lawyer, always a lawyer. If facts couldn't be confirmed they could be substantiated well enough to not pose a threat. He mentioned tumbleweeds, and she remembered tumbleweeds from the Google Street View of his hometown and the couple of YouTube videos she'd found of people driving around it. He mentioned dust, his high school football team, and loving his dead grandma. She nodded, having looked at pictures of all three, although the grandma mention did perk her up. There was something sweet about a guy who mentioned his grandma on the first date. The soda water still irked her, with its threat of sobriety, but his dead grandma tried her damnedest to cancel it out.

She grew up in a series of worn-down apartments on the edge of the fourth-drunkest city in America. A cold city in the center of southern Wisconsin where people drank out of boredom and the civic pride that springs from constantly hearing that you live in the fourth-drunkest city in America. Drinking wasn't part of the culture, it was the culture. She was an African-drinking-American, happy to aim all the suspicion she had in her at anyone who abstained. Where did sober people meet people? How did they celebrate births or deaths or Tuesdays? But Aaron was looking at her in a patient way that moved her off drinking and onto thinking about telling him about herself.

Normally she held in as much of her life story as possible, tell-ing guys what they might want to know only when the conversation wouldn't make sense otherwise. Her last ex nicknamed her Victoria's Secret, and when she got pissed about it, she'd throw her underwear at him instead of answering whatever question he'd asked her about herself. Being a lawyer intimidated everyone, and her parents' story terrified the rest. But this time she sat there, inspired by the liquid interest in Aaron's eyes, telling him about herself without help from a second limeade.

Her work. "I'm a lawyer. Corporate. The kind pretty much every-one cheers against." Her childhood growing up in Wisconsin. "New York is my beach the minute it hits fifty degrees." Her best friend. "Nia was the only other Black woman in my dorm in college. Thank god she turned out to be cool." Her dead parents. "Car accident. Deer hunting season. They got gored by one antler apiece, even though they were already dead by then," a statement that always took her back to an accident she had not witnessed but could picture perfectly in her head. She looked down into the half glass of soda water she had left, where the two offending antlers had stationed themselves at the bottom.

Over the eleven years since her parents died, the antlers had ap-peared in glasses, bowls, mirrors, grass, and in the eyes of people she didn't like. She went on to the native Wisconsinite glory of feeling cool air on her flip-flopped toes at forty degrees and the point in a deposi-tion when she'd backed the person she was questioning into a corner and waited for the kill. Yet the antlers stayed put, waiting until she got distracted enough to forget they were there. Her parents were people who drank and slow danced around their living room to Stevie Wonder and took her on picnics where her mom packed homemade Lunchables "because buying them at the grocery store is so expensive when I can just cut up meat and cheese my damn self," she always said, and her dad whipped out his banana pudding, one of three dishes he made, along with chili and collard greens—and red punch, if punch counted as a dish. And then that deer turned them into a pair of fucking antlers.

"I should have had the chance to eat the deer, as revenge," she said.

"I guess that rule woulda stuck me with cancer," Aaron said. "Waddaya think cancer tastes like? Chicken fat?"

"Your grandma died of cancer?"

"My mama."

"So your dad raised you?"

"My grandma. My dad apparently wasn't that into the havin' kids part of knockin' people up."

He didn't have any parents! Aretha almost took her right hand out of her lap to pump her fist on the tabletop, but remembered just in time that it was tacky to openly celebrate parentlessness. When she thought about the bad dates she'd been on in the past, she blew up all the horrible things the guys had said and shrank the part where they cringed when they found out she didn't have parents anymore, like a piece of paper folded in half until it disappeared from view. Yet the paper always came flying back at her from its hiding place, ready to slice its way across her finger and draw blood.

The last guy she'd dated was a white lawyer. A fighter. A guy who could win an argument in the morning and plan out the next six months of his life by night. She liked the version of herself that sprang up when she was with him: Happy to make fun of bad movies and compete her way through video games against him, because he understood that winning at work could be seamlessly transferred over to winning at life. He didn't blink an eye at her whole parentlessness thing. But when he took her to Connecticut to meet his parents, they shook her hand and stared at her with a little too much concern. In the kitchen, while

Aretha chopped onions haphazardly and his mom with precision, she'd asked if Aretha thought parentlessness was a huge problem in the Black community. Aretha loudly blamed the onions that went up her nose and watered her eyes for her hustle out of the kitchen and into the bathroom, and credited herself for her quiet walk back out to her car to drive herself out of their lives. But here she was, sitting across from a guy whose parents would never rematerialize from dust to ask her shitty racist questions about why she didn't have any parents. She was free. She could pump her fist under the table, out of sight.

"So between us we don't have any parents," she said.

"None."

"This is kind of exciting," she said, unable to calm herself down.

"Yeah, other people don't really get it."

They both smiled. She sipped her soda water, which tasted less blank the more of it she swallowed. She liked him, this guy with no parents who loved his dead grandma and actually fucking listened to her. And then he mentioned his roommates.

"They're kinda weird," he said.

"What do you mean by weird?"

"Well, Brittany built a little house in our backyard."

The name Brittany ran through her head with the force of an alarm, as if all roommates were romantic partners lying in wait for your date to work out so they could steal him from you.

"To have tea in or something?"

"No, to live in, in case the main buildin' goes down."

"Because of another hurricane?"

"Or whatever else."

"OK."

"Don't worry. I don't believe in livin' in little houses in the backyard."

"Got it."

"And James kinda hangs out by himself, in his room, openin' weird tabs on his laptop."

"People get lonely."

"Yeah, loneliness is an alternative lifestyle now."

"BDSM is an alternative lifestyle. Loneliness is as edgy as buttered toast."

Even though she went to her fair share of parties and happy hours, as someone who lived alone she knew loneliness. But more importantly for the kind of person she was, she'd read up on it, and was ready to spit out all the googled loneliness statistics Aaron needed to hear. Yet the conversation shifted, allowing her to feel the warm glow of interrupting her sometimes lonely lifestyle to temporarily entertain living some other way.

•

DEEP IN THE PENNSYLVANIA WOODS, A COUPLE HUNDRED MILES away from the house they shared with Aaron in Brooklyn, Brittany and James were living their actual alternative lifestyle, which Aaron, as a rule, never did more than hint at during first dates. They stood inside a darkened garage, looking at a table full of guns for sale. Brittany picked up an AR-15 and put its butt under her chin.

"I could shoot this from right here," she said.

James mentally yelled at himself for letting Brittany's gun-on-chin trick make him hard again. He tried, as the house's body man, not to have feelings during gun runs, because feelings got in the way of what he thought of as pure business. Money and physical things exchanging hands, usually in garages just like this one thanks to guys just like Jim. Older and white and armed enough to try to make a little money off spare guns. And James, a little bit away from the actual exchanging of it all, waiting there in case anything went wrong.

Nothing had, to date, ever gone wrong, so he spent his time during gun runs questioning his purpose in life, and trying to ignore the half of him that knew his purpose was journalism, which he wasn't allowed to do anymore. You lift two fucking sentences about fucking climate change at fucking three a.m. for your fucking four a.m. deadline for your fucking article about climate change that not enough fucking people are going to read because fucking climate change isn't sexy enough for them for whatever reason other than that their impending drowning death due to ocean melt just isn't something they care to ponder, and suddenly you're being dragged out by security, one fucking guard per arm, zero chance to grab the year's supply of peach tea you kept in your cubicle to even out your mood, because he was Georgian enough to believe his tea should be peach, even though he didn't take it sweet.

He had gotten all the way to the fucking *Washington Post* from a shitty alt-weekly in his bumblefuck Georgia hometown, goddamnit, and he should still fucking be at the fucking *Post*, gently explaining Miami's not so gradual transformation into palm tree soup for the kind of people who thought they had a hundred years to beat climate change because they didn't see it happening now. But it was healthy to have a job again, he told himself, even if that job didn't have a cubicle or sources or the opportunity to write a sentence that could slash across thousands of people's brains like lightning. He had an assignment at this new job. To protect the Brooklyn house. And because they were the only people who'd given him a chance after the plagiarism bullshit, he'd protect that house until he died.

Anyways, as she'd mentioned repeatedly whenever he made the mistake of giving her a too-warm look, Brittany wasn't into white guys. So James straightened his back and took a deep breath and thought about cold showers and ice cubes and frozen-over lakes and bad, non-peach kinds of tea that he didn't understand why anyone liked, like Earl Grey and shit. But what really calmed him down was the knowledge that just like on all the other gun runs they'd done, nothing would go wrong.

"Do you want the gun, or are you going to shoot it off your chin in my house?" Jim said.

"Give me three of them and I'll juggle," Brittany said.

She pretended to throw the gun she held into the air. James grabbed her arm, lowered it, reached into the bag they'd brought, and handed over the cash.

"No recoil," Brittany said. "That's why I could have shot it off my chin."

Jim ignored her to take an extra-long look at the money.

"What the fuck kind of money is this?" he said.

He held a handful of James's favorite alternative currency, which was called Sunny Delight, after the drink he'd liked as a kid. Sunny Delight was a type of metal coin covered with a yellow emoji smiley face.

"Well," James said, "I figured that, as a member of the community, y'all would accept community payment."

"What fucking community?"

"Jesus, man, the community," James said, sweeping his arm across his body to signal the deeply obvious existence of the community: the survivalists. The doomsday preppers who insisted on sticking that hokey *doomsday* into their name instead of picking the upbeat vibe of the word *survivalist*. The underground gun and weed dealers. The anti-government activists. The militias. The regular-ass libertarians, even though James considered himself leftish because he wasn't afraid to be a vegan since he didn't want to have to kill animals when everything eventually went to shit. The community had all the people who'd been kicked out of polite society, like he had, or at least had the good sense to reject it on nights and weekends.

"C'mon," Brittany said, "let's give him the money that actually works."

James reluctantly gave her a stack of green bills that were so obviously on their way out of circulation that their technical name hadn't occurred to him in months. When that cursed word *dollar* tried creeping into his head, he'd bat it down like a swatter on a fly. Brittany counted out a stack of hundreds twice before handing them over. She was just about to stuff the guns on top of the duffel bag of cash when they all heard it. The police siren. Wailing down the block and stopping right out front. Something going wrong.

Brittany looked at James. This was his moment. The time when he'd save the two of them from whatever shit was making its way to the fan. He felt a great rush of adrenaline that he knew would translate itself into action any second now. Jim pointed at the garage's back door. There it was, the plan that James totally would have come up with if Jim had given him a couple more seconds. They sprinted from the doorway out into the woods in back of the house until Brittany told James that sprinting was too loud, so after that, they power walked to a hiding place between the trees. James felt the mosquitoes before he saw them. A couple pricks below the end of his polo shirt sleeve. They would get a little further into the woods, and he, as the guy who knew what to do when it all went wrong, would execute his grand plan to scratch himself.

"The police weren't after Jim, right?" he said.

"I wouldn't make any assumptions about the people we buy from," Brittany said.

"But he seemed nice."

"You mean he gave us guns for money."

"Yeah, that's pretty nice."

"For all we know he's into crime. Traffic tickets. Misdemeanor jaywalking. Felony line-dancing."

"Dancing is a crime out here?"

"Dancing's always a crime when you leave the city."

Flashlights swept the air in front of them. James scrambled up a tree, figuring that Brittany would understand that the plan was to climb trees now, but she stayed stubbornly flattened on the ground, immune to his ability to solve problems. The flashlight beams swept closer.

It was quiet enough where they hid that even James's breaths felt like thunderclaps going through his ears. He slowed down his breathing to try to quiet it, but that didn't work, so he gripped the branch in front of his right hand until his knuckles hurt. He eyed the closest beam like he could beat it back with a hard stare. The flashlights receded. Everything went dark again. He and Brittany sat silently until the police footsteps disappeared and the squad car went flashing back into the dark. James dug his nails into his right arm. The scratch felt like a scream. And then he wet himself. Right there on the damn tree. Out of relief, which made all the sense in the world as long as Brittany didn't notice. He hadn't peed that loud, he said to himself right as her eyes turned towards him, horrified. She's flipping out about something else.

"Let's go," Brittany whispered beneath him.

She couldn't have possibly noticed.

They took a wide berth around Jim's house to their car. Brittany gunned it east through the wide-open Pennsylvania night sky into Jersey, where the highway grew from two lanes into four. They snaked past diners and drive-throughs and hugged the curves that led them to the turnpike, where they turned north for the last great lurch back into NYC.

"Next time I'll bring you a diaper," Brittany said.

James glared at her.

"Real heroes have the courage to pee themselves while the cops are still there."

He balled his hands into fists, like he was planning to fight their car's windshield for giving him up.

•

TWO AVENUE BLOCKS FROM THE BROWNSTONE WHERE Brittany and James would show up in fifteen minutes sat Aaron and Aretha, still at the bar. Aaron had finally brought up his coffee business, and Aretha listened patiently, as a person who investigated everything in her life except what the liquid she drank every morning might have in it. She pictured all the other words she'd googled that started with C: *cup, cinnamon, cervix, cordial,* which led her down a road full of polite people and impolitely disgusting fruit-flavored liquors that should be banned.

"I got fired from the bar, but I was sick of bein' a bartender," Aaron said.

"I'd be out when my coworker stole my tips," Aretha said.

"I was done. I don't mind stayin' up late, but I'm not actually nocturnal. Bartendin' is for people who are their best selves at one in the mornin'. If I wasn't drunk I couldn't fall asleep at six a.m., when I finally got home from work. I stopped drinkin' after the hurricane, saved a lot of money, learned about coffee, and found a businesswoman and investor who lives with me."

"Lives with you?"

"Oh, we're not together."

"Really."

"You'll meet her. I don't think she could ever be with anyone. It would wreck her style."

"You'll meet her" echoed through Aretha's ears after Aaron said it. She floated on the future of the *will* in it, the promise that they would sit around whittling away time together after she met his roommates. A perfect feeling but for that *her* at the end, and the mystery of whatever she did in their backyard. But they'd sat around at the bar for a couple hours now without a single reminder of bad dates past cropping up in her head. Her mind felt quiet and smooth, well prepared for whatever she might encounter in Aaron's home.

"OK," Aretha said. She took another drink of her second limeade, which she'd ordered after deciding she didn't want to quit drinking forever on a first date, even if she liked him. The bartender had mixed it heavy. Aretha felt the normal wave of drink number two ball itself up into something larger on its run towards shore.

"Let's go meet 'em. I can show you around the machines, if you're curious. Since we own the buildin', we roast, pack, and ship in it."

"Really."

"Yes."

"Who the fuck owns a building?"

"You can officially call me the fuck."

"Do you live near here?"

"Two blocks."

"Let's go."

Aaron offered her his left arm when they left the bar, and she hooked her right arm around it. They turned off the main street and walked onto an avenue full of a late-September humidity that weighed down the trees standing in the dark. Aretha looked up into the apartment windows they passed, half lit and half not, and imagined everyone in them to be as happy as she was. The wind sounded musical to her ears, the ground obliging under her feet, Aaron's arm steady in her grip. They walked past a restaurant named Bambi, where diners determinedly stared at each other over candlelight. Aaron led her to the stoop of the building to Bambi's right, and she looked up. Three vertical rows of brownstone windows shone down on her. People their age didn't just go around owning entire houses in Brooklyn unless they were royalty or had gotten millions of people addicted to opioids, but here he was, owning a whole big-ass house. Aaron reached for the keys, opened the front door of the building, walked up a set of stairs to the second-floor landing, and unlocked a door. She followed him in.

"Oh my god," she said.

The coffee. The roaster sat squatly in the middle of the room, an octopus with metal legs. The smell was everything. Roasted, caramel heaven. She inhaled again. She heard footsteps. A lanky Black woman stood in the corner of the roasting room in a track jacket and track pants. Angry Flo Jo gave Aretha a look.

"I didn't realize we were having guests," she said.

"Aretha, this is my roommate and business partner, Brittany."

Aretha reached out her hand for a shake. Brittany didn't take it. She turned her back and went marching back up the stairs she'd come down.

"She just takes a while to warm up to people," Aaron said.

"OK," said Aretha.

She noticed a stack of full coffee bags in the corner of the room. "Tactical Coffee," they said, "because you don't want to fall asleep during the apocalypse." The guy on the lower half of the bag was sprinting away from something in terror, with a full cup of coffee in one hand and a hunting rifle in the other.

She, a person who never freaked out, channeled her reaction to the gun on the coffee bag into a very long exhale. Before she could ask Aaron what kind of apocalypse he might be planning to shoot, a blond guy came in and stopped on the landing of the stairs Brittany had just taken up. He gave off a sour smell and stood stooped to one side, thanks to the oddly pointy duffel bag over his shoulder.

"James," Aaron called to him. "Come meet Aretha."

James put the bag down on the floor and offered her a handshake. Aretha looked at the pointy end of his bag, picturing the baseball bat or skinny yoga mat that had probably distended it. But he looked like he'd given up on exercising. She said hello to the ring of flesh around his middle that made him look permanently stuck in a hula hoop. Then she caught a whiff of him and wrinkled up her nose.

"Y'all into coffee? Or prepared?" James said.

"Prepared to see the coffee," Aretha said, mentally congratulating herself for being quick on the draw.

She caught James's look over at Aaron, a mix of confusion and laughter that she knew was meant to stay over her head. How had she gotten it wrong?

"Just back from the gym?" she said, pointing to James's duffel bag.

"Definitely got myself a workout," he said.

She looked pointedly at James's hula hoop and then back to the roaster. She didn't figure him out with her eyes.

"Welcome to the house, Aretha," James said on his way up the stairs, "stay safe."

She watched him disappear.

"Safe from what?" she asked Aaron.

"Oh, we had a break-in once. It kinda freaked everybody out, so we keep ourselves safe."

"Safe, huh," she said.

"It's not like we can call the cops."

"Of course not," she said.

In her head she'd multiplied the thing she thought was probably a gun in James's bag into an entire army's arsenal. But Aaron's
completely reasonable fear of calling the cops while Black shrank the
field of guns she'd created in her head down to a hard-core but reasonable number—like two. She didn't like guns, but she grew up in a
house with them because her parents insisted they might, like tons of
Wisconsinites, want to go hunting someday, which turned her into a
person who didn't think guns would affect her if she didn't see them.

"A break-in. That's terrible. What'd they take?" she said, ready to
move on.

"Some frozen hash browns and a couple of pounds of coffee."

"Your coffee's so good people steal it?"

"We ran with that as our slogan for a couple of years."

Aretha felt pity wash over her. This guy had lost his mother and
suffered through a break-in and rising floodwaters? The feeling reminded her of times when, growing up, her parents couldn't pay a
bill and they'd sat around in the dark or used a hot plate for weeks
until they rustled up the money. The coffee smell rose up to inter-
rupt her musing on catastrophes, sending a fresh round of itself up
her nose.

"How does it work?" she said to Aaron, pointing to the roaster.

"Well," Aaron said, pointing to the side of the roaster, "we put the
beans in this drum, and then the machine spins 'em around in a circle
on top of an electric flame."

"A drum circle," Aretha said.

"Minus the hippies," Aaron said. "Then we run cool air over the
beans, and let 'em rest before we brew up a sample batch. Come on
down to the kitchen."

She followed him into their kitchen, which looked like a kitchen,
other than the counter filled with machines.

"That's a plain old drip," he said, pointing to the only coffee maker she'd seen before. "But we've also got an AeroPress," he said, pointing to a plastic tube with a plunger that made her think of the female condom, that tragic plastic sleeve that looked like a surgical glove gone wrong. "A V-60," he said, pointing to a ceramic cup with a funnel inside, like a coffee cup had decided to throw a tea party.

"What's that?" she asked, pointing to the machine that looked like an hourglass with a dainty wooden ribbon tied around its waist.

"A Chemex."

"How does it work?"

"You pour water on top of ground beans for pretty much all of these."

"And they all just make coffee?"

"Different coffee. It tastes very different. You wanna try some Chemex? I have fresh beans."

Aretha looked at her watch: 11:38 p.m.

"Isn't it a little late?" she said.

"A half-inch won't keep you up."

She was going to say yeah. To midnight coffee. A decision that might turn her night sleepless and her morning into a mental walk through wet sand. But everything had already gone off-kilter ever since Aaron decided not to suck three hours ago. He poured cold water into a kettle that he placed on the stove. He ground a handful of beans into powder with a hand crank. He laid a paper coffee filter over the top of the Chemex. Aretha watched him move with a grace she associated with Olympic swimmers. He put in grounds, then a light round of hot water, spinning his wrist in a circle like he was slow dancing with the machine. He put in another taste of hot water, then one more. This wasn't coffee making. Coffee making, as Aretha knew it, was the robotic insertion of grounds into the automatic drip machine on her kitchen counter before she went to bed so she could wake up to a familiar dark sludge she never thought about. It didn't have technique, or daring, or romance.

He poured himself a full cup, to prove his dedication to the cause. She accepted the inch of coffee he gave her. She committed an act she never had before: she smelled it.

"Oh my god," she said. "It smells just like . . ."

"Blueberries?" Aaron said.

"No."

"There's a little bit of toffee, right there at the beginnin'."

"Nope, that's not it," she said. "It's more like a summer day with a good ocean breeze."

"You mean the milk chocolate notes."

"No."

She took her last sip and swished it around her mouth with pleasure.

"This is amazing, but I have to run," she said to him. "We should do this again."

He grabbed her hand and kissed it. She carried her suddenly warm hand all four blocks home, past brownstones, the heavy trees that hung over them, and the war in her head between the parts of it that adored Aaron and the parts that thought the whole Tactical Coffee thing was a little much. Why did they put a gun on the front of a bag of coffee? Who wanted to be reminded of the possibility of the apocalypse at the bleary hour people got up to get caffeinated? If they weren't afraid to put guns on their coffee bags, did that mean James's duffel bag was full of guns? How good did that coffee taste? Why couldn't she focus on the gun on the front of the coffee bag instead of going back to his hands and his wrists and his lips? He'd said he wasn't into living in little houses in backyards, but did that mean he wasn't into anything else that people who didn't mind living in little houses in backyards might want to do?

She and her kissed hand and her coffee-flavored mouth went through all these questions on her way up the stairs to her apartment. She went into her kitchen and grabbed a bag of the ground coffee she always put into her drip machine before she went to bed, ready for a hit from sniffing it now that she knew coffee could smell transcendent. She opened the bag. She sniffed. Mud. She gave it another sniff, like maybe the coffee would wake up. It didn't. She obediently poured coffee into her drip machine and looked down at its old, reliable self, the Stonehenge of her kitchen counter. They'd been together through years of law school and late nights at the firm, far too long for her to think about replacing it with a Chemex. But back then she'd resigned herself to dying alone, too. She brushed her teeth and changed into her pajamas and fantasized about drinking better coffee. And pondered Aaron, the charming guy who ran a coffee company with a theme that seemed kind of dark.

She got into bed, looked up at her ceiling, and thought about how Saturday afternoons after brunch with your best friend were a perfect stretch of hours to do that second round of googling on the guy you liked, and how she'd be able to do that tomorrow. The round of googling that would surpass the first round in every way because it would drill down to the true heart of the matter of whether she should bother going out with him again.

She trusted the internet. She had become an expert at plowing her way past its piles of shit for the glimmers of useful information it hid in strange archived websites and databases too boring for normal people to look through. She could write down a list of pluses and minuses about him, like weirdos did, or she could enter the bowels of the internet and dig up his house deed, his criminal history, his credit rating, and everywhere he'd been for the last couple of weeks. In a less enlightened era, this might be stalking, but in a world where it was all at her fingertips, she was just curious. In an ideal world, she'd find enough evidence of what James meant when he'd asked her if she was prepared, and if all this preparedness included Aaron, no matter how much he shrugged it off. Weapons, supplies, hopefully a decent picture of their backyard, complete with anything that looked like a bunker. If it existed, she could find it. At work, she turned this power into finding obscure Supreme Court cases from the 1940s that said what partners wanted them to say, and at home, she used it to reduce uncertainty in her life.

•

THE NEXT DAY SHE ROSE FROM BED AND PUT ON THE FIRST dress she bought after she started practicing law at the firm. An orange slip dress meant to remind her of the existence of weekends. She walked ten blocks to have brunch with Nia, who waved hello from a back booth. Nia looked like Nia, and Aretha took comfort in her refusal to change. Nia sat tall and round-faced with a short afro and an equally short portion of weed-filled vape pen poking out from her shirt pocket.

"You look happy," she said.

"I . . . I . . ." Aretha stammered.

"Made partner?"

"Right," Aretha said flatly.

"Had a great third date of the week," Nia said.

"How do you know?"

"Because you would never have missed last night's party for any other reason."

"True."

"You missed out, girl. Me and the crew took over the dance floor. We shook, we shimmied, we even did the crab walk."

"No."

"Yes."

Now Aretha felt wistful. Sure, she'd had a great date, but she loved the nights when Nia gave up on all the reasonable shit people did in clubs and danced herself straight into orbit. Pretty much the only time Aretha ever took a vacation from being a rules-based person was when Nia talked her into doing some dance everyone else on earth had forgotten about fifty years ago to a rap song from yesterday.

"You never know what'll go down when therapists get together," Nia said.

"Therapy?" Aretha said.

And Aretha's wistfulness died. She never mourned all her friends who'd left town harder than she did on therapist nights. Nia was cool, but the other three of them floated from never liking their drinks to hating the music to deciding everyone else in the club was dressed wrong to psychoanalyzing people based on their dance moves. Aretha went out to relax, not to hang out with people who were born with a tree up their ass.

"Yup, right there on the dance floor. But enough about last night. You look real fucking high for a person who doesn't believe in weed."

"You got me."

"What's he like?"

"Well, I told him a lot of stuff about me."

"On the first date? Whoa."

"I know. Anyway, his mom's dead, so he kind of gets me. And he's a coffee guy."

"A coffee guy," Nia said.

"Yeah, he owns a coffee business."

"Is the coffee good?"

"So good."

"What's his company called, so I can look for his stuff?"

"Tactical Coffee."

"Why's the coffee tactical?" Nia said. "Does it defend his place?"

"Not yet. I'm sure he's working on that."

"Why? Is he a tactical guy?"

"No, but I think his roommates are."

"What do you mean?"

"Well . . ."

"Wait, I think I've heard of him. Is he the guy whose coffee has the gun on the bag?"

"Yeah."

"And the bag says something crazy on it?"

"'Tactical Coffee, because you don't want to fall asleep during the apocalypse,'" Aretha said.

She remembered the horror she'd felt the first time she saw their coffee bags, but in the diner's bright light, falling asleep during the apocalypse sounded hilarious. Even comforting. A cozy apocalypse that would lull her into a nap. Nice.

"The coffee stuff is bad," Nia said.

"You hate coffee?"

"They put a gun on the bag. They're riffing on the apocalypse, but how the hell do you know they're not serious?"

"His roommates are more into the apocalypse stuff. He just humors them."

"I'm sure that's what all the survivalists say."

"Look, I googled his company."

"And?"

"They're a legit business."

"No one puts 'survivalist' on their incorporation documents."

"Yeah, I know."

"You don't know what survivalists are?"

"I'm not worried about them."

Nia looked at her.

"OK, I'm kind of worried about them. But I like him. I don't just go around telling anyone about the antlers."

"No," Nia said. "The antlers?"

"Yeah, the fucking antlers."

The antlers, who loved to come when called, did a circle around her mind and disappeared, like Aaron had showed up to fend them off. He and his roommates had a break-in, Aretha said to herself. They didn't want to have any more break-ins. They couldn't exactly call the cops. Maybe Nia, as another Black person who understood that Black people couldn't call the cops, would understand the break-in thing. But Nia's parents were so rich. Aretha remembered the first time she went with Nia to visit them. After they took the exit that led to their town, Aretha spotted what she thought was a cop car with a slightly off logo.

"What's that," she'd asked Nia. "The cops?"

"Private security," Nia said, waving to the driver, who waved back. "Our cops."

"Do you pay for them?"

"The neighborhood does. My parents chip in their share."

Aretha had looked out the window back in the direction of the private security car, and not gotten it. Intellectually she understood what Nia said, but viscerally she didn't get the idea of hiring private security for a neighborhood. Why would anyone want a second layer of almost cops in their lives on top of the regular kind?

"Lemme tell you about a client of mine," Nia said. "So I'm in my office when the doorbell rings and my four fifteen shows up. I buzz the client in, take a seat in my chair, and this wired-looking white guy in an army jacket comes to sit on my couch. I'm looking at the army jacket and his ramrod-straight, military posture and thinking maybe we're going to have a conversation about ways I can help him work through his PTSD. Instead, he tells me that the army jacket is the last tie he has to his survivalist days. He's changed cities and names and professions to get away from his old friends, who built bunkers in their backyards on weekends and spent half their free time training themselves to use weapons in remote private gyms."

"What were they training for?"

"He said they were convinced Obama would suspend the Constitution, but also that the training could be used for anything. Invaders at your door. The fallout of a global pandemic. Raccoons that wouldn't leave your yard. The total subway collapse we all know is going to happen someday because no one's shelling out money to fix the trains. He ate mostly dried astronaut food and slept outside in a sleeping bag in sleet to prepare himself for extreme conditions. He climbed hills for stamina and staged fake emergency drills where he'd climb down his fire escape at three a.m. and jump over and back over his building's backyard fence. He stopped sleeping and started staying up all night, because he never had enough hours in the day to finalize his plan.

"One day, he was at work, and someone spun a pencil, and he thought that was fucking *it*. That the pencil spinning was the beginning of the end. He ran down the fire escape stairs to get air. And then he threw out all his survivalist gear and skipped town to sit on my couch, shaking and pale, wondering what the hell anyone does if they don't have a plan for the worst possible future. Honestly, I didn't know what to do with him. We talked about his thoughts and feelings. His sense of self outside of the version of himself that spent years preparing for nothing that had actually happened to him. And then one day he just didn't come back."

Their waiter came over. They ordered. Aretha turned back to Nia with her arms extended on the table, like the rest of what Nia had to say to her would have to go straight up her veins.

"Have you seen him since?" Aretha said.

"No."

"What do you think he's up to?"

"I don't fucking know. Probably finding some more stuff to be afraid of and weighing whether he wants to build an entire fucking lifestyle around being afraid of it or not."

"I couldn't imagine doing that."

"Actually, I bet you could. You still don't like roaches, right?"

"Who likes roaches?"

"Right. But you scream and run away from them."

"Look, roaches are terrible."

"If you found out that your favorite slice joint was crawling with roaches, would you go?"

"Hell no. I don't know if I'd walk on its side of the street anymore."

"Look at you, making a plan to avoid something you're terrified of. So what's your next step? Having a shootout with the roaches in an alley somewhere?"

"No."

"But your new guy, see, he's a shootout-with-roaches-in-an-alley type."

"No, he's not. He's a coffee guy. They believe in protecting their business."

"With rubber spatulas?"

"C'mon, you know Black people can't call the cops," Aretha finally said.

She looked at Nia.

Nia looked at her.

They said nothing.

Their food came. Nia dived into her eggs, but Aretha side-eyed her plate of pancakes before cutting herself a bite. The other dining tables had enough people talking at them to create a din full of the excited chatter of people psyched to have two weekend hours off from work. But for Aretha, the loudest noise in the room was the silence that had set in between her and Nia. It was time for Nia to move in for the kill. And Aretha respected her for this. What good were friends if they never twisted the screw on you when you were out there maybe making bad decisions? Still, Aretha had to fight back. They'd been friends for so long that she couldn't imagine dating a guy Nia didn't approve of on some level. But she'd bucked up and told Nia about the not-calling-the-cops thing. She could win on Aaron, and they could go back to relaxing at brunch. Nia put down her fork. Aretha took a deep breath.

"You don't want to date this guy," Nia said.

"We're just hanging out."

"Hanging out with that big-ass glow all over your face."

"Hanging out. We don't have plans to see each other again."

"Oh, I bet your plan guy will come up with a plan. And his plan will have guns, and dried food, and a bunker, and zero logic whatsoever. And you're going to be there when he hands you a gun to shoot the apocalypse, and you're going to tell him that you can't shoot nuclear waste because you're a lawyer and that's illegal, and he's not going to give a shit."

"Are you telling me you don't set an alarm every night?" Aretha said, a little surprised at herself for defending a guy who hadn't made it to a second date yet. Who was she? What had happened to her?

"Oh my fucking god," Nia said.

"You plan stuff. You were just talking about planning to avoid roaches. You're acting like I told you we were getting married. I just like him. Besides, I don't know that he's even into the guns and bunkers and fake tactical training part of all of it. He probably just named his business Tactical Coffee to take the hard-core people's money."

Aretha saw the Tactical Coffee logo in her head and took a mental dive back into the world it came from, full of delicious coffee and a guy who understood the dead-parents thing. Maybe Nia didn't get it because she had parents. Rich, supportive, alive parents who loved her in true only-child style. When they came to visit Nia in college, they took the two of them out for the absolute fanciest Italian food southern Wisconsin could offer. They'd get seated, and Aretha would be humbled by the spectacle of people eating twenty-two-dollar lasagna while Nia and her parents spoke a three-person secret language full of charity dinners and pool renovations, with occasional breaks to translate for her. When the law firm Aretha was hoping to work for called to offer her a job, she pictured falling into Nia's parents' sort of lifestyle, where she produced a kid who was a seamless extension of herself and took that kid to live in a house full of mysterious, unexplainable rich-people shit, like gazebos.

"Why do you like this guy?" Nia said.

"We just clicked."

"What do you mean by *clicked*?"

"I could talk to him forever."

"Can't you talk to someone forever who doesn't run a killing-themed coffee business?"

"And who are you with again, queen of relationship advice?"

Aretha, who felt sure she'd landed a slightly too big hit, watched her blow reach across the table and roll off Nia like rain down the side of a building. If you looked up the meaning of the word *single*, Nia would pop up at you, grinning, with the vape pen intact in her pocket. She'd barely hooked up with anyone in the fifteen years Aretha had known her. "I'm good enough for me," she'd said whenever Aretha asked about her male hookups, or her female hookups, or anyone Nia brought up more than once who wasn't one of her clients.

"I'm in a healthy, committed relationship with myself. And I give damn good relationship advice. Rule number one is don't get with some guy who doesn't seem completely opposed to killing people. It's an easy rule to follow. I follow it every day!"

Aretha glared at her.

"I'm not visiting you in the bunker."

"I'm never going down in the bunker," Aretha said, "so we have a deal."

Nia ate, and Aretha ate, and a second round of silence descended on their table. Aretha spent that silence thinking about how she and Nia met, on the second day of college in their Wisconsin university town, where someone in their dorm started a fire that was officially explained away as a typewriter that self-ignited.

"Gotta be weed," Nia had whispered to Aretha, as they stood outside shivering in the cold, with their coats hastily thrown on over their pajamas, waiting for the fire department to give them the all-clear to go back inside.

Nia handed Aretha a fresh joint from her pajama chest pocket and a lighter. Aretha took a hit.

"The dorm room," Nia said, making a dismissive gesture with her hand. "At least I didn't lose my spare," she said, pointing at the joint. "You know how hard it is to find a decent fucking dealer in this town who doesn't look at me like I have three ears just for being Black? Don't tell anybody it was me."

"I like you," Aretha said.

"Great, 'cause I need a new roommate."

One conversation turned into four years of hungover dorm breakfasts and sober between-class lunches, and the two of them arriving at parties together with their arms linked, and sudden trips to Chicago when Nia was willing to whip out her car, a mint-green Fiat her rich therapist parents bought her as a welcome-to-college gift. Nia would pull up in the car, and Aretha would hop in. The Wisconsin cold wore off under the force of car heat. Nia's usual mix of Ja Rule and Missy Elliott and Destiny's Child kicked in, and Aretha would get the first lick of the elation that would fully land on her when they got there. Three hours later Nia would pull into a hotel parking garage so they could check in, get dressed, meet up in the bathroom to do their makeup and debate where they should go out.

They'd pop out for pizza and call themselves a car to drop them off in a line, where they'd shiver until a bouncer removed the cord blocking their way and thrust them into a second world of heat and music. They'd grab drinks and survey the scene, and Aretha would feel the transgressive hit of going to Chicago, the city her parents had left for a safer but dull Wisconsin life, to hang out in clubs they couldn't possibly have imagined might exist someday, if she wasn't cursing herself for not having parents rich enough to give cars out like candy. And then the death car and the deer tied to the top of it came to claim her parents right before graduation and kicked off a stretch of feeling guilty that she'd ever decided they had faults.

After college she'd moved to New York for law school. Nia came back to the city, where she'd grown up, to set up her own therapy practice. The two of them still showed up at parties with their arms linked, even though the parties had moved from comfortably broken-down Wisconsin college houses and Chicago clubs to the upscale Manhattan and Brooklyn apartments of the people who occupied the same social strata as they did. She and Nia settled everything that ever needed to be settled over brunch. Aretha always declined the weed after they moved to the city, out of a sense of obligation that set in after her parents' death, a way of looking for their approval in the afterlife mixed with a need to not be the weed-smoking Black lawyer at work and stick out even more than she already did. And Nia had upgraded to what she called a "more adult" vape, its white plastic tip poking out of her shirt where the college joint used to be.

In college, Nia and Aretha had hashed everything out. They'd gone over each detail of Aretha's parents' deaths and what Nia's parents' money meant. They analyzed news, the movies, the weather, how to vote. Their friendship needed everything to be settled out loud. Before she'd entered the restaurant, Aretha knew Aaron could survive a healthy round of debate. But one round in, something curled up in her stomach when she pictured herself and Nia launching into a second round. She wanted another couple of days to google him and figure out if he'd gone survivalist in any of the freaky, possibly illegal ways. Normally she'd ask for Nia's advice on this, but everything didn't need to be decided with your best friend, a position she'd adopted exactly one pancake bite ago.

"Yeah, you could talk to him forever," Nia said, "but if he truly turns out to be a bad idea you're getting rid of his ass, right?"

"Of course," Aretha said.

"You mean it, right?"

"Would I lie to you?"

"Don't lie to yourself."

What was the internet supposed to cough up about Aaron that

would outweigh how she felt sitting across a table from him drinking his coffee? Aretha argued with herself from her bed, where she sat looking him up on her laptop three hours later. She'd worked her way through Tactical Coffee's publicly filed business registration documents. Aaron's nonexistent criminal history. His credit rating. She'd taken a look at everywhere he'd ever lived that she could find on Street View, except for the apartment building that had been destroyed to make way for the bigger dreams of a taller apartment building. She'd checked out his other dating profiles, his employment history, which included the bar he'd told her about, and one blurry photo of his mama, who truly was just as dead as her mom, thanks to the relentless hand of ovarian cancer. The internet didn't make him seem dangerous, or obsessed with anything that could be called survival techniques, or even particularly interesting. It was always unsatisfying to find the online history of the kind of people whose lives hadn't produced any entertaining hits. Just a set of addresses and employers and changing ages indexed by people search sites. When she switched her focus to Brittany she got even more bored at the formulaic set of information about her business ventures (coffee, yoga mats, clunky "running" sandals) and her personal life (prep school, Harvard double, both undergrad and MBA).

The closest she'd come to unearthing anything interesting lay with James, the former climate reporter whose career had gone up in the smoke of twenty-five plagiarized articles. His hits were pure gold. The plagiarism itself. The backlash to the plagiarism. The hand-wringing about whether a plagiarist reporter reflected the diminishing moral fortitude of an entire country. Maybe an entire civilization.

She kept reading about him, and some columnist brought up the fucking Magna Carta. "The inability to select the words of your choosing is just another form of tyranny," the columnist droned on.

Yeah, Aretha found his column on the internet, but she could feel the live, spoken drone in it. The lecture that started from 1215 to Rousseau's social contract in 1762, to the present, letting her picture the columnist as the kind of blowhard who would gladly talk for eight hundred years straight. James's borrowing some words, the columnist claimed, couldn't possibly constitute a breach of the agreement under which we all formed a society.

More of James's odd defenders, a set of people who argued that competition was competition no matter what way you chose to compete and he'd won by getting more attention paid to his article than the people whose original words he'd lifted. In a world in which internet hits were currency, James was the slot machine that kept paying out. Maybe she'd try again with the Aaron stuff tomorrow. In the meantime she could go swimming in the infinite pool of James hits, floating from indignation to condemnation and back.

She hadn't had this good a time searching someone's bottomless supply of online hits since her parents died and she went hunting through their articles as if looking at enough seven-hundred-word summaries of what happened to them would bring world peace. The media had lost its shit over a straightforward three-car wreck that had killed everyone involved. "Hunting season," reporters said breathlessly in their reports from outlets hundreds of miles away from places where anyone hunted. "Antlers!" screamed article after article after article. But the coverage that ended up annoying Aretha the most was the "can you believe Black people live in Wisconsin" angle, turning her previously flesh-and-blood parents into a pedantic lesson on demographics happily promoted by dipshits who'd never heard of Milwaukee, or Racine, or Kenosha.

Her phone buzzed. It was Aaron, texting her to ask if she wanted to go out tomorrow night. She sat her phone down. She pumped her fist. All that worrying about whether she should go out with him again killed by the euphoria that set in after a single text. She'd wait an hour or two to text him back, just to seem chill. Aaron's internet self was boring, but James had a dropped breaking-and-entering charge from *The Washington Post*, right after they'd fired him. Nothing like a dissipated criminal charge to turn a mild-looking nobody carrying a duffel bag into a member of the dark side. She could see James, hustling angrily down a sidewalk in the dark, hoping to find the kind of office that never totally shut down empty enough to loot. And then James failing, his fists clenched and his jaw tight as security moved in like a broom on crumbs. Her phone, which had the annoying habit of flashing a text on its home screen until she opened it, coughed up Aaron's text again. Ah, fuck it. "Of course," she typed.

•

THREE YEARS BEFORE AARON MET ARETHA, HE AND BRITTANY bought the house on Vanderbilt. They used her savings, with a hair of what he'd stashed away from bartending, a little bit of what they'd earned together from selling coffee, and a very healthy donation from her parents. It was three stories of brownstone fading gently into disrepair, but they could fix it up. He'd fixed his mother's apartment windows in West Texas, and she'd tinkered with the pilot light in her family's gas stove in their house outside of Boston, which made them sure their history of little repairs could easily be turned into big ones. When that didn't work out, they got used to the cracks on their new house's walls and ceilings, and dealt with an inconsistent boiler that left their winters flipping between cold and boiling hot by keeping extra blankets and box fans on the side of their beds. Right before they moved in, Aaron sat awake at night fantasizing about the thrill of having his own walls, and Brittany dreamed happily of the tax implications of buying a house. They'd been using a friend's roaster and wanted to expand, and she couldn't imagine anything sexier than writing that business expansion off. Even though Aaron couldn't imagine living with someone who mainly took joy in taxes and rules, he was sick of waiting for the day when he'd inevitably get kicked out of his apartment on 9th and C.

He got fired from the bar because the bartender who stole his tips successfully claimed it was the other way around. Ever since, he'd been not drinking to spite them, sleeping until noon, and spending his afternoons and evenings trying to hustle up more work before his banker roommate's girlfriend kicked him out. He could feel it coming the second she looked at him with the same skeptical face that she aimed at the bathtub in the kitchen, the dirty clothes all over the floor, and their half-black but deeply loved shower curtain. She didn't understand that a little shower curtain mold brought people together, especially the kind of people who felt terrified by all the choice at shower curtain stores. Where was the job that would get him out of there before she threw his ass on the curb?

He shook down the handful of college friends he still sort of kept in touch with, but they'd all moved on to the kinds of office jobs that looked askance at just-fired bartenders. He tried other bars in his neighborhood, but they all seemed to have enough people pouring drinks for them, and his newly sober self felt disgusted by alcohol anyway. He swallowed a layer of pride and walked around the neighborhoods next to his, but they didn't think he could cook food because running the deep fryer at his old gig didn't count. He didn't exactly have retail experience so it would be weird for him to start selling clothes tomorrow, wouldn't it? No, he said to deaf ears and closed mouths, no, it'd be perfectly natural for me to just pop in here and hand people shirts and take money for 'em. When he finished saying his piece, they would call his accent charming and shoo him out the door. The bodegas were family-run. The grocery stores had a couple hundred other applications to sort through before they could possibly even think about maybe getting back to him someday.

A Lower East Side art gallery hired him to make half his bartending cash to sit silently behind a desk, because his six-four, dark-skinned self looked intimidating enough to make people think twice about walking out with the art. And when he wasn't making shitty money babysitting art, he worked a few hours serving burnt coffee at the only East Village coffee shop that didn't mind that he didn't have barista experience, an internet café holdover from the early 2000s that ran Windows 95 on all its house computers as a parlor trick and had an old-school tenement bathroom overtaken by a claw-foot tub full of white, cubic, dead computer monitors from the '80s.

For three weeks, he thought he'd figured everything out, since his roommate stopped making him pay rent, and his roommate's girl-friend seemed to be ignoring him instead of asking him to leave so the two of them could be alone together. But a month into his roommate's girlfriend's tenure in the apartment, everything sprouted plants: a rub-ber tree on top of the dresser in their room, a fiddle-leaf fig in a pot on the living room floor, tiny cactuses in pots everywhere. She could green them into respectability. She flipped out the half-black shower curtain for a new one covered in palm trees. Aaron saw himself as the next unnecessary moldy-shower-curtain sacrifice. He could see his end coming in the whispering she did to his roommate when the three of them were watching movies together on the Thursday nights when Aaron wasn't serving terrible coffee or saying absolutely nothing to the people who entered the gallery and the couple had forgotten to plan anything else. But he wasn't giving up on free rent, so she was going to have to carry him out of the apartment on her back.

For entertainment, when he wasn't third-wheeling himself into watching movies with his roommates, he did what he could afford to do: walk. Three or four miles in, he could forget that he didn't have much money or that he'd gotten fired from the bar for a completely bullshit reason and just focus on the act of moving down the street. But eventually he'd end up at home, a place where the water stains on the wall reminded him that a hurricane had come for him there, and the plants reminded him that he was fucking up the vibe of the apartment by not having a girlfriend too. Or friends, really, since the nocturnal bartender life had put him out of touch with all the people he used to hang out with who worked during the day.

After he met Brittany and they sold enough coffee to get their money together, he saw the house on Vanderbilt as a chance for him to become someone else. A coffee roaster. A respected businessman. A person whose life didn't depend on the financial generosity of his banker roommate. Someone who flipped off all the assholes who let him drop into the flooded portion of his life without offering him a lifeboat. A person who didn't need people he didn't live with.

Even if it was mostly Brittany's parents' consulting money that bought the place, the two of them had their business. Their blood and sweat. Their joint trips on airlines that dipped ticket prices by not allowing checked luggage on flights to Honduras and Brazil and Colombia to source beans, where Brittany tried to seem as social as possible without saying anything and Aaron did most of the talking, because years of bartending had left him completely cool with making conversation with people he'd just met, and he wanted to be the Black guy in the white world of specialty coffee. The guy you could trust because he looked more like the people who grew the beans, even if no one in business really trusted anyone else.

He went to Colombia and Uganda and Jamaica and met growers and listened to their speeches on growing conditions. He bent down to smell fresh coffee beans. He offered to pay growers just a hair more than they'd been getting from other roasters. He shook hands and held babies and ate dinners in growers' houses and explained how he and Brittany had come to form a company. Their chance meeting in the coffee shop he worked at after she'd angrily hung up on a yoga mat buyer who had called her to cancel his monthly order. Their collective confidence that they could make coffee better than the shit they were drinking. "Too bitter," Brittany said. "Over-roasted," Aaron said, remembering the years-long piecemeal lecture one of his bar customers had given him about coffee, and the thrill when he finally started to taste everything the guy told him existed in a cup.

Meeting her was the highlight of his time at that coffee shop. He'd just eased into the boredom that set in after the morning rush when she came in. She ordered a small black coffee, and they got around to talking about how terrible, but cheap, the coffee was, and how she loathed selling yoga mats and wanted to have a business she didn't hate.

"Have you ever dealt with yoga people?" she asked him.

"Nope."

"They're a cult. They sweat on the mats and send them back. They send me shots of themselves doing yoga on my mats, and then they send me follow-up shots where they give those same damn mats one-star reviews. They meet up in the comments on my site to tell each other how to do yoga better, like I'm running a recipe blog. They show up at the stores that sell my mats when I'm dropping off fresh supply to poke them like they're worried the cake isn't done yet."

Before the yoga mats she'd taught yoga herself, part-time. "I didn't bend well enough to get bumped up to forty hours of stretching under hot lights a week." Before that she'd sold shoes. "All feet figure out their own way to be ugly." Before that she'd worked for one of those firms that sold weird financial instruments no one understood until the crash, when everyone decided on the exact same day that weird financial instruments were worth nothing. In between jobs, she'd interviewed for what felt like hundreds of other jobs, "but I probably never smiled enough." She couldn't put on the pleasantness that gets women hired. She didn't put exclamation points on her emails or try to make other people seem comfortable beyond bringing up what they might have in common, but even if she had, she feared her five-ten, dark-as-hell self wouldn't pull off that just-saw-a-puppy vibe people seemed to want out of her.

She was born without a smile, and it suited her, Aaron thought to himself from behind the counter where Brittany stood, tracksuited and determined, at peace with having no chill. Another customer came in, and he wandered back over to the cash register to take their order. After he turned out a mocha with enough extra hazelnut syrup to make it undrinkable, he looked back over at the table where she typed, and she looked up at him with the kind of relaxed face that might have passed for a smile on someone else.

She kept coming back to the shop. He looked at her jaw and her arms and face and kept the conversations to coffee, because hooking up with her would feel great, but getting out of 9th and C would feel so much better. A couple of months into their coffee business he congratulated himself for successfully tamping down the cruder version of himself that might have thrown their arrangement away for a shared night on a mattress.

She went over to his apartment and met the roommate and the

roommate's girlfriend, and he went over to her place and met her optimized soy protein bars, which were called Life Preservers, and her nunchucks, which she nicknamed Bertha after her mother and kept mounted on a wall for easy access just in case. "I lost so many jobs and so many friends who didn't want to hang out with someone who didn't have a job," she said, "so I only have me, and I decided to protect myself." And as a person who'd gone through enough trying to get jobs and getting blown off by his more successful friends to feel like he only had himself, he understood her completely.

She came up with the coffee bag design. At first it freaked him out, but after looking at it a couple more times, he found it funny. People would see that guy running away from doom with a gun and a full cup of coffee, and they'd laugh too, he figured. Then they'd buy it. And they did. Tactical Coffee was written up for the quality of the coffee they sold, sure, but no one could resist the bag's design. "Delicious coffee packaged in a delightful satire of our culture of overwork," one newspaper said, sending thousands of coffee bag design enthusiasts to their website.

The business bloomed into a brownstone with a second-floor roaster for Aaron, a first-floor bedroom Brittany could use as an office, and three upstairs bedrooms that dropped their morning commute down to a set of stairs. On move-in day, Aaron thought about the hundreds of employers who had rejected him and Brittany. All the workplaces they mysteriously didn't fit into. The emailed dings. The nonresponses. The looks that interviewers gave him when he showed up, as if he were an alien sent to fifth-dimensionally destroy their jeans department. All of those nos that had turned into a house. After dropping off her last bedroom box, Brittany went into her bathroom, shut the door, looked into the mirror, and thought pleasantly about how she would never bother to smile for anyone ever again.

Brittany spent that first fall they lived in the house digging out a corner of the backyard to build a bunker. "The ground's going to go hard in January, and then we'll just be stuck if anything happens," she'd told him before she bought a spade and some sheet metal and started spending her weekends outside. "There are so many bunker-building videos on YouTube," she said, when Aaron reminded her that she'd just broken the handle off one of the kitchen cabinets and glued it back on so crooked it looked like a unicorn horn. When she was a kid, she'd built Barbie houses, and gingerbread houses, and wooden shacks in shop class instead of the candleholders they were supposed to make. The wooden shacks could hold pencils or pens or spare change, instead of merely candles, assuming nothing dropped through the mysterious holes in their bottoms. But she was a better builder now. She could build a bunker that didn't have holes in it. "I'm just going to will my way through it," she said anytime he didn't make his bunker-building objections specific enough.

Aaron chewed on a Life Preserver, which didn't taste that bad if he spent less time thinking about just how bad it tasted. He watched Brittany dig from the back window of the roasting room, which became his favorite place in the house almost immediately after they set it up. One silver roaster new enough for its gleam to brighten his mornings when he walked in to remove the beans that had roasted the previous night. A couple stacks of twelve-ounce bags with his company's logo on them, ready to be packed with coffee beans and shipped. His company. The company that had saved him from a future where only a few inches of rising water stood between him and a total breakdown. All he had to do was fight off the quarter of his brain that feared a bunker would turn them into the armed guy on the bag front. The pile of dirt next to the hole Brittany dug grew to pumpkin height. Bicycle height. Aaron told himself it was a basement extension, then a cellar, as if either of them knew anything about cellars. But when Brittany insisted it was a bunker often enough for him to give up pretending, he switched to assuming they'd never actually go down in it.

"It's a hobby," Brittany would say anytime Aaron seriously attempted to ask her about where she was going with the whole survivalist thing. She always held a spade in her hand and had a handkerchief tied around her forehead that matched that day's tracksuit.

"But a hobby is playin' chess or knittin' or pickin' up the guitar."

"We only do this part of the time, unless, of course, something happens."

"It feels more like all the time."

"You have a go-bag. You have a plan. And besides, you don't want to get stuck in another hurricane again. Or do you?"

She gave him the look. It always turned him back into the broke guy living in the apartment with the bathtub in the kitchen on 9th and C who'd been reduced to hiding from four inches of hurricane water by crawling on top of his roommate's dresser and crying because he didn't know how to get any further away. He stood still, resisting the urge to touch his legs to see if they were cold again, like they'd been from the stormwater that flowed in through the walls. His breaths went shallow and quick. He went from a man to a panicky toddler with long legs, convinced he was destined to die facedown in a kiddie pool's worth of water.

Brittany clapped a hand on his shoulder.

"I didn't think so," she said.

The water in his head receded.

She went back outside.

Aaron watched Brittany dig and contemplated the perfectly reasonable contents of his go-bag: A thin, foldable fleece blanket for the cold. A tent. A water filter. A ham radio. A first-aid kit. A copy of *The*

*Thinking Man's Guide to Self-Defense*. Two flashlights. Two flares. A flint-and-steel set for when he inevitably needed to start a fire in a deserted postapocalyptic Brooklyn. A month's worth of camo-colored Life Preservers in all-caps wrappers that loudly said eating two a day could reduce the risk of death. He went to the kitchen and grabbed a Life Preserver that hadn't made it into a go-bag. He unwrapped and chewed and took in the optimized soy protein and felt his risk of kiddie-pool death lowering itself right on down to zero.

He went back to the window and watched Brittany deepen the bunker hole. Aaron had picked up his walking habit from a third-grade friend he was allowed to walk around the block with after school back in Texas, and his short-lived bluegrass obsession from a bluegrass-obsessed friend in college. You hung out with people and they rubbed off on you. It was only natural that he'd become more like Brittany, since they lived together. He ate Life Preservers now. He had a go-bag. Was a bunker so bad? He could ignore it, just like he ignored her gun collection. She kept the guns in her bedroom, and her bedroom door shut. If he never saw them, they were almost not there. He didn't have to look at the bunker. Sure, the bunker wouldn't work in a hurricane, but they had a roof for that. If he ever had to go into the bunker he just wouldn't think about it too much. He was the one who went around all unprepared for hurricanes, but Brittany had a plan for everything. If he didn't have any plans, he might as well roll with hers. She'd turned him into a man who had thoughts about self-defense: namely, that if it all went to shit, he should defend himself. The bunker was just a self-defense building. He practiced coming to terms with it by looking at the hole and thinking of it as a brown, crumbly pair of brass knuckles.

But the week before she started building the bunker, when it all went to shit for the two of them, he wasn't even there. He was crawling around South America looking for beans when a masked weirdo in black spandex held Brittany up at gunpoint in the house for two pounds of coffee and a bag of frozen hash browns. Brittany gave a single interview about the break-in that she closed by saying that apparently they made coffee good enough to steal. They printed a run of baseball caps that said "Tactical Coffee" on the front and "Good Enough to Steal" on the back, and put them on stoops around Brooklyn, where people stole them, took pictures of them, and put those pictures online, as they'd intended. Their sales skyrocketed.

After the break-in, Brittany shifted. She bought a doorbell that would annoy the dead, a video intercom system, and another two years' worth of Life Preservers. She doubled her gun stash from four to eight. In the backyard, her bunker hole grew bigger. "For some reason I called the cops after the break-in," she'd told Aaron the second he came back from his trip, with her right hand shaking around a mug of chamomile tea that she insisted was calming her down, "and they fucking laughed at me. 'Are you sure you didn't just rob yourself,' one of them said. 'Because, you know, sometimes your people like to take things.' Yeah, I just took my own fucking coffee and hash browns and threw them in the garbage can at the end of the block and decided to get the cops involved anyway. No one gives a shit about Black people. All we have is ourselves."

Aaron couldn't disagree with that. But he winced as she took them through the survivalist version of Maslow's Hierarchy of Needs. Of course the business should be secured. But not with guns. He spent half his free time lying on his bed trying to come up with some other way to protect themselves, and the other half soberly meeting women in bars who didn't think about guarding themselves 100 percent of the time. They all seemed lovely and charming and a little soft, compared with Brittany. When he met Aretha and saw that same steel in her eyes a match lit up in his chest.

Why did his mind blank itself out every time he tried to brainstorm how he and Brittany could protect themselves without turning into John Wick? He pictured alarm whistles. Mace. The black pepper his grandma put on their car to scare off cats. Could he switch Brittany into letting him sprinkle pepper on their delivery van for the human cats of the world? Probably not. They had to defend the business because people might be after them. With guns if they had to. It was what they had, this coffee that saved him from being an East Village charity case or an unemployed wanderer, ducking into shops to ask for a job, lasting five seconds, and finding himself back out on the street. He was proud of who he'd become and he wasn't going to let a little hang-up over how to guard the house get in the way of that.

He'd also learned to live with the version of Brittany who stood in her bedroom with her shades drawn, armed, running drills just in case anyone casually stopped by the house to shoot up a coffee company. Brittany acted as both the head of the numbers-and-money side of the business and the body woman, physically prepared to head off all the subsequent break-ins that never happened. Aaron had a lot of thoughts about her body-woman side when she first mentioned it to him, a week before they closed on the house. Thoughts like: Since it never works out when Black men want to arm themselves, why would a Black woman have a better chance of getting away with carrying guns?

"I come from three generations of Black Massachusetts natives who successfully protected themselves from outsiders and each other," she'd say, and when his eyes went wide at that, she worked him back down to the home-defense side of things.

"Another intruder," she said.

"I'd punch 'em."

"Or her. Women can intrude too. We can do anything."

"OK, I'd punch her, too."

"You'd hit a woman?"

"You'd shoot 'er?"

"If I had to."

"Thing is, I'm six-four. When I make eye contact with most women I can see 'em tryin' to figure out if I'm gonna tackle 'em next. I think I can handle whatever might come to our door."

"What if you're not here? What if you're in South America, sourcing beans again?"

"You don't believe in better door locks?"

"What if they're not enough?"

Brittany had no fear that couldn't suddenly balloon into a bigger fear. Aaron got tired of fighting her fears, the dark clouds that shaped their lives and filled what she called their defense budget, so he gave in to them. It wasn't like he could turn himself into a snake plant and go back to 9th and C to live with his old roommate and that guy's plant-freak girlfriend. If Brittany wanted to live in the Pentagon, he'd get used to the fifth wall. He put together the go-bag the first time she mentioned his hurricane to him. He watched her build the bunker with anguish, then indifference, then calm. When she went outside to dig, he watched her and mentally went over the house rules she'd insisted on when they moved in.

"Why do we need house rules?" he'd said.

"It's best to spell out what we expect of each other while we live here."

"We won't do fine just respectin' each other's space?"

"See, Aaron, that's so nebulous. It doesn't mean anything. It's not specific."

Brittany grew up in a house where rules came as naturally as air.

"Sure, my parents hugged my brother and me once every couple of years, but we mostly showed each other love by following rules," she'd say. "My brother and I knew when to serve everyone lemonade, when to ask for help on homework, when to take out the stray dog that kept invading our yard."

"Take out, huh?" Aaron said.

"Yeah, that's what I said."

"So you'd just kill dogs on Tuesdays, then?"

"We solved our problems."

He gave her a look. She beat it back with a stronger look.

"Rules work, Aaron," she'd tell him if he balked at one of hers.

Or she'd go with "Just look at us, Aaron. We made some rules, and we followed them, and now we're pretty much the only people in their thirties in this city who didn't come from money and own a house."

"Your folks have money," he'd say.

"Not that much," she said.

"Enough to give us three-quarters of the down payment."

"Do you want them to take their money back?"

Aaron shut up. If he closed his eyes, he could see the people who made her. The mother and father and sister and brother who could afford prep school and fancy college and house down payments and made and deferred to rules as naturally as she did, even though he'd never met them. He knew he never would. He suspected there was something about them that would cut against her carefully cultivated track-star-with-nunchucks vibe. They probably smiled at other people or had sex or showed weakness.

Did she even talk to them anymore? He'd never entered a room and found her deep in conversation with them on a phone or in the middle of a line of texts or seven minutes into a Skype chat. They never stopped by the house, and when he paid attention to all her family stories, some of them had clues, like dial-up internet, that made it seem like she hadn't talked to them in years. He was friendless and familyless in a natural, organic way, thanks to death, distance, and time. But Boston was just up the road, close enough for her family to accidentally be in town whenever, ready for their bunker tour. She didn't have a single framed picture of the people from whom she'd inherited the impulse to shape any potential conflict imaginable into a neat, bullet-pointed list. When she suggested making house rules, he'd pictured a list of steps that would tell both of them how to clean the bathroom, or a reminder of things to remember when running the roaster.

"All that stuff you keep mentioning about chores is kind of obvious," she said, holding a clipboard and pointing the pen at Aaron's head as she spoke. "We're going to write down the stuff we won't actually remember."

"Like what?" Aaron said.

"The stuff we won't want to say out loud to each other over and over again."

"Again, what?"

In the end the set of house rules they wrote down would only make sense to them.

"In the closet in Brittany's room," Aaron wrote in a blue cursive even he could barely read, a series of angry slashes and loops.

"Your handwriting looks like it just came back from a three-state killing spree," she said to Aaron. The two of them stood in the kitchen toasting the finished bunker, with soda water for Aaron and a half-glass of red wine for Brittany.

"You'd think a dog killer would be OK with homicidal hand-writin'," he said. "Let's grab them flashlights."

They went out into the backyard, where Brittany pointed out the bunker door, which she'd covered with Astroturf so it kind of blended in with the backyard grass. They lowered themselves inside. They turned on their flashlights. The light bounced off the bunker's sheet-metal walls, which Brittany was proud to have welded together herself after watching the right videos online. When she shut the bunker door, Aaron thought of playing house as a kid. The euphoric sense that hiding under a blanket could protect you forever. The bunker was only about three times the size of the biggest blanket houses he'd built as a kid, back when he'd just thrown a blanket over enough lawn chairs that the whole thing could fit, big enough to hold him and a handful of other giggling kids from the neighborhood. The inside of the bunker looked like his go-bag turned into a metal studio, with survival equipment piled everywhere, other than under an enormous red, black, and green flag mounted on one wall so they wouldn't forget what race they were. He remembered the version of himself that had objected to the bunker and laughed. What had he been so afraid of?

"In case of emergency," Brittany wrote on the household rules list in bright red pen, in smaller and neater handwriting than Aaron's. She stood alone in the kitchen, since Aaron was in Ecuador sourcing beans and James was a week away from walking into their lives, proud of herself for settling on what she figured to be the final plan, well suited to any emergency she could think of. A plan to spite her family, who she hadn't heard from since they gave her the down payment for the Vanderbilt house, a sum of cash her parents called goodbye money so they wouldn't have to deal with her rules anymore. Especially the rules that led her to thinking about building a bunker in the backyard of her then future house, an act they associated with white guys out West with mullets and a willingness to shoot whoever crossed them just because they could get away with it. But she felt equally ready to junk her family's rules, namely the rule that said her dream of building a bunker couldn't possibly expand into their dream too. They'd all gone their separate ways thanks to divorce and disdain, yet she felt an urge to keep something of them going inside her. She'd carry on their tradition by putting an armed white guy on the roof and a bunker in her backyard and daring absolutely anyone, including her fucking family, to come get her.

Six months before Aretha entered their lives was the sixth month after James showed up. He drifted into the kitchen, all hopped up on the vodka-spiked peach tea he'd shotgunned for hours, having successfully given in to the aversion to coffee he developed the second he moved in. He felt haunted when he took a breath on the roasting-room floor of the house, or saw the freshly roasted bags of beans lying on the floor, or the always warm pot of Sanka on the counter, the stuff Aaron had been drinking since he snuck samples out of his mom's coffee cup at age ten, but now filled the gaps between the fancier coffee he drank most of the time. The V-60 stuff and the cups of AeroPress he gently pushed into being, like birth, if instead of a baby you got a bitter black puddle of mud that tore up your stomach.

He went to the sheet of house rules. Because Brittany told him to, he wrote the phrase "James knows what to do," even though, as usual, he was pretty sure he didn't. But hopefully he could figure out what she meant. Brittany did the books and the business strategy and even drew most of their ads herself, slim little stick figures escaping from emergencies while getting high as hell on caffeine. Aaron talked to people, and sat with them, and added a tall, gentle vibe to whatever needed it. And James spent his days shadowing one or the other of them and his nights sitting up alone in his bedroom, switching between peach tea and peach vodka and pleasantly dreaming about killing his old coworkers. Everyone dreamed of taking out at least one person they'd worked with, right? he'd say to himself in his weaker moments, when he questioned the sanity of his dreams of ending a newspaper and the people within it. What kind of weirdos lived an entire work life without fabricating some fatal grudges against people who'd dragged their bad breath into work, or their smelly lunches, or their pathetic need to fire him for lifting a few words for a few pieces?

He could see himself going into Brittany's closet, borrowing one of her guns and fixing the main thing that had gone wrong in his life. His old boss, dead between the eyes and up the nose and in the mouth after James shot him in the face. His old work wife, back when he was domesticated enough to believe in shit like work wives instead of the wild animal he'd become, a tech reporter who taught him about the deepest, darkest corners of the internet, a set of sites that proved irresistible when he had all day free to sit around and look at them, full of other people who had been fucked over like he had and nothing better to do than talk about the people who'd fucked them. He'd enjoy killing her, too. And anyone else who sat near him and his old work wife at work. Whatever security guard was on duty on the building's first floor, all of them, in his head, an interchangeable mass of dead lumps in blue uniforms too lifeless to ask anyone who entered the building who they were there to see. Anyone on the street afterwards with the wrong look to them. Himself, at the end, with the gun sending its final click into his mouth to finally clear his head of revenge. But first he would teach himself to protect the house, as a warm-up. He'd develop his instincts. Wait for the right moment. Stop peeing himself when things went to shit.

He went into Brittany's abandoned bedroom and opened her closet, where her guns sat in haphazard piles. He picked up what he thought of as a beginner gun, because it had a bubble-gum pink Hello Kitty stock, and aimed it at the wall. He turned off the room light, and in the darkness he crept over to the window, pointed the gun at it, and watched the gun wobble under his drunken hand. He imagined looking out over cornfields or dust or endless stretches of concrete. A line of sight that would make any intruder clear. But what he saw was the crowded jumble of Central Brooklyn, where brownstones fought with blocky high-rises and modernist buildings for their very own piece of the sky. What a mess of shit to have to shoot a gun into. But if he had to, he would. Now all he needed was some aim.

•

**"SO," NIA SAID.**

"So," Aretha said.

The two of them were at brunch on Saturday, seven days after Aretha first told Nia about Aaron, in their usual booth. The late-September heat had shifted, without warning, to an early-October chill, so their coats were wadded up next to them. They'd switched orders. Nia dawdled over pancakes. Aretha cut into a plate of sunny-side-up eggs.

"You first," Aretha said.

"I have a new client, and she's a fucking plant chick. All she does is buy plants."

"Why? You can't keep plants alive in our tiny, lightless apartments."

"See, she thinks she can. She doubled down on cacti and succulents and all that other shit you can't kill."

"You can kill all of that here! My old roommates, the catering girls, might have killed twenty plants trying to keep them alive in the summer heat and the radiator heat and the cold. We used to say that the city's real motto was 'If you can kill it here you can kill it anywhere.'"

"I know, girl. But she doesn't. She has a plan."

"You mean a plan beyond buying them?"

"She keeps saying buying them is her plan. She needs something to keep her mind off all the depressing political look-who's-suddenly-proud-to-publicly-hate-Black-people shit, so she has a plant plan."

"Why do you think everyone needs some kind of plan lately?"

"Trendy way to pretend you have control over your life."

"But we do."

"Not to the bullet-point level people seem to want."

"God, what's the fun in that," Aretha said, dreaming of the un-planned parts of her life. After she left the office, she'd grab coffee or take walks or respond to one of Nia's texts or get on a train to come out of a station and end up in a neighborhood different enough from the one she left to qualify as another world, fresh air on her limbs, little to nothing on her mind. She could let Saturday and Sunday just unfold from hidden, strobe-lit, EDM-filled Brooklyn warehouses to brunch to the after-hours bar that served her and Nia's drinks with a free hit of coke that she always politely declined, to brunch, to one of those '70s parties she and Nia loved because they could wear bell bottoms and imagine their parents as disco royalty while pretend-ing to be disco royalty themselves. There was a routine to growing up working class that Aretha didn't miss for a second. The frantic tackling of the errands on days that weren't filled with work. The struggle over the bills. The constant calculation of how much of life could be conducted for free to reduce the stress in the rest of it. The law had given her enough money to very slowly chip away at her law school loans and otherwise not bother with planning out the life she lived outside of it, so she didn't. And when the weight of her previ-ous precisely measured life dropped down upon her, she brushed it away. Aaron appeared over the horizon of this entire line of thinking, winking at her as a reminder of his existence, which relaxed her, and plans, which did not.

"What's plant lady's real problem?" Aretha said.

"General stress."

"She doesn't link it to anything?"

"She just keeps saying she's busy and inviting me over to see her plants, and I keep gently reminding her that boundaries exist. We are working on getting to the root cause of her busyness."

"You mean it's deeper than her actual schedule?"

"Yeah, there's something existential about it. And what's up with you? You planning for an apocalypse of love?"

"It's not really like that," Aretha said. "He calls it more of a pre-paredness hobby and says his roommates are really more into it than he is."

"That's a way to keep you around until he unveils his fucking tank and explains that he practices for war every weekend right in the middle of Brooklyn."

"I still like him."

Nia groaned.

"Why is he so great again, exactly?"

Aretha took a mental spin through her entire week to answer the question, past the rumored threat of a new associate to compete with at work, and into the act that made her forget about that: joining Aaron on the street corner between their places so they could walk together for date number two, which they'd spent entirely on their feet.

"I'm not usually much of a walker, but this is nice," Aretha said, fifteen blocks in. They'd headed north out of their neighborhood into Fort Greene and down the hill to the Navy Yard, where Aretha, who'd never been to this side of town, eagerly took in what she could make out of the cranes and shipping barges hidden behind a tall industrial wall.

"Your driver takes you everywhere?" Aaron said.

"No. I just walk four blocks to the subway, go up two sets of subway stairs, enter my office, leave my office, wash rinse repeat. I work a lot of weekends. Most parties aren't that far from the subway. If I work super late, I can expense a hired car."

"Fancy."

"No, fair compensation for me making them millions of dollars and not getting paid anywhere near that. But go on, tell me about your Olympic walking career."

"Well, I was ten the first time someone noticed my skills," Aaron said. "I was goin' down the road to the candy store I was allowed to visit only on Sundays when some old guy whistled in my general direction and said, 'Boy, you sure can walk. You ever thought about joining a walkin' team?' After winnin' the junior walking championships I destroyed everyone else in the under-fifteen world walkin' championships, and before I knew it, I was holdin' a gold medal and tearin' up on the podium while they played the national anthem. And then they followed it up with 'Walkin' on Sunshine.'"

"I hope you at least got a key to your hometown out of that. A gold key, with a key chain shaped like a power walker."

"I think bein' an Olympic walkin' champion is a bigger deal than you think it is. My hometown mayor didn't bother with that key-to-the-city shit. They gave me a big ol' gold-plated door knocker to the city so I could bug anyone I wanted to whenever I felt like it."

Aretha linked her arm in his. They wound their way up to Williamsburg. She imagined their combined arms as a shield protecting them from—she looked around—people in beanies and baseball jackets standing in line outside bars. Was he getting to her with the survivalist shit? She did think of safety, as a woman who was sometimes alone, but only on the rare occasions she took uncrowded sidewalks through deep residential Brooklyn, not when she was walking with someone. Except this couldn't be a survivalist sense of safety, since he hadn't laid out the gritty details of what that meant. Just a general sense that the two of them were safer together that had never set in during her other relationships. Maybe it was just his height, which straddled the border between tall guy and human shield. They walked up to Greenpoint for ice cream, which they ate on a bench overlooking the East River.

"How'd you get into survivalism?" Aretha asked him.

In true lawyer style, she'd waited for what she considered to be the right moment to ask the question. He'd probably been mentally doing all the calculus that people did while walking: how far have we gone, is that car coming straight into this crosswalk and going for my knees, why have those people been camped outside the M&M store long enough to smell like someone made a beer out of armpits—stuff that kept people alert. But one scoop into a two-scoop ice cream cone seemed like the perfect moment to let yourself mentally relax enough to be questioned about your household's habits.

"You mean preparedness," he said.

"Do I?"

Aretha had long ago decided on a gentle questioning style. People just loved to keep talking if only someone let them.

"You do. There's a difference between havin' a plan in case somethin' goes catastrophically wrong and decidin' that you're just gonna be out there while the world burns down around you, holdin' a sword or somethin', only thinkin' about fendin' people off."

"Is there?"

"I think you think I'm gonna suck you into a bunker and tell you to come out and reenact *Mad Max*. I'm a coffee guy who doesn't want to get surprised by another hurricane."

"I'm sorry about your hurricane."

"You should ask me about somethin' less heavy, like my dead mom," he said.

He had the smile of someone who knew he'd steered his way out of trouble. Aretha's killer instinct didn't want to let him escape, because she never let people flee her questioning. When she looked back upon her legal career she saw a lot of unearthed case law and a healthy number of people on the other side of conference room tables pleasantly answering her questions until they realized they'd entered an unescapable trap, and then not escaping. But her other side pictured him in rising water in a shitty apartment again. If dirty hurricane water had crawled up her legs, she'd make sure it wouldn't happen again too.

"OK, I will. But what exactly is your plan the next time a hurricane comes around?"

"I have a go-bag. We don't live in one of the evacuation zones, so the next hurricane I'm worried about is the big one. And all I mean by go-bag is a bag of supplies I can take with me to whatever hotel I'm gonna have to hole up in until the water goes away."

"That seems reasonable," Aretha said.

What had she been so worried about?

"Told ya," Aaron said.

"So, your mom? What was she like?"

"Well, she died when I was pretty little, so I mostly think of her as someone with a big fluffy cloud of hair who hugged me sometimes. And your mom?"

"In Wisconsin it always felt like people only talked to the corn.

There are guys I knew there who I'm pretty sure would be willing to go years without saying anything. She was the opposite of that. Big hand gestures. Big ideas. We had an apartment, so we didn't have that much space growing up, and she ran a full garden off of our window-sills anyway. Geraniums, petunias, begonias, and English ivy."

"She sounds great."

"She was great."

"Corn sounds great too, if you want to stop by the grocery store on the way back."

"Hell, yeah."

The grocery store they went to had some decidedly early October corn for sale: undersized kernels, off color. But they bought a three-pack anyway and went back to Aaron's house for their vegetable nightcap. Sitting at his kitchen table with mediocre corn in her teeth reminded Aretha of all the good corn of her childhood. But Aaron kissed her with roughly the same amount of corn in his teeth and all the shitty corn they'd eaten turned sweet in her mouth.

"Well, like I've said, some of it is that he's a member of the dead parents club," Aretha said to Nia, back at their diner, because talking about dead parents sounded so much more objectively reasonable than talking about the fact that she'd dreamed about kissing Aaron with corn in both their mouths three times since it happened. Nia didn't get corn, since she'd only gone to school in the Midwest in-stead of actually being from there. She didn't track her way through spring and summer by noting corn height whenever her parents took her out for a country drive, or popping over to somebody's yard to watch her household's corn grow in the tiny garden a friend had rigged up. So Aretha brought up the dead parents thing again, not that Nia would probably get that either. How could she? Hers were alive and well, probably puttering around their Long Island house stacking their therapist cash, or on their way to Nia's place to stack hers.

"It's a very exclusive club, as you know," Aretha said. "Our bouncer's a hard-ass."

"His parents are dead?"

"Well, his mom is. And his dad wasn't really around. But it's not just that. He just seems in control of his life as opposed to all the guys I've bothered with who are pretty sure they're going to win the lottery or become famous even though they spend pretty much every minute awake working some job where they're basically a glorified intern."

She took a second to think of her white ex who knew how to win, and remembered how angry she felt all the time when she was with him, even in the midst of all their winning. The problem with their combined level of competition was that instead of leaving her need to defeat opponents behind at work, she had to defeat movie choices and restaurant picks and any theory he floated whenever they talked about anything. And sure, she enjoyed the rush that came with enacting a ten-point plan to subvert his need for the bad Thai takeout near his place, but over the run of their relationship she celebrated her victories against him and mourned her defeats so hard that she stopped sleeping.

Aaron was an upgrade, with his dead parents and his profitable coffee company and his sweet, let's-just-walk-for-hours demeanor. She felt herself becoming so much less of a clenched fist posing as a person when she was with him, and sometimes even without him. She'd started doing shit like smiling in the break room at work instead of aiming the usual mix of haughtiness and force at everyone she worked with. And she even, if she gave it a chance, liked his preparedness. Wasn't being ready for disaster just another name for having your shit together?

"And the rest of it is just a feeling. You know I have all those charts for the guys who didn't pan out. All their pluses and minuses facing off in columns and everything. But I just stopped somewhere in the middle of the second round of googling for this guy."

"What? You didn't give him the full three days of background check?"

"My heart wasn't in it."

"You're broken."

"No, not at all. Just different."

"I'm going to miss you when you go live in the bunker," Nia said.

"So, soon, because everyone always moves into the bunker on the third date."

"Second date, girl. You guys are behind."

Aretha felt changed from head to foot, as if she were running on a milder, Aaron-like setting. Nia seemed to have backed off, which always made her feel better.

On Monday she put on a pencil skirt, a shirt, a coat, and a hunter's orange knit hat, as a shoutout to the Wisconsin she couldn't forget no matter how much it reminded her of her parents' deaths. The antlers came. She remembered her walk into Greenpoint with Aaron. The antlers went away. She joined the flow of people to her subway stop, got on a car, and looked around to see if anyone else appeared to be running on a looser keel like she was, but they all had on workface. That eight a.m. steeled, half-tired look of dread that seemed to eat people up the minute they got out of the shower. She blocked them out and floated through six subway stops straight into the underground tunnel that led directly to her office building.

Hi to the security guard. Press the button on the elevator. Get vaulted fifty-eight stories into the air as a physical reminder of the heights she aimed to achieve at work. Wave to the deal lawyers and the tax lawyers all the way down to her office in litigation, a medium-sized square that signaled her place in the middle of the associate ranks. Its walls held her framed law school diploma and a blown-up picture she'd taken on her phone of a taxi that, thanks to a reflection off the glass she'd taken it behind, looked like it was running into itself right in the center of the Columbus Circle fountain, which lurked over the middle of the shot. She liked the optical illusion of it, and imagined the other lawyers in her office would feel drawn to the implied destruction of it running into itself as a hint of what they could do to people who opposed them.

She dropped her bag on her office chair and went to the kitchen for coffee. Put the coffee cup in the machine, click it shut. Survive the nearly interminable wait for it to brew and the disappointment that would inevitably set in when the coffee wasn't as good as Aaron's, even though it had no reason to be. A navy-pantsuited woman she hadn't seen before walked into the kitchen with a face full of optimism unusual for law firms. She took a brew cup and waited her turn at the machine Aretha was using.

"Hi, I'm Mum," the woman said.

"Aretha."

"Nice to meet you, Aretha."

Aretha shook her hand and mentally went through all the ways she could ask Mum why exactly she was here in the kitchen without seeming too rude, and when she ran out, flipped seamlessly to all the questions she couldn't ask about her dumb-ass name.

"It's my first day," Mum said.

"That's great," Aretha said.

"I'm in litigation."

Which was fine, Aretha thought, as long as she wasn't an associate, because the associates already had a pecking order by law school graduation year and an assumed pecking order based on ability that everyone tried to shake up without much success on their assumed march to partner. The one thing they didn't need was a new associate who would fuck up the eventually-making-partner math. But the bad signs were there. The pantsuit. The balls to walk up to someone who looked like a lawyer and say hi. Secretaries and copy people kept their heads down and their motions quick, as if one accidental round of eye contact with a lawyer would get them fired, which might be true, since they were prone to disappearing without notice. But as the Black woman lawyer at the firm, Aretha was afraid to show concern for secretaries or copy people, no matter their fates, for fear someone in charge would decide to snap their fingers and make her one.

"Me too," Aretha said.

"So I guess I'll see you at the meeting at ten."

"Yeah," Aretha said, trying to relax her smile so it seemed real.

"Great."

Aretha left with her coffee. It was amazing how fast a good mood could be wrecked. One minute you're gliding up to your office on a cloud because dating the right guy has emotionally fortified you for the warfare of the workweek, and the next you're a pilot in an airplane falling back to earth because some bitch in a navy pantsuit has coolly walked into the cockpit to be unafraid of you. The ten a.m. meeting was for litigation lawyers only, so Mum was a fresh enemy. The office already held so many enemies. Who the hell needed another one? Sure, they talked about themselves as being part of teams that worked on cases, and they showed up in unified packs to happy hours and charity dinners and legal-awards ceremonies, but everyone knew that was bullshit. An iron-clad barrier stood between the millionaire partners trying desperately to hold on to their books of business since the economy crashed, and the associates, hungry enough to steal the clients or any work that might lead to career glory if any partner left an opening, and happy to take down any other associate that stood in their way. All of them played a version of musical chairs that would leave the winner with millions of dollars and a level of power that Aretha imagined was accompanied by an actual physical sound.

To heighten the competition, the head litigation partner liked to pit the lower and mid-level associates against one another to find case law. It was the world's geekiest Olympic event, and yet, whenever he announced a new round of competition, Aretha went feral, ready for the hunt, with a hunger that she could taste on her lips and in the back of her throat. She felt a new round of case law competition coming on, since Mum had arrived the week after half the associates had been put on the brand-new Hurricane Sandy apartment-damage case. At ten a.m., all the litigation associates gathered around a conference room table. Aretha thought she spotted the itchy look the head litigation partner always got before he announced case law competition, like sending associates to look for law might leave him with a very exciting rash.

"Welcome to Mum, which is short for Chrysanthemum, right?" he said.

"No, but that's all right," Mum said, giving Aretha a window to mentally rip on Mum, both for being new and for ending up in a profession full of professional talkers with a name that meant silence.

The partner moved on, energized by fucking up Mum's full name.

"You're lucky, Mum," he said, "because on your first day you get to participate in one of the most exciting traditions we have around here: the case law hunt. Six of you get to leave this meeting to find me the case that will prove central to our argument. The case that shows, as much as a case not exactly like ours on the facts can, that it would be completely ridiculous for our client to have to pay out a bunch of claims for people who've lost their houses through absolutely no fault of their insurance company."

Aretha felt a note of dizziness, far up in her forehead, easily chalked up to nerves. After claiming victory in the last seven case law hunts, she felt ready to nail number eight. She rolled her pointer fingernail over and down into the stretch of skin between it and her thumb, and when the pain hit it brought with it a speck of brightness that left her primed for the win.

"We're hoping to get rid of this case at the motion-to-dismiss level, so please try to find cases that decide 12(b)(3) or 12(b)(6) motions. I want, if possible, cases that failed because the plaintiff, even if all the facts were assumed true, didn't prove that anything that might be considered an act of god qualified for insurance coverage. On your mark, set, go!"

He waved his hand: the starting flag of all their case law races. Aretha, Mum, and the other four mid-level associates took the track back to their offices at the fastest walk possible, since the building would have to be aflame before it became dignified to run. Aretha shut her office door, pulled her chair up to her computer, placed her hands on the keyboard, and typed. The first round of searches pulled down cases that dealt with hurricanes but not insurance, or insurance but not natural disasters, and the later ones dealt with both, but the insurance coverage had very different terms, or the house damage didn't sound similar enough. But the actual case she wanted kept its fucking distance from her, just like the cars that drove all night on the street beneath her bedroom window. Where was it? She got up and grabbed a cup of water from the kitchen water cooler and sat back down, trying to will the right case closer. Outside her office a more complete silence than usual had set in. A silence that refused to fall prey to lawyers' footsteps shuffling past each other on carpet or the usual round of secretaries whispering about which partner was mean-est, most demanding, so technologically behind that he still wanted all his emails printed out.

Aretha searched until the cases began to circle around one another, like she'd been taught, the same handful of them popping up over and over again no matter how she framed the search. But instead of that small pack yielding up the right one as it usually did, the four or five cases that came sort of close to what the partner wanted stubbornly remained sort of close. Not close enough to pull and print for him and go running down the hallway, claiming the win. The not-good-enough cases swam in front of her, mocking her with their inadequate facts, which she'd already gone over three times. She punched in an-other search and heard a siren behind her, where, fifty-eight stories below, an ambulance dragged itself across choked-up avenues at a pace she could beat on foot. It was amazing that people bothered to have emergencies in Midtown, a place where traffic could dependably move at one mile per hour for an entire day. She often found herself looking at ambulances trying to dart past six lanes of cars with their lights flashing and hoping the sick or hurt people trapped in the backs of them weren't super-dedicated to making it to a hospital.

"She found it!" yelled the head partner from down the hall.

Shit.

"She found it!" the head partner yelled at Aretha, after sticking only his head into her office, tortoise-style.

Aretha found a fresh hangnail to work on after he disappeared, a flap of loose skin that could easily be bitten down to just before the point where it would draw blood. She waited for the *she* of the partner's sentence to take her victory lap, as the only associate who wouldn't be sadly staring at her computer, wondering why it had failed to cough up the answer. The victory lap wouldn't be a real lap, definitely not run, or even quickly walked. A stroll down to the bathroom or the water cooler undertaken with barely suppressed glee. Other than herself and now Mum, there was one other female litigation associate who'd been sent on the hunt, and Aretha cheered for her to be the winner, since it would be in bad taste for Mum to win on her first day of work. But Mum won. Her quiet steps padded past Aretha's office in triumph, since everyone who didn't win had the good sense to sit quietly at their desks in shame for a moment. And then Mum returned to Aretha's office doorway.

"We should grab lunch sometime," Mum said. "I'd love to ask you a few questions about the office."

"Sure," Aretha said, with an extra-positive spin on her voice to bring it back to within the normal range of how people were supposed to react to asshole requests like wanting to have lunch within the window of time when she'd still be able to remember that Mum won on her first day. Oh, they'd have lunch all right. And Aretha would do her best afterwards to fill Mum's head with the finest misinformation about the office she could dream up. If Aretha did her job right, Mum would be showing up at all the wrong times. Missing key meetings. Filling her water cup backwards.

"How was work?" Aaron asked her.

It was seven hours after Mum's victory, and he leaned against the wall in front of Aretha's office building in an Arcade Fire shirt, a chill look on his face that officially declared worrying passé, and a vape that peeked out of his shirt pocket, just like Nia's. Aretha took a look around the lobby, convinced she'd find a security guy eyeing the vape like it was a bloody steak for him on a plate just out of reach. Aaron had a medical prescription for it. "I said I was anxious, and then I twitched for effect," he'd said once, "and it worked."

But Aretha could feel the perceived illegality of it radiating from his shirt. They moved away from the door, and she took a relieved breath.

She was a magnet that just kept on attracting vapers. She texted the number one vaper in her life to confirm their next brunch date, and went back to number two. This would be the perfect day for her to discover, in the privacy of Aaron's house, out of sight of the cops, that weed chilled her out. She'd spent seven hours trying furiously to win at something other than finding case law. But she didn't end up as the fastest coffee pourer or the person who sent the pissiest email to opposing counsel. Or even the person who sulked hardest after Mum's win. That honor went to a male third-year associate who pretended he was vaguely related to the Kennedys because he was rich and from somewhere near Boston, two qualities that Aretha knew meant he didn't really have anything to bitch about in life, whether Mum won at work or not. If he didn't make partner, he'd crawl home to get swaddled in money and connections until his family came up with another successful career for him. Aretha had no one to slink home to and no other dreams for her life, just a desire to not end up homeless if they passed her over.

Aretha hooked her arm around Aaron's and tried to sound happy about losing at work, because she didn't think the three-week mark was the right time for her to dump two hours of frustration over her fears of not making partner on him. Maybe in week four she'd feel OK about interrupting his permanent relaxation. He only had idyllic-sounding days, full of roasting coffee beans and talking happily to bean suppliers on the phone. He never had to leave his house or sweat over the stress of working for someone else. But he never seemed like the kind of person it was worth being angry at for maintaining a state of ever-present calm. Getting upset at him would be just as worth it as getting pissed at a pear. The pear would remain chill, and she'd be the person who'd wasted all the energy getting mad.

"Mum, huh," he said when she'd finished.

"The stupidest name in existence."

"She could be named Juicy, or Baby Please."

"A lawyer named Baby Please would probably win everything, because they'd seem nice, and that niceness would trick people into thinking they had the better argument, since we're all professional assholes."

"Rename yourself Baby Please, then."

"Done. Now I'll make partner."

"Go on, baby, please."

They walked down from Midtown along Sixth Avenue, from office buildings to residential ones but for the cafés crammed into their ground floors, past Bryant Park into the unknown-to-Aretha streets below it. Aretha, who'd never walked more than a street from her office thanks to food delivery and the subway tunnels that snaked around Rockefeller Center and made the sidewalk optional, couldn't believe what the blocks south of work held. Halal meat smoking its way up her nose as its vendors flipped it over on grills in front of lines of customers that snaked down blocks. The bead district of the upper Thirties, sending her back to all the years of summer camp where they had nothing better for girls to do than make different kinds of bracelets. Entire families dressed in matching lime-green sweatshirts so they could find one another if the forces of darkness conspired to separate them after a matinee performance of *Mamma Mia!*

"Have you been here before?" she asked Aaron.

"Yeah. When I was broke as shit back in the East Village, I entertained myself by walkin' the length of the island."

"This is amazing," she said, looking directly into the maw of a Macy's revolving door which spat hundreds of people out per minute.

"You wanna see somethin' amazin'? Come back at eight a.m. and you'll see a DMV line that stretches from here to the moon."

"Aaron, with DMV line updates on the eights," she said, in her best imitation of 1010 WINS.

"You know it."

"So what'd you do today?"

"The usual. Bagged up some freshly roasted beans and dropped 'em off at grocery stores. Took the train out to a couple of coffee shops that just started carryin' our beans and did a brewin' demo. Talked to a coffee bean seller in Mexico who promised to barbecue a whole goat when I come down to visit 'im next week."

"That sounds delicious."

"Come with me."

Aretha let herself imagine a world in which she, a person who'd never taken a vacation thanks to a childhood lack of money and a working-adult lack of time off, went with him, greatly helped by every video clip she'd ever seen of Mexico. She pictured one enormous taco, twenty beaches that sat on top of one another internet-tab style, and a farm where someone had put the coffee beans she bought at the grocery store back on trees.

"Take your trip to Mexico when I get that half-day off for Thanksgiving."

"You should come over for Thanksgiving. We go all out."

"What does that mean?"

"James bakes eighty kinds of pie, and Brittany makes somethin' Puritan, and I grill brisket out in the backyard 'cause I can't stand turkey. We throw ourselves a little party because we're sort of our own family."

Brittany and James. Members of the club. Even if they didn't like her that much. Aretha shaved off a good 20 percent of the disdain that she felt when she thought about the night she'd met them: James and his odd pointy bag, Brittany's open hostility. Anyone who didn't have someplace to go to be surrounded by family on a holiday felt like kin to her.

"I'd love that."

Aretha clenched her right fist before remembering just in time that she wasn't going to pump it just because she'd been invited to a Thanksgiving full of familyless people like her. Openly celebrating other people's familylessness felt tacky. But in her head she listed all the reasons why going over to his place for Thanksgiving would be perfect. She usually went with Nia to her parents' house out on Long Island and watched the three of them, clad in turkey sweaters, talk about the neighbors, who her mom disdainfully called "new money," and her dad insisted were relatable because they watched football. Aretha watched all of them, petri-dish style, with great interest, since they taught her bits and pieces of a language that had proved useful at work when she needed to cover up her working-class background with the upscale personal presentation that made more sense in fancy law firms. But it would be cool to take a year off from people who had won more at work than she had that week and spend the holiday with normal people eating normal food in a more normal-sized house instead of Nia's parents' palace, where she sometimes worried she'd break everything right down to the forks. Of course Brittany and James would be normal. Holidays normalized everyone by turning them into food-serving, table-sitting, carbed-out mounds in chairs. She was gonna eat herself silly and veg out in that gorgeous house. And Brittany and James would warm up to her after the shared experience of getting way too full.

"You're cheating on our family Thanksgiving?" Nia texted her back later that night.

"Your family's Thanksgiving."

"Aw, come on. You know my parents think of you as their daughter from another mother."

"No they don't. They think of me as a very nicely dressed charity case, because of my parents."

"Nope. They were gonna make buttermilk pie for you."

"No fucking way."

"Yes way. I'll bring you a slice."

"Thank you!"

"And you bring me some buckshot from your dinner."

"You've always seemed like more of a brass-knuckles chick."

"I accept all gifts. We still on for post-Thanksgiving brunch?"

"Hell yeah."

For the month before the holiday, Aretha and Aaron hung out every night. They met up outside her office and inside coffee shops where he gave baristas brewing tips. They walked Manhattan, Brooklyn, Queens. They rode around in the coffee van Aaron used to drop off bean deliveries, an unmarked navy-blue boat that smelled like a diet version of the roasting room. For Halloween, they dressed up as Lil' Kim and a tall, skinny Biggie to hand out candy from the front porch of the house with a costume-appropriate soundtrack playing on Aretha's phone. They slept on each other on the subway and learned that they were both the kinds of people who always miraculously woke up before missing their stop. They crammed themselves into ferry seats and tucked themselves around each other, rocking as one with the boat's bounce over the water. They had sex in her apartment, in his bedroom, in unisex bar bathrooms, in the back of the coffee van after they'd parked it on a dark residential street between deliveries.

Sometimes, right before Aretha went to sleep at night, she hallucinated up the feeling of Aaron's hand on the small of her back when they walked down the street.

He whipped out pictures of his grandma. Texas. The early days of his coffee company, when he and Brittany dressed up as broken mugs to call more attention to their coffee at coffee conferences. Aretha put her head on his stomach when they sat on park benches and told him about law school, the firm, speeding to Chicago in Nia's green Fiat, the parties she loved going to, even if a more crushing than usual workload and her new Aaron obsession meant she'd stopped going to them. They went to the aquarium on a cold, windy day and shivered together as they watched the outdoor seals strut around like bored prizefighters. She memorized the twitch of his shivering and how it was unlike hers. They went from the aquarium's chill to the nose-prickling radiator heat of the inside of a Coney Island pizza place to the steaming heat of the first slice of pizza burning the roofs of their mouths. Their waitress took their picture to put up on the happy couples' section of the customer wall. Aaron went to the bathroom right before they left, and Aretha gazed at their shot, where tall him hulked down to get in the same part of the frame as smaller her, the two of them matched only in their million-watt smiles.

Aretha rose early on Thanksgiving Day to pick out wine for the drinkers in Aaron's house, as a gift. She walked the quiet residential streets of her neighborhood until she reached Flatbush, land of liquor stores. To her right lay the cheap place, to her left the expensive place, right in front of her the right place, the place between cheap and expensive that would signal she wasn't trying too hard. Now all she had to do was pick a wine that also tried the right amount.

As a hard liquor drinker by choice, her reward for finding the wine section of liquor stores was a feverish round of trying to remember what she'd ever learned about wine, which mostly came from tipsy conversations at firm happy hours. The lawyers she worked with loved to yell "I'm not drinking merlot" at one another from some movie she'd never seen, so she should probably rule out merlot. She'd only ever seen prosecco drunk by the kinds of people who accompanied it with one carrot stick, tops, to avoid gaining weight, so it couldn't possibly taste good. In the end she went with a pinot noir, since she remembered seeing an African American flag on one of Aaron's house walls, and knew that *noir* meant "black." The militant wine choice, she said to herself. The Black Power fist of wines.

The correctness of her wine selection carried her the six blocks between the liquor store and the Vanderbilt house. She arrived on Aaron's porch and rang the doorbell. He scooped her up into a kiss and led her inside, where she took in the house for the first time since their first date. The roasting room gave off an orange note that Aretha gratefully inhaled twice, and the rest of the house smelled like something she couldn't label until the two of them made it to the kitchen and she saw three pies cooling on the counter. She moved a little closer to take in the smell of freshly baked crust, and then she saw the bowl of brown glop down the counter.

"Is that gravy?" she asked Aaron.

"Pilgrim puddin'. Brittany made it. I think it's got cornmeal and molasses and pure New England motives in it."

"I love a good dessert full of motives."

"Don't we all?"

He pulled a tray of meat out of the fridge, headed to the back of the house, and opened a door that deposited them in the backyard. She took a look around and found a hammock still wet from the previous night's rain, a bright green square of Astroturf that cut up an otherwise seamless browning November lawn, and a smoking grill large enough to double as a spare planet in a pinch. She took a long look at the Astroturf, but he headed to the grill and flipped it open. Instead of the charcoal bricks she associated with grilling, Aaron was burning wood.

"What kind of wood is that?"

"Mesquite."

"Why are you using wood?"

"'Cause I don't want my meat to taste like outer space."

"What kind of meat is that?" Aretha asked, pointing to his tray, which had all sorts of meat she swore she'd never seen before.

"Well, over here we have brisket and hot links, and over here we have goat."

"I have never had any of that."

"First you're gonna try mine, and then we're gonna get you down to West Texas."

He kissed her and started putting meat on the grill. She imagined their idyllic future trip to West Texas. Sunshine, oil fields, tumbleweeds. The excitement that came from visiting a place she'd never been within a thousand miles of, even though, other than the meat, he called it boring. She was firmly in the middle of the how-boring-could-anything-possibly-be-because-it-has-to-do-with-him stage of their relationship. She was going to get right off the plane and hug a tumbleweed, and it was going to hug her back.

She heard footsteps from across the lawn. Brittany walked over in a festive tracksuit. Black, with a floral ribbon that ran from her shoulder to her sleeve. Aretha smiled at her, and Brittany didn't bother smiling back.

"Hi, I'm Aretha."

"I know."

"Thanks for inviting me over for Thanksgiving."

"I didn't invite you anywhere."

"Well, thank you for having me anyway. I brought some wine," Aretha said, handing the bottle over.

"Thanks," Brittany said, as if thanking people hurt her physically. "Did he give you the full tour?"

"Not yet," Aaron said.

"Are you going to give me the full tour?" Aretha said.

"No. I'm just going to point stuff out. Back there we have three stories of house," Brittany said. "And over there we have our bunker," she said, pointing at the Astroturf.

"Your bunker," Aretha said.

"Our bunker."

Aretha looked at Aaron. We had a deal, she said to him silently. A deal where we hung out with each other and had a damn good time doing it in a way that didn't mean we ever had to think about your bunker because you said you weren't really into shit like having a bunker.

Instead of saying something that would fix the moment, Aaron just smiled. Aretha took her left hand, pulled it behind her back, and balled it up into a fist before she remembered that she wasn't the kind of person who let anyone speak for her. Now all she needed was something to say.

If only she could run over there and pull at the Astroturf, which had to be covering a trapdoor. If she could get in the bunker and look around, she'd know how to feel about it. Until then, what was the point of trying to make conversation about something she hadn't even seen? But Aaron was still here, on her right, flipping meat and watching the two of them, so she stood still for a minute, trying to figure out what to say about the bunker. She looked over at Aaron and watched him watch her. This was obviously some kind of test.

Had they really spent every day together for a month so she could give a thumbs-up to a psychotic hole in the ground? If he really wasn't that into the survivalist stuff, why didn't he say something dismissive about the bunker? Bunkers were for people who wanted to spend their whole lives worrying about a doomsday that would probably kill everyone in sight if it happened. A bunker would have nothing to do with Aaron's hurricane fears, unless his big hurricane plan was to drown before everyone else got the chance.

"A bunker, huh," she said, figuring Brittany would find her dumb and start talking about what the bunker held so she could make up her mind based on its contents.

"Built it myself."

"You're a structural engineer?"

"I dabble."

"So what's in there?" Aretha asked, annoyed, because guiding people towards talking their way into trouble had worked on pretty much everyone else she'd ever met.

"Oh, you know," Brittany said, amused. "Bunker stuff."

"Want a taste of brisket?" Aaron said.

"Sure," Aretha said, thrown off, but hungry.

He held out a slice of meat to her, and she ate it off his fingers. She tasted brisket salt and brisket fat and finger salt. All that fat and salt took her away from the bunker and straight into a world where the only thing that mattered was the taste of that meat.

"Can I have one more piece?" she said.

He held out a second cut, and she did it again, went straight to Brisketland, far away from the backyard and everything else she'd ever tasted. It was hilarious that they had a bunker out here, because this, at its heart, was a house of pleasures. That coffee smell. Those pies cooling on the kitchen counter inside. This meat. The feel of her legs tucked between his on his bed, right before they went to sleep. She didn't have to make a decision on the bunker this instant. She could hang out, eat more meat, maybe go down and check it out herself when no one else was watching. Besides, who was she to not take Aaron's fears seriously? She feared car accidents thanks to her parents' deaths, and not making partner in a way that would leave her unemployed and on the street. If anyone dared to dismiss her fears she'd find a way to politely tell them to fuck off. He'd been through shit, and he was afraid of shit, and part of the reason she stood in this backyard was because she knew what that was like. So what that he had a little fort in the corner of the backyard.

"I think it's great that you have a bunker," Aretha said to Brittany.

"Fantastic," Brittany said.

She headed back towards the house, clutching Aretha's wine, but at the last minute she put the bottle down on the back porch and went in without it.

Fuck Brittany. Aretha wasn't afraid of her or her fucking bunker. She didn't go around being afraid of people, and she sure as hell wasn't planning to start now.

"Sometimes Brittany's a little spicy," Aaron said.

She'd mentally thrown enough anger in Brittany's retreating direction that she'd forgotten he was still there. She put a hand on his shoulder, and felt grill smoke waft over her fingers.

"I think we're going to end up getting along fine," Aretha said.

She grabbed the wine off the porch, took it inside, and put it in the center of their dining room table.

A few hours later, when she, Aaron, Brittany, and James sat down at that table to eat with the opened bottle of wine at its center, she felt the familiar glow of refusing to lose. After they'd eaten the first round of food and everyone's faces relaxed from it, she went with her first rule of getting to know people and asked them about what she knew they cared about so they could talk about themselves. She asked Brittany about the business, and Brittany answered with a good 10 percent more interest than she'd ever showed in Aretha's presence. She asked James about building security, and he talked doorbells and cameras and his lookout point on the roof, and she allowed herself to be fascinated with the mechanics of making sure no one broke into your house.

Aaron told stories about his last couple of trips to buy coffee beans in South America, and Aretha laughed along with the rest of the table at his tales of PowerPoints awkwardly displayed over the pictures of family on bean growers' house walls. Hundred-degree days that he spent sweatily trailing people who wanted to show him their coffee fields. "All I could find in late June was one of those big straw hats with a pink ribbon tied around the base, so I was out there lookin' all Mary Poppins down in Ecuador tryin' to keep the sun outta my eyes, and the Ecuadoreans were laughin' their asses off at me." Aretha could look across the table at Brittany and James and feel something resembling warmth. She could watch Aaron telling stories about Ecuador and know she was in the right place, to his left at the kitchen table, enjoying the shit out of being with him.

They ate more food than she'd ever seen before. The grilled meat. Brittany's potato salad and collard greens. James's apple pie and sweet potato pie and whiskey buttermilk pie, which tasted like Nia's parents' buttermilk pie with a little extra zing. Brittany's Puritan pudding, which tasted like being told you should never enjoy anything in bowl form. "The humbler the food, the closer the God," she said. Aretha silently threw her support behind food with an ego. And miraculously, after dinner, the three of them went upstairs, one by one, to nap everything off, leaving Aretha awake and alone downstairs. She waited for three sets of snoring and crept out into the backyard.

Outside she greeted the Brooklyn night: a black sheet lit through with orange streetlights, framed by the low hum of traffic. She always appreciated the streetlights, which made her feel safe crawling home alone after late bar nights, but that night she really appreciated them for lighting up the backyard enough for her to tiptoe through it. She made it all the way over to the strip of Astroturf and pulled on it. It didn't budge. She ran her hands over it like she was drawing a grid, square by square, until she found a hidden latch, which gave when she pulled on it and swung what looked like a trapdoor up into her hands. Startled, she paused a second before sliding herself down through the doorway to the ladder that led from the Astroturf to the bunker floor. The door clicked shut behind her, and she was in the terrifying pitch-black underground. Brooklyn didn't do pitch-black. No matter what kind of blackout curtains she bought to sleep with and however tightly she pulled them, orange streetlights and white headlights crept into her bedroom with a vengeance. At least she could still hear traffic streaming by.

She wished she could replace every step she took down the ladder with a step back up into the light, but she hadn't come this far to not figure out what they kept in the bunker. So she moved her hands in slow circles around her. She could feel her way through this. Besides, they couldn't possibly be planning to spend the rest of their lives underground in total darkness. She touched fat lumps and skinny pointy lumps and one wide, soft lump that had to be a bed, before she remembered that she had a flashlight on her phone and flipped it on.

She stood inside maybe four hundred square feet of metal-walled bunker. Her feet clicked on its floor like she'd taken up tap dancing. She saw water. Blankets. A copy of *The Thinking Man's Guide to*

*Self-Defense.* She flipped it open to chapter 8, "Understanding the Enemy Within." She closed it. She flipped it open again, to chapter 12, "Man: The Most Dangerous Game." She closed it again. She wiped her hands off like the book was covered in worms. She saw a constellation of flashlights attached to a metal coatrack that looked like a tree. She opened the duffel bag at the base of the flashlight tree and stared at hundreds of batteries nestled inside, hard plastic butterflies in their cocoon. A bed, a folded air mattress, a battery-operated radio. A stack of canned split-pea soup next to a can opener. A neatly folded set of extra blankets. A pile of extra clothes. A crisp red, black, and green striped flag, so two of the three people who lived in the house wouldn't accidentally forget what race they were in the middle of the end of the world. She imagined Brittany and Aaron tinkering with the Black national anthem until they ended up with "Lift Ev'ry Bunker and Sing."

They had more bags of coffee than anyone else would possibly store in a bunker, with their armed coffee drinker plastered on every single one. A hand grinder sat next to the coffee, and a French press, too, the biggest one Aretha had ever seen, home to six or maybe even eight cups when full, right alongside a pan deep enough to heat that much water, and a hot plate. And the weapons. The swords mounted on walls, the nunchucks piled in a corner, the safe that, when she wiggled it, sounded like it had at least a couple guns inside.

Why the fuck was she here? She had fears, sure, and so she kind of understood the hurricane that had rented an apartment inside Aaron's head, and the break-in that haunted all of them, but she remained a lawyer. A logical person, controlled by reasonable deductions based on facts and evidence. She didn't run on fear, or rounds of useless humoring of that fear, or the crystallization of that fear into probably structurally unsound underground sheet-metal boxes full of food and weapons. She sat on the metal floor, realized she didn't want to sit on their weird-ass metal floor, got up, and worked her way back up the ladder into the relative normality of the backyard.

From the yard she crept back into the house, where she headed for the roasting room. She sat on the floor and breathed in some coffee fumes. The roaster wasn't on, probably for the holiday, she thought, so the steam layer of the smell she remembered from the night of her and Aaron's first date had gone, leaving just the coffee itself, warm and sharp. She stood up and walked around the roaster, trying to discover more about a part of the house that didn't bug her, like the bunker did, but the roaster just sat in the middle of its room, a hunk of metal that didn't plan on explaining its secrets. She could sleep on the bunker issue and figure out how she felt about it in the morning.

She crept upstairs, to the bedrooms, where, behind the first door on the right, Aaron slept, still smelling of brisket. She climbed into bed next to him, sleepy thanks to his bedroom's calming failure to resemble four hundred square feet of underground sheet metal. She closed her eyes. One of his fingers brushed her lip. It still smelled like brisket. She took the finger into her mouth and sucked on it as if she could pull brisket fat right out of his skin. He gave her another finger, and another. They took their clothes off.

The next day she woke up and stared at him, wondering why she always woke up feeling brighter next to him, like the mere act of sleeping tucked under his arm made her 10 percent sun. She took in his sleeping face and waited patiently for his knocked-out self to tell her how she should feel about the bunker before he woke up. No dice.

She kissed his forehead, whispered that she'd text him in a few hours, rolled out of his bed and right back to her apartment for a shower and a change of clothes before meeting Nia at brunch, having returned only the brunch text of the pile from Nia that sat on her phone. The other texts asked her questions she didn't want to answer about Aaron and the Vanderbilt house. She'd really thought Nia was cool enough with Aaron, but there was nothing like a few glasses of wine at Thanksgiving dinner to make it clear that she wasn't. Shit. She could see Nia's texts even when she wasn't looking at her phone. "Having gun-shaped pie for dessert?" one said. "Packing a go-bag of love?" read number two. Aretha scoffed at the Aretha of one month ago, who was sure she'd escaped Nia's anti-survivalist disdain. But the worst text sat on top of the pile: "So how many guns does he have?" It was a question she still didn't have the answer to. Yeah, she'd found the safe in the bunker, and James had that full black bag, but she'd be a fool to decide that was it. Did Aaron have guns? Someday she'd have to search his bedroom.

If only you could just google how many guns someone had. You could stick in their name, and, say, "3" would pop up along with a designation like "moderately armed," if owning three guns counted as moderately armed. Like an air-quality report, but for guns. Aretha had no idea how many guns people who owned guns in the city tended to have, or how many guns would sound like too many, if Aaron ever spit out a number for himself.

Maybe one wouldn't seem excessive, she thought on the walk up the block to the restaurant. Especially if he had a license for it and kept it in a safe. Also, if he did have a gun, would it be hot? She pictured him in a wide stance in the cowboy boots he wore everywhere, with a gun holstered to his waist. She needed to lie down. She tipped her head, as if the part of her that felt ready to allow him one gun could be drained out of her ear. In what world was she a woman who'd put up with her boyfriend owning a gun? If she needed to date a gun guy, she should have stayed in Wisconsin, where people could at least theoretically hunt deer, even if they didn't really do that anymore. There was nothing to hunt in Brooklyn but other people.

If only Aaron could figure out how to suck, which would make her verdict on his permitted number of guns so much easier. She could hate his terrible manners or eternally unwashed clothes or an insatiable cheating habit instead. She tried to imagine him aiming a gun at someone but he popped up in her head eating sweet potato pie and calling himself Mary Poppins again. Her sunny self came back. Nia was already at their usual restaurant booth when Aretha blew in, red-lipsticked and happy.

"What is it?" Nia said.

"Nothing," Aretha said.

"You don't fucking believe in lipstick."

"Maybe I do sometimes."

Nia gave Aretha a look.

"Maybe every once in a while."

Another look.

"Today's a lipstick day."

"It's a great lipstick," Nia said.

"Thanks," Aretha said, slouching back into her chair in relief. "So, what's up with you?"

"No, you first."

"You can go."

"I have a feeling you're going to be the one with the news."

Aretha looked down at her sweater sleeves, which had grown bits of lint that had to be picked off right then. It was late November, but not really cold enough to qualify as sweater season yet. She'd put on the sweater as a kind of fuzzy moral support so she and it could face down whatever Nia threw at them.

"Come on," Nia said.

"I want to move in with him."

"Yeah, that's what the lipstick said, too."

"His house is perfect," she said.

"Not him."

"Yeah, it's mostly about the house. He's optional."

"Actually, wait a minute," Nia said. "He owns a fucking house? You never mentioned that."

"I didn't?"

"No."

"It's a whole three-story house."

"And he's our age?"

"Yeah."

"And the house is here?"

"Yeah."

"Where the hell did he get the money to buy a house here?"

"His coffee-roasting business, I think."

"But we all made a deal we didn't want to make by moving here in the last couple of decades. Everyone that's about our age. No owning houses in places like here. The deal is you live here until they raise the rent on you enough that you have to leave, like a lobster in a boiling pot."

"You own an apartment."

"I don't own a house."

"Well, he does."

Aretha described the roasting room. The bedrooms. The lush green backyard, carefully removing all mention of that square of Astroturf and what lay underneath it. The monument to coffee in the kitchen. One entire counter filled with a labyrinth of coffee grinders and brewing machines, of which she still worshipped the simplistic Chemex, the first machine she'd met, for its throwback to a simpler time of coffee brewing. Water over ground coffee inside transparent glass.

If she forgot about the guns and the bunker, thinking about the house made her feel like people looked like they felt in cruise ads. Flip-flopped feet thrown up on boat-deck lawn chairs like the people attached to them had developed an allergy to worrying. What stood between her and a house was the six figures of law school loans that she and everyone she knew had taken out as the first step to a lifestyle that might still pan out if she was allowed to keep practicing law for a while.

When she was a kid, the adults in her life had told her that all she had to do was get the right amount of education, land the right job, and then bam! She'd end up with a house. Landlords could kick you out of an apartment or give you the eye for bothering to be Black and trying to rent one, but you could pay off a house and stay in there forever. Never mind that her parents had escaped Chicago only to end up in a rich Wisconsin city where houses remained expensive and distant, and New York was even worse on the house-cost front. Aretha still believed in the gospel of owning a house. But the people she went to law school with had been dropping like flies, suddenly disappearing from their firms right around the time they were supposed to make the final push to partner, which theoretically came with the kind of job security that would let you end up with a house. Aaron's house had Aaron in it, and pounds of excellent-smelling coffee. It also proved that what she had been taught was possible.

"So he's rich," Nia said.

"No, your parents are rich."

"There's own-a-house-on-Long-Island rich, and there's own-a-brownstone-in-the-middle-of-the-fucking-city rich."

"He says it was a fixer-upper."

"Is it falling apart?"

"No."

"Well, he fixed it up into being rich, then. Are you happy?"

"Yes," she said, bringing Aaron to the front of her mind and pushing the heightened competition at work to the absolute back of it.

"Can I meet him?"

"Would you want to?"

"Yes!"

"It's that you've been so negative about the whole him thing."

"You mean the guns?"

Nia said it loud enough that a good quarter of the restaurant turned around to eye them in terror.

"We should get out of here now that everyone thinks we're going to shoot them," Aretha said.

"Just wait it out."

"Somebody will call the police on the two Black women who are talking about being armed."

"Not if we don't whip any weapons out."

Aretha took a look around the dining room while moving her eyes as little as possible to avoid attracting even more attention, but the crowd looked pretty Central Brooklyn: a collection of people from enough of the colors and backgrounds that didn't award themselves trophies for summoning the cops. Many of them had phones in hand, sure, but to stare dreamily into them as usual, not for the thrill of dialing 911.

The moment passed. Their food came. The usual eggs for Nia, but Aretha had sprung for French toast. Food with a backbone to back up her sweater in its defense of the rest of her. Bread never betrayed you. She took a bite, and it tasted great, but why did she need backup? She remembered waking up with the sunniness lodged in her head, and she let it propel her to where she truly wanted to go.

"They have a couple of guns," she said.

"Are you worried about that?" Nia said.

"Sometimes. They have a bunker, too."

"The fuck?"

"It's a little Astroturf-covered underground square in a corner of their backyard with food and guns in it."

"That'll get flooded if we get an inch and a half of rain."

"They swear it won't, but they haven't taken it through a hurricane season yet."

"Are you freaked out by it?"

"I go back and forth on that. The way he and his roommates introduced me to the bunker felt like a challenge, and you know me, I'm up for any good challenge that doesn't involve a bunker. But he lives with two other people, and they don't have family, and he invited me over for Thanksgiving so we could not have family together, and I fucking loved that he got me that well. So I'm torn, but leaning towards deciding that the bunker isn't going to get me."

"You're not worried that they'll use their guns on each other, or you."

"No."

"Who the fuck are you now?"

"I don't know," Aretha said.

"Well, girl, if you need me . . ."

"I'll let you know."

How had she become a person who threw her instincts in the garbage? Her instincts had gotten her to the fifty-eighth floor of a Midtown office building where even if Mum seemed promising Aretha swore she could win more often than not because she was a winner, to her austere studio apartment with nothing on the walls, as she liked it, and everything she needed in the closets, from suits to jumpsuits to the kinds of dresses it took a miracle of gravity to get into, to this life that she had largely shared with the friend who sat across the table from her, wondering why she had become someone else. She loved her sensible self, the person who could always research her way to an answer that made sense. The person she'd known forever, who made sense all the time, knew that bunkers were bullshit. Yet every time she hung out with Aaron she failed to find the right moment to run away screaming.

Her newer self went back to a daydream she'd had lately, at work and at home and at this diner, sitting in front of this plate. The daydream where she lived in his house, next to him, the source of all the sun she'd absorbed lately, burning up everything that bothered her, from the guns to the feeling of generally losing to Mum at work, to Nia's continued resistance to him. Aretha and Aaron had spent twenty-nine straight days together. She kept a toothbrush in his bathroom and a set of clothes in a corner of his closet and a box of spaghetti in his kitchen cupboard. They practically lived together already.

She'd never wanted to move in with a guy. She'd liked picturing most the rest of the ones she'd bothered with alive in their own separate squares of apartment and subway car and office, only intersecting with her when she wanted them to, but definitely not for shit like weeks at a time. She'd reluctantly agreed to move in with her last ex right before his mother had lifted a hammer and split their relationship like a wall, and she'd taken her failure to do it as evidence of the superiority of living alone. And here she was, ready to give up on the five years of solitude she'd lived in ever since she moved out of the apartment she shared with the catering girls after a couple of them got knocked up and the third found a catering job thousands of miles away in the desert, where Aretha pictured her putting cactus on toothpicks, spikes and all, for the appetizer daredevils of the world.

But no one she'd ever met before had made her feel it, the sixth sense that kept her aware of where she was with regard to where Aaron was at all times, or the air that kept her head aloft instead of cynical. At work everyone had started mentioning that she seemed happier, with the disdain that they might have used for someone who'd just cheated them out of fifty thousand dollars, since they didn't have a happy profession. And yet she couldn't stop herself. She felt like a sleepwalker, if sleepwalkers forever felt the one decent high she reached in college. The time she'd taken a pull off one of Nia's joints and understood that she could fly.

"Tell me more about your survivalist patient," Aretha said.

Nia sighed.

"OK. So, I've had three of them, and they could all put on a respectable face. But when the end of the world comes, they're going to shoot it," Nia said.

"I thought you only had one survivalist patient."

"I didn't tell you about the other two, because they're freaky."

"Go ahead."

"Fine. The second one was an army vet who was looking for shooting buddies and thought the rest of it was like long-term camping. The food-replacement shit. The bunker-building. Everything right up until they formed a plot to shoot a congressman who wanted to introduce a bill to ban assault weapons again. They were going to shoot the guards, dress in their uniforms, then go in and take out the congressman. The idea being that they needed to do this so they could keep the guns they needed to shoot the end of the world when it came. The guy still comes in every week, dressed in fake fatigues, ready to mark his feelings up on a whiteboard he always brings with him. Every time I ask him why he still wears the fatigues, he just looks at me like he's a Christmas ornament someone smashed with a hammer and glued back together wrong. Sometimes I'm worried he's going to kill himself. He's never really replaced being like that with anything else.

"The third one just kind of disappeared before we really had a chance to get into the issues she came to talk about. Her strict family, their emphasis on five hundred seventy-three rules for every situation, her inability to make or keep friends because of an emotional distance she thought made her seem tough. If I had to guess, I'd tell you she was still out there living that life."

Aretha immediately thought of Brittany and the friendless house she lived in. Three stories of them and their coffee, blocking people off in the same way. But they hadn't blocked her off. Well, at least Aaron hadn't.

"Did they go after the congressman?"

"No."

"Why do you think the woman went back to it?" Aretha asked, waiting for Nia to describe the mysterious woman as tall, black, giving off vibes of Cruella De Vil as an aging track star, and extraordinarily preppy.

"Hey, she could have gone to see another therapist. I'm working on a hunch, since she told me what she wanted to talk about, worked through those issues for a couple of sessions with good progress, and then just up and disappeared. But who knows? Maybe she's happily running a fishing boat in Florida."

"People leave here to fish all the time."

"Maybe she owns a casino in Vegas. Maybe she spends most of her days on the moon."

"Of course. A moon person."

"Living with all the other fucking moon people."

"Eating dried food out of little plastic bags."

"Calling the act of waking up one giant step for mankind."

"I've just never understood why people need to spend all their time planning for some emergency that will never happen."

"I think of it as a control thing. Like anorexia, but with guns."

"Wow. I don't think I could ever become that much of a control freak," Aretha said, while wondering if that was true.

They went back to their food. Aretha waved their server over to order a limeade. Nia ordered a mimosa. Their Saturday brunch did what Saturday brunches are supposed to do around the hour mark: make the weekend days on which they happen feel infinite and golden, just for not having work in them. Aretha looked back at the version of herself that was raised by a house cleaner mom and a security guard dad, neither of whom made it to college. They ate most of their meals as homemade work sandwiches and warmed-over dinners prepared quickly during their slivers of free time and consumed no further than several feet away from their kitchen. She thought if her parents had been alive, they'd have found her alien, with a law degree and only the mildest shame about spending fifteen dollars on egg-covered bread. Yeah, other people pictured aliens as green-skinned things that talked mostly in beeps, but they'd forgotten about the kind that could afford expensive French toast.

"So how is work?" Nia said.

Aretha moaned.

"There's fresh blood," she said, before going on at length about Mum, who'd shown a disconcerting tendency to win case law competitions and say the right things in meetings. Partners looked at her with confidence. Younger associates too. She'd grown a tail full of baby lawyers that trailed after her from water cooler to desk to meeting, as if respected lawyer vibes could be absorbed through air.

"I'm going with a two-part strategy: try even harder to kick ass at work, and get my recruiter to get me out of there so I can find someplace else to make partner in case my work foot doesn't make contact with enough ass."

"Since when do you want to make partner?"

"Look, I've thought about it, and . . ."

It's what comes next, Aretha didn't say, because she didn't think that sounded convincing. How else am I going to pay off my loans as a person who spent too many years spending money partying felt depressing to think, much less say out loud. But she needed to blow off steam from work, and forget about having dead parents, even if it took a boatload of sixteen-dollar drinks and twenty-five-dollar covers to dissolve the darker parts of her life. "Making partner is the only way to truly win at work" didn't feel like the right thing to say, since Nia always won at work. She owned her own therapy practice, so no one could fire her. She owned her perfect two-bedroom co-op apartment, so no one could kick her out of New York. Aretha owned a closet full of clothes and some shame about how much less she owned than Nia. She pictured Nia's apartment, with its tasteful wall art of Black people being Black throughout time and asked herself why she couldn't have her piece of Aaron's house. "I want to make partner because I don't like where showing up at work seems to be heading otherwise" would come too close to admitting that she probably wouldn't make partner, even though the odds were against her anyway, and the number one rule in the law was to never admit that you might be flunking out of it, because that would seem less successful, and one of the keys to making partner was to give off constant, consistent vibes of success. I want to make partner because it's the only important job in the law, she didn't say out loud, since she felt sure Nia would point out some other legal job that she thought had to mean something to the lawyers who did it. Sure, there were smaller firms, and the feds, and in-house positions at companies, but to take those jobs after six years at a large law firm would be like cutting off her left leg at mile 18 of a marathon. Also, they paid less.

What else was there to want other than partner? The feds never won millions of dollars for an identifiable person, just the nameless, faceless general public. And their basically nine-to-five hours lacked the urgency of the firms' late nights and weekends. Smaller firms could win money, but sentenced lawyers to a less-glamorous existence, full of printing their own copies and emailing their own documents. In-house jobs left the real action to outside counsel, the front line of the legal army, the people who wrote the briefs and made the arguments and did the winning while she would be doomed to sit there, in an office, answering questions for the dipshits in marketing, with their perfectly coordinated outfits and empty heads.

Even if she didn't necessarily adore defending the companies who wrapped themselves into pretzels to avoid paying for hurricane damage that was probably their fault, or arguing in favor of defective products that had almost certainly chopped off people's legs, there was always the prospect of winning, attached to the potential to recover enough dollars in damages to coat the entire practice of law in glory. There were arguments to shape and favorable decisions to earn, and the only way to keep the adrenaline rush of both flowing was to keep hiking up the mountain towards partnership.

"It's just what I want," she finished, leaning back and crossing her arms as a buffer against Nia's raised eyebrows.

"You've never really sold me on that being what you want," Nia said.

"I'll get there."

Nia redoubled her eating efforts, even though Aretha felt ready to hurl whatever she could at the idea that trying to make partner was an unworthy goal. She needed an adversary, and hers was suddenly much too busy with her food to keep up the fight. Aretha's French toast looked tired now that she wasn't going to have to defend herself anymore, sagging in its syrup like old skin. But Nia hadn't pressed her too hard on the guns. Maybe she'd gotten away with one.

When they'd finished eating, she waved goodbye to Nia and congratulated herself for not setting a firm time for her to meet Aaron, who was waiting for her two blocks away, in the middle of the Vanderbilt strip, on a corner in a direction Nia wouldn't walk. Aretha and Aaron had to meet up because their twenty-nine-day streak of meeting up couldn't possibly stop at thirty. They went back to his place to throw a new set of beans in the roaster. They visited a couple of coffee shops that had bought beans so Aaron could demonstrate a couple of brewing tips, and Aretha felt warm while she watched his hands work, from pulling to tamping to pouring, with the finished product sliding darkly out of the pot with a concentrated version of the same rich roasted smell she linked to his house. Then they were free to walk around Prospect Park, where an early cold shock had turned the trees orange and yellow. This is such a stereotype, she thought as they walked along the edge of the running path, hand in hand, while the orange and yellow trees pumped the sky full of energy. Liking this walking-through-the-fallen-leaves shit is like liking Paris. I am not a basic bitch.

Aaron gently stopped her, mid-stride, and clasped her right hand in both of his.

"Aretha," he said.

"Yes," she said.

"Will you move in with me?"

"Oh my god, yes," she said.

"I love you," he said.

Something inside her flipped on, like a light switch.

"I love you too," she said.

He whipped out a yellow bracelet and slid it over her wrist like a very big yellow rubber engagement ring. She felt the same sense of flight she'd felt at the diner, but this time she took off, leaving Nia and her silly getting-too-worried-about-the-bunker concerns on the ground.

"A promise bracelet," Aretha said, laughing.

They hugged. They resumed their walk.

And then she took a good look at the bracelet, which screamed TACTICAL COFFEE from her wrist. If she wore it to work, from a distance, her coworkers would think the bracelet meant she opposed cancer. If anyone asked, she could explain that they leaned on the more strategic side of coffee, and a good 75 percent of her coworkers, being the kind of people who thought they could outfox a tiger if they needed to win a case, would accept that. Strategy was always an OK way to frame your goals, no matter how bloodthirsty they were. At work she could stand up and announce that a legal defense plan involved killing off all the remaining giraffes of the world, and no one would flinch as long as she phrased it in technical terms like "reducing giraffes' global emissions by pursuing a one hundred percent elimination of their carbon footprint."

But she was sure as hell going to take that bracelet off before she went to brunch with Nia again, or at least slide it up high, under a sweater. She and Aaron finished their park loop and turned back towards Vanderbilt. She leaned into the basicness of the moment. She was going to live with her wonderful boyfriend and his roommates who would become wonderful the second she moved in. Brittany and James would understand that Thanksgiving went well enough that they could allow themselves to shave another hunk off their dislike of her. And then they'd slide into friendship. They'd take crazy road trips to deliver coffee beans together. They'd watch funny movies and look at each other in total mutual understanding with each joke they agreed was hilarious. They'd look back, six months or a year from now, at that completely ridiculous period in their lives when they weren't tight and laugh at their previous inferior selves.

She dropped Aaron off at his door.

"Four weeks," he said.

"So you've been listening to me when I mentioned my lease is up in December."

"My ears are right here, open as hell."

At home, she emailed her landlord to let him know she wouldn't be renewing her lease. She packed between trips to see Aaron at the Vanderbilt house and trips to meet up with Aaron on a street corner and eat dinner or see movies or walk to the waterfront and watch the East River churn. She looked into her closet and saw all her party stuff hanging in a corner, ditched since she'd met Aaron. She ran her hands over dresses. Skirts. Two sequined jumpsuits that took her back to an era of frantic nights on the dance floor, because if she bothered with a jumpsuit, she was gonna get down. She swore she'd drag Aaron out to party some night.

She packed while getting hit with memories of the apartment she'd agreed to ditch: the glory of finding a decent place to cushion the sting of having to move out of the apartment she shared with her three caterer roommates who kept their kitchen so full of free white wine and congealed hors d'oeuvres that she had to keep her food in her bedroom but were always up for going out on a Thursday, or a Tuesday night, or a Sunday afternoon after-party to the Sunday morning after-party to the Saturday night start of the whole thing; celebrating the raise she'd gotten at work with Nia, an ill-advised pre-party bottle of rum and the taxi driver who reversed backwards down a narrow street at forty miles an hour to avoid a stopped ambulance; getting ready to go out to a party in her apartment's tiny, badly lit bathroom and accidentally gluing a set of false eyelashes just far enough away from her real ones that she looked like she'd started knitting a blanket to cover her face. She had lived alone here, sure, but in retrospect she'd liked it. She packed between rounds of work where she casually misinformed Mum about the tiniest things just so she'd look dumb: where they kept paper clips, staples, salt. What font a particular partner liked to put briefs in.

The thought of moving in with Aaron gave her the strength to go after Mum. During the ten-second gap every morning after she passed through the last round of building security but before she landed at her office door, she could feel her destructive powers coming on. The elevator thrust itself upwards, sending a tingle into her arms that inched her ever so closer to becoming a human lightning strike. She could be the blast of light and heat that would send Mum crawling back to whatever hellhole firm she came from. At work, Aretha found cases and wrote memos and talked to juniors about how to do their jobs without fucking up in million-dollar ways, but the only thing that truly made her happy was overhearing a confused Mum get corrected about all the steps the firm usually took to make sure a brief was filed by five p.m.

Alongside the growing pile of boxes in her apartment lay the duffel bag Aaron had recommended she bring, and inside that bag sat an emergency blanket, a couple of weeks' worth of protein bars called Life Preservers, two flashlights in case one ran out of batteries, and the smallest radio she could find online. She had become good at looking at the go-bag and thinking of it as a go-bag instead of her go-bag. Just a go-bag that would live at Aaron's house with its go-bag sisters so they could all grab one on their way out of the house like those families with tons of kids who grabbed one lunch off a counter full of lunches before they went to school. Aretha assumed those lunches were probably perfect because those families could always afford a crisp new brown paper bag to put the lunch in and an endless supply of actual Ziploc brand bags to put their sandwiches and fruit in instead of using one of the leftover plastic bags her parents kept in a pile from when they went shopping.

Aaron had convinced her that she needed a go-bag, just in case a hurricane wrecked the city. The hurricanes are comin' up further and further north these days because the water's too warm, he'd said. When winter disappears, people as far up as Maine are gonna get threatened with water every week. Don't you want to be prepared? She didn't necessarily want to be prepared, but she wouldn't mind having her shit together. Like he did. The falling-apart climate did throw hurricanes and fires and floods at everyone, and that hopefully only once-in-a-lifetime Brooklyn tornado, and when shit happened to her she didn't expect help. Her parents had died, and other than Nia, no one said anything comforting or sent money. Only the antlers showed up, happy to put their bony selves on her shoulder whenever she didn't want to be touched.

In packing her go-bag, she shoved aside her biggest fear: mysteriously getting fired from her law firm and never finding anything else to do with her life. Why couldn't she pack a go-bag that would protect her from total career failure? Oh, you know, a duffel bag with a time machine she could use to saunter back into the past and be born rich. The firings had started when everyone from her law school graduation

year had been practicing for two years, and the professional guillo-
tining marched on every year after that, usually at a psychologically
convenient time like Thanksgiving or Christmas. Thanksgiving had
passed, so at work everyone passed one another with suspicious eyes,
looking for some sign that they'd be called into a meeting to talk
about profits and how they hadn't quite contributed enough to them.

Five years in, and seven case law competitions lost to Mum later,
she wondered how long she had left. Not only were lawyers not really
making partner anymore, almost none of them got close, while older
partners went on at length about how much easier it was to make
partner in the '70s, a deeply relevant piece of news for everyone coping
with a shrinking profession forty-plus years later. The loan companies
marched on with their four-figure monthly bills, making fun of all
the young lawyers for picking a career that everyone at law school
insisted would stand the test of time but turned out to last roughly
as long as they'd survive in the NFL. But the nonlawyers she knew
got fired plenty, too. The journalists and bartenders and retail workers
had all chosen professions deemed as temporary as hers. Each casualty
went back to school for more loans, or on the internet to try to create
a mysteriously glamorous persona that could possibly kick other kinds
of work in their direction.

What would she pack to deal with getting fired, other than herself, some clothes, and a bus ticket to nowhere? She pushed that fear
down to the netherworld where she stored her thoughts on Aaron's
nonhurricane fears: The dark, when he wasn't passed out in it. Fires.
Riots. Race war. They're never going to like us, he said, meaning the
latest wave of white Americans that thought people like her and him
should go back to wherever in Africa they were really from, even if
slavery had wrecked any notion of where that might be. That's true,
they aren't ever going to like us, she thought, an opinion of his that

she didn't disagree with but wouldn't do anything about, because she couldn't beat anyone in any kind of war. She was too squat and too scared to physically fight anyone when she wasn't escaping a bad date.

But Aaron's hurricane speech had gotten to her. She'd done some googling to double-check what he told her and spent hours looking at color-coded maps that showed the hurricanes arcing north more often since the planet had been put on the stove to boil. She'd found charts detailing the progression of northern hurricane season, which had grown to almost six full months of keeping watch over the ocean. She'd watch the forecast videos of hurricanes with generic-ass names swirling around the Caribbean and wonder if the next one would crawl up to their stretch of coast, even though she spent most of her time on the fifty-eighth floor of a building, fifty-seven stories too high for hurricanes to bother with. If she couldn't prepare herself for the emotional and financial insult of getting fired, she could at least figure out how to escape some rising water.

•

IS THERE ANYTHING BETTER THAN WELCOME SEX? YOU'RE-going-to-be-here-for-a-while sex? Just-loaded-your-last-box-in-from-the-car-so-we-can-maybe-live-together-forever sex? Aretha didn't think so. Aaron put the last of her dozen boxes down on their bedroom floor. She shut the door and gave him a look good enough for him to rip three buttons off her shirt. Afterwards they lay on the bed, panting and sweaty. Aretha listened to her heartbeat in both wrists and took in another lungful of delicious post-sex air.

"I'm goin' to Honduras to talk about buyin' some beans tomorrow," Aaron said.

A section of Aretha's good mood flew out faster than the rest of her, up from her body like steam.

"For how long?" Aretha said.

"A week. I have a couple different farmers to visit."

"So I get to hang out all by myself with the crew," she said, pointing in the direction of their bedrooms. Brittany's right across the hall and James's down at the end of the hallway, across from the upstairs bathroom. Both of them far enough away, thanks to the solidity of the upstairs walls, that Aretha, who couldn't hear them, could pretend they weren't there. Aretha was a fixer, and a solver, and a foot stomper if her fixing didn't work immediately. Somehow after three full days living in the Vanderbilt house she hadn't become best friends with everyone. Maybe it would take four.

Instead of remembering that they'd kind of gotten along on Thanksgiving, Brittany eyed her with a pity she didn't understand, the kind of look more appropriate for three-legged dogs and terminal cancer victims than happy lawyers who'd just moved in with their boyfriends. Aretha thought James spent 100 percent of his time behind his locked bedroom door, but she heard a noise above her early one morning and climbed the attic ladder in one of her work skirts to find him perched on the roof with a rifle at his side, searching the other building roofs. She remembered that he'd mentioned keeping watch from the roof, but didn't expect to find him there looking like a rabid dog hunting for someone to bite. She scanned the world beyond their house to see what fire or flood or approaching army James aimed to fend off, and saw nothing but the sun rising meekly over Crown Heights.

She sat down next to him.

"What are you looking for?" she said.

"Nothing," he said.

"Bullshit," she said.

He just kept silently looking for it, whatever it was, with his eyes shifting from side to side at nothing that she could make out. Why the roof? Houses in the city didn't feel like they needed to be guarded from roofs instead of from behind front doors, unless he thought someone would come flying up at him from a fire escape. He feared a Catwoman, she thought, or a Spider-Man. Someone in a mask who didn't mind scaling fire escapes to taunt him. When Brittany wasn't freezing her out at the breakfast table, and James wasn't ignoring her on the roof, they spent their time not talking to her from behind the bedroom doors they closed when they saw her walk by.

So maybe she'd spend Aaron's work trip week with her bedroom door shut against the threat of Brittany not talking to her in the bedroom hallway, or James not saying a damn word to her on his way up to the roof to glare intimidatingly at the sunrise.

"They love you," Aaron said in their bedroom, two days before his trip.

"They hate everyone."

"Sometimes I feel like they kinda hate me too."

"So that's why I'm here. I'm your buffer against your roommates."

"They're great business partners," he said, recovering from the kind of slip he almost never made. Bean suppliers were great and coffee shop clients even better and his paranoid, judgmental roommates the absolute fucking best. Aretha seethed at the relentless sunniness of his worldview, and her failure to imagine what she could do to fit in with the rest of the house.

She didn't want to talk to Brittany or James or look at them or eat what they called "nutrition" at every meal. In all the times she'd been over to the house since she met Aaron, how had she not noticed what the other two ate? She'd moved in with visions of backyard grilling and soul food sides in her head. But she only ever saw them eat the circular, camo-print, optimized soy protein bars called Life Preservers that promised to lower your chance of death. On a search for the next box in her bran flake kitchen stash, she opened a cabinet above her head and stacks of Life Preservers fell on her, in their brown and green and camo plastic wrappers, making fun of her for not preparing herself for a kitchen ambush. She pocketed a Life Preserver and waited until Aaron went on a trip to Indonesia to test it out. She unwrapped her bar with great anticipation, took the first bite, and rolled it around in her mouth the way she imagined wine tasters did, working her way through plastic and gummy notes before the bar's true flavor arrived: sawdust.

She refused to think about the drills they conducted in the back-yard, for fires like she remembered from elementary and middle and high school, and for floods, and high winds, and how to attack in-truders in hand-to-hand combat, which made Brittany and James whip out a variety of fake martial arts moves. Punches and kicks that sometimes hit air and sometimes hit each other's arms and legs and sometimes sent one of them tumbling to the ground. Aretha, when her curiosity wouldn't let her rest, asked Brittany if they were doing karate, and Brittany explained that they were practicing a mix of ka-rate, Krav Maga, jiujitsu, muay Thai, and judo, just to cover all their bases. Aretha felt a new feeling roll up into her stomach. A turf war between emptiness and nausea that made her temporarily swear off talking to Brittany, just in case stupidity was contagious.

But she loved Aaron. Before his suddenly extensive round of Janu-ary work trips, they spent their nights trying new roasts he worked on during the day and their evenings walking the streets, where he'd spin every basketball game and darkened underground party they passed as evidence of a pervasive December happiness in Central Brooklyn.

Since she'd moved in with him, Aretha felt the maybe-there's-a-bright-side-to-everything side of herself shine through and insist that she and Brittany and James would get along beautifully while Aaron was busy tromping around coffee fields. Aaron looked amused. This was a house full of people dedicated to plans, and Aretha was just as stubborn about sticking to hers. She'd get along with them or die trying.

"Don't throw out your back or anythin' in your quest to make friends," Aaron said.

"We'll work it out."

The next morning Aretha woke up and rolled over to the cold side of the bed in disbelief that there was a cold side of the bed. She looked at the time, hugged a pillow, and tried to go back to sleep until she heard the shower going off down the hall. She got up and grabbed a bundle of clothes and bounded down to the downstairs shower, taking the steps two at a time, convinced that this was the first day of the rest of the part of her life where she and Brittany and James got along. After she showered and changed, she went to her room to grab her work bag, and to the kitchen for breakfast.

She heard someone rattling around in the cabinets, and prepared herself to have an uplifting conversation with whoever it was in a way that would only make the two of them closer. Brittany and James sat at the kitchen table chewing their morning Life Preservers and looking at their phones. When Aretha appeared they looked up at her without interest and back down. Just like that, all her dreams of becoming best friends forever curdled up. She, a person who'd turned to an all-bran-flakes diet for inner fortitude the second she arrived in the house, found her bran flakes in the cabinet, poured some fresh milk over a bowl of them, and tried to think about something more uplifting, like how if the world ended today, she, unlike the rest of them, would go out while regular.

"Good morning," she said.

Brittany kept staring at her phone, and James sank further into himself, shoulders hunched. Why the fuck did she bother? When she'd eaten half her bowl, they looked at each other and got up from the table at the same time. Aretha heard only one door shut. She waited what she thought was a reasonable length of time, grabbed one of the glass cups that worked best for listening in on other people's conversations, and went upstairs. She found them whispering behind Brittany's closed bedroom door, and put the cup up to it. Somewhere on the other side of the door lay the reason they wouldn't talk to her, but she would figure it out.

"Since she wants to hang out with us so bad," James said, "she can go on the next run instead of me. I don't want to do it anymore."

"But you're part of the team. You do runs. Why the hell would she be useful on one?"

Aretha's head snapped up. Of course she was useful. She could run, even if the last time she remembered doing it was an ill-fated New Year's resolution that ended in her drinking more instead. She owned running pants. At least, she thought she could run in them if she needed to, since her running pants were made of spandex and all, and spandex theoretically stretched to run with you, even if it had been a few months, or maybe a couple of years, since you'd tested it out. But most importantly, she was always useful. She blocked out the last seven case law competitions she'd lost to Mum and pictured her usefulness as a note of heat in her chest, no bigger than a pin, ready to reach out and burn whatever she needed it to. She closed her eyes and saw it. Glowing and alive. To fully take in the sight of her own usefulness, she leaned back into a wall that turned out to be Brittany's bedroom door.

It fell open, dropping her on the floor between Brittany and

James. Brittany eyed her forcefully enough that she half-expected a wind to push her back out of the room. James sat slouched on a desk chair. He stared at the floor, like he used to be part of it and wanted to go home.

"Oh my god," Aretha said, hustling to her feet. "I'm so sorry . . ."

"That you were listening to us," Brittany said.

"What, me? Never."

Brittany pointed at the glass cup, which had fallen to Aretha's left, and which Aretha had forgotten existed somewhere in the haze of feeling her usefulness rise up within her.

"People still try to listen in on other people's conversations by using cups?" James said.

"She does," Brittany said, lowering the full weight of her disgust for Aretha into a single glance.

"What is this, 1957?"

"Jesus Christ, no, I wouldn't ever . . ." Aretha said.

"Shut up," Brittany said. "You're in here now, so you're going to be made useful."

Aretha grasped for the usefulness that she'd felt outside the door, but it was gone.

"I'm actually just going to leave," she said.

"You're not."

Aretha looked at James, who passively looked back, with nothing on his face that might serve as a lifeboat.

"You're here now," James said. "Just like I am."

"Since you're here," Brittany said, "the three of us are going on a field trip tomorrow night."

"I have to work tomorrow."

"You don't have to get off work early. We're leaving at eight."

"That's early for a lawyer."

"Look at the little lawyer, James," Brittany said, "who's too busy to ride in the back of a car."

"But I have to go to bed that night, just like you."

"You can sleep in the car."

"What? No."

"At least I won't have to go, since y'all are going," James said.

"You're going too," Brittany said.

"No, I'm not."

"What is this about?" Aretha said. "Groceries?"

Brittany laughed, a bitter sound that told Aretha it was time to get up and run. If only she had someplace to go. She dived for the door, but Brittany pulled her back with a level of force Aretha never thought skinny women capable of, a yanking-the-big-fish-out-of-the-pond-with-one-arm kind of tug. Aretha stumbled, and ended up right back on the floor where she'd started. Brittany doubled her facial disgust. James just looked tired.

"We're going to go buy guns," Brittany said.

Aretha felt like she'd gotten stuck under Niagara Falls. Her arms and legs had lost their bones and melded with water. Soon she'd collapse. They had guns, and she'd calmed herself down about moving into the house by telling herself that since they'd already bought the guns they needed, they'd never need more. But apparently they had to fuck her up by needing more guns.

"Why? You think the neighbors are going to shoot you?" Aretha said, picturing the neighbors. The friendly older Black homeowners who liked to go on about the dangerous '70s. Their bougie kids. The other bougie Black people who clearly felt drawn to the neighborhood's bougie Blackness like flies to sugar. The young white investment bankers who hid their bankerness on weekends under thrift shop sweaters and skinny jeans. None of them seemed to want to fuck up a squeaky clean neighborhood in a city that had, per capita, about the same amount of crime as Boise, Idaho.

"No, no, I've got it," Aretha said. "You think someone's going to steal the coffee. They're going to run in here with burlap bags and take a week's worth of your inventory, and they're going to pay for the crime of inconveniencing you for a couple of weeks by getting blown away."

"We had a break-in," Brittany said. "They did steal coffee."

"And you're going to freak out about that for the rest of your life?"

Aretha clapped a hand over her mouth to avoid laughing. And then she gave up. If they really needed to pretend that the people busy marching from home to job to grocery store to bodega to bar were secretly spending every minute of every day planning to break into their house, who was she not to laugh at that? She let her arms and legs go limp on the floor. Her laughter roared through her body. Her stomach heaved. Her eyes teared up. Brittany knelt down until she was eye-to-eye with Aretha and slapped her.

Aretha gasped, and stood up, scared.

That's right.

They had guns.

There were guns in the bunker.

There were probably guns in the house, too.

They were armed and they hated her.

Nia had fucking warned her, and she'd just blithely insisted to herself that she was up for living with a militia.

Brittany had said "field trip" so casually, like buying guns was a carefree fifth grade class visit to a museum. How the fuck had Aretha come to live here, among armed people, without figuring out how armed they needed to be? They never left the goddamn house to give her a moment to take inventory. Her parents had owned a hunting rifle or two, in case someone invited them up north to shoot deer, and she'd looked at James's bag and figured the house belonged to that same rifle-or-two school of gun ownership, but these people talked like they needed an arsenal. Googling people's backgrounds didn't kick up anything about how many guns they hid in their closets, or, she thought, looking around the room, in their dressers or under their beds. How many did they have? When she moved into her last apartment, she'd searched it, front to back, for anything anyone had left there. Even though that search had only turned up a book of dead matches, she felt emotionally complete when she finished looking in every corner. Even though Brittany and James never left the house, someday they'd be on the roof or in the backyard long enough for her to go through their rooms.

She cleared her head. They didn't need twenty guns, because no one needed twenty guns. They probably had three or four, like she'd suspected, and they were planning to take this trip to pick up number five. She didn't support this decision, but she didn't need to pass out over it.

"So you're coming tomorrow," Brittany said.

"I'm a lawyer. I can't break the law. You have one of the maybe ten permits to own a gun in this city?"

"No, I don't. But I know your bar number and am happy to email your ethics board and tell them that you commit crimes if you don't come with us."

"How the fuck do you know about ethics boards?"

"I get around."

Aretha focused on her breathing. Everything was still going in and out like she was used to. She just needed to check. She didn't want to fuck with Aaron's roommates, but how dare they? Ethics boards helped lawyers stay in touch with lawyer values by almost never punishing anyone for their lawyerly sins. Maybe Brittany knew someone on an ethics board who actually cared that Aretha dealt with guns, but she'd happily assign a 95 percent chance to the possibility that Brittany didn't. The only problem with probabilities was that they left room for uncertainty. The 5 percent that Aretha couldn't account for crawled into the room with the three of them. That low percentage turned itself into a cold finger doing a crawl up her spine.

"Look," James said. "You can stay in the car. Nobody'd want you coming in and talking anyway."

"But you are coming with us," Brittany said.

"Thanks for giving me a choice," Aretha said.

The next evening, at seven, Aretha snuck out of work. She left her office lights on and her computer set to never power off so anyone who passed by her office might think she was still there, just on her way to the bathroom or the water cooler or a conference room to meet with someone with edgy opinions on when to schedule meetings. She took a train home, changed into sweatpants, and took the stairs down with Brittany and James, right into the backseat of their car, where she sat alone, but for the black duffel bag she was pretty sure she'd spotted over James's shoulder that first time she'd met him. This time it lay empty.

Brittany drove. Aretha tried to pretend they were three friends taking a lighthearted January road trip to wherever people took lighthearted road trips in January, the most obviously lighthearted of the months.

Aretha looked out her car window. Brittany crawled through the silver-high-rise-lined, traffic-choked mess near the Holland Tunnel and sent the car flying out the other side in Jersey, where leafless trees framed aging factories, smokestacks, and houses with faded paint that made them look like they needed a nap.

Winter. The dead season. Here we are racing towards death,

thought Aretha, with her hand on the doorjamb just in case there was an opportunity to toss herself from the car and end up in OK-enough shape to run away. Brittany drove fast, with her chemically relaxed ponytail flying behind her, as the meanest of the cheerleaders of the world, her preppy face hardened and darkened into something even more feral than usual. Aretha missed Brittany's regular threatening preppiness. The forever half-upbeat, half-entitled angriness of it that made her the skin-covered equivalent of polo shirts without all the dark enthusiasm she brought to taking sketchy car trips. James formed a pile of dough in the front seat, somehow whiter in the seven thirty p.m. pitch-black night. A little swollen-looking around the jaw, like Life Preservers had put weight on him, even though protein swore it would never do that to you. He drank something that smelled like rotten peaches out of a brown glass bottle and eyed the road with the same dead stare he'd given to other people's Brooklyn roofs up on their roof.

"So how long's the drive?" Aretha said.

No one responded.

"What's the name of the town we're going to?"

"What, are you going to map it in case you don't think I know where I'm going?" Brittany said.

"Just trying to make conversation."

"Don't."

James yawned and stretched his closed fists out, like a cat. They were both cats: he was a sleepy cat and Brittany an angry cat, and neither one of them gave a shit that she was in the backseat. But they didn't have to talk to her for her to have an absolutely great time. If she looked at the passing suburbs hard enough, she could turn dead grass into almost sort of uplifting dead grass. The diners looked energetic, the factory towns productive in their constant belching of industrial smoke. Soon enough they'd probably get to some countryside full of fresh air, and she would blissfully inhale the half breath of it she could get from behind her closed car window. Until they got there she was going to get the dopamine rush she'd assumed she'd get by talking to them from looking at her phone.

Twitter. Instagram. Facebook. Email. A quick answer for the first-year associate at work who wanted to ask if a chart she found in a pile of documents established anything they didn't know about how Hurricane Sandy had hit the Rockaways (it didn't). A technical question from one of the partners on how many inches of stormwater were found in one of the hurricane case's plaintiffs' basements (36). Another congratulatory email from one of the partners thanking Mum for winning yet another case law contest, as if the rest of them needed to be re-reminded that they'd lost six hours ago. Fuck that. She went back to the rest of her phone and received a happy emoji-laden text from Aaron about the glories of Honduras, where it was warm and he wasn't driving around with two people who refused to talk to him. She closed her eyes to imagine him at peace in the middle of some coffee fields, with the sun shining down on him like a gentle hand on his shoulder, but the Jersey darkness outside her eyelids snuck in and wrecked the view. She did her weekly calculus on the odds that she could get him to move out of the house, or kick both Brittany and James out and find a new Brittany to do the books, or a new James to do whatever the fuck he did. But the thing about zero was that it resisted all attempts at addition, subtraction, multiplication, and division.

Aaron had the kind of vaguely terrified respect of Brittany that Aretha, sitting in the backseat, unable to stop her right hand from clenching the armrest every couple of minutes as Brittany whipped around curves in the road, now understood completely. James seemed like the kind of guy who might recline into a chair forever if Aaron asked him to move out, and Aaron seemed like the kind of guy who'd feel a little too bad about that. And neither Brittany nor James brought up their families, or left happy pictures of them as their phone wallpaper, or disappeared on the weekends to go visit them. The three of them had their survivalism, and their house traditions, and their coffee. She'd never get Aaron away from his family. So Aretha switched to another fantasy that would never pan out. The one where she and Aaron magically had the house to themselves because Brittany and James had independently decided to leave, with Aaron's permission.

She'd skip through all three stories of the building, lighter than air, on her way down to the kitchen to paint it a color other than red, so it didn't have that just-cooking-up-the-blood-of-my-enemies look. White? Cream? Anything less violent. Who the fuck left their kitchen red? What previous owner had decided to paint the kitchen after reading *Massacre Monthly* magazine? Except she could see Brittany selecting the red paint, carefully taping over the edges of the walls to prevent drips, explaining it away as a classic New England shade of blood. The Puritan blood of America's Puritan ancestors, here to keep our intentions pure. The coffee in the kitchen was already violent in its way, dark and pooled. Not that she'd want to get rid of it, just to change the red walls behind it that made the coffee look almost as homicidal as they did. They kept every set of shades in the house closed except the ones in the roasting room that overlooked the backyard, and the minute Brittany and James disappeared she'd run through the house, opening them all up, letting light in.

To the garbage with Brittany's striped polos and her framed family crest and her plaid down comforter, all of which looked like she'd inherited them as a member of the fourth generation of an all-Black lacrosse team that might secretly double as an army. To the backyard with all of James's stuff, where she could burn it. His room smelled like he was trying to turn all the clothes in it into mushrooms by getting them damp and letting them stay that way forever. The beaten-down white T-shirts that might have gone under collared shirts if he had a job that made him leave the house. The bottles of peach liquor he kept in the corner near his bed, visible from the door but half hidden under a couple dirty T-shirts in a way he probably thought was completely hidden. The stack of metal CDs, as if anyone needed to listen to either metal or CDs ever again. How old was he? For some reason the wiki of a person who'd enjoyed two solid months of plagiarism coverage listed his birth year as approximate.

Maybe he'd plagiarized his birth certificate, she thought, looking out the window into the windows of a diner that looked kind of amusing: purple walls, red lamps. But the next diner looked amusing too, in an all-white way, and the next, while she mentally flipped around the fake birthdates he could have given everyone. He was old enough that he hadn't thrown out his CDs, she concluded, right when Brittany drove them out of town into another stretch of flat Jersey darkness.

But more than getting rid of all their shitty stuff, kicking them out of the house would give her the mental headspace to actually relax when she came home, instead of the spidery crawl that went up her arms whenever she stuck her key in the door, now that they'd black-mailed her. Living with Aaron was supposed to feel fulfilling. And sometimes it did! They went ice-skating in Prospect Park, where Aaron crawled around the outside of the rink, holding on to its edge, and Aretha dragged him out to the center to skate in lazy circles while he dug his fingers into her arm as if it were the side of a cliff. They walked east to one of the Trini food stands of Bed-Stuy, bet each other on how much scotch bonnet pepper sauce they could stand to put in their doubles and walked home under the spell of their pulsating mouths. It was great to look into his eyes every night and plan vacations, even if they'd probably never take them because January gave him a work schedule worse than hers, between sourcing and testing and selling coffee beans. Not that she knew how to plan vacations, since she'd never taken one, but coming up with a list of imaginary places to go and imaginary things to do when they got there had an excitement to it. Then she'd run down to the kitchen after a particularly loving round of vacation planning and face a pair of glares for her offensive, nonsurvivalist existence, and whatever she could hold on to from the dreams she and Aaron came up with upstairs would disappear.

Sometimes she caught herself imagining the glories of living in the apartment she'd just left, listening to the rap and R&B and indie rock she could put on at full blast thanks to her neighbors, who made too much noise to notice hers. Or the apartment before that, where she and her three catering-girl roommates had split leftover mini-sliders on toothpicks before they huddled in the bathroom to get ready to hit the bars as a pack of four, jockeying for mirror space between their flatirons and eyelash curlers instead of judging one another for not eating sufficient amounts of optimized soy.

Jersey countryside turned into Jersey towns littered with delis and fast-food places and cut up with avenues filled with the same three or four iterations of box house built in the '50s then turned into Jersey countryside again. Brittany hit the gas right when Aretha started enjoying the view, clearly as revenge. The charming towns outside Aretha's window swirled into a neon-hazed darkness as Brittany pushed them deeper into the countryside and James fell asleep heavily in his seat, further cursing the car with a buzzsaw of a snore. Aretha watched her window, waiting for another town to cut up the blackness, but

Brittany gave up on towns and pushed them off the divided highways to the winding two-lane country roads.

Mailboxes came out of nowhere like enormous baseballs frozen in flight. The car slid down and rolled up streets, and finally landed across the street from a house. A two-story wooden number that looked like all the two-story wooden numbers they'd passed for miles, other than that they hadn't stopped in front of the rest of them. Brittany cut the engine. Without inviting Aretha, she and James, who'd thrown the duffel bag over his shoulder, walked up to the front door in synchronized steps, even though Brittany walked crisply, like a drum major, and James loped, like a horse.

Aretha looked for some sign that the other two wanted her to get out of the car and come with them, but they knocked on the house's front door and went inside without her. She looked down at her phone for a text, and it took a few minutes to realize Brittany wasn't going to hit her up with an invite to tonight's exclusive party. If she didn't have to go inside, could anyone prove she'd gone along on the trip? Brittany and James would have to testify against her. Brittany might be up to that, but James seemed too generally drunk to hold up on the stand. But Aretha was born to take Brittany down in a courtroom. What the fuck did Brittany know about the law other than that she clearly hated it?

Aretha could see the beautiful courtroom where she'd beat Brittany. Its gleaming wooden benches. Its kindly judge, who'd be thrilled to meet the one of the two of them who understood what was going on. Your honor, she would say, I was blackmailed, which means I wasn't legally in their car, helping the two of them commit a crime. Brittany, spirited into a situation where her rules meant less than Aretha's, would melt into a steaming yet preppy puddle. This was absolutely the best-case scenario for a practicing lawyer who'd

been threatened into a road trip, other than the whole still-physically-
being-stuck-in-the-backseat-of-the-car-while-they-bought-guns-that-
it-would-be-illegal-to-take-back-to-the-city thing.

A yellow fishtail of light lit up the bottom and sides of the closed
garage door. The living room TV flashed through all the versions of
TV color that could be seen from across the street in the backseat of a
car. Blue, then purple, then white, then blue again. How much meaning could she wring out of lights? How long could it possibly take to
buy a gun off someone? Did they stop in the middle of the deal to per-
form a play? She grabbed on to her door handle like Brittany had hustled them around a curve fast enough to freak her out, and when the
car didn't take the hint and start moving again, Aretha grabbed the
handle harder, until her knuckles hurt.

She moved on to the only mental game that it made sense to play:
living room or garage. They had to be in the garage, for sure, not
just because the garage light had flipped on, but because she couldn't
imagine anyone buying guns in living rooms, which she imagined as
temples to televisions and fireplaces that actually worked instead of
the nonfunctioning one she'd had in her solo apartment, thanks to
one of the infinite numbers of landlords who assumed most tenants
showed up with dreams of arson in their heads. Whether fireplaces
worked or not, they were supposed to be shrines to framed pictures
of relatives looking very seriously into cameras, which she fantasized
about as a person whose dead parents didn't, in life, believe in talking
to their relatives, and never got the money together for a house.

Owning a house. The dream. The freedom of never getting kicked
out by your landlord that came with having enough money to buy
one. The possibility of having an entire fortress around yourself. She'd
grown up in a series of cheap apartments in the kind of white Wisconsin town where the white kids she'd gone to school with had held

up homeownership as a cudgel to be whacked across her back if she said anything wrong in history or biology or English class. "She lives in an apartment," they'd whisper, as if apartments were bad instead of cozy little collections of people and rooms and, on lucky nights, warm cooking smells from her mom's and dad's collections of memorized soul food recipes. Cornbread. Greens. Fried chicken. But there were rules in the town where she grew up, and one of them was that you were supposed to live in a house, even if your parents didn't have house money and their parents didn't either and there weren't that many people that would sell a house to people who looked like you. So she envied all the houses that other people owned and tried and failed to squirrel away leftover money after she made her massive law school loan payments and prayed for the financial luck of becoming partner, even if that dream seemed to be moving further and further away, one lost case law competition at a time.

Where were Brittany and James? It had been forever since they went inside, even if forever, according to her phone, had only lasted seventeen minutes. Entire fucking civilizations had probably ended in seventeen minutes. She saw no movement in the house lights. No other cars passed her on the street. No one walked by on the road. Nothing came crunching through leftover snow. Brittany hadn't left her the keys, so the car heat would run out. It had already started seeping out the doors, replacing itself with completely unnecessary freezing New Jersey winter air. She rubbed her thighs, which didn't work. She clapped her hands together.

"Come on," she said.

She closed her eyes and tried to will Brittany and James out of the house. She got to the part of being cold where you can only think about how fucking cold you are. She blew onto her legs, which kept them not quite warm for a handful of seconds at a time. She zipped her coat up to her mouth. She stuck her head between her legs in the fetal position. Twenty degrees, her weather app said, assuming they were somewhere between Trenton and Philly like she thought they were. Hurry the fuck up.

The driver's door flew open and slammed. James stuck the duffel bag next to her in the back and hustled into the passenger seat.

The gun bag thumped her left leg, fuller this time.

She recoiled.

Brittany jackknifed the car across the black Pennsylvania night with the heat back on.

Aretha inched the gun bag away from her leg so it rested on the other side of the backseat.

When enough heat had filled the car to calm her down, Aretha unrolled herself from her crouch and relaxed, well aware of where she wasn't: in her bed, in pajamas, flipping between checking email and aching for Aaron's missing warmth next to her. In her office, with the night at her back, shifting through online files and the occasional paper one to try to win a prize for a company that didn't give a shit about her, in order to please partners who sometimes spent hours reminding her and the other associates via email that they hadn't won a case law competition. Following what everyone had called "the path" back in law school, that supposedly seamless trip from associate to partner and the money and the house and the 2.5 kids and the meaning that it was assumed came with it, that we've-finally-found-out-what-Christmas-is-really-about feeling that Aretha figured naturally came alongside success but had only really felt when she met Aaron, which is why she'd moved in with him and planned to stay there, no matter what, even if that *what* was sitting in the backseat next to her. What if there wasn't anything at the end of the rainbow? What if she didn't make partner? What if Mum, who seemed to win more and more every day, scored the ultimate victory over her? What if she'd just made some money and written some briefs and her boat never took her, river-style, into a greater body of water?

Brittany hustled through another highway turn. The gun bag bumped Aretha's leg. She recoiled again. But Aaron, and Brittany and James whether they ever talked to her or not, had found a way to live untethered to the path that seemed to be failing her. They had worked Life Preservers and preparedness exercises and coffee into a philosophy for them and by them that only seemed marginally more depressing than spending seventy hours a week grinding away in an office, trying to shape weeks of research into twenty pages that might end up, in their final form, as a single footnote in a brief. She didn't have to transform her life into gun runs and martial arts training, but she wanted something else. She sighed with great pleasure as they came back to the Jersey towns, which grew into the wide swaths of Jersey suburbs and the unblinking night eye of the city, bathed in orange streetlight and filled with boot-clad people marching across its surface looking convinced, just like her, that better things lay in front of them.

•

IN THE PASSENGER SEAT, JAMES WAS SITTING AROUND AN-
noyed that his crawl back up to the light wasn't going well. He wanted to be the hamster on the wheel performing a task day in and day out amid a mass of other hamsters doing the same thing. Someday he'd breathe in dry office air again and eat bagels that tasted like they'd sat on a catering tray for three days and go to happy hours to talk about how gorgeous somebody's ugly baby was. He wanted to rejoin the society that had kicked him out its front door onto a curb by writing

stories they couldn't refuse. But first he had to convince people that he wasn't a creep anymore.

He'd settled on the only correct plan: journalism school, an idea he would have laughed at in his actual journalist days but now seemed like the kind of professional sucking up that could reboot him. He'd spent November and December typing up application forms and attaching one of his clean pieces to them, a tidy little article about sunny-day flooding in working-class Miami neighborhoods full of people he'd called to talk to about how their basements flooded on special occasions, like Thursdays. The moon grew full and the tides rolled in a little high and made themselves at home in people's basements for weeks. The most incredible thing about meeting Aaron for the first time was that Aaron had read the article! He remembered it!

"Hurricane Sandy taught me that climate change floodin' out your apartment is the worst thing ever," Aaron had said, with his hand on the rack that held roasted and not yet shipped beans inside twelve- or sixteen-ounce sealed sacks that screamed TACTICAL COFFEE at James in a way he thought might be kind of weird. Why did coffee have to be tactical? But Aaron had read the article, which remained one of James's last links to a version of himself he liked better. A version that wrote articles that people read and that made them angry for a good five minutes about all that water seeping into Miami basements over and over again, with the tides. When James wrote a good article he could hear a victory bell in his head. When Aaron talked about that article, he heard it ring again, a reminder that while he'd generally fucked up in life, he'd gotten some things right.

"You can't escape. But it feels like you should be able to, especially if the water looks kinda low," Aaron said.

The glow that set in after Aaron started talking about the article seeped into James's bones like a space heater on a five-degree day. He basked in it, even after he realized that his thrill might have lasted so long that he didn't hear Aaron blow through the description of the job he'd come to interview for. But here he was, in the front seat of the car after yet another fucking gun run, serving as the muscle of their scheme instead of writing marketing copy for the coffee or ads they could put online or anything else that would use his actual skills.

Too bad his main skill these days seemed to be attracting rejection letters from the kinds of j-schools that normally just sent emailed rejections but needed to tell him off via handwritten asides on the bottoms of form letters. The top of his desk held the latest one, from an Ivy League school whose name he wanted to erase from the earth thanks to a dean who'd scribbled "you're a worthless, plagiarizing sack of shit" below three sentences of boilerplate. He had owned the letter for exactly twenty-one hours and twenty-five minutes, since he came back from a grocery run and found it in the pile of mail on top of the kitchen table, in an envelope that confused him, since they'd already dinged him online. Where was the acceptance email that he hadn't received yet? He craved three or four sentences of promise that he might be admitted into the world at large again.

I am a sack of shit, he'd repeatedly said to himself in the day since he'd received the letter when he wasn't going through his life story since the plagiarism for the holes in it. In the six years since he'd lifted all those stolen words, he'd given a few talks about ethics in journalism, signed up to teach high schoolers how to write essays and reported pieces, and bagged groceries. He'd turned himself into a shining beacon of morality to whom employers and schools had an inexplicable allergy.

He'd tried smaller papers. A paper run out of someone's garage. A style magazine that, as a guy who owned seven white T-shirts, six pairs of relaxed-fit jeans, and a parka, he dreamed would look past his lack of style to let him write about other people's. He had so much extra time to follow this quest, since his righteous-as-hell, conformity-obsessed suburban parents swore to any reporter that would listen that they didn't teach him to copy anyone else and therefore weren't up to talking to him anymore, and all his friends had fallen off like dead skin in a bathtub.

Brittany drove over the Brooklyn Bridge, and James saw his friends and family drifting away into the water right when his fired ass had all the time in the world to hang out with them. Brittany drove up Flatbush, which was still lit for Christmas. All these snowflakes and ribbons and wreaths that couldn't possibly be making anyone happy, since it was January, the month when everyone looked as depressed and dead-eyed as him. Who the fuck had morals anyway? He read the news, where governments were making journalists they didn't like disappear just because they didn't like them, and everyone rich seemed to be taking money from the coal industry because they didn't care if they were alive in twenty years, and people found all the reasons in the world to rip brown children away from their parents. The winning future plan was to give up all the existential weight attached to having a soul.

Especially because he couldn't convince anyone he had one. You've really never done anything terrible in your life, he wanted to ask every single person who told him no, he couldn't stop being the shitty body man for an extremist coffee company. Really? You've never fucked up? Brittany took the Grand Army Plaza circle, and James found the one broken wreath hanging above him, its green ribbon only half-lit. His wrecked wreath, since they were both sacks of shit. He sat up in his seat to look at it in all its disappointing glory and spotted the dangling black wire that had probably left it powerless. Brittany made the turn onto Vanderbilt. The broken wreath disappeared from view. They were almost home again, the place that gave him whatever purpose he had left. Tomorrow morning he would go back to the roof to resume his watch. Someday he would see a threat, and then he would shoot it, as a favor to the only people who'd seen fit to employ him after his great fuckup.

Aretha shifted in the backseat, and his thoughts shifted to her. The righteous lawyer, somehow sucked into their drain. He hated everything about her, from her stiff suits to her perky suck-up face to her very obvious strategy of trying to get A's all the way through life. She was rich, and successful, too, so successful that her business cards didn't make any sense. Her job title was associate, which made it sound like she'd joined a mob that passed politely through security every day to plan murders while eating Chex Mix in a conference room. Journalists informed people about the world, but lawyers were just mercenaries, happy that their piles of money saved them from having to believe in anything in particular. But he could fuck her up. Make her resell the spare guns with him. After she put a couple of guns into other people's hands, she would be wrecked just like he was. He would enjoy watching her give up her professional purity. If he couldn't be happy anymore, he could watch her suffer.

Brittany parked. They all got out of the car. Even Aretha's walk seemed self-righteous. Quick and up on the balls of her feet. He'd wreck that walk. Her feet would come back to the ground like the rest of her. She'd already come on one gun run, so there was an opening, and soon he'd drive a truck through it.

•

ON THE SATURDAY BEFORE VALENTINE'S DAY, AARON LEFT BEfore sunrise to catch a flight to Colombia, and Aretha, who had spent the balance of her life sure that Valentine's Day was a holiday for hopeless romantics and people with an urgent need to singlehandedly prop up the greeting card industry, put on the gray yoga pants and white yoga shirt that had become her weekend uniform instead of the clubwear she used to live in and told herself that she didn't care that Aaron was spending the tasteless chocolate holiday several thousand miles away from her. Besides, she liked the novelty of not telling Aaron that she'd gone on a gun run when he went on yet another trip as a change-up from the regular vibe of not telling him that she'd gone on a gun run while he was at home.

On the ride back from Pennsylvania, she swore she'd tell him the next morning because she was done keeping secrets in her relationships, but then work slammed a few fourteen-hour days at her in a row, and before she knew it a couple weeks had passed, and every time she thought about telling him she came up with a heavy list of excuses not to. Gotta get to work, her head said every morning. So . . . tired . . . from . . . work, she said to herself every evening. Besides, they'd settled into a comforting when-Aaron-isn't-there routine, where he texted her about how Colombia or Tanzania or Costa Rica sounded wonderful, and she responded with three exclamation points she tried to will herself to feel by typing them into existence, and who was she to wreck their texting rhythm by bringing up unimportant shit like driving around buying guns with cash. Besides, if he didn't deal with the guns, would he give a shit that she did? To take her mind off thinking about telling him, she asked herself, once fully dressed in her yoga clothes, why she'd looked down upon the idea of wearing athleisure 24/7. You absolutely never knew when you were going to have to run away from something, and stretch pants left your legs limber enough to dash away from the rest of your life. Living in the Vanderbilt house sometimes reminded her of the possibilities of escape, especially since no one else who lived there other than Aaron had taken a liking to her.

Aretha looked over at Brittany and James the second they all got home from that gun run, ready to see a sign on their faces that they'd shared something together in all those hours of driving. She was greeted with no change in Brittany's high-energy sourness or James's drunken boredom, and no eye contact from either of them. T minus two hours until she was due to meet Nia for brunch. Aretha went down to the kitchen in search of a bowl of cereal, but she wandered through the roasting room first to take in its smell, and saw James and Brittany practicing their martial arts medley in the backyard, in boots, on top of the snow. This was it. Her opening to search the house.

She started with James's room. A plagiarist had to be shady in ways that would explain what the gun runs were for. They couldn't just be buying guns to stockpile guns. Yeah, he'd said "just in case" when she asked him why they kept them around, but there had to be more to it than some interminable wait. At work she constructed entire narratives out of a couple of implicating emails and a handful of cases, and she could do the same thing at home if she found the right set of clues.

She quickly got bored with James's piles of plain white T-shirts and dirty jeans, and the sickly-looking peach liquor in the corner, but at least the Georgia flag tacked up on the wall explained his peach fetish. He didn't keep any of the guns in his closets or his dresser. Just a set of rejection letters from journalism schools, which she found odd, since he'd been a journalist already, so why would he go back to school for it? No guns under his bed. Not a one in the sheets.

She quietly padded across the hall to Brittany's room, and shut the door behind her. What could she learn about someone who only seemed to run on black coffee and rules? When Aretha moved in, she'd noticed the cryptic list of rules tacked to the kitchen wall, right below one of the cracks the other three occasionally acknowledged but never seemed up to fixing. The first rule came back to her in a flash. In the closet in Brittany's room.

Brittany's room had a labyrinth of closets behind a cloth curtain. Tiny little doors that sat under and on top of medium-sized and large doors, all of which were padlocked. They collectively filled up all the space where one normal-sized closet would have gone. Aretha swept through the room again, and fixed on the closet full of clothes. She opened its door. On the floor lay a handful of rifles and handguns, haphazardly resting on one another. Aretha took a step back. When they'd done the run, she'd assumed the point was a gun for each of them, tops. How many guns could one house need? The pile on the floor said the answer was at least fifteen. Maybe twenty. When she tried to count them the numbers froze up in her head. She took another step back.

What were they going to do with all these guns? Aretha had assumed people owned guns for a specific purpose, usually hunting, since she'd grown up with hunters. Or near hunters, anyway, the kind of people who took a week off from school or work around Thanksgiving to go up north and shoot deer that they roped to the tops of their cars to drive home and humiliate her dead parents by impaling them. Growing up in the middle of hunting culture without going hunting had taught her that there were rifles, and handguns, and no real urgency to own the second, since you couldn't hunt with a handgun.

Her parents didn't hunt, but they'd owned guns anyway. Two rifles for all the deer hunting they were going to do someday, and two handguns for, as her dad said, that space between the time an intruder entered the apartment and the police showed up. Her dad, the closest she'd come to knowing these kinds of people before moving in with them. Another guy who just knew that whatever danger came knocking on his door in the night, he could solve it himself with the right weapon. Looking back, Aretha felt amazed by her dad, the Black man who thought he could get away with shooting an intruder without ending up in jail himself. When she'd questioned him, he'd lovingly explained that this land was his land, right on down to the Second Amendment, and when she scoffed, he gave her a long history of it, going all the way back to stagecoaches. After that, during the middle of a picnic or an argument, she'd picture him heroically keeping a stagecoach from getting robbed while dressed in a powdered wig and those pants guys wore back then that looked like they'd been inflated with a bike pump.

She discovered her parents' guns at age twelve, just within reach on the shelf in their bedroom closet if she stood on her tiptoes. She'd taken down one of the rifles, as if by touching it she'd come to a greater understanding of why it kept waiting for her parents' nonexistent hunting trips. She reached down to the floor of Brittany's closet to pick up a rifle like she might have held a baby she didn't want to drop on a floor, with one hand under the stock and the other seven-eighths of the way down the barrel. The gun felt heavy and awkward in her hands, ready to tip back towards its stock at any minute. Twenty years had left her no closer to understanding how people moved from holding guns to shooting them.

Downstairs, the backyard door slammed. Aretha put the gun down as fast as she could without dropping it, shut Brittany's closet door, and went flying out of that bedroom to hers. She face-planted on the bed. Time to pretend to be a normal person who put on her coat and shoes and left the house for brunch without being too worried about her gun-stockpiling roommates. Were they an army? Had she missed recruitment? Were there twenty fucking people training in that backyard every weekend that she couldn't see? Were they starting a war against bodegas? Her breath came faster. She half-ran, half-walked downstairs to the coatrack just inside the front door.

Outside she walked as fast as anyone had ever flown on two feet. Even if he wasn't into the guns, was he worth it? She hurled herself down sidewalks at a rate that proved no match for the race she ran inside her head. Did it make sense to live with a guy because of a November and December that they spent practically sewn together if come January he'd disappear, leaving her alone with the crazy people he lived with? He said he wouldn't live in a bunker, but did that mean anything in a house that armed? She looked down at the Tactical Coffee bracelet she'd never taken off since she put it on that day in the park, and its cheerful plastic kicked her brain into a place she didn't know existed, where it said things to her like "What the fuck do I have to do with these gun-owning freaks who don't talk to me," and "If they don't talk to me, can't I just search our room for guns, put anything I do find in one of their rooms, keep the door locked and shut when Aaron goes on trips, and never end up in the middle of whatever the fuck their plan really is?"

For a few glorious seconds she mentally carried out the last plan. She got the imaginary guns she hadn't found in their bedroom out of it and locked the two of them in while cops searched the rest of the house because some neighbor with X-ray vision had seen all the guns through the walls and called in backup. She and Aaron waited under the bed until Aaron gave her the all-clear and she got the two of them out of there, to a spacious apartment that could fit one coffee roaster and zero weapons. They'd think about having fingernail clippers, and Aretha would come down against the ones with blades.

Except she'd gone on a gun run with Brittany and James, and it was exciting. She slowed her walk. She rifled back through her memories of herself, from the seven-year-old too terrified to not do her homework to the thirteen-year-old who stood a reasonable distance outside the candy store while her friends shoplifted, terrified that placing a single finger on a gummy worm would mark her as a potential criminal, to the eighteen-year-old who didn't drink for half of freshman year, since it was illegal, to the law student who sat in class, happy to divide the world between the purity of the law and the nothingness of opposing it. The world shifted back towards normality. The restaurant windows no longer glared at her for having roommates with guns. She could walk at a pace that didn't make her think of seniors determined to finish their seven a.m. mall loops. She remembered everything about their trip to Pennsylvania. Grabbing the doorjamb while Brittany whipped the car down the road like it was a racetrack. The gun bag poking her leg. Was it a crime that after thirty-two years of following the rules, she wanted to feel something?

Aretha made it to the block that held her and Nia's favorite diner. Nia was so prim and proper and well-manneredly rich, with her family money and her long waiting list of people dying for her therapy. She loved Nia, but Nia had no idea how it might feel to throw life's rules in the garbage because they weren't working for you. She had grown up rich, and went to college, and done what her rich parents did, and found fulfillment in that.

She entered the diner. Nia sat in the furthest-back booth, with her afro freshly picked out, and a sweater that covered a shirt with a collar so crisply ironed it looked like she might try to break a window with it. Her vape stuck up at its usual angle, which meant that the sweater had forced it into her bra. They hugged. Aretha put on her best calm face and thought heavily about trying weed again. Maybe right in the middle of the restaurant. If she got high enough she could forget about the part of herself that looked forward to the gun runs of the future. Her rational side understood that there was no excitement in cruising down Jersey highways and zero thrill in watching a couple of guns poke the side of a duffel bag and even less of a charge in picturing whatever the hell the people they sold guns to might do with them.

They both ordered French toast. Cold-weather food for the coldest of days. For the first time, brunch felt interminable instead of luxuriously slow. What the fuck was the point of brunch? What about ordering fifteen dollars of egg-covered bread was going to make her feel alive? The diner's orange carpet was tacky, and the people who sat in every direction went on forever about their boring lives of work and home and bars and hangovers so bad they just had to tell someone about them. Their waiter came to drop off silverware. The voices around their table rose in volume as people got more animated in their retellings of the dull stories of their weeks. The silence between Aretha and Nia threatened to turn infinite. Nia looked at her. Aretha fought the urge to look away.

"You first," Aretha said.

Nia looked amused.

"I bought a rubber tree," she said.

"What? I thought you'd never give in to plants."

"This is what happens when you spend two hours a week listening to a plant lady. I was walking past this plant store on the way home, and one of the rubber trees got me."

"Got you?"

"You know. I had that feeling people probably have with babies, only with some leaves in a pot."

She whipped out her phone and showed it to Aretha, who saw the rubber tree resting in Nia's kitchen with its branches extended towards the sun, like a handshake, and wondered how she'd let so much time go between trips to Nia's apartment that Nia had gotten into plants. She used to spend a couple weekend days a month there, trying on heels and dresses and pants Nia didn't feel like owning anymore, since they were the same size, or getting ready to go out, or giving up on going out because the weather outside was shit and waiting for delivery pizza on Nia's couch, or on the floor in front of the nonoperational fireplace she kept stocked with a fake log that felt convincing anyway.

"The heat," Nia would say, waving her hand at the log.

"It's so hot," Aretha would say, moving a couple inches closer to the AA-batteried glow.

Instead of just going over to Nia's, like a normal person, she'd let herself get sucked into Gunland. She loved their diner, but if she could have traded the food that would show up in half an hour for an afternoon on Nia's couch, she would have done so happily.

"Is the rubber tree a lot of work?" she asked Nia, as the kind of person who thought plants were only a hair less complicated than brain surgery.

"No. I water it once a week, fertilize it once a month, and plan to give it a hearty trim next year at around this time. Then it'll spit more leaves out at me."

"Can I come see it sometime?"

"Sure, but since when are you into plants?"

"I'm not not into them."

Nia took Aretha through that week's set of unbelievable clients. The welder who came to talk about why he gave up on ballroom dancing and his mother. The food blogger who came to talk about her distant, professional axe-throwing boyfriend and her mother. Her personal favorite, the plant-growing lawyer who came to obsess about her distant plants and her mother. Aretha listened while kicking herself for not just saying she was into plants, even if it wasn't true. Being into plants might have set her on a more sane path than the one she'd taken a couple of steps down.

"Thank god my mother's dead, so I don't have to talk about her," Aretha said.

"That's never fucking stopped anyone else," Nia said.

The plant-growing lawyer was worried she wouldn't make partner. Aretha felt relieved that someone else out there was suffering in one of the exact same ways she was before she remembered that she'd stopped worrying about making partner somewhere around the gun run. Oh, she still wanted to do it, but her trip from terror at getting trapped in a car in Pennsylvania and her almost immediate swing to excitement over the illegalness of what they'd done had grayed out her reaction to work. She traveled her usual loop between her office and conference rooms and waited for the acts she performed for pay to feel exciting again.

She picked up a pro bono litigation case about a prisoner whose prison had stopped feeding him. She coached her new, chiller self into winning three case law competitions in a row. She put on a convincing performance of fake camaraderie with Mum by having lunch with her once a week, an act she used to hate and now didn't mind, once it became clear they were going to bitch about things Aretha had always wanted someone else at work to bitch about with. The hours. The nonexistence of female partners. The signs that one partner was going through a divorce: sudden weight loss, hastily acquired orange fake tan.

"You could probably use some plants," Nia said back at their table. "I think, even though plant woman talks about her plants like they're kids who don't call home, that there's something about lawyers and plants that works out. You're all stressed, and they don't have anything to do with all your briefs and arguments. They work on another corner of your brain. Start with a couple of succulents."

"I'm not as stressed about work as I used to be."

"The new man?"

"You could say that."

"How is your coffeehead?"

Aretha saw all the coffeeheads in bits and pieces. Aaron pouring her a half-inch of coffee on his last new roast Tuesday night and telling her about the time when he, a brand-new bartender who had no idea what a Sex on the Beach was, mixed someone a rum and Coke. Aaron texting her from Brazil, where he'd accidentally eaten the banana leaf that came with a plate of fish. Her calling him "my leafy greens," and promising to have the recommended three to five servings a day of him when he got back.

And Brittany and James swinging their arms around for backyard training exercises, in ways that would intimidate no one who didn't know they owned too many guns.

"Are you OK?" Nia said.

"Never better," Aretha said.

She thought of the hum of the roasting machine going off in the background while she and Aaron took a rare mutually free Saturday morning a couple of weekends ago to sit in bed and talk about pancake recipes. Ah, pancake recipes. A cheaper way to re-create the brunch experience that also took out the part of brunch where Aretha had to leave the house for further rounds of Nia questioning. She imagined making pancakes with Aaron. Her making batter, flipping them better than she'd ever done before as a serial pancake burner. Him cheering her on while he fried up bacon and held one of the mugs of coffee that doubled as his third hand. Him handing her the gun in his holster and telling her to flip with it, spatula-style. Her deciding that flipping pancakes with a gun was hot.

"You're doing it again," Nia said.

"No, I'm not."

The guns in Brittany's closet rose up in her head, trying to freak her out, but Brittany's voice rose up in her head, to tell her not to fear them. The house walls took their place, reminding her that they seemed to be developing bigger cracks than she remembered them having when she moved in. But who's to say she remembered correctly? She worked late enough to hallucinate up cracks in walls, and imaginary mice, and pancakes flipped by guns, and ominous shadows cast by their decidedly un-ominous living room couch, a green velvet number that matched the retro quality of Aaron's T-shirt collection and the Roots and TV on the Radio and Beach House posters he'd tacked up in their bedroom. He'd picked up the couch while the other two took a rare recreational trip out to a gun range in Jersey for target practice.

"It's about coffee, but it's about the look, too," he'd said, pointing out the art deco touches of the coffee bag design after he put the couch in place.

Aretha saw it after he explained it to her: the vaguely '50s quality to the gun-toting, coffee-carrying man. The Miami house that the bag man had to defend and the 2.5 kids and the picket-fence feel of the life she'd imagined he was defending, reunited with the violence that brought bag man to life. Really, it was art.

"They're all doing well," Aretha said.

"Well, that took you forever. Did you ever figure out if they're the armed kind of survivalists?" Nia said.

The whole room floated. Spun. Wobbled on its axis. Aretha could open her mouth and answer the question, but she wasn't sure if words would come out. Maybe just air, like a fish.

"You know, I have no idea," she said, looking at her phone. "Shoot, I've got to go call someone at work. Next week, same time?"

"Sure," Nia said. "Are you OK?"

"Just fine."

Aretha left three-quarters of her French toast on the table to congeal when she got up and promptly forgot that she'd ever been hungry in the first place. She couldn't eat anyway, since her stomach seemed to be made out of ocean waves that kept crashing into whatever qualified as shore. She left the restaurant and hurried down the sidewalk to the Vanderbilt house, the refrigerator door to her magnet self. On the other side of the front door her stomach waves stopped.

When she got up to her bedroom she googled the history of the house, as the last background check she planned to run on the bunch of them, as a farewell thank-you to Google, her eternal ally, who couldn't help her any further down the path she'd chosen. Built in 1896, renovated in 1950, home to a Broadway actress and ten different sets of musicians before the gang had moved in to make coffee. A brownstone among brownstones that looked just like it: faded red brick, floor-to-ceiling windows that looked like eyes stretched open with a toothpick. Framed by the sky above and restaurants below, and buildings that resembled it in all directions. Only a hair back from Atlantic Avenue and its murmuring sound of nonstop medium-to-heavy traffic. Big enough that four people could practically have their own existences in it, even if two of them had chosen to stick together. She went up to the bedroom and sat on the bed and looked out the window and watched a blue jay pick at what was left of a leaf.

Her stomach rumbled. She went down to the kitchen for cereal. Half Froot Loops and half bran flakes, for balance. James came down from his room to chew sullenly through a Life Preserver, but for the first time since she'd moved in, he looked at her between bites. She looked back at him. Was this it? The magical moment when he started talking to her, and they became friends? But he didn't follow the look with any words, so she didn't say anything either. They both just sat at the table for a while, chewing and taking up space, until he broke the silence.

"You ever thought about being more of a part of the house?" he said, sitting back and crossing his arms in a by-house-I-mean-empire kind of way.

She'd answer a real question if he asked her one, but she hated this kind of fucking around.

"I'm terrible at jiujitsu," she said, waiting him out.

"What we do in the backyard isn't really jiujitsu. It's a mix of jiujitsu, Krav Maga, muay Thai . . ."

"Right. Brittany told me."

Their fucking martial arts gumbo.

"I'm not a coffee pro, either," she said. "I can't roast anything for you."

"That's not what I was thinking."

"Go on."

"I need to run an errand and was wondering if you could help me with it."

"What is it?"

"I think you know what it is."

"What the hell does that mean?"

"You know when you took that little trip to Pennsylvania with us?"

"Yeah, I do," she said.

"We need to take another trip like that."

"OK."

"I know you're probably scared," he said, "but . . ."

"What the hell would I be scared of?"

She put her right fist on the table to back herself up. James blinked at her for a few seconds. If he didn't understand the feeling in the air, she did. There's a point in a deposition when the mood shifts if the lawyer's doing a good job, right after they ask the question and right before the other person gives the bad answer that they know they were backed into giving but can't find a way around. Aretha couldn't believe this feeling had set in because she'd agreed to go on another gun run, but James had the right look of surprise on his face.

Aretha got up and walked upstairs, to the bedrooms, where she spotted Brittany spackling a wall.

"The walls are OK, right?" Aretha said.

Brittany gave her a look, the latest in a series of Brittany looks, all of which meant the same as the ones before it, yet somehow conveying a small range of levels of disdain.

"I'm prepared, Aretha. For whatever."

Aretha kept walking until she reached her bedroom. She shut the door, thought better of it, got up, opened the door, put on socks, and marched down to the living room to chill on its couch in her socks. She wasn't afraid of these people. This was her fucking house too. She put her feet up on the couch and lay down on it the long way to take up as much space as possible. For the first time in months, her head was clear. She pulled out her phone and read through Aaron's cheerful texts from Colombia. The people were great! The houses colorful! The arepas warm! He was having an absolutely fantastic time wandering around the countryside in a slightly less ridiculous-looking hat! She responded to his texts with a brightness that came from knowing she would no longer be bored during his trips. She would work, and she would ride in cars with Brittany and James and see what came of that. She was a lawyer who wanted to see what lay on the other side of the law.

At work she looked at people, because they no longer scared her. Everyone who passed in front of her got a forceful round of eye contact. Work, where force worked out. She was meaner to the plaintiffs' attorneys and crueler to the document reviewers, asking them to go faster and faster until she could see them twitch. The trick as a woman in the law was to be mean enough to get everyone to snap back by doing things for you immediately but not mean enough to be called a bitch. That week she congratulated herself for walking right down the center line.

At home, to reinforce this feeling of newfound inner toughness, she splayed herself all over the house purely to take up space. She lounged on every couch. She lay lengthwise on the floor of the roasting room, closed her eyes, and breathed in its smell. She put on her yoga pants and yoga shirts and went down to the living room to do something completely ridiculous in them: yoga. She did all the yoga she could remember from the single yoga class she took a couple of years ago. Downward-facing dog, up-dog, half-pigeon, pigeon. She flexed her arms and legs and felt them gathering strength. She switched her cereal mix from half Froot Loops and half bran flakes to all bran flakes, and her soy milk to almond milk. The warmth from exercising control over all the things she could control grew inside her. She could power a small room with it. Maybe even a whole house.

An axe-throwing bar opened up neighborhoods away from the house, and she spent her Tuesday nights there, drinking limeades, throwing axes, and feeling even more like a person who'd just decided gun runs were exciting. At home alone under the dark bar lights, with a cold glass spitting dew into her drinking hand that she'd wipe off before she sent axe after axe flying towards the target. She felt the floor quake under her feet when they landed, and a rush not unlike the one that came from winning a case, especially if she imagined each axe as a round of sex with Aaron. Watch-the-world-bend-to-my-will-just-like-the-ground-an-axe-hits sex. Maybe-we're-conquering-the-world-just-by-fucking-each-other sex. Thank-god-I-found-a-way-to-spend-a-couple-hours-drinking-alone-because-I-feel-bad-about-doing-it-in-front-of-a-sober-person sex. On Tuesdays, he roasted beans late, so she'd come home from the axe bar and they'd have all the sex she'd already had with him in her head, and then they'd pass out together. And then she'd wake up and go to work and wait for James to summon her. But he did not.

She waited four weeks. On the twenty-ninth day, she rose before dawn to eat her bran flakes and report to the train so she could arrive at work early to finish up the summary judgment brief for the Hurricane Sandy case. Both sides had produced, in total, five million documents, and those documents had been sorted like hair under a fine-toothed comb into neat little electronic piles called helpful and unhelpful. This stubborn-ass case had survived a motion to dismiss and thirty million smaller motions about what documents and witnesses to produce and where the witnesses should be deposed. Aretha and Mum and the other mid-level associate on the case had flown around the country to do the depositions, which forced Aretha to miss Nia brunches to wake up in dull hotels and eat eighteen-dollar client-subsidized eggs and report to windowless conference rooms and ask the same questions in dumber and dumber ways to try to get witnesses to fall for them. At least she could add too busy flying around the country to the list of reasons why she never got around to telling Aaron about her gun run.

But that was all over, and they were down to the absolute last set of arguments and documents that might prevent them from having to stand trial over the issue of whether her clients would have to pay out insurance claims that they didn't deserve to have to pay out for people who'd unluckily lost their houses to a hurricane in a way that had absolutely nothing to do with the people who were paying her to defend them. The only problem was that somewhere along the way she'd started thinking of the plaintiffs, and their houses, and their now houseless, beached-whale-like lives, full of temporary apartments that contained the tenth of their stuff that they were able to save. Or the plaintiffs who'd saved nothing. Living in the Vanderbilt house had fucked her up by making her sweet on houses.

The Vanderbilt house didn't matter, she told herself as she double-checked every argument in the brief. These people's houses don't matter either. Behind her, the first ray of morning sun crawled up from the horizon to lick her computer screen, which contained fifty pages of perfect words that would win it for them. And maybe take those people's houses, whispered a part of her she could tamp down. It was control time, after all, where with enough effort she could get rid of everything that bothered her. It was just a job, she said to the section of her head that went back to the depositions she'd taken, how people described living after they lost their homes, even though she'd filled the pauses in their answers about living two or five or ten or thirteen people to an apartment with objections about relevance.

She took another hour to look over the brief before she declared it done, saved it, drafted the email to the head partner and attached it, and slipped outside to wait the hour until it would be acceptable to send the email. Around her, Midtown woke up. The first morning round of halal meat hit the grill. The juice trucks smashed fruit and vegetables into plastic cups. The by-the-pound delis sold plates of breakfast to tourists who videotaped them, determined to play back the videos for their families who were less convinced of the mystifying powers of twenty-two-dollar yogurt deemed magical because it was eaten in NYC. The office workers crawled out of the subway and found new purpose when they hit the sidewalk, their shoes clicking determinedly past everyone standing in groups waiting outside a bakery to eat cake at eight a.m. because a television show had once dressed its characters in the kind of tulle that showed everyone who didn't eat that bakery's eight a.m. cake that they were idiots. Aretha turned into the Diamond District, where its vendors gently placed trays of diamonds in window displays that, to her, usually looked exactly the same as all other trays of diamonds. But finishing that summary judgment brief meant she and the diamonds matched. They were both glittering and perfect.

She floated back to the office on that diamond air, ready for another day under her control. Even the office lobby was with her. Its normally dull tan carpet sparkled. Its usually generic framed landscapes chose today to remind her of the limitless scope of photography. She sat down at her computer, sent the email, and enjoyed the bubble of accomplishment that sets in after sending really important emails for a good three hours.

For their lunch Mum picked a new fast-casual place near the office called bumblehive, specializing in bee-pollen-based foods, which were said to strengthen the immune system by exposing the body to the powerful biological moment when bee met flower. She ordered a bee-pollen salad. Aretha ordered a bee-pollen-flavored meat loaf slice, and the two of them sat down for another round of firm gossip.

"The smoker looks very orange today," Mum said, referring to a corporate partner who'd taken out all of his frustration with the custody dispute part of his divorce in an indoor tanning booth.

"He's a week away from being a tangerine with a hairpiece," Aretha said.

She tried to remember the days when she hated Mum, but they'd faded into this new world where they had lunch together. Aretha had reluctantly decided that Mum made for OK company, as another person who watched everyone else in the office closely enough to understand the appeal of gossiping about them. The male lawyers barely had time for Aretha; they spent their days and their happy hours working on winning Olympic gold for sucking up, and their weekends doing ridiculous shit like playing golf with one another free from the company of any of the women in the office. And Aretha knew it would look bad if she hung with any of the female junior associates, who were beneath her. But Mum understood the appeal of partners' bad tans and male associates' terrible striped dress shirts and the once-in-a-while hilarity of some lawyer finding some way to insist they were cool, as if there was some hip way to wear wingtips while arguing about sections of the U.S. Code. Besides, as the associate who'd just written the brief for the most important case in the department, Aretha was feeling generous.

"Orange partner wants those kids that badly?" Mum said.

"I think he just wants it to stop," Aretha said.

Their food came. Aretha took a bite of her meat loaf, which tasted just like everyday meat loaf if everyday cooks coated their beef in wax, and gave what she thought was a pretty damn good dramatic performance by pretending it wasn't gross. Mum's salad had waxy-looking cubes all over it that she swore tasted delicious.

They moved on to the litigation partner neither of them ever worked with who'd lost a case in front of the Second Circuit last week, and the first-year corporate associate who wore white sneakers with her skirts, a power move that said she was completely unafraid of being fired, no matter how many times everyone pointedly looked at her feet in meetings. Aretha felt odd, like someone had turned on a space heater in the middle of her chest, but she took a fresh bite of meat loaf anyway.

"Someone's going to have to spill coffee on them," Mum said.

"Oh no. Then she'll come back to work with a spotless new pair of white sneakers. She's never going to let anyone mess with her look," Aretha said.

"I can't believe she has time to worry about making that much of a fashion statement at work."

"Especially in a profession where the frontier of fashion is starched jeans on casual Fridays with ironed creases so sharp you could cut your lip on them."

"I should mess with everybody by wearing white shoes when I argue the summary judgment motion."

"Which motion?" Aretha said.

Maybe the feeling crawling up her chest into her throat was suspicion. She'd turned in a fifty-fucking-page summary judgment motion that it took her two weeks to write and circulate to the partners and edit and polish, and Mum was not fucking going to tell her that she was going to argue that motion. Her motion. Nope. She crossed her arms and sat back, waiting for Mum to tell her all about the other fucking case she was going to do it for. The other case where Mum wrote the brief. They had a rule at work. If you wrote the brief it was your motion, unless a partner took it from you because, say, that partner wanted to notch a Supreme Court argument under his belt. But not everyday federal district court motions like the Sandy one. These were not stolen from the Arethas of the world.

"The Sandy one."

"Congratulations," Aretha said, taking care to avoid clenching her teeth. Her throat moved to full-blown hot from merely irritated. She put down her fork and went for her glass of water, which didn't solve the problem. "Have you ever argued a motion before?"

"No," Mum said brightly. "It'll be my first time."

"That's so cool," Aretha said.

She choked.

"Aretha?" Mum said.

Aretha couldn't breathe. This was what happened when you dared to trust other lawyers enough to go to lunch with them instead of doing the right thing and never leaving your office or speaking to anyone else unless you had to. Who the fuck knew losing at work could literally close your throat? She clutched at hers with both hands.

"I'm going to call 911," Mum said.

Aretha slumped over in her chair. Fuck Mum, the bitch who could even win at getting an ambulance to show up. And the fuckers who stared at her with their bugged-out eyes, as if not being able to breathe was an act that should be watched with total concentration, like a solar eclipse. One minute they were all gaping at her in a big semicircle, and the next minute she wasn't looking at anything at all.

•

SHE WOKE UP IN A BALL OF LIGHT WITH A NEEDLE IN HER LEFT arm, facing a doctor who held a clipboard. She tried to get up, but the needle held fast.

"Thanks for everything," she said, "but I have to go back to work."

"Don't worry," the doctor said, "they know you're here."

She looked deep into the doctor's long white beard, angry that Rip Van Winkle didn't seem to get it.

"I think you think that's a good thing," Aretha said.

"Everyone understands an allergic reaction, Aretha."

"Right. So what the hell am I allergic to?"

"Bee pollen."

"Fuck."

"Just don't eat it. It's pretty easy to avoid. Unfortunately, you're also allergic to bees."

"So I can't eat them either."

"Unfortunately not."

"I'm going to have to cancel tonight's dinner plans."

"We want to keep you here overnight for monitoring, anyway."

"No," Aretha said, picturing the twelve hours of work that would go on without her, alongside the rumors. "Aretha had some kind of breakdown," the senior associates who didn't like her would whisper to the juniors. "Some people just can't handle the workload," the partners would say to one another in the backs of their hired cars. Here she comes, a fired weakling unable to gut through swelling and a blackout at the office. Complete with unfixed hair and sweatpants she'd never change again, with nothing else to do but come up with a new name so her student loan company couldn't find her.

"Yes," the doctor said. "Sometimes these reactions come back a few hours after we first treat them, and we'd like to keep an eye on you to make sure we can treat you right away if that happens."

"Fine."

The doctor left. Aretha picked up her un-needled arm to test it, and her legs. She felt a little light-headed. Not affected enough that she couldn't go back to work, just a hair off. Without the doctor, the only sound left in the room was the low rumble of medical equipment. Where the fuck was her phone? She scanned the room until she spotted her work purse sitting on a chair near the door in all its acceptably office tan, flat-bottomed glory, way out of reach.

Aretha had spent almost all of the last six years looking at her phone, a legal document, or someone else, and had no idea what to do with herself if all three were taken away. What did people do who were stuck in hospitals longer than overnight? How many hours a day could a person spend trying to entertain themselves by listening to machines beep? She closed her eyes and breathed deeply, trying to put herself to sleep, but she felt the restlessness that meant she'd probably spent too many hours passed out already. The doctor had shut her door on his way out, which meant she couldn't ride this out by listening to other people's conversations, and no one had the decency to discuss something salacious while glued to the area right outside her door. Not that she had any idea what salacious hospital conversation might be. Hot Band-Aid tips?

When Aaron walked in after she didn't know how many hours of boredom, she teared up out of relief. He leaned in to hug her around her IV. Under his weight she felt real again.

"What happened?" he said.

She took him from the finished brief to the bee-pollen meat loaf, to Mum's assignment, to the summary judgment argument in no time at all, the words falling out of her mouth like drool.

"First things first," he said. "You need to give Mum a nickname that makes you feel at least kinda better."

"That's what you think is first?"

"C'mon, hun. You've had a day. Are we callin' her Mute, or Silent, or Dandelion, or what?"

Aretha laughed.

"Can we do all three? I'll hold up cue cards and you'll flip through them? I'll draw a mute, silent dandelion? I'll carve one out of clay and stick needles in it," she said.

"I'll go huntin' for clay. You should probably find another job."

"No."

"They took your motion."

Aretha groaned. For some reason she'd imagined that solving boredom by dropping off guns with James would knock out the key issue in her life. But now she pictured the future, all covered in shit. The recruiters who never had leads on anything any self-respecting lawyer would want to do. The interviewing partners who hadn't seen sunlight in seven years and carefully scrutinized everything she said to make sure she'd never heard of hobbies or having free time. The smaller firms, excited enough by the prestige of her law degree to offer her the scintillating possibility of doing the same property disputes and divorces over and over again. Was there a company someplace, or better yet, one of those government jobs where she could work nine to five, make a decent amount of cash, and not kill herself mimicking the sheer effort it seemed to take to practice law at her current firm? Never mind that the fucking president had put a hiring freeze on government lawyers. There had to be someone down there with the feds who could hire her under the table.

Who she envied the most were the born-rich types who could just take a year off to "figure it out" and end up in Bali teaching yoga part-time while painting homemade mugs and taking the exact same picture of the ocean every day. She would love to kill a year doing the kind of shit people looked cool doing on Instagram, without bothering to put any of it on online. Instead she was going to hope she had a year left at her firm to take bad recruiter phone calls, sock away as much of her salary as humanly possible, and be thankful she didn't have to pay rent.

"You wanna come work for us?" Aaron said.

"Maybe," Aretha said. "What would you have me do?"

"How do you feel about spendin' your days up to your waist in fresh coffee beans?"

"I don't know."

"Sleep on it."

"The second I make it home, I'll stick a bag of beans under my side and pass out."

"That's my girl. Well, hun," he said, "I have to make it back to put the beans in for the evening roast, and do a round of deliveries, but you're goin' to be fine."

They kissed.

"Could you hand me my bag?" she said.

He did, and left.

She took a few minutes to think about bathing in coffee beans. Surrounding herself in that smell would be sublime. Right up until she got sick of being alone with the roaster. She'd waved hi to Aaron sitting alone next to the roaster too many times. On top of that, she'd never wanted to fuck a single one of her bosses, ever. It was a form of losing. A concession that they held the cards by fucking you and you'd never replace them because they only saw you as someone they fucked. But really, roasting coffee beans would feel like taking the L. No one to compete with, nothing to win. Aaron went to South America and Africa and Asia to try to outtravel his competitors in the battle for the best-tasting coffee, but on the roasting side she'd mostly be battling her own boredom, sitting in that room, smelling coffee beans heat up.

She dug out her phone. A flurry of texts, mostly from Aaron, and forty fresh emails. She ignored the juniors, scanned the mid-levels for the traces of glee that she expected, and found them in not-so-cleverly-camouflaged expressions of support, and memorized every word of the head partner's "srry to hear this.. be well soom," the typos expected in an email that didn't have to go to someone outside the office and could therefore be dashed off in his trademark "I have thirty seconds tops to deal with you" way. They didn't give a shit. No one she worked with gave enough of a shit that she'd had an allergic reaction bad enough to send her to a hospital to send an email or a text that sounded like they cared that she hadn't died. Mum had sent four worried, long-winded emails, as was her style, but Aretha had no time for those who won at work. If she ever had lunch with Mum again, it would be because Mum held a gun to her head. James had sent her two puzzling texts. "Where are you," read the first one, as if they were tight enough for him to be updated on her every location, and "We'll talk soon," which, since they didn't really talk, made her cold enough to futilely hunt for a blanket warmer than the millimeter-thick one that lay on top of her legs.

The hospital let her go the next morning. She walked out to the nearest Duane Reade to hunt down the Benadryl the doctor said she should always carry with her from now on, in case bees thrust themselves into her life again. Pink pills in hand, she followed the weak February sun to the subway. Her B train chugged over the Manhattan Bridge and stopped. No one on her train car looked up. Aretha looked out at the Brooklyn Bridge, with the tourists that walked over it at all hours reduced to grayish dots, thanks to distance. She watched them walk over the water and stop to take anything from compulsively frequent selfies to full-blown photographer-assisted photo shoots, where from her position the cameras mounted on tripods looked like tiny black spiders. The people on her car got restless, flipped through pages of reading, annoyedly clicked things on their phones. "There is train . . . mmmrr . . . bbbffrr . . . ," the conductor said, providing them with one of those unintelligible train announcements that thankfully always happened when you really needed to understand what the conductor had to say.

The train car lights went out. Everyone looked at one another, a pack of deer without headlights, wondering what the fuck was up. "Mmmmmm . . . power . . . mmmmmm," the conductor said. Someone in Aretha's car swore. The B train loved to suddenly lay over on the bridge for stretches of up to ten minutes at a time, but this B train had been stuck for eighteen. An eternity. A baby started to cry.

Aretha looked out the door window, which lay tantalizingly close to the pedestrian path. People texted, their angry fingers banging on their phones. She'd give it ten more minutes. Fifteen. Half an hour even. She grabbed her pole and watched ferries go north and police boats crawl south towards Battery Park.

She zoned out. She zoned back in. She checked her phone. Forty-five minutes had passed. The older kids on the car had graduated to complaining, the adults to whispering and looking at one another with worried eyes. A couple of people yelled "Open the door!" She tested her arms and legs. Still weak, but OK enough. She walked to the back of the train car, opened the door, stepped out, and grabbed on to an exterior pole. "Lady, stop," some guy yelled. She didn't. The car door shut behind her. She looked up towards the front of the train and saw wafts of smoke, weak enough to look like a daydream, specific-smelling enough to be real.

To her horror, Brittany began talking to her from the inside of her head again, in a tone Aretha thought of as Brittany's instructional voice.

"Go away," Aretha said.

"I'm going to help you," Brittany said. "I don't like you, but I can get you out of here. Remember what I told James while we were training in the backyard, about how to escape a stopped Manhattan Bridge train, back when you used to listen to our conversations from the kitchen window instead of with a plastic cup?"

"I do," Aretha said.

"You probably don't, since you don't believe in our methods."

"Go ahead, Brittany."

"To your left, there's a chain-link fence. You don't even have to step on the tracks to get there."

Aretha walked over to the fence and stepped into its links.

"Lady, stop!" someone yelled from the inside of the train.

Aretha didn't. Instead, she climbed the chain-link fence. The weakness in her arms and legs from the aftermath of the allergic reaction came back, so she grabbed the fence harder. She paused and looked at the smoke again and worked her way up the fence with the fresh energy that comes from wondering if the tunnel on the Brooklyn side of the Manhattan Bridge might blow up. She paused at the top to look at an angle of the Brooklyn Bridge she'd never see again, several dizzying feet further up in the air than anyone belonged. She climbed the fence and lowered herself down the other side, with new life from having escaped the train. She stuck her feet into gaps in the blue carved railing that sat below the chain-link fence and down onto the welcoming concrete of the Manhattan Bridge footpath, where she threw up her fists in triumph.

"We did it!" she said to the Brittany in her head.

"Watch out for the runner," Brittany said.

"What?" Aretha said.

She went flying onto the concrete, hands first.

"Stop talking to yourself on the bridge," an angry white runner said, cheeks red with exertion, body spraying sweat all over hers.

He ran off.

She grabbed on to the chain-link fence to get herself back up. Her hands and knees felt like someone had taken a cheese grater to them. She called herself a car from an app and shuffled in the Manhattan direction to catch the car at the furthest point from the smoke.

"I listened to you," she said to the Brittany in her head.

"Yeah, so?"

"I'm not sure that's a good sign."

"I'm a completely unbiased person who thinks you're doing the right thing."

She lowered herself gingerly into the hired car. The driver flew at the same rate that the pain flowed back into her ripped-up knees now that she'd left behind the thrill of climbing over a subway fence. Her car left the shifting shadow of the bridge for the light.

She went back to her old friend Google, to ask what happened to her train. The searches pulled up nothing and nothing and nothing and nothing until one hit screamed "track fire!" They didn't know who started it. Maybe someone living in the tunnels? It didn't burn that big, just enough to stop seven or eight trains and reroute the rest of them onto already crowded tracks for hours. In her head Aretha saw everyone on those other trains sighing and waiting, like they had on her train before everyone's mood went dark from the wait. The rest of them were probably still waiting up on that train car for some more nothing to happen before they'd be allowed to leave. But she'd done it. She'd escaped. She knew how to leave a stalled train car.

Everything felt perfect until her car arrived back at the Vanderbilt house and she had to stand on her gimpy knees and shuffle to the front door. The house looked at her as it always did, with its three stories of brown calm. She checked her work email on her way up to her bedroom and decided to give herself a night to feel like a person again instead of an angry beehive. Instead of throwing herself all over the living room couch as usual, she shuffled up the bedroom stairs with a bowl of bran flakes and locked her door. The silence in the house meant Aaron was out doing deliveries and Brittany had left the house to meet with their tax lawyer or their accountant or one of the other boring-ass business people she dealt with sometimes.

And James? She heard nothing, but he had no habits, rhythm, predictability. He could be up in his room working off a hangover by getting another one started or silently taking up the downstairs bathroom, as he liked to do, magazine in hand and bathrobe on, cosplaying as a '50s dad. He could be in the house or the backyard or some mysterious place between them. But he was somewhere nearby. She knew it. She'd locked her door as her last defense against him. For twenty-nine days she had exercised perfect control over her life other than that stopped train, and for almost all that time she thought James was the answer to her problems at work, but work was the answer to her problems at work. She would show up there tomorrow and do a much better job at the whole working thing without getting waylaid by bee pollen. And then she remembered that doing better at work was an old impulse that made more sense when she thought the people she worked for might have given a shit about her maybe almost dying. Let James come and find her. The bran flakes tasted like air, but she'd declined enough hospital food to find air delicious, so she picked up a Life Preserver as a chaser, and its sawdust finally did the trick. Between bites she listened for James. She heard nothing.

She bucked up enough to take her empty bowl down to the sink to wash it out, and right when she put it on the drying rack and turned to leave, James rose up in front of her like a bloated ghost. She gave him her usual disappointed once-over before remembering that she wanted to see him.

"Aretha," he said.

"Yes?"

"We're going tomorrow," he said.

She saw everything Brittany had threatened rise up between her and James. The ethics board, a phone call to her boss. But more than that, she saw the true end of the path, if the path could be called the world where she cared about the blowing up of a career that hung around her neck like a fifty-pound weight. She was going to have to become a different kind of person anyway, even if inside she was kicking and screaming about it. A person who didn't work at her current law firm, because they didn't let her argue her motion, and she knew what that meant.

There was no path. In her head she went back to Pennsylvania and sat with herself in the backseat of Brittany and James's car, enveloped in hours of the thrill and terror of not knowing what would happen next. If the law had turned its back on her, she could return the favor.

"OK," she said. "I'll go. But first you're going to teach me about your guns."

James walked upstairs. She followed.

He went to Brittany's empty room, and over to her closet. He slid the curtain back and opened the biggest safe. The guns sat in a pile, with their barrels pointing in all directions. Aretha thought of potpourri in a vase.

James picked up the Hello Kitty gun.

"This is a twenty-two," he said. "I shot rabbits with it when I was a kid growing up in Georgia."

"You did?" she said.

"Well, no. But other people do."

Did he have any idea what the truth was?

The next day she did twelve hours of work and everyone treated her as if her entire body was a broken leg. "Are you OK?" they kept asking, like morning birds chirping directly into her ear. And all she could think about was seven p.m., when she was due to meet James. The day ticked on, like a time bomb, with James's voice in her head instead of Brittany's.

She would go to the break room for coffee, and hear him, so lightly Southern that she knew he'd worked most of the accent out of his voice in order to move to New York, like she had with the Wisconsin tone she didn't know she spoke with until she'd arrived in the city. Both of them polished their voices with the hick's hope that they would somehow miraculously come off as not hicks. She put her K-cup in the machine and heard him talking to her about .357 Magnums, an oddly big handgun for city people, or people who lived near cities, or people who could feasibly drive to one.

"Some people like making a statement a little stronger than 'I can hide this in my pants pocket,'" he'd said, before raising the gun up to Brittany's bedroom window like he planned to shoot it out.

She did a little research for a client so rich she couldn't imagine the files she organized doing more than dropping a penny into the water fountain of the company's life. In her head, James came up behind her, in her office, close enough for the hair to rise on her neck. She felt hot. Excited. "This is a Glock," he said, with his lips an inch from her head while she looked up cases about arbitration that had language she could use to strike a poetic note about the glories of forcing someone who bought a defective lawn mower to sit down in a room with someone who'd come on behalf of the product's manufacturer and a third party, the arbitrator, officially neutral but almost always selected by the company, because why leave the act of winning to chance? "Cops like them," James said in her ear. "People who aren't cops like them because lots of non-cops like to pretend that they're cops. You can stick one of these in a pants pocket. We sell a lot of Glocks."

"Wait, you sell guns?" Aretha had said.

"Yes."

"I thought you only bought guns."

"We sell guns too. Our spares."

How many fucking spare guns did they have?

"Why do you think I know so much about guns?"

"Wikipedia?"

"No."

"But . . . ," Aretha said. "You know, fingerprints."

"What are you, the FBI?"

She talked to a client and a contractor and a junior associate on the phone. She forked the last piece of prosciutto, the last piece of melon, and the last asparagus spear from a mostly empty catering tray left over from someone else's meeting onto a paper plate. She shut her office door and sat back down at her desk with her plate. She stuck the first bite of food in her mouth. James leaned into her ear.

"This is a forty-four," he said, holding up a gun big enough that it would have to go into a man's interior jacket pocket, or a car's glove compartment, or underneath the passenger seat. "I think of this as the Dirty Harry gun, but everyone around here calls it the Biggie gun, because Biggie rapped about it on his second album. People like buying these for Brooklyn pride, even if they have no idea where Brooklyn is, really, because they've never left Pennsylvania."

She flashed back to Aaron dressed up as Biggie for Halloween, as un-Biggie-like as he looked, but Aaron's Biggie had nothing to do with the .44 in front of her.

"I don't deal with the guns," he'd said when she'd mentioned what Brittany kept in her room, at the tail end of an axe-throwing and coffee-roasting night, right before she was finally going to tell him that she went on a gun run. "They do. And if they tell you anything about the guns, don't tell me." So she didn't tell him anything.

Aretha left the office and walked to the subway. On the platform she could feel James's breath in her ear.

"This is an AR-15," he said.

She closed her eyes and saw the moment when he'd handed it to her and she'd accepted it. Her warm hands. Its cool stock.

"The gun for school shooters and copycat school shooters alike," he said.

"What's the difference between a school shooter and a copycat school shooter?" she'd asked him, just to see what he'd say.

"Well, one of them had to come first, in the year 1600 or whatever, in one of those Pilgrim schools that just had to be very slowly shot up with a musket. And everyone else has just been copying them."

Her train rolled into the station. She entered it. James vanished. She left the train, the station, the streets she didn't live on. She walked into the Vanderbilt house, up the stairs, and into her bedroom. She pulled out a pair of black stretch pants and a black stretch top that she'd bought two years ago, when she thought she might become a runner for more than the two weeks after New Year's, and said hello to Aaron's empty side of the bed, since he'd gone to Colombia. She was fucking sick of his empty side of the bed, since lately if he wasn't in Colombia he was in Ecuador, and if he wasn't in Ecuador, Kenya had called his name. There was only so much texting you could do with someone before you felt like they mostly lived in your phone. But he wasn't there, and it made more sense to think of him when he was, so she turned off the Aaron part of her brain and waited.

James knocked on her bedroom door. He took the wheel of the car. Aretha sat in the back and congratulated herself for creating the three-foot gap between herself and his stale-smelling clothes, even though the car had done most of the work. The guns they had to sell tonight sat in the backseat next to her, in the same black duffel bag she saw James carry upstairs on the night she met him, but when it bumped her, this time she didn't flinch. She let it sit on her. Metal against canvas against her left leg. She unzipped the bag. Two AR-15s, long and lean like early corn, ready to make them a few hundred bucks apiece. Holy shit. She was driving somewhere with a guy she barely knew to sell guns.

"We'll get protection money," James had said.

"Protection for what," Aretha said.

"The house."

"What do you mean by protection? Do you need a lawn chair to sit on the roof to finalize your guarding-the-house setup? Do you not have lawn chair money?"

He started the car in response. She hoped desperately that he wasn't drunk, since his old-clothes smell had a hair of his maybe-been-drinking smell in it. But he sent the car into the dark without a wobble. They headed east, into deep Brooklyn, and north and east, into Queens, where the addresses turned hyphenated and the businesses seemed to stack themselves in tighter bunches to Aretha's not particularly Queens-trained eye.

James sped down straightaways and looped around corners and parked in front of a ten-story building as tan as a '70s suit. He opened his car door. She opened her car door. He swung around to her side of the car to take the guns, threw her the keys, and told her to drive if anything happened. She shut her door, climbed into the driver's seat, and failed to picture herself as a successful getaway driver. She took a breath of car air she didn't expect to take, because she should be inside right now, with James, holding the bag or accepting the money or both, since she'd bothered to come along. Well, if it didn't work out, she wasn't legally in the car this time either. "They blackmailed me," she'd tell the judge. And then she'd wait to win. "But you went twice," the judge in her head said, as if blackmail were a coupon that would expire in a week. Why am I in this car again? If I can't get out of the car, I'm risking it all to be bored.

Since this time they hadn't left the city, she looked around to double-check that she didn't know anyone outside the car. Not that she thought she'd know anyone in Queens, since her coworkers moved in a straight line between their offices and the Riviera Maya or Buenos

Aires or Istanbul or whatever trendy lawyer vacation spot was in that year. But Queens could suddenly develop a pocket of expensive, tasteless food, and before she knew it, it'd be crawling with people she tried not to make eye contact with every day in the office, their faces flushed thanks to hundred-and-fifty-dollar bottles of wine, their suit jackets thrown over chairs in an attempt at casualness as if they hadn't been born unable to relax.

She checked the entire area around the car, but James disappeared into a whirlpool of activity that didn't seem to have any lawyers in it. Aretha had seen so many people vanish into crowds in the ten years she'd lived in New York, yet somehow she'd figured the guns James carried gave him a neon glow in the dark as a person who was obviously fucking up. But he looked just like the other people who walked the sidewalks and drove cars past the car she sat in. In sight for a few seconds, and then gone.

Maybe he'd transferred his fucking-up glow to her. She could feel it, in the dark, like if she touched her arm she could light up the car. She scanned the passing cars for anyone curious enough to look into her car and see that she'd fucked up, but no one out there gave a shit about anything happening outside their climate-controlled utopias. All the visions she'd had about fucking up before that moment in the backseat involved fucking up at work. She'd file a brief late, or miss some incriminating statement in an email, and the doing-a-bad-job-at-work gods would strike her with lightning. She never figured she'd fuck up at home, a place where everything was supposed to proceed according to plan if you kept paying rent.

The windows in the building James entered mostly stayed lit, like torches held above the head. In Pennsylvania, she'd stared at her phone, but here she sat and memorized everything around her. The buildings, the people scuttling by in the dark, the highway overpasses that hung above her head as ugly gray concrete chandeliers. Nothing happened, and nothing seemed about to happen. After a while she got used to the nothing, which felt so much better than the Pennsylvania nothing since she had the keys and could turn the car on and get some heat instead of slowly freezing to death. The buildings refused to spit James out, and after a while she stopped thinking about him or even her phone, which was busy pinging with new emails, as it normally did, but she didn't have to read them just then. She finally had something else to do other than be available at a moment's notice.

She flinched when James dropped himself heavily back on the driver's seat, since she'd fooled herself into thinking the silence she lay in would last forever. But twenty-nine minutes after he left the car, he threw the duffel bag back into the backseat, where it landed on her legs and slid onto the floor, lightly lined with money. James handed her a few twenties. She took them.

When they got home, she went over every square inch of the money and didn't see anything odd in it. It just felt odd to be holding it. Gun run money. She tucked it into her wallet, where she imagined it blackmailing the rest of her money into driving around for hours to sell guns. She brushed her teeth, changed into pajamas, and went to bed, sure that the ebb that usually set in after getting home would knock her out. But she lay awake in the dark for hours, charged up like she'd plugged herself into the wall. After a lifetime of studying and sucking up and trying to get rich, she'd almost sold some guns.

In the morning, right before she left the house for work, she heard footsteps behind her. She turned around, saw James, and impulsively gave him the nod. He, in a sign that he'd assimilated after years spent living with Black people, nodded back. Their mutual nodding habit stuck. They'd nod to each other when they entered the house and left it. When they spotted each other in the kitchen or coming out of the bathroom or the roasting room. Brittany still wouldn't talk to her, but James's thawing out meant she didn't think of the Vanderbilt house as a site of constant inter-roommate warfare anymore, even when Aaron wasn't there. She hadn't had a friend that wasn't Nia in years, and James didn't quite count, but the house vibe lightened up anyway. She could linger in the kitchen. Stare out the back window of the roasting room. Chill in her own bedroom with the door open. Deep-six Nia's texts in plain sight of everyone else.

"Brunch?" Nia texted her the night after she went on gun run number two.

Aretha hit delete.

"C'mon, I fucking miss you," Nia said.

Delete.

"You still hanging out with those fucking survivalists?"

Delete.

"And all their fucking guns?"

"Our guns?" she typed, trying on a more daring side of herself, before returning to the safer world called "their guns," and then deleting that to go back to the tried-and-true strategy of nonresponse. Nia wouldn't get it. Aretha couldn't tell her about her roommates buying guns in Pennsylvania, and selling guns around the city with James, no matter how Aretha tried to lightheartedly phrase it in her head, sounded even worse. So Aretha hid out in the Vanderbilt house and practiced pressing delete. Good riddance to the era when they went out for brunch. It didn't feel right to hang out with anyone who didn't live in the house anyway. They didn't get it.

"You should get out of the house with the guns," Nia texted.

Delete.

"And call me!"

Delete.

"No one throws away the friends they've had for fifteen years because of some shit man."

Delete.

"You're going to text or call me when this is all over, and I'm not going to give a shit."

Delete.

"Girl . . ."

Delete.

"Come the fuck on!"

"I'm drowning in work," Aretha texted Nia, "but I'll totally hit you up when it lifts."

"You are so full of shit," Nia texted back.

Thank god she heard someone at the door. The telltale sound of a suitcase came clanking along the floor downstairs. She ran down to meet it and saw Aaron, with his hat covered in snow, freshly arrived home.

"I'm so happy to be here," he said. "After spendin' three days meetin' every single extended family member who helped a woman grow some coffee beans, I am one hundred percent psyched that you're not goin' to come at me with a PowerPoint about growin' conditions. Shade versus sun. Rainfall. Irrigation. Packin' materials. Shippin' speed."

Aretha threw her arms around his neck.

"Actually, I've got a coffee PowerPoint right upstairs, on my phone," she whispered into his ear.

"In our room?"

"Yeah."

They went upstairs to their bedroom, where she pushed him down on the bed, straddled him, and kissed him.

Her phone beeped with a new text from Nia. She picked it up, deleted it, and went back to kissing him. Her phone beeped three more times.

She reached over to turn it off.

She undressed him, grabbed him, pulled him inside her. When she woke up and left the bed, her walk had a nickels-bouncing-around-in-a-sock looseness that sent itself inside to the rest of her, making even the moment when her Q train got stuck going over the Manhattan Bridge a pool of calm. Everyone sighed around her with the weight of starting their Thursday late, but she just spent their eight-minute delay looking at the speedboat hurling itself at the sun coming up over the East River and felt the rush other, simpler people felt when they looked at inspirational posters. When she got home that night, she passed James in the hallway on the walk up to her bedroom. He whispered "next Tuesday" in her ear and she went warm, like he'd crawled inside her chest and lit a match.

Could Aaron tell? She felt like she was walking around every day with her chest fire giving off a glow that anyone could spot from miles away. When contractors threatened to deliver documents late, or plaintiffs' attorneys sent angry emails at six p.m., or Mum bragged about preparing for oral argument, or her frustration set in at being split between trying to help win the Sandy case from the sidelines and secretly hoping it would sink, and the plaintiffs would get insurance claim money to rebuild their houses, all bothered her to a hangnail-picking degree, she'd calm down, take a deep breath, and remind herself that she had a hobby.

That's what she was calling it. A hobby. Some people knit scarves, and she went with James to deliver guns in the dark. She'd somehow survived all her years on the planet without even being tempted to leave the path. The straight-A's-to-good-law-school-to-grinding-herself-away-at-an-office-in-the-quest-for-partner path of being a good person who would also end up successful. Or maybe a successful person who'd end up good. But there had to be other kinds of people out there living other kinds of lives that were less grueling and pointless than her life of getting paid a lot to shuffle papers around for large companies that really only lightly gave a shit about any given case in particular, other than the mild threat of having to fork over millions in damages they could afford to pay. Lawyering had suckered her into living a life that resembled a permanent stupor.

Now that she wasn't stuck in a car getting bored while waiting for James to come out of an apartment building, she felt the excitement in delivering guns without touching the guns or the bags or the money or even leaving the car yet remaining a key part of the delivery process. At all moments when James wasn't silently driving her and a backseat bag, she knew she'd be more daring next time he texted her or knocked on her bedroom door. She wanted to feel the heat of fucking all the way up.

"I'm going in this time," Aretha said while James drove them to their next run.

She'd put a pair of leather gloves in her pockets in case she got the chance to touch the guns, because fingerprints, and she could feel them warming her pockets in anticipation.

"No, that's my job," he said.

"If I'm going to keep coming on these, I should have a role."

"You have a role. You drive away if something happens."

"That's not a role."

"OK. I'll do the money. You're just going to display the guns. All you have to do is put three handguns on a kitchen table, or a living room table, or wherever the client wants to see them."

"Oh, so I'm Vanna White."

As the only person she'd ever met who'd apparently seen zero episodes of *Wheel of Fortune*, he eyed her with a virginal blankness. He U-turned and drove south on Vanderbilt. She took a second to look at him and found him arranged into his usual formation: dirty T-shirt, rotten peach aroma, dull forward stare.

"Why do you do this?" she asked.

"Brittany has me sell off the extras," he said. "Sometimes I buy, too."

"Why does she buy so many extras?"

"Asking her questions like that isn't part of my job."

"Are you trying to be more like the people you sell coffee to?"

"I don't sell coffee to anyone. I sit in my room, drink, and do things for Brittany."

"Why do you do this for her?"

"Because I love protecting the house."

"People say no to people all the time."

"Not Brittany."

What the fuck was it about Brittany that people didn't say no to? They drove east down Atlantic like they were going to JFK, past bodegas and hotels and basketball courts in the dark. Aretha watched every block of the drive. The frozen boredom on people's faces as they waited to cross the street. The smeared neon signs of the restaurants that couldn't remain legible thanks to the speed of the car. They turned away from the airport. James sped off onto Long Island, where Aretha lost track of wherever the hell they could possibly be.

The city made sense after the nine years she'd spent living in it. She knew the rivers and the bridges and the taller, famous buildings by sight, and had a general sense of what neighborhoods were which by their mood and their architecture. But even GPS didn't do anything for her on Long Island, where the town names were unfamiliar and unpronounceable, and the towns themselves looked more or less the same other than the sizes of the houses and the colors of the people there. It reminded her of Jersey, with its towns that disappeared into woods that disappeared into towns at random to her ignorant eyes.

James parked the car in front of a house.

They got out.

Aretha took the bag from the backseat.

It poked her side.

She jumped before remembering what she held.

She and James walked up the gravel driveway to the house.

She put on her leather gloves and half-expected to walk into a lion's mouth, but after James rang the doorbell the two of them entered a bland suburban house. Large, square rooms, decorative sticks in a vase, framed family pictures on the fireplace mantel. The small brown woman who let them in led them into her living room, where she had a medical drama on her television and an indifferent cat creeping across the floor. The whole scene reeked of suburban normality, except the part where James took the bag from her shoulder and pulled out the guns. But that was normal too. Aretha thought of the suburbs as alternating between boredom and violence thanks to her parents' childhood stories of the white people who showed up to throw rocks through house windows when Black people moved into previously all-white Chicago suburbs, and modern bouts of people stomping each other to death at the entrances of stores on Black Friday and then claiming "It can't happen here," even though it had just happened there.

"What do you have," the woman said.

Aretha put the bag on the living room table.

"Rifle or handgun," Aretha asked.

She'd never felt clearer-headed.

The woman gave her a look. James did too. "They don't say very much," James said in her head, repeating a conversation they'd had in the kitchen while Aaron crawled through Kenya looking for coffee beans and texted her about seeing lions so she could text him back and pretend anyone would voluntarily want to see lions when you worked with lions who wore blazers for ten hours a day, and Brittany kept herself shut up in her bedroom. "They don't take that much time. They make their request, they hand over money, we leave."

Fuck. They probably didn't answer questions. But Aretha found it hard to stop asking them. Lawyering had taught her that all problems could be solved as well as they were probably going to be if she fired enough questions at enough people, and her question-asking habit had leaked over into the rest of her life.

"Handgun," the woman said.

"Are you looking for anything in particular?"

"Who are you, Walmart?"

James poked Aretha in the side. She shut up, put all the handguns in the bag on the woman's kitchen table, and watched the woman look at them, thinking about what it would be like to be James, or Brittany, or the woman who stood in front of her, full of an unshakable confidence in their ability to gut through some mysterious disaster with a weapon and a dream.

The woman gazed at the guns like they were an alternate sun. Didn't she have any questions? Aretha would never buy a gun, or a couch, or anything that cost more than five bucks without asking the seller something. There had to be something this woman wanted to know about what they'd just put on her table.

"This is a Ruger LCP," Aretha said, pointing to the first gun. "It's small, light, accurate, easy to hold . . ."

"How much?"

"Two hundred."

"That's all I need to know."

"But I have other specs," Aretha said.

Let me make the argument, she said to herself. Let me convince you. This is what I do.

James shot her another look.

"I don't care about specs," the woman said. "I'm just looking to buy something."

The woman picked up the gun.

"Buy that," James said.

She handed him two hundred dollars.

James took it.

"Do you have two of them? One for each hand?"

James handed her a second, identical gun. She forked over another two hundred.

The woman lifted the second gun and aimed it at her television.

Aretha blinked and saw the television explode. Dark glass flew and electrified light flashed and the hole the gun blew open in the TV looked just like a hole in the head and the room went spinning around tornado style. She clutched the woman's couch arm hard enough that she could feel her fingernails trying to fight their way off her hands and wished for deer. Just enough to fill the woods between the houses they'd driven past on their way here. Fat-flanked deer, thicc from eating their fill of acorns and grass, ready to serve as more comforting, logical targets than whoever this woman they'd just sold some guns to would end up thinking was coming to rob her. But she knew deer had gone out of fashion to shoot, and been replaced with intruders. Back when she used to go to Wisconsin to visit college friends, she saw that shift happen. The usual talk about deer hunting season had been joined by posters that went up in the corners of bar windows and that said "Please don't bring your gun in here." The deer that impaled her dead parents popped up to remind her of its existence as an animal someone had chosen to kill instead of a person, as if her parents hadn't died that day too. Its antlers appeared and multiplied to sit all over the woman's living room floor.

Aretha blinked. The antlers disappeared. The woman's television lay untouched. It hung as flatly and blackly on her wall as it had when she and James walked in.

James handed her the bag. She obediently put it back over her shoulder. The two of them waved goodbye. They got back in the car. She took off her leather gloves. In her head, the woman's television absorbed another shot and reassembled itself. She grabbed ahold of the car's armrest hard enough to stop thinking about anything other than the pain in her hand.

James handed her a hundred dollars of the four hundred he'd collected. She took it with pride. She'd fought through fear and nerves to leave the car and put guns down on a table. Her nervous, gun-selling self beat the living shit out of being her nervous, wondering-why-Mum-had-passed-her-at-work self. James drove them home along the wide stretch of Atlantic they took to get there.

Next time she'd ask for half.

•

APRIL BLEW IN, LUSH AND GREEN, BUT ARETHA MISSED THE dead winter grass that matched her mood. Her quest for another legal job sent her on a merry-go-round from calls to job interviews, to enthusiastic job-interview-ending handshakes, to silence. Turning her back on the law to sell guns felt perfect until she thought about facing an infinite stretch of time with nothing to do during the day except wonder why she had nothing to do. She shook up her worrying about job interviews by worrying that she didn't seem happy enough on her and Aaron's axe-throwing, bean-roasting late nights. The job hunt left her feeling like an insincere exclamation point that wore shoes. But Aaron seemed as happy as ever. Twice in the last week, he'd brought up how they'd lived together for five months, as if the act of making it through not quite half a year of cohabitation deserved cake. She always assumed, as someone who'd never lived with a guy, that if she stuck it out for this long she'd hope they'd get married tomorrow. And maybe she would have if going to work didn't feel like walking into a hostage situation, waiting for the bomb to go off, or worse yet, waiting for everyone else to figure out how to defuse the bomb before she did so she could lose at one more thing. When she wasn't celebrating her job-search failure by lying awake in bed, she spent the dark hours of the early morning worrying about the details of gun runs with James, which spiraled back into worrying about looking too thin and severe in job interviews. A perfect doom loop.

She couldn't quite get out of her own head at home, so she spent Aaron's work trip nights honoring their walking tradition by ambling around their neighborhood and the neighborhoods around it, looking for anything uplifting. Seven or eight walks in, she spotted a blank spot between two brownstones that turned into a community garden whose daffodils looked orange under the streetlights when she approached it. The daffodils sat next to some green stuff too leafy to be grass and too unformed to be anything else in particular. How did her mother figure out plants? Or Nia's plant lady? Or Nia? Aretha pictured them all solving plants the way she'd do it: smelling some dirt, finding some app that could tell her which seeds were which, trying to find the names of plants on the internet by describing them as best she could, even if that meant she'd google stuff like "green ram's head with a falling-off mouth," or "plant that looks like it wants to eat me." Normally when Aretha looked into a green field, she felt confused. But that night, watching plants fight gravity calmed her down. On other walks she noticed other community gardens, with their daffodils and early tulips and unidentifiable piles of other green stuff, but every couple of nights she made a point of going back to the first garden to see if it had changed.

At work, she resumed lunching with Mum, because it killed time and took her out of the office, where everyone gave her the wrong kind of eye contact. Normally everyone complimented anyone who lost weight, since skinniness was one of the socially acceptable steps towards world domination, but everyone looked over her suddenly defined jaw and unearthed cheekbones with total dismissal.

Mum picked a new lunch spot that served Mediterranean food.

"You mean they can put pasta on the menu somewhere, maybe cut it with hummus, throw some olive oil on top of the whole thing, and convince everyone it's exotic," Aretha said after the hostess seated them.

"No, I think they grill stuff. I think grilling is Mediterranean now," Mum said in one of her new suits. Before the partners announced that she'd be doing the oral argument, Mum wore slightly dowdy suits to work: brown and gray and tan beasts with wide lapels that never should have left the '70s, all in a size too large. But now her suits were modern, slim, and sharp, like the jackets meant to poke anyone who looked at them in the eye before they wandered over to a museum to be part of an exhibit on lawyer fashion. She'd updated her hair, too, from its lank brown shoulder-blade-length dullness to a razor-cut bob that ended right at her jaw. Mum was propelling herself into the future. A dominant future. And Aretha was drowning in a heroic effort to stay afloat in the present.

She ordered the hummus, which came grilled, with grilled yogurt on top and a grilled cucumber mint garnish. Mum's grilled kabobs were topped with a tiny grilled banana and had a dish of grilled saffron rice on the side.

"Our straws have grill marks on them," Mum said.

"Dedication is beautiful."

They took a few bites in silence.

"Keds girl finally bought a pair of heels," Aretha said.

"Oh my god! I haven't looked down in a while."

"They're good heels. A nice, solid oxblood color that's office edgy."

"Office . . . edgy."

"You know what I mean."

"I do. I think going-through-a-divorce partner finally got divorced."

"Why?"

"You know how he used to sleep on his couch?"

Only partners had space in their offices for couches, a layout that older paralegals told years' worth of stories about. "My god," one of them would start. "The eighties," another would say. "All that coke." "You never knew when you'd walk in on someone having sex, right there behind frosted glass. And they wouldn't stop for anything, not even me dropping off a final copy of a brief." The '80s didn't fucking exist, Aretha would think the second they got started telling stories. Never mind that she was born in them. The '80s were so far away from the staid, having-one-drink-at-a-long-business-lunch-might-be-too-risqué era she inhabited that they might well have been erased from the historical record. In the meantime, everyone could at least refuse to bring them up unless they were willing to bring enough cocaine to the office for everyone. Aretha could do cocaine at work. From everything she'd ever heard about it, it was the perfect drug for someone who could barely handle a cup of coffee. No better way to solve all your problems than to have a heart attack next to the water cooler.

"He leaves at six now," Mum said, drawing her back into the present.

"Right. So he's dating someone."

"Nine more months until he brings a twenty-year-old to the holiday party."

"Three more months until she shows up to summer intern and proves that she's completely useless since she has no idea what cases are."

"The thing is," Mum said, "word on the street is that you're sadly not necessarily going to be here for either one."

Aretha sucked a lot of air into her throat. Where was she? It looked like a restaurant, except it seemed full of knives, ready to stab her. Her eyes teared up, and then she remembered where she was and who she was with and found yet another level of inner reserve, because lawyers never admitted they'd lost anything that wasn't in print in a court decision or coming out of a judge's mouth. Except she'd lost. She'd fucking well and truly lost. What the fuck was she supposed to do now?

"Why are you telling me this?" Aretha asked.

"Because I like you and I think they're treating you like shit," Mum said.

"OK," Aretha said tentatively, still not sure she wasn't going to cry.

Lawyers didn't like one another. Come on, Mum, how much lying were you going to do? You're not being nice. You're enjoying this. We're drinking through grilled straws so you can throw yourself a lunch party to gloat at me. Aretha could see Mum's glee in her new haircut and suits, and the slightly upturned corners of her mouth. Mum even forgot to do the right thing after announcing the news and tactfully look half-dead from stress.

"I have a friend who . . ."

Mum went on in the benevolent tones of the victorious. Aretha couldn't hear the rest. Mum's friend had a fucking job, and soon, she, Aretha fucking Jackson, would not. Yeah, there were probably some technical details in there about what kind of job Mum's friend was giving away, but did they matter? She'd end up saying yes, get me a fucking job with your fucking friend who does litigation or boring-ass contract work or shoe selling or anything else short of mowing lawns. And if Mum's friend offered the job, Aretha would take it. Maybe she'd even fucking mow lawns. She only owned athleisure and going-out stuff and lawyerwear, but surely people could mow lawns in athleisure, and if that didn't work out, maybe she'd hit up her jumpsuit collection. Mowing lawns was the kind of not-quite work-out athleisure promised would be the pinnacle of human existence. A minute ago, she'd been a proud litigator, and in the future, she would be a proud woman who found some way to work so the student loan people wouldn't start calling to threaten her. She had loans and she didn't have a mysterious parental fountain of cash, so she'd take any job anyone slung at her to stay in New York, since all she had other than New York was Wisconsin, a fucking black hole with antlers in it. Once upon a time Aaron had offered her a job roasting beans. She could do it. She would learn to roast beans tomorrow. She should leave this lunch and take the train home and ask Aaron, on the spot, how to roast beans.

Mum had stopped talking, and looked at Aretha with an air of professional concern. Her facial expression had less warmth than a friend would have offered, but more than anyone else she worked with. Aretha didn't really work with people. Their souls had melted right into their suits a few hundred thousand dollars ago.

"Are you OK?" Mum said.

"How do you know this is going to happen?"

"They've been inviting me to these meetings about oral argument, and in one of them, a partner slipped."

"And said something vague?"

"It was pretty clear. He apologized, even."

"An apology. Wow."

"I know."

"When are they planning on telling me?"

"I don't know."

Maybe the restaurant could grill her. They grilled everything. Why not a person with no fucking future? They could just put her on top of the grill until she developed the telltale marks. They could cut her up and serve her. Hello, we have a new special today, it's called the Futureless Lawyer and it comes with a side of fries. If she became a lunch special, she wouldn't have to go through the Faustian struggle of trying to find a new job in an era when no one cared to hire lawyers with a medium amount of experience. They cost too much, firms said, when we can just keep on younger, cheaper first years until they get too expensive. We can't make anyone partner, because the partners refuse to retire, and we don't want to fire them because of their expertise, firms said. There are a lot of people with your résumé, firms said. We see a lot of you Ivy League types, and you all kind of look the same on paper. Yes, we know the Ivy League was supposed to make each one of you into a special snowflake, but it didn't. Yeah, you took out a couple hundred thousand dollars to get that law degree, but have you ever thought about doing something else?

"Are you OK?" Mum said again.

"I'm fine," Aretha lied.

"Do you want me to talk to my friend about a job for you?"

"Absolutely."

She turned back to her food, which had all the taste of air. If she threw her plate across the room, she'd feel better. She'd throw it hard enough to shatter. The noise would mess with everyone else's power lunches. For a second they could all feel as fucked up as she did before they went back to running the world.

They finished eating. Mum paid the bill. They went back to the office, which had changed. It was colorless to begin with, but for Aretha the lunch had sucked out any color that remained, leaving everything with the appeal of a soup drained of broth.

Back in the office, everyone's eye contact drained her, too. They sucked out any sense of who she still was just by looking at her. They marched along on their inevitable paths to success. She perfected her fakest smile whenever she had to talk to any of them. She felt her face turn into a polite plastic sheet when she asked a contractor to hurry up and look at some documents. A first year dropped in to ask for some tips on how to write a memo about a court decision that was bad for a cosmetic company client's ability to force one of their clients into arbitration by including an arbitration clause on a scratch-and-sniff plastic sheet on the outside of the shrinkwrap they packaged their moisturizers in, and Aretha helped her shape that yes-but-in-a-noey-way tone appropriate for clients that wanted to live right on the edge of the law to make more money and would fire a firm that gave them a straight-up no.

It turned out she could do her job on autopilot if she needed to, with a face dead enough to hide her worries. She worked hard to bring out her inner robot. A partner called her into his office to offer her a minor assignment. A write up of a couple of paragraphs of case law on the permissibility of letting your long-haul trucker employees freeze to death in the central Midwest so long as the employer could find a gentle way to blame the employee for turning off the engine while parked to sleep, or using the bathroom at a gas station instead of peeing into a cup during a seventeen-hour shift. Aretha accepted the assignment with her brand-new robot face: eyes calm, jaw loose, mouth set to convey a sense that all the world's pleasures were mere distractions compared to the ideal act of staring into the middle distance at absolutely nothing while memorizing the exact way in which the partner would like to burn a long-haul trucker who gave a shit about stupid things like staying alive.

At home she took her mechanical self on a gun run with James, and felt amazed at how much easier going places with someone who didn't talk went when she didn't try to talk either. In silence, they were equal partners, asking the exact same amount of each other while their car rolled down city streets and raced down highways. I'm going to do this until I find something more normal to do, she thought as she handed a brown-haired, acne-scarred white Washington Heights guy a Glock 19, and he handed her three hundred bucks. When she took the money fire shot up into her leather-gloved hands. How did I ever think I was a robot? When she got back into the car she took off her gloves and touched the doorjamb. It felt liquid and alive.

James drove them to Paterson, New Jersey, so they could sell an AR-15 to a Black guy whose kids played loudly in the house next to the garage where Aretha armed him, their giggles and shrieks alternating seemingly on cue. The doorjamb feeling from the car stuck, and so Aretha looked excitedly around at his garage and listened to his kids. She thought about how happy the guy must be to own his first gun, since she was prone to imagining the first time she met someone as an equal level of beginning for both of them.

When she spotted the guy's other guns, piled on a homemade-looking shelf above their heads, she forgot to steel herself for a second, and imagined the kids finding the shelf in the middle of one of their fights and shooting each other. But just as neatly as the idea had entered her head, it left when the guy handed her a stack of hundreds, neatly replaced by the same mantra she uttered to herself whenever shit got dark at her office. This is somebody else's problem, she silently recited to herself as she gave him the nod to close the deal. She sat in an office and decided things were someone else's problem, and now she stood in an alien living room, seamlessly transferring a problem to someone else. And then she froze up. Why had her work self melted into her gun-selling self? How had she become a person who was OK with any of this? She could turn it off, right?

"Why do you guys sell these?" she asked James when they were packed back into the car and she was aiming them towards the George Washington Bridge.

"Well, I sell them to make money."

"I thought Brittany made you sell them."

"She did, at first. Then she said I could do whatever I wanted with them, and I chose to sell them."

"And you make money off the coffee."

"I sell them to make sure our people are prepared."

Our people. She looked at him after he said it, and found him at his absolute calmest, with none of the boredom or disinterest she usually saw in his eyes. Their grandfathers probably would have joined bowling leagues. Their parents might have met people at a bar. But in the shotgun seat of the ancient blue Volvo that the household kept around in case the delivery van went down sat a guy who thought he was building a community of armed people. Fear sliced into Aretha's chest, cutting her neatly in half. She looked down at the two parts of herself and marveled at their miraculous act of continuing to drive the car. But no matter what she thought about his motives, she sold guns too. And she refused to give up the bright, clear feeling she got when she handed someone a gun or took their money.

"We have four tomorrow," James said.

"Whatever you need, I'm there," Aretha said.

"Even if you need to get off work early to do these?"

"Who the hell is around in the middle of the afternoon anyway?"

"OK, but if someone was, would you be ready?"

"What the hell wouldn't I be ready for," Aretha said.

"You tell me," James said.

"Nothing," she said.

That conversation came back to her the next morning at the breakfast table, when Brittany casually nodded at her over their identical plates of optimized soy protein, because Aretha had gotten into eating Life Preservers a couple of times a day. That conversation returned to her at night, when Brittany did the same over everyone's plates of what she called her "festive" dinner, Life Preservers that she served with a lemon vinaigrette dipping sauce. The smell of vinegar mixed with soy wafting in Aretha's general direction made her feel like deoptimizing all the soy in her stomach right back up onto the kitchen table.

She tried her usual trick of simply imagining they were eating something else, which was also an excuse to daydream about the meals she'd eaten before she'd decided to calcify her guts for the apocalypse. The pan con lechón she'd grabbed at a takeout window uptown, with pork that juiced in every bite and velvety buttered and toasted Cuban bread. The perfect slice: yeasty crust, sharp basil, milky sweet mozzarella. The greatest hits of her mother's cooking: cornbread, fluffy sweet potatoes, collard greens laced with ham. All those other meals that cost more than the free Life Preservers she could bum off everyone in the house. If she wasn't going to work at her firm anymore, the least food could do was cost less. Someday Brittany would present her with a bill for the soy, but she hadn't yet. And if she didn't think too hard about eating it, it tasted great. Not at all like sawdust. The more of it she ate, the more she sensed a salty creaminess. So this was soy. Pure and practically unadorned.

Her conversation with James came back to her that night, when she and Aaron sat in bed with the lights off, waiting to fall asleep. Aaron eased into the slower breathing that meant he'd soon be down for the count, and Aretha sat, wide awake, looking at the ceiling and wondering just how many other people Brittany and James planned to arm. Aaron had told her never to say anything about what they were doing with the guns, but how could she not tell him? She rolled over and touched his arm.

"Did you know," she said.

"Uh-huh," he said, sleepily.

"That they're selling . . ."

"I will never have any idea what you're talkin' about," he said.

He rolled over. He went quiet.

Aretha waited.

He started snoring.

How on earth could he not care?

"I really appreciate that you're helping out around the house," Brittany said to Aretha the next morning.

Aretha sat up from her breakfast soy, startled both because Aaron's indifference meant she'd slept badly enough for a pin drop to send her flying across a room and because something seemed to have gone wrong with Brittany's factory settings. Usually when she spoke to Aretha, Brittany's tone kept an edge, like maybe she'd kill her on the spot if she had to. But when Aretha looked across the table, she saw a sweetness and light that had to be fake. If only there was a way to test out someone's face, maybe by pressing into it with the tips of her fingers, or spitting squarely into its center, to see if they were kidding.

These were the soft, comforting tones of someone who knew she'd talked to James about why he sold guns.

"Thanks," Aretha muttered quietly into her bowl.

"No, I mean it," Brittany said, sticking her right elbow on the table so she could lean in closer.

Aretha, out of habit, flinched backwards.

Brittany took her last bite of food and stood up to put her bowl in the sink.

"If you ever want to do a little more around here, let me or James know."

"OK."

Brittany climbed the stairs, rustled around in her bedroom, and came back down dressed in the solid black tracksuit that meant it was martial arts time. She opened the back door to do at least two hours' worth of stretching, breathing exercises, punches, kicks, and sweeps in the grass. Aretha watched from the kitchen and thought of her axe-throwing nights. Arm back, forward throw, sweat. Maybe she and Brittany weren't that different.

During the day, she completed office tasks with a half-dead smile on her face, and at night she lay awake with her head on Aaron's chest. She stared into the ceiling. She listened to traffic. She listened to every creak the house made. Her lawyer self knew why people didn't want to know about the illegal things their roommates did. She pictured the three of them in court, with Brittany and James across the room from Aaron, who was patiently explaining that he was just a coffee guy who didn't know they sold guns, or had guns, and actually, he wasn't even sure he'd met these people before. How could she trust a guy who had that much of an escape plan if everything went to hell? Whenever it all went down he'd grab his shit and go, and it would be like they'd never met. He couldn't be serious about giving a shit about how long they'd been together if he lived his life with one hand on a go-bag.

What did she want him to say? She didn't know, because the things she didn't want him to say had crowded them out. She'd make road maps in her head about other things she could bring up when Aaron materialized, magician-like, on a schedule she didn't remember anymore, to entertain her by reciting minutiae about coffee bean growing conditions. He never seemed to recall what he ate or what else he did on his travels, and half the time he only had five ecstatic minutes in him before he collapsed into a jet-lagged sleep. She'd lie in the dark next to him, listing all the things she couldn't say when he wasn't snoring hard enough not to hear them. "I know what you mean when you talk about how good the soil people grow coffee beans on tastes, in a way," she never said to him. "I feel that way sometimes right after I've handed someone a gun and right before they hand me a wad of cash. The air between us always changes then. It gets thicker. We both know it. The other person's face brightens, even before we're done. The ground has shifted under our feet."

"Sometimes, after a run, I look over at James," she said into her own head while he snored next to her, "and I feel something. I don't know what it is, but . . . I know what it is. I want to fuck him, even though that would almost certainly be the worst decision in a life filled with shitty decisions, like deciding the straight-A mentality had to come with me through all the parts of my life that haven't had a school in them. I eye his bag-of-flour-looking ass during a gun run, and I think why can't we fuck up together one more way? For some reason it's not enough for me to fuck up with him by driving guns that are almost certainly illegal to people who almost certainly don't have permits to own them, to sell them under the table. I want to fuck up by fucking him, too. I want to hit bottom. I want to fuck up things

with you. You're so fucking perfect, Aaron. Your trips and your kind-
ness and your insane levels of happiness and your sobriety and your
coffee and your insistence on staying out of the gun stuff. But because
I'm fucking up, sometimes I can't stand looking at perfect you. I want
someone else who likes fucking up. His fuckups are a lot worse than
mine, but you know what I mean."

"I miss having friends," she silently mouthed at his back in the
dark. "Not necessarily Nia, because she doesn't understand why I live
here, but a perfect, imaginary friend who would get it. Someone who
would look at me celebrating Christmas with you and me eating Life
Preservers and sometimes taking trips with James, and note that I've
evolved by leaving myself open to new experiences. Sometimes I think
Brittany and James are the only friends I have left, even though they
don't talk to me that much. They've blackmailed me, but they don't
judge me anymore. We do terrible shit together, and I like it."

She blinked again, and woke up in the dark, with no one sleeping on her right. Maybe she'd imagined Aaron the whole time? His
suitcase wasn't in the closet, and a stack of the retro-printed T-shirts
he always wore on trips, "to look relatable, in a fashion-forward way,"
he'd said, had disappeared too. But most tellingly, his cowboy boots,
which he called his only link to West Texas other than his mom's
gravestone, weren't in their usual resting spot by the bedroom door.
They had dark brown bodies and lighter, sun-worn toes, and gave him
a click she could hear from upstairs. She used to associate the click
with strength and a retro manliness, and now every time she heard
it she thought of him as the last piece of a puzzle clicking into the
place he really belonged: outside the house, probably on his way to a
plane to fly somewhere and come back to continue not saying a damn
word to her about the guns. But this time he'd taken off without even
telling her. She waited for the text he'd inevitably send her about how

he had to scoot off to Hawaii in a rush to source beans that someone roasted with volcanic rock while doing a handstand, so she could respond with an extra, even more insincere exclamation point. But the entire day flipped by without her phone buzzing once.

In May, Aretha checked seventeen days off her calendar and reported to federal district court early in the morning on Friday, the eighteenth, to support Mum's argument with the rest of the team. Fifteen lawyers greeted Aretha as she walked up the courthouse steps in a black coat and a black skirt suit two sizes smaller than she'd been the fall before. Almost white girl skinny, she'd griped to her bedroom mirror after getting dressed that morning. Ready to disappear.

Her coworkers stood in groups loosely organized by law school graduation year, except for the partners, who huddled in a small, authoritative clump that spanned almost a quarter-century of law school degrees, and Mum, who stood in the center of them, with the giddy flush of a girl reporting to prom on the arm of the prom king. She alternated between talking to the partners on last-minute strategy points and gleefully greeting the other associates in anticipation. Aretha found Mum on the steps and gave her a sympathetic forearm squeeze.

"Thanks for the great brief," Mum whispered in Aretha's ear.

"Anytime," Aretha whispered from behind clenched teeth.

So this is how she delivers her kill shots, Aretha thought as she watched Mum take her beaming self over to other groups of lawyers. With a smile.

Mum released Aretha into the world she belonged to: the world of the other sixth years who weren't delivering the most important argument their litigation department had this year. Their smiles fake, their bitterness real, they huddled tightly as a pack of three against the wind, which blew from the southwest, settled itself in their heads, and swirled with their anticipation of occupying the Mum position on the stairs. At other glorious times. In other radiant places. Most definitely at other firms, where the respect they would be treated with would threaten buildings with its force.

Aretha's mood lightened. As the one of the three of them due to face the chopping block first, she felt free. No more worrying about what the partners or anyone else thought of her. No more putting her entire heart into case law competitions or raising her hand first at meetings. No more gentle sucking up at happy hours, ironically titled events that underscored just how fucking miserable everyone was who attended them, with their smiley-faced sandwich boards and their happy-ass bartenders, professionally ready to pretend five p.m. on a Tuesday was actually one a.m. on a Saturday night.

Wow, she missed Saturday nights. Sure, she loved walking around on them with Aaron, up Washington or Flatbush to the bars, where he'd order water and she wouldn't, but she craved an old-fashioned Saturday night, where she put on clothes tight enough to hurt and worked her way down, with Nia, to the middle of the dance floor. They copied dance moves from other people. They made stuff up. But the year Aretha remembered the fondest was the year they agreed, no matter what, to do the jitterbug at two a.m. Aretha might be hanging out with a guy or huddling in a pack with her catering roommates, eyeing everyone else. Nia could be talking to someone she knew lightly from other parties who she seemed to run into every third party or so, the therapists and lawyers and writers who, like Aretha and Nia, went to parties to feel a little less stiff on weekdays. But the hour would come down on the two of them and they'd meet up to do a dance so ridiculously out of style that it felt like theirs.

She looked down, half-convinced in the time she'd spent think-ing about going out that her suit might have done her a favor and turned into something sequined. But nope. She was still stuck on the courthouse steps in a dull-ass suit, a couple minutes closer to death. Since the other probably not chosen sixth years were Midwesterners like her, and they had time to kill until one of the partners gave the sign, the three of them caught up on weather, traffic, and crops. They Midwesterned, right in the middle of the steps of the courthouse for the Southern District of New York, where the only crop was bird shit, free to be harvested at any time. But they talked about other crops: corn and soybeans and sugar beets that could be harvested and eaten or thrown at mailboxes in a barely sublimated metaphor of what they all wanted to do to Mum, the anointed one.

A partner jerked his head towards the door, and the other fifteen of them trailed him inside, snaking their way through security and up to the fifteenth floor, where their assigned courtroom sat, a quarter full of other lawyers who looked just like them if you didn't look too closely. Roughly the same black and navy and the occasional, daring, dark-sand-colored suit, usually worn by the kind of partner both powerful enough to give up on being restricted to pedestrian black or navy and old enough to remember an era when tan suits were hip. Mum moved to the most hallowed courtroom position. Up on the aisle, at the end of a row of partners, so when their case was called she could swiftly stand up and walk to the defendant's table, along with the head partner, who'd sit next to her as support.

The judge walked in, one of the handful of Black federal judges in the district, with his shiny bald spot forming a halo on the top of his head, like Aretha's dad's right before he died. "My holy bald spot, hallowed be its space," he'd say to her as a wink to the baptism they'd both shucked, but Aretha's mom hadn't, baking with more fervor for church sales every year, and adding Wednesday Bible study to Saturday to score more points with God. Aretha looked up to see if the judge would look at her, and when he did in the count-the-Black-people-in-the-room way she'd also done ever since she could remember, she shot him an of-course-I'm-the-one-who-should-actually-be-arguing look that he ignored on his way to the bench.

This is it, Aretha thought as Mum stood up, it is really fucking over. She felt herself becoming a very large block of ice. Mum began to speak, slowly at first, but then faster, like her argument had to run downhill, about the upsides of cheating people out of rebuilding their houses for technical reasons. Aretha recognized her own words, lifted straight from the brief. She closed her eyes and she was Mum, up on her feet, unrolling the best parts of the argument she'd put on paper. The case about denied insurance coverage because the plaintiff filed a lawsuit instead of going to arbitration, breaching their contract. The exact-match signature requirement that had invalidated so many people's insurance claim paperwork in another case. "Denying people compensation for their losses at the lowest point in their lives isn't what we aim for," Mum said while Aretha mouthed along, "but it's an unfortunate consequence of what happens when we apply good law to bad facts."

Aretha squeezed her left hand until her fingernails left moons in her palms. If only she could draw enough pain out of her hand to survive this. She dug a nail into the weak flesh between her thumb and her pointer finger. She aimed her left hand's nails into the skin between her right knuckles. What would really hit the spot, she thought to herself, would be grinding all my teeth into powder right here on the floor and throwing all that fucking powder on them so they all look like they had an accident in a quarry. This is my brief and these are my words, and this moment should be mine too. What if I got up on the table and fucking screamed out the rest of her argument? Just yelled it over the top of her voice so they could hear me? She has one fucking minute left and I will fucking pinch hit this shit because I cannot live with her taking any more words right out of my mouth.

But the worst thing was that Mum was fucking standing up there winning. Since she'd written the brief, this was Aretha's case to win. As a litigator, she had been trained in the art of winning and was at peace with the lessons she'd learned from it. No matter how much she tried to tamp it down, there was a part of her that sat down to dinner in the days before she'd turned to the soy diet and daydreamed fondly about defeating the steak on her plate. Being a lawyer started out as a profession and ended up a blood type. A great need to win attached to all the cells floating under her skin, constantly creating its own antibodies to losing. Yes, it was kind of a shame that their opponents probably wouldn't get the money to rebuild their homes. But was it really even about that? It was about the winning. If she had done the argument on top of the brief and someone had ordered her to individually tell all the people on the losing side that they'd lost, she'd savor every single goddamn fucking minute of watching their faces cave in the second the judge legally erased the existence of their homes from the record.

"Time's up," the judge said.

Mum waited for the first question. Aretha slowly unclenched both her fists and looked down her row of lawyers to confirm that no one had noticed her having a moment. Their eyes were all fixed on Mum, who answered softball questions with aplomb. Aretha blinked three times and Mum was done, gliding back towards the courtroom doors with a gladiator's confidence while the rest of the lawyers formed a waterfall behind her.

In the hallway, the partners were exuberant. They fist-bumped, making contact a record-high half of the time. They issued awkward, joyful high-fives. They clapped Mum on her back. They said partner things, like "I think we have a good shot with this one," and "Obviously we don't know, but I feel really good right now," and one of them said, "You nailed it," which that partner followed up by whispering to another partner while staring at Mum, yet well within Aretha's earshot, "Haha, nailed." Aretha put on a more fake pleasant look than usual, to fit in at work by facially saying it was great that Mum was probably three weeks away from that partner getting drunk enough at a happy hour to stick his hand on her thigh.

Aretha suffered through a group lunch and a subway ride back to the office before the head litigation partner called her into his office. His sidekick, litigation partner #2, who'd gone to law school with him, sat drumming his fingers impatiently on the arm of his chair, which sat to the right of partner #1's desk, halfway to the window. Aretha looked outside and saw the entirety of Central Park, rendered as one dizzyingly green rectangle with roads cutting across its center like a belt on a pair of pants. Aretha sat down in the only other chair in the room, right in front of partner #1's desk.

"I think you know why you're here," the head litigation partner said.

"I have no idea," Aretha said.

The second partner laughed, an awful sound, like a seal dying after being crushed by a bear.

"Come on, Aretha."

"I had a really great time this morning," Aretha said, "listening to Mum deliver an oral argument that lifted . . . every . . . word . . . from my summary judgment brief. I thought she crushed it."

"You didn't write that brief."

"Weird, I swore I spent at least a few nights here, typing it on my computer."

"We took your name off it. As far as anyone is concerned, you never wrote it. And really, you haven't done much of anything around here for the last six years."

"What are you doing?"

"Letting you know that Mum wrote that brief, along with me."

"What? I . . . I . . ." Aretha searched for air.

"Shouldn't have taken that day off."

"I was in the hospital! Having an allergy attack!"

"And somehow getting zero work done."

"Almost dying is a sign of laziness?"

"You are only going to officially be employed here for one more month. You may find it useful to spend your time educating yourself about what other legal opportunities exist for you."

"But why?"

"You weren't chosen."

The second partner stood up, walked over to the door, and opened it, waving his hand from his waist to the door to let Aretha know it was time to leave. Aretha stood up and obligingly stumbled in the right direction, her feet having turned to rocks. She had psyched herself up for this moment ever since she had lunch with Mum, sure she'd survive it in great style, and now it was here, and everything had caved in. She arrived back at her office, shut the door, and did the one thing no one, especially women, was supposed to do at work. Cry. Crying in the office marked you as weak and womanly. Possibly ready to have your period right there on the fucking floor.

Six fucking years of her life, doled out in sunny mornings and wintry afternoons and Thursday-night briefs and Sunday-afternoon memos. All so they could judge her on an allergy attack instead of anything she'd ever done or not done for them. She knew all about at-will employment and its lack of need for rational reasons to surgically separate people from their jobs, but Jesus. They were so full of shit. She saw younger iterations of herself hunched over the computer that sat inches from her balled-up hands, finding cases. Searching and calling people on the phone and typing in skirt suits and pantsuits and the occasional pair of sweatpants. Oh, the relaxed dress code of weekend typing, where the office filled with the hushed air of the clicking that came from every third office and the weighty silence that descended over the rest of the space, since no one called anyone on weekends.

Here she was, thinking of the pleasures of weekend typing after they fired her like some kind of goddamn dunce. Yeah, she probably looked like an onion from all the crying, but it was time to try to sneak out of the office anyway and go walking, which always solved so many problems, the key problem here being that she wasn't physically tired enough to stop thinking of the asshole top partner down the hall. She would not think of him. Thinking of him granted him another fucking victory beyond the victory of giving her the axe. She rescheduled some calls and saved a couple of documents. Could she postpone everything she was scheduled to do at work until the end? Well, she was certainly going to fucking try.

She put on her coat, and stuffed two pairs of heels in her purse in favor of the loafer-sneaker hybrids she hid under her desk. The loafer part kept her looking sharp, and the sneaker part acknowledged that she spent her day walking between offices and elevators and subways and street blocks and stairs. She took a look around her office for anything she needed, in case they changed their mind and didn't let her in the building tomorrow, but all of it, on second look, seemed so disposable. The pouches of green tea, which she whipped out whenever she felt the mild internal wobble that meant she was getting sick. The spare fork, in case the kitchen had run out of the plastic kind. Some papers they'd probably give to the first year who replaced her about cases the first year wouldn't have the legal experience to understand.

A bunch of stuff she really didn't recognize but must have deemed important at some point: a couple of straws, six boxes of paper clips, a swimsuit from one summer retreat's beach party. This was a life? This collection of shit?

She stood up, mentally planned her route, and took it, from her office through the copy room through the kitchen, making sure to take the time to dump an entire box of almond milk from the fridge all over the homemade banana bread someone had left on the counter. The milk sloshed off the counter and onto the floor, where hopefully her boss would slip in it and break his back twice. Outside the far kitchen door, she turned right and then left, passing three right-hand offices. Two lawyers looked up and saw her, and she imagined the total exhilaration of going back to the kitchen, picking up the almond milk, and throwing it in their faces. Instead she walked on, as an onion in retreat.

Right outside the last of the three office doors but before she reached the hallway with the elevators in it, she reached into her purse, grabbed a handful of receipts, tore them into pieces, and threw them all over the floor, confetti style. A couple of months from now she wouldn't work with a single goddamn one of the people who sat in the offices she'd just passed. She would not gain any friends from the firm, or acquaintances, or even people she fondly remembered putting up with. She would try to forget how often everyone in the building was encouraged to go to war against one another. She would never google a single damned one of them to figure out if they'd achieved what she hadn't. In six months, in her head, they wouldn't exist.

Outside, on Sixth Avenue, the warm smell of cooking halal meat mingled with exhaust, tourist sweat, the plasticky insides of clothing stores, and the gluey smell of all the stickers opposing the president that people sold from sidewalk tables. She looked in her bag, where her two pairs of backup heels lay, one navy, one black. She grabbed the navy heels by their heels on her walk down the island, aware of how much she'd always hated them. They had a fucking T-strap, like her foot needed to be covered with a kid's ugly playground swing to not fall out of the front of her shoe.

She walked downtown, determined to hurry through forty blocks of scurrying office drones until they thinned out near Union Square. After that she could walk to Brooklyn at a more recreational pace, down and over the Manhattan Bridge towards home. The goal was to feel like total shit once she got there, too run over by the soreness that set in after walking that many miles to be able to form a coherent thought about being fired. But first she had to keep her head down so she could see anything other than people looking at her onion face. If only she was the kind of person who could cry subtly. Dab her eyes with a tissue once or twice after letting a few picturesque tears fly. She could feel the eyes on her, with the concern common to people who lived in a city that bailed out its women if they looked attractive enough to bother. When one person stared at her for too long, she flung the navy heels at the starer, a balding middle-aged white guy. The heels struck him squarely in the chest. She took off running and he went after her, yelling. Hey. Hey! HEY!

Together they sprinted through the Twenties, where the flower shops spat their plants greenly onto the sidewalks out front and the hotels and stores and office buildings kicked out people who didn't look miserable. In the Fifties and Forties, whenever she'd dared to look up, she was greeted by the sight of perfectly ignorable tourists and office workers who looked only a couple of orders of magnitude less melancholy than she was, their faces pinched as they hurried down the street between elements of their routines. Midtown wasn't a center of happiness, just bustling activity. She'd taken great comfort in everyone else's inability to look content as her work situation deteriorated. She'd descend from her office in the rain or snow or cold or dark, and everyone would look just like she felt.

How dare these people in the Twenties seem sort of satisfied! She mentally redid their faces in mid-dash, touching them all up so they looked as miserable as she did. As miserable as she thought she might have looked two blocks ago. It turned out flinging your shoes at some asshole with a staring problem actually felt pretty fucking sweet. "Go to hell!" she shouted brightly at her pursuer, thrilled that he'd lightened her mood by continuing to try to catch her. Behind her she heard a thump, and she looked back to find no one chasing her. He'd found his way to the version of hell that manifested as the side of the building he'd run into. He sat at the point where building met sidewalk, rubbing his head while three people asked if he was OK. She turned left at the next street to lose him for good and made her way to the subway, since she'd run out enough of her anger to figure out where she had to go next.

At Union Square she caught an L train to Brooklyn. She sat down. The train took off. Somebody had left the window open. Wind came rushing through her ears at the train hustled through its tunnel. She felt good. She felt fine. She was in no way going to throw up. They fucking took my name off that brief. They pretended I didn't spin fifty fucking pages worth of cases and facts and argument into gold. They fucking fired me. They are all slipping in that almond milk right now and fucking up their ankles forever. They are losing teeth after falling face forward into it. They are blackening their eyes.

The train sent her past the East Village and through the long tunnel that connected Manhattan to Brooklyn. She got out at Lorimer and walked up Metropolitan with her hips swinging and her shoes thumping all the way past the diners and the vintage clothing stores to the axe bar. The bartender gave her a nod and a limeade. She put her driver's license down as a deposit, picked up an axe, and went over to the targets. She took a long cool sip of the limeade and sent her first axe flying just off target and into the wall with a satisfying thwack.

Three limeades later the bar had settled into a wave, and everyone else's voices had a delay. The television mounted in a corner spoke very softly about the night's sports scores. She paid her tab, collected her license, and looked longingly back at the axes, looking for a spare for one last throw. Someone had left one on a corner of the bar floor, almost hidden under a booth, like they knew she'd need it.

She gave the last axe of the night a windup and a throw spirited enough to land smack in the meat of the left hand of some guy who'd popped up to block the perfect line between her axe and the target. He had the walk of someone who saw the bar in waves like she did, and yelled at her in the same mumbly blare as the television. And hearing him yell at her felt great. He'd gotten in the way of her axe, and she'd fixed that. She'd just gotten fired, and she'd responded by firing her obedient self. She calmly walked out the front door of the bar into the crowds of Metropolitan Avenue and understood that it wasn't an accident that she'd ended up in a house full of people who solved their problems with force if they needed to.

She went back down in the subway and up out of the subway and across Atlantic to Vanderbilt. She'd done it. Her feet ached. Her shoulders had gone stiff from all the axe throwing, like they were 10 percent saltwater taffy. There she went, past a glassy apartment building put on earth to bring higher rents to their neighborhood, even though it lay three-quarters empty. Up past the Mexican place and the Thai rolled ice cream place and the old-school soul food place and the place that used to be one hundred square feet dedicated to the purity of artisanal mayonnaise before it became one hundred square feet dedicated to the purity of artisanal watches.

Up to home, where she put her key in the door, shakily ascended two sets of stairs, and walked down the bedroom hallway in search of her abandoned bedroom, ready to happily text Aaron about how she hoped he was killing it in Panama just like she'd killed the meat of that guy's hand at the bar. She almost ran smack into James, who mumbled an "I need to talk to you" in her general direction at the same speed she could talk, all those limeades later. Fuck. The point was to never end up as drunk as he usually was. He shuffled back to his bedroom, kicking off as much alcohol aroma as she probably did.

She tailed him past her empty bedroom and Brittany's empty bedroom, nervous about being in his bedroom with him as opposed to poking around in there herself on the rare occasions when everyone left her alone in the house. She shut the door after herself, and slowly lowered herself down on the only chair in the room, a desk chair that belonged to a desk covered in liquor and marked-up clippings from *The Washington Post* that probably contained thousands of words he hadn't written personally. He sat down on his bed, with his head against his headboard and his feet aimed straight out in front. Fuck it.

"What you drinking?" she said.

"The usual."

"Can I have some?"

He pulled out a plastic Atlanta Braves cup, poured a few inches of the usual into it, and handed it to her. She took down a solid mouthful of peach liquor sweet enough to wreck her teeth on the spot.

"Can you do five runs tomorrow night?" he said.

"Yeah," she said.

"Even though we'll have to start in late afternoon?"

"I'll talk to people at work, shift my schedule around," she said, mentally planning to redistribute 100 percent of her work to some of the suck-up juniors who hadn't been fired yet.

"It's good that you're this dedicated to the cause," he said.

They sat in the silence that overtook them when she failed to answer, staring at each other from opposite points in the room. I've already lost pretty much everything, she thought as she wobbled over to his side of the bed and kissed him. Why not throw the rest of it in the fucking garbage? He tasted like peach liquor, and she tasted like peach liquor, so they sort of canceled each other out.

God, you look like a stale bundle of pizza dough, she didn't tell him when he'd taken off all his clothes. She had never been attracted to him, and she waited patiently for that to change, since she'd decided to fuck him anyway. Why the hell couldn't making shitty decisions feel more glamorous? From now on, I am making all my shitty decisions in a club somewhere, under a disco ball, while wearing a sequined jumpsuit. He slipped on a condom, which made him a stale bundle of pizza dough with a rubber cock, and entered her. I am being fucked by an uncooked pizza, she thought, lifting herself up on her elbows underneath him so she could see the moment when the fucking became interesting, if it was going to. Pizzas taste better cooked, she thought, as he settled into a rhythm that reminded her of a public access television show about sawing. I miss Aaron, who has abs. Aaron was busy becoming one with coffee twelve hours away by airplane instead of having abs across the hall and generally being available to stave off the making of shitty decisions like this one. Aaron was busy being a coward in Panama, getting out of what his roommates did as a hobby by getting on planes. Oh thank god, she thought when James rolled off her, having set the land speed record for sex.

"I love you," he said hurriedly, like he had to get it out before he threw up.

"That's great," she said.

He slapped on his pants and shirt and ran down the hallway to the bathroom. Aretha put on her clothes and crept into the hallway. Behind the closed bathroom door, she heard retching sounds. OK, that was enough. He didn't actually have to throw up. From the bedroom hallway, she heard him go back into his own bedroom, lock his door, and pass out, as evidenced by the snoring loud enough to cut through two sets of bedroom doors in a house where a coffee roaster ran for half the day. She went into her bedroom, sat on the bed, and noticed that the waviness of the bar had followed her home. Her stomach joined the party, which sent her down the hallway to her own bathroom to puke.

She closed her eyes and woke up terrified on the roof. James's domain. She must have walked to the back of the hallway between the bedrooms and up a ladder, while drunk. Well, she said to herself, I'm still alive, and when I wake up tomorrow, James and I will have been too wasted to remember how we fucked up.

She scanned the whole scope of the roof, a flat, concrete-colored thing with a high-enough railing that they could have had deck chairs or roof parties if they had been different people entirely. She walked over to the only thing they did keep on the roof: a small zipped black tent. She looked into the side of the tent, to confirm its lack of people, and unzipped it. It held only three things: a bottle of peach liquor, a handgun, and a rifle. She entered the tent. She sat down. She picked up the rifle. It fed its reckless energy into her arms. Is this why people want to fire these things? Because they lift them and feel charged up?

She put the gun back down, zipped the tent up, hustled down the ladder, and fled to her bedroom, where she passed out.

Twenty-four hours later, she sat, dosed up on aspirin, in a car with James, who wouldn't look at or speak to her. For the first time in months, she didn't try to talk him into talking to her, because she didn't want to hear him say anything again for a while. Possibly ever. She didn't want to talk about the roof or what happened in his bedroom or that night's destination. She never wanted to hear his drunken voice again.

He silently drove them to the Bronx. Queens. Secaucus, New Jersey. A red-brick building on the edge of the Westside Highway. A quiet street on Bay Ridge filled with apartment buildings and one donut shop that sent so much fried dough smell wafting into the car that Aretha couldn't help but breathe it in and relax. She didn't bother explaining the features of a Smith & Wesson M&P Shield, a Sig Sauer P938, a KelTec 9mm. People bought the guns because they planned to shoot things with them, not because they needed to hear a list of specs or watch her face fall when she realized they wouldn't hunt animals either. What they shot was up to them. She was a conduit, connecting people with something they needed. She performed an essential service by handing over the guns, and James, too, by accepting the money. Way more essential than pushing paper for some suited fucks who probably hadn't broken any bones in spite of the almond milk she'd graciously spilled for them. In addition to helping their city and suburban neighbors, they could two-step their way through an entire night of gun runs without bothering to open their mouths about what they'd done in his bedroom right before their trip.

Could a pool of shame be large enough to sink into? Right there, in the passenger seat? She'd struggled to think of it as the passenger seat instead of just calling it shotgun, like she had when she had lived in shotgun land growing up, and she and the other kids in the world made it a game, yelling "shotgun" while they raced to be the first one to sit in it. As an adult who used to oppose guns, she had told herself to think of it as the passenger seat in order to not encourage the homicidal side of car culture. But now that she sold shotguns, she was free to think of it as shotgun again. A tougher name to match her newly tougher self, able to walk into someone's living room with a rifle slung over her shoulder and make cool '70s, almost blaxploitation-esque eye contact. The shotgun seat. The rifle of the front seat of the car. In the shotgun seat she could simultaneously feel invincible and bathe in shame for having slept with James. She could dunk her head down in it and never come up for air.

They didn't talk once James parked the car. They entered the house in a mutually assured silence that made talking seem exactly as logical as loading seven pounds of garlic onto an apple pie. They walked to their bedrooms in the quiet. They shut their doors. Aretha flinched when she spotted Aaron sitting in their bed with his legs lightly crossed in front of him in total repose. Aretha mentally slung an axe into the meat of his hand. This was the first time she'd ever wished Aaron gone. Just for another week or so, so she could get her head together about how badly she'd fucked up. Or maybe longer than that. He looked like himself, in his retro Pabst Blue Ribbon T-shirt, which he wore to convince coffee people he might have drunk in the not too distant past, and skinny jeans, carefully selected to make him look like an off-duty indie rocker. She just looked at him and his face that said that no matter how much of a survivalism game he talked, he'd never really freaked out about anything other than that hurricane he survived. She thought of her lost job, and Nia, who she couldn't bring herself to text right now to tell her how hard she'd fucked up, and James. She fed herself off her own loneliness and shame.

"Honey," he said.

It took all the strength she had in her not to hit him. Him being nice to her was too much. She realized she'd hoped that he'd become a mean person in Panama. Like her. Meanness was what she felt up to dealing with just then. And then she remembered that he was no better than her. She'd fucked James, and he was a coward who hoped to ignore the guns they sold so he could walk off with everyone's coffee money in the end. They could be assholes together. She deserved him.

"Sweetie," she said, offering up her entry to their couple's nickname game.

"Darling," he said.

"Sugarplum."

"Johnnycake."

"God, I want a johnnycake," she said. "I'm so fucking hungry."

"You've only eaten Life Preservers for two months."

"It's a defense mechanism that's defending me from the horror of having to select other food."

"You're eatin' like, eight hundred calories a day. If I ate like that, I'd probably end up killin' someone."

She left the doorway to go lie with her head tucked into his armpit. She listened to his bean-sourcing stories with interest, trying to make the attention she paid to him transform her into the person she used to be before she met him. A better person. Or at least a little less fired.

•

IN CALIFORNIA, ON A VISIT FOR WORK A COUPLE OF YEARS AGO, Aretha deposed a witness and went outside afterwards to find herself in the middle of the first and only earthquake she'd ever experienced. Everything had turned to Jell-O around her, a mild but consistent twitching that was over nearly as soon as it had started. She thought of that earthquake as gravity's mildest tantrum.

But gravity didn't throw itself on the floor and shake its fists in New York City, which is why she couldn't believe it when she felt a similar wobble in the house, right after she left the shower, in the middle of toweling off her legs. She wrapped one of her towels around her chest and another around her hair and went to investigate, but found nothing. Just a temporary disturbance that she might have imagined, but for a continuing sense of vertigo. Five minutes later even that had disappeared, and she was left to the ordinariness of a Tuesday in May where she was forced to confront another dying day at a job that had turned itself more robotic than the stiff face she'd stupidly thought she could maintain forever. The other lawyers had given up on whatever warmth they'd ever put into making eye contact with her. On good days she took solace in having upgraded her catering tray taste to cold cuts other than prosciutto. On bad days she thought even the wall art was looking at her with pity, as a fired person who was finding new, innovative ways to screw up job interviews.

She was too late to them. Too early. Interviewers judged her shoes for being too black for her navy suits. Not black enough, in that she hadn't bought them yesterday, so they'd had time to fade. She'd racked up all the disappointed stares. You're too tall, interviewers' judgmental eyes told her five-foot-six-inch self. What a shame that you're too short, too. Have you ever thought about being less Black, firms said by wondering out loud why she was from Wisconsin instead of someplace they thought would make more sense, like Chicago, and sending out their all-white interview slates that took place in all-white offices that quietly whispered to her that maybe she'd survive two years tops, if they let her do anything beyond looking at documents. She'd stubbornly put "drafted summary judgment brief for winning motion" on her résumé as a signal that in a previous life she'd been allowed to do true high-class-associate stuff, despite the risk that they might call the office and be falsely informed that she hadn't, in fact, drafted the brief. She'd sworn off drinking until she found a new job. And until she could be sure that she could drink without throwing axes into anyone else's hands. Or sleeping with anyone else. Aaron had gotten to her by repeatedly insisting she didn't need to pour booze all over the stress she already felt, and he'd bought them a weighted blanket, which she'd been excited about since she needed something other than stress crushing her in order to sleep. Except it usually didn't work. Maybe she could pay someone to sit on her every night.

She got off the subway three stops early to shape her evenings by putting some exhaustion into them. She watched people enter the beauty supply store, the bodega, the sushi place. She looked into shop windows and felt nothing. She turned off the main street into the residential streets to be alone with trees and buildings, and found herself doing a loop past the first community garden she'd spotted back when she started taking these walks. She stopped in front of it and put her hands on its chain-link fence to peer in. The daffodils were long gone, leaving some aging tulips and a couple of trees bleeding purple flowers onto the ground, where unidentifiable green stuff sprouted up next to the flowers. A Black woman with a bandanna tied around her bun wet the mysterious green stuff with a watering can, walking the grounds in measured lines. She looked up and saw Aretha, who let go of the fence to walk away.

"Hey," she yelled.

Aretha looked around her, assuming the woman meant someone else.

"You. In the suit."

The woman walked up to the gate and opened it.

"Come on in."

Aretha entered. Inside the garden the trees blocked out overhead light, leaving her alone with the plants on the ground, whatever they were, and this woman who bothered to deal with people in suits.

"Do you have any questions?" the woman asked.

"Sure," Aretha, said, pointing to all the plants.

"Lilac trees," the woman said about the purple-flower-spitting canopy above them. "Corn," she said about four rows of green stalks that Aretha felt straight-up dumb for not recognizing right away, being a native Wisconsinite and all, even if she was the kind who grew up in enough of a city to think all the farmland that surrounded it might as well be Mars. "Tomatoes," the woman said about the plants staked to the brick walls of the neighboring buildings. "Green peppers, jalapeños, pumpkins, down the road, closer to September," she said, pointing to the neat rows of plants she'd just finished watering.

"I'm Aretha."

"I'm Tonya."

Tonya held out her hand for a shake, and Aretha shook, coming away with a light sheen of dirt.

"So, you eat all these vegetables, when they're ready?"

"No. We give them to a group of families who asked for them and live in a section of the neighborhood where there's only bodega food."

Aretha looked all around herself again. How was it possible to feel so much better just from having left the sidewalk? Her white sneaker-loafers sank into dirt, pleasantly wrecking themselves. She looked up again, to the canopy of lilac trees that hung above them, purply fucking up her plan to walk around hating herself.

"Do you need volunteers?" she said, in a voice she didn't recognize, because she had never in her life volunteered for anything. But if Tonya agreed to let her come here and help out, she'd have a place to go that wasn't work or the house.

"Sometimes," Tonya said, getting out her phone. "Give me your name and number and I'll text you if we need anything."

"OK."

Aretha thanked her and left. She looked admiringly at the dirt on her shoes, rubbed the dirt on her hands on her suit sleeves because fuck suits, and headed home. Was it being outside? The weather, after she took her jacket off, was firmly in that golden three-week period after winter gave up and before the air turned into a sopping-wet dishrag. The plants? She'd remembered her mother's garden fondly for the handfuls of flowers it produced every summer, and how relaxed she felt every time she smelled them. Maybe it was just briefly being around someone who didn't know she'd been fired and wasn't asking her to sell guns or desperately hiding from the guns she sold. She took out her phone to find the only other person she knew who fit that description.

"Hey girl," she texted Nia.

"What's up?" Nia hit back.

"Do you want to come over sometime? See the house? The coffee?"

Aretha waited and watched the three dots that meant Nia was typing. She'd probably say no. She couldn't imagine Nia kicking her suspicion of the roommates hard enough to get herself inside the house. And they hadn't seen each other in months, which always raised the possibility that they didn't want to see each other again ever, despite the sheer length of their friendship. But Aretha felt a yearning for a time in her life when things had gone better than now. In all the space those three dots gave her to think, she flipped back to college and her and Nia's early years going out in the city. If she couldn't re-create those days, she could at least hang out with the other main person in them.

"You could meet Aaron . . . ," Aretha added.

"Absolutely," Nia said.

"I'm so glad. I know we haven't seen as much of each other as we usually do, so let's fix that."

"I'm looking forward to it, girl."

"Next Saturday?"

"You got it."

This gave Aretha five days to mentally prepare herself for Nia's visit, which would go perfectly. Sure, Nia had her doubts about Aretha's house and the people who lived in it, but they'd be swept away the minute she made it inside. Aaron had already charmed Brittany, who made other misanthropes seem like the life of the party. Surely he could win over Nia, who was several thousand times more chill.

Aretha spent the hours before Nia's visit surreptitiously cleaning the house's common areas to avoid summoning Brittany's insistence that she was doing it the wrong way, and huddling up with Aaron to plan Saturday down to the inch, like they'd planned their family-free holidays. If they could celebrate Christmas without family, they could throw the world's coolest housewarming for exactly one person. Aaron cycled a particularly aromatic coffee bean from Honduras into the roasting rotation to give the house the best possible smell. Aretha baked lasagna in the kitchen with the windows open, giving in to her Wisconsinite need to greet a guest with something homemade and cheesy from a thirteen-by-nine-inch glass pan. The doorbell rang, and Aretha took one last triumphant look around the house before going to answer it.

"Are you ready?" Aretha said.

"Born ready," Nia said, on the porch. "Might have even been ready before that."

"You're going to love the tour. And Aaron."

"I'm already getting a kick out of Bambi, which looks like a restaurant that sells some really high-class dead movie deer."

"The highest. I'm so happy you came."

"Of course I'd come meet my main girl's man."

They hugged and walked up the brownstone steps. Aretha watched Nia's eyes go wide immediately upon stepping into the second-floor doorway and taking it in. The long rectangular swath of living room, decorated with Aaron's beloved green velvet couch and two framed pictures: a shot of farmers picking coffee beans in Ecuador in the '50s on one end, and a Kenyan family celebrating their 1972 harvest on the other. The roaster in its room, with its octopus arms and legs working a butterscotch scent into every corner.

"It's really a house," Nia said.

"What did you think it would be?"

"Everyone's dream house. You know, a house that's actually an apartment that doesn't have that many rats."

"We have three entire floors."

"Show me."

They went downstairs first, to the slightly cooler first floor, where Brittany liked to invite business guests, and Aretha sometimes used to pretend she lived alone, with its untouched backup kitchen, pair of often-ignored couches, and the sliding glass doors that overlooked the backyard. Aretha thought of the backyard stories Aaron had told, about Brittany picking all the previous owners' weeds and overgrown collard greens out of the yard to get it down to grass and her bunker, and her mouth watered in tribute to the missing greens, and to the corn she'd seen in the community garden the other day. The bunker sat out back, covered by the patch of Astroturf that Aretha found more obvious than the other members of the house did. But despite Aretha's distaste for the bunker, she felt her chest puff up with pride at being able to show the yard to Nia. Real houses, the kind she and everyone she grew up with thought they'd be able to buy someday when they were real adults, came with yards, and now she'd lucked into getting hers.

The backyard had the medium-green flush of mid-spring, with a couple of old oaks authoritatively guarding one corner and a hammock tied between them. When looking outside, Aretha mentally erased the bunker and highlighted the hammock. And even if she'd never sat in the hammock, since the slowly dying cold season had only granted the yard a handful of hammock days, the relaxed promise of its cloth body softened her up inside.

"Come on!" Nia said. "Let's go sit in it!"

She unlatched the glass door and slid it open. The two of them dashed outside, giggling like kids. Nia stuck her foot into the hammock's middle too fast, and the hammock picked her up, swung her a foot across the yard, and dumped her on her back in the grass, still laughing. Together they stuck a foot in apiece and balanced the hammock enough to end up on their backs in it, side to side, looking up at the sky.

"So you're out here all the time," Nia said.

"Never."

"Why not?"

"I just . . ." she said, trailing off into yet another unwanted thought about the bunker, that stainless-steel boogeyman a short walk from where they lay, ". . . will get out here more often," she added, looking over at Nia.

"I should have gotten out here before this," Nia said.

"But I thought you didn't want to come over."

"I thought so, too. But I also thought you'd be living in one of those apocalypse movies instead of a cool-looking house that doubles as a coffee shop."

"Well, the house's legal name is 28 Days Later," Aretha said.

"Girl, really?"

"Nope, I'm just fucking with you. But c'mon," Aretha said, climbing out of the hammock. "Let's go see two more floors of house."

"And then the bunker, right? I've never seen a bunker."

"You don't want to see a bunker," Aretha said.

"I do, girl. I am really excited about your bunker."

Aretha took a couple extra looks at Nia as she herded her inside and upstairs. Nia was loving this in a way that made Aretha wonder who she planned to laugh about it with later. Once upon a time that person would probably have been Aretha, and they'd have done their laughing over brunch plates at their diner eight hours after they crawled out of a warehouse elevator deep in Queens at sunrise in smudged makeup and sweaty clothes. But now Aretha could feel herself becoming the subject of all that laughter, and she hated it. Nia thought she was getting a tour of an amusement park called Six Flags Underground, where the Ferris wheel was full of guns. And Aretha was dragging behind her on the stairs, thinking, This is my fucking life you're snickering at.

Upstairs they bounded into Aretha and Aaron's bedroom, which gave off the hot-mess vibe of people who cleaned for company but not themselves. Sheets and blankets thrown across the bed, socks sprinkled all over the floor. Aaron's collage of overlapping coffee maps and indie rock and hip-hop posters up on his side of the wall. Hers blank, just as she liked it, free from all the statements of tasteful professionalness she felt she had to make on her law-diploma- and tasteful-photograph-laden work walls.

"No-picture Aretha strikes again," Nia said.

"She's a silent killer," Aretha said.

"Is that a claw-foot tub?" Nia said, poking her head into Aretha and Aaron's bathroom.

"Yeah, but we never use it."

"Why not?"

"Do you know how much time you have to have in your life to take a bath?"

"Uh, ten minutes?"

"In your world."

"Yours, too," Nia said, bouncing across the hall to Brittany and James's slightly open bathroom door, which Aretha had never opened.

"Now, that's a fancy ceiling," Nia said.

"Yeah, I guess it is fancy," Aretha said, looking up. She didn't know how to think dreamy thoughts about ceilings. Just floors and velvet couches and hammocks and backyard roasted meats and retro pictures of people gleefully holding coffee beans. Nia had to be talking about the ceiling's borders, which looked shaped out of whatever bullshit must have passed for clay in 1907. "Come on downstairs," Aretha said, stepping out into the hallway.

Nia followed, and pointed at Brittany's and James's shut bedroom doors.

"I don't think they're home," Aretha said.

She held her breath, waiting for one or both of them to move around and prove her a liar, but enough time passed for her to get lucky. She took Nia down into the roasting room.

Aaron met them there, looking fresh in a vintage Blackalicious T-shirt and jeans. Aretha admired him, the wood he stepped on, and the blissfully still-shut bedroom doors she saw behind him. She introduced Aaron to Nia, and felt pleased when Nia broke into a smile. She did it! She officially qualified for the trophy that magically appeared the second anyone brought the two key people in their life into the same space without one of them finding the gun stash.

"What kind of coffee is that?" Nia asked, pointing at the roaster.

"So the other day I flew down to Honduras, and met this family who'd figured out how to grow a hybrid of these two already killer beans . . ."

Aaron gave a brief speech about coffee varietals. Then he took a couple of steps, gestured, picked up a handful of unroasted beans, and held them out under Nia's chin. She sniffed.

"Wow," she said.

Aretha and Aaron exchanged a look of pride.

"So there's a little butterscotch on the nose, and some blueberries on the back end," Aaron went on.

He walked into the kitchen, grabbed a cup, poured some freshly brewed coffee into it, and handed it to Nia. She took a sip.

"This is incredible," she said.

"We've come so far in roughly a decade," Aaron said, "from those second-wave, bitter Starbucks coffees that people had to add milk and a half-dozen syrups to in order to choke it down, to the modern third-wave stuff. Smooth right off the bat. Best enjoyed plain so you can taste the layers in it."

The three of them migrated to the living room, where they all sat with coffee and started talking. Aretha allowed herself to relax, since the other two seemed to be getting along. Nia, ever the therapist, drew Aaron out of himself. She worked her way from his childhood in West Texas to the hurricane's nadir, to the coffee expert perched between them on the couch, while Aretha listened and occasionally interjected with a story or a correction, but mostly scanned the flow of information occurring between Nia and Aaron for anything she didn't already know. She couldn't turn off the switch inside her that always scanned for new facts. Everyday life in the house was unlikely to kick up anything she didn't already know, but Nia could. The half of Aretha that wasn't content to sit back and watch Nia work waited for the person who'd figured out that Aretha had truly met someone because she wore lipstick to brunch once to suss out everything that was wrong. If Aaron tipped his head, would Nia figure out that he traveled too much, giving Aretha enough time alone at home to leave herself open to the temptations of gun selling? If Aretha winced, would Nia understand that she'd fucked up with James? If either one of them sneezed, would Nia figure out that Aretha had failed at work? Aretha had developed a book's worth of strategies to keep Nia from finding the gun stash, as if that were the only shameful secret in a house full of them.

While she waited for Nia to complete her investigation, she played one of her favorite mental games. The one where she deposited herself into Aaron's life to live it for him while he talked about it. There she was, watching the tumbleweeds roll by in Aaron's otherwise scenery-less Texas hometown. Driving past oil rigs and beef cattle and through thunderstorms and away from tornadoes. Wait. He'd never mentioned the tornadoes.

"They'd just come flyin' in out of nowhere," he said to Nia. "You'd have a few minutes to get yourself under a desk or somethin' and there they'd be, darkenin' out your living room and freakin' the shit out of your mama. Not me, of course. I was never freaked out. Just terrified."

Nia just sat back on the couch with her coffee, listening. When Aaron went deep into the tornadoes, Nia's empty hand rolled up into a ball, like she could beat back all the pieces of wood that flew at him when the wind got up. Tornadoes, that hurricane. Poor guy was a magnet for disasters. Aretha squeezed her coffee mug between her hands in sympathy.

When Aaron switched from hurricanes to the dark side of bartending, Aretha left him with Nia and went to reheat the lasagna. After she put the pan in the oven, Aretha saw the tornado drills she did in school, undertaken halfheartedly because the lake on the edge of town sent tornadoes flying around her hometown instead of through it. She remembered curling her head into her lap and tucking her whole body under a desk. The tornado Brooklyn had a few years ago didn't turn it into tornado central, but Aretha felt ready to face another one if she had to, warm and fuzzy about the house's stored soy protein, the infinite supply of great coffee, and the relief of curling up with Aaron every night now that they could be terrible people together, even if they hadn't figured each other out yet.

Out in the living room Nia and Aaron had moved on to Nia's plant lady client.

"She sends me pictures of the plants once a week, like I'm her mom and the plants did really well at their spelling bee."

Plant lady herself appeared in one of the pictures, with her face hidden in shadow, and Aretha thought she looked kind of like Tonya. She tried to remember why she thought bringing Nia over to the house wouldn't work out, but that distant self was gone, brushed away by a breeze during their stay in the hammock, or burned off like germs in the oven with the lasagna. She lifted the pan out and inhaled deeply. The other two came into the kitchen. Aretha cut them squares, and the three of them sat down for lunch. Aretha took a handful of peaceful bites before she recognized the creak that meant someone had opened one of the upstairs bedroom doors. She forced herself to keep chewing. Everything would be fine. Cheese fixed problems.

Brittany wound her way down the house stairs, tracksuited and sullen. She entered the kitchen, grabbed herself a soy protein bar from the stash under the sink, and sat down at the kitchen table, right in front of Aretha, who worked up a lawyerly smile. The kind she whipped out every time she had to talk to a client about super-fun things like individual items on that month's legal services bill, or the unpredictability of the judge who'd been assigned to their case.

"Hey, Brittany," Aaron said.

"Hello," Brittany said.

"Brittany," Aretha said, "this is Nia."

Nia stuck her hand out to Brittany, looking for a shake. Brittany clasped the last couple inches of Nia's fingers with hers, and wiped her shaken hand off on her track pants. Nia, ever the professional, greeted Brittany's rudeness with a three-hundred-watt smile. Something seemed wrong. Aretha mentally rifled through their texts and their brunch conversations, looking for clues, and finding none, she went back to Brittany's tracksuit. Brittany had gone flamboyant. This tracksuit would just have been a solid black swath of polyester had it lacked two vertical body-length stripes: a garden-variety white one and its gold disco cousin, aflame in the afternoon kitchen light. The tracksuit. Nia had said something about a tracksuit at brunch one week. A patient who . . . wore . . . tracksuits. "Flo Jo, without the hair, or the nails, or the Olympic records," Nia said in Aretha's head. "But chock-full of plans no one needs."

Aretha settled in at the table to watch them, with her sweating hands down out of sight in her lap.

"So what do you do for a living, Nia?" Brittany said.

"I'm a therapist."

"Do you find that fulfilling?"

"Very much so."

"Even though therapy doesn't really help anyone?"

Aaron shot Brittany a look. Brittany ignored him and doubled down by putting her elbows on the table, cupping her face in her hands, and leaning forward. Aretha squeezed her hands together hard enough in her lap that they shook. Nia zeroed in on Brittany, like an eye doctor adjusting the sample lens until the patient could see again.

"I think the best thing about therapy is that you get to dedicate a section of your life to making a sustained, incremental effort to understand yourself better. No one figures themselves out overnight," Nia said. "But why don't we talk about you, since you're already sick of me? What do you do for a living?"

Brittany clenched and unclenched her fists, grabbed her Life Preserver, and ran up the stairs. How had Nia and Brittany sat across a table from each other for minutes at a time, let alone long enough for Nia to end up with stories about her? Nia was born patient. She let flies land on her until they chose to back off. She was the only New Yorker Aretha had ever met who stood perfectly content at traffic lights with zero urge to wander out into the street, even if it was clear of traffic, until the crossing light summoned her. But Brittany believed in motion. She tapped her feet, her arms, wiggled her legs, built bunkers, worked out constantly, ran upstairs to hide at the slightest provocation. Upstairs, Brittany slammed her door. Aretha put a hand down on the kitchen table to stop its wobble.

"Brittany's a little testy sometimes," Aaron said.

"Huh," Nia said.

"But the food's good, right?" Aretha said.

Nia looked down at her plate of lasagna for a beat too long.

"Yeah, I . . . ," she said.

Something thumped once. Twice. James came running down the stairs with an AR-15 strapped to his shoulder. He ran into the roasting room, picked up a Tactical Coffee balaclava that Aretha had forgotten existed, put it on, and ran all the way back upstairs, to the roof, where she heard his boots against the tiles. Business as usual on the guarding-the-roof front. Aretha went back to her lasagna, thinking of how James might as well have been wearing his name on his face, only to be distracted by Nia's fingers digging into her arm.

"What the fuck was that?" Nia asked.

"Oh, nothing really," Aretha said.

"Who the fuck was that?"

"Just James, running upstairs," Aaron said.

"To do what?" Nia said.

"Guard the roof," Aretha said.

"So you don't think this is a big deal?"

"I don't get the part about wearing the balaclava with the company name on it, but he does the rest of that all the time."

"It is weird," Aaron said.

Aretha looked at him, since he'd suddenly become someone who criticized James, wondering what else this person she didn't know might say.

"But it's his thing, and I'm not sure I could stop him if I tried to."

He'd thought about stopping James? Aretha felt months of relief wash down on her head. Maybe they could finally talk about his roommates.

Nia put her fork down on her plate.

"Aretha, I gotta go."

"Really? I thought you'd stay until at least after lunch."

"I just remembered I have an appointment."

"What appointment?"

"An important one."

"You don't have an appointment."

"I do."

She left the table and hustled her way to the front door.

"I'll text you," Nia said.

"We're still on for Saturday brunch, right?" Aretha said.

"Absolutely," Nia said, shutting the door behind her.

Aretha flew over to open the front door and ran outside, to make sure Nia was OK. Nia had stopped just beyond the house, terrified, like a ghost had flown into her face.

"You have to get out of there," Nia said.

"Nah, I think you just don't get it," Aretha said.

"No, I got it, and you should fucking get out of there."

"I know that looked a little weird, but . . ."

"You don't love him enough for that."

"Nope, I love him."

"When you're out of there, text me," Nia said. "We'll go out."

"I'm not leaving, hun."

"Oh yeah, you will."

They hugged.

They let go.

Nia turned up the street.

She just didn't get it.

Aretha went back to the house. She opened the door, walked to the kitchen, and found Aaron there, still eating her lasagna. She left hers to congeal on the table, rustled around in the kitchen cabinets, and grabbed a Life Preserver.

"I didn't plan on whippin' out my whole life story, but you were right," Aaron said. "She just kind of wheels it out of you in this calming way, like you're doin' a good deed by tellin' her everythin'. But I get why she's allergic to the house."

"I think the Tactical Coffee balaclava was a little much."

"Honestly, me too. There's guardin' the house, and then there's tellin' everyone who sent ya."

"Are you going to talk to him about it?"

"Yeah. I think we might need to talk about a lot of stuff."

Not too much stuff, Aretha said to herself. Just the balaclava stuff. Keep it to that.

"I could sit with you two while you do it if you want," she said out loud.

She pictured a lovely future where she casually brought up that carrying guns to the roof generally seemed like a bad idea and James didn't mention that they'd slept together because Aretha was right there when he and Aaron had their big talk, looking James in the eye, making it extremely awkward to go there.

"Nah, I think this is more of a business thing."

Running around in the house in a fucking balaclava is business?

"Well, good luck," she said.

•

**INSTEAD OF MOVING OUT, ARETHA MOVED FURTHER IN.**
She and James drove the boroughs three times a week to get rid of their gun stash and sometimes pick up more. As she'd requested, he'd upped her cut of their sales to 50 percent, a number that turned her on about as much as holding the guns did. It was hysterical that she'd once thought she needed Aaron to hold a gun to feel this alive, she thought, while walking to a house in Hackensack with the duffel bag slung over her shoulder. On their drives she tapped the car floor like she might get up and dance. Sometimes James opened up about climate change, and she pictured the world he described, where the southern sections of Brooklyn got less and less regular subway service when the water slowly came in to eat them. And sometimes Aretha told James about flying all over the country to try to get businessmen in suits to hang themselves with words under fluorescent lights.

Her head insisted that she, as a person who'd never cheated on anyone before, should shut down around Aaron. But instead of re-doing herself as an out-of-power phone, she kept their walking dates. And the part of her that thought she'd never sleep with him again thanks to shame watched the rest of her throw her head back in joy on the Tuesday night Aaron found something new to do with his tongue. Just because she wasn't perfect didn't mean she had to throw herself in the garbage.

To show gratitude for her housemates, she bought the other kind of optimized soy protein she could find online, a brand called Soy Team 6 that sent her a variety pack: plain, cinnamon, and habanero. Unlike the bottle of wine she'd brought for Thanksgiving, Brittany greeted this present with a squeal and a hug.

"I always thought putting flavor in with my soy would make it taste too busy, but this cinnamon stuff isn't bad," she said, perched at the kitchen table during one of her and Aretha's more frequent hangouts. They'd started doing martial arts in the backyard together, sweating and shifting their way through up to three hours of backyard aerobics. Aretha's former axe-throwing self loved the exercise of it, even if she didn't understand most of the moves. But the weirdest part of all this had to be Brittany's sudden openness. They started with small talk about how to land various stretching positions and hits. They segued into the upsides of not having a family (or in Brittany's case, never talking to hers): 100 percent fewer awkward holiday din-ners spent discussing some weird internet theory some gullible rel-ative had gotten into, zero judgment on whoever you might bring home, absolutely no one to tell unemployed you to look up the ad-dress of the company you wanted to work for and just show up there. Brittany told her to come to the last hour of the workout so they could have lunch afterwards, and Aretha, who'd realized after all the walk-ing and the axe-throwing that she liked working out, declared herself game for spending an hour after their workouts in the kitchen, eating and talking about whatever came to mind.

Brittany would perch herself at the head of their round kitchen table, which was a good visual trick, since a round table has no head, but something in her bearing and posture created one. In another life maybe she'd have been a ballet dancer, or a gymnast, or someone who made money off her walk, Aretha thought whenever Brittany sat down, all delicate limbs and grace, in front of the Soy Team 6 bar that clashed with her by sitting in a rough chunk. Brittany still made Aretha nervous, no matter how much they hung out, so it took her a few days to start asking questions. By then Aretha had added a sliced banana to her soy diet, which made her feel downright decadent compared with Brittany's plain camo-colored brick.

"So do you have any other friends?" Aretha asked Brittany.

"Sometimes I meet people at other preparedness events and we get to talking."

"But they never come over."

"They're too busy getting prepared."

"For what?"

"Hailstorms. Rainstorms. Hurricanes. Avalanches. A total, permanent loss of power. Internet outages. Poisoned water. Poisoned food. Food shortages. Land sinking under water forever. Earthquakes. Tornadoes. Martial law. Pandemics. You know, the stuff all of us worry about every day."

They're getting prepared for whatever James is going to do on that roof, Aretha didn't say. Right that second, James sat above them in his usual lookout spot, next to the tent, armed and ready for whatever enemies the blank roofs of their neighborhood could throw at him. James and Aaron had talked about something, even if Aaron never told Aretha what, and her cup trick didn't work on James's bedroom wall. But James had stopped wearing the balaclava, and smelled about half as drunk as usual. If he had to be up on the roof, at least he was doing it more clear-eyed. And maybe he didn't plan to do anything dangerous up there. After their mistake she'd developed a mild affection for him, like they'd scaled a mountain together, broken all four of their ankles, and had given up on mountains ever since. They'd shared an experience. But she couldn't afford to be less suspicious of him. Even if he never ended up doing anything up there, he could still tell on her for what they'd done.

"Yeah, I worry about stuff," Aretha said.

"We all do," Brittany said. "Do you have a go-bag?"

"I do."

For Aretha's birthday, Aaron had bought her a copy of *The Thinking Woman's Guide to Self-Defense*, a book with a cover that featured a can of mace tied up in a big pink bow.

"What?" she'd said on unwrapping it. "I thought you didn't really believe in this stuff."

"I don't really," he said, "but I wouldn't want anythin' to happen to you while you're walkin' home alone."

"You must have forgotten that we don't live in Aloneland."

"People go to bed here, too, leavin' the sidewalks empty."

She'd rolled her eyes and swore she'd never read it, dooming the book to the dust in the corner of her closet, but every once in a while, when she couldn't sleep, she fished it out and read it while hiding under their sheets with her phone flashlight. Chapter 2: Men. Chapter 3: Other Men. Chapter 5: Dark Streets, Possibly Filled with Men. The book had made it up from the closet floor to the top of her and Aaron's shared dresser, and now spent most of its days resting on her go-bag, which she kept under her side of the bed.

"So what's in your go-bag?" Brittany said.

"Mace, a knife, a water purifier, some Life Preservers, a fire-starting kit, a couple changes of clothes."

"Not bad," Brittany said.

Aretha usually focused on all the stuff she didn't put in there: enough money to survive life on top of her monthly loan payments, a stable job that wouldn't fuck her over for missing a day thanks to an allergy attack. But for what she could control, her go-bag wasn't too bad. She still couldn't see herself using most of the stuff in it. But she figured no one who packed one of these could. If a hurricane came, she could wait it out for a week or two on higher ground. If some poison worked its way into the water supply, she could probably filter it out. And if fruit magically fell down at her feet, she could peel it with the knife.

"I didn't think you believed in our stuff," Brittany said.

"I don't think there's anything wrong with having a plan."

She said it, and then she realized it was true. Brittany smiled with approval. Aretha got up from the table, suffered through another week of not finding another lawyer job, and reported to the backyard to swing her arms and feet in tandem with Brittany again.

"Up," Brittany yelled, lifting her tracksuited arms. Aretha raised her arms above her head and swung them in circles in what Brittany claimed was a capoeira move, one of many the enslaved Brazilians used to make it look like they were dancing instead of plotting their escape. "Down," Brittany yelled, and they shifted into downward-facing dog right there on the grass. "To build the leg strength we might need to flee," Brittany had told Aretha when she asked. "To the side," Brittany yelled, and she and Aretha swept their arms to their left and punched with their right fists, a move Brittany could not explain.

They shifted their weight into planks and squats. They stood on one leg. Their arms defended the rest of their bodies from humid summer air. Aretha failed to keep herself from becoming distracted by the beauty of the backyard. If you ignored the bunker entrance in the corner, which she always did, the yard was an unbroken paradise of green. The bunker served as Aretha's last stand against a full embrace of their lifestyle, even if, as she hung out with them every day, she felt her resistance to their underground lair weakening. Brittany and James were her friends, and she supported her friends. Back in the day Nia fed her need to go out until two in the morning to temporarily become something greater in the middle of the dance floor than an overworked lawyer with dead parents. And now the part of her that had given up on texting Aaron during his frequent international coffee bean runs because of their frequency gravitated towards Brittany, who understood her need for backyard exercise, and James, who understood their mutual attraction to guns.

"Aretha," Brittany said. "We're moving on."

They settled into what Brittany called the thunderbolt pose. Legs spread, knees bent. "So you can spend a long time being ready if you need to," Brittany told her the previous week, when she'd asked about it. Aretha centered her weight over her knees and seriously pondered readiness. She was ready for the phone call that would shake her out of her current employment stasis. A job offer that would surely be coated in gold and accompanied by a full brass band, marching alongside her to celebrate her triumph. Brittany was so fucking lucky. She had a job! She worked alone on the business books, so she didn't have to try to beat out other people, and she did most of her job from her bedroom, so she didn't have to see anyone else.

Actually, fuck that, Aretha decided as they conducted a series of sweeping kicks. No one to beat means you don't exist. I am here, defeating the air in this backyard with every kick, and very ready to win at something professional other than sending panicked emails to my recruiter that I spend an hour editing to make sure they don't sound too panicked. I will beat out as many people as I need to in order to be a lawyer again. Never mind that I'm six years out of law school and people are asking for my grades and getting freaked out by the single B in there. I can fucking do this. Now if only her recruiter would email her back. It was June, so obviously her recruiter was just taking a lot of time off before Flag Day.

Brittany called out more positions. Aretha moved her hands, her head, her face. She battled the backyard air, and the air fought back. Her legs ached. Her arms, too. Brittany said they were done. She went inside and upstairs to her room. Aretha lay on her back in the grass. The sky mocked her by looking clear, cloudless, untroubled. The plants laughed at her for not having a purpose, since she would be jobless in three weeks and they'd still be there, growing up to the sky. What was Aretha destined to do? All the lawyers she knew who knew lawyers who worked at places that weren't hiring right now but just wanted to talk set her up with people who had no idea what she was up against. They'd say stuff like "Well, back in my day it was easy to find jobs," as if the only reason she hadn't solved her job problem yet was because she hadn't bothered to transport herself back to 1981.

The grapevine of the people from law school who she still talked to once in a while told her that the grapevine itself was in bad shape, since people got fired and couldn't find jobs again and disappeared. The deal she'd made with law school was that getting a law degree would allow her to permanently escape the world in which she'd grown up. No more memories tainted by trips to Aldi, where they'd buy canned ravioli in bulk and send it with her to school for lunch in warm thermoses, since it was cheaper than school lunch, even if the smell freaked out all her classmates enough that no one ever sat with her in the cafeteria. No more waking up and remembering how the benefits office people used to yell at her mom for not filling out the forms right. She could remember her parents as fountains of pure love, untainted by money. She'd been a little too proud of rising from the primordial shit, so life threatened to slingshot her back.

Instead of going back to her bedroom on the way up from training, Aretha ascended one more level to the roof, where she found James sitting right outside his black tent. She'd wanted to watch him watch over whatever the fuck he monitored up on the roof, and he didn't disappoint. Instead of the ever-present bottle of peach liquor that she thought of as his third arm, he sat next to a hot mug of coffee, weaponless. He handed her the mug, and she took a four p.m. sip, an act she would never have committed in January but that felt right now, since she no longer worried about how tired she'd appear at work. When she sat down on his left, he grabbed a gun out of the tent and put it down next to his right leg.

They looked over the Brooklyn roofs that surrounded them, which held nothing, since it was an hour when people took to the streets, like most hours other than the middle of the night. The view had some drying laundry and a selection of lit windows and fire escapes hanging off the backs of buildings. Below them lay traffic, up to its midmorning weekend sound, no honking, not much stopping, just the constant sound of cars going from one place to another that framed their lives and let them sleep free from the threat of total quiet.

Suddenly, Aretha spotted a guy on his roof looking over at them. James looked at him and then back to her.

"That motherfucker really likes looking at us," he said.

She got up to leave. Despite her lingering, half-disgusted affection for James, she didn't want to watch him do whatever the fuck he might do next.

"Downstairs," he said. "You know when."

She took the kind of breath she'd have taken if someone told her it was all the air she'd get to survive underwater for a minute.

"It didn't happen," he said. "Or at least I won't tell anyone."

"Phew," she said.

She spotted another wall crack on her way back down to her bedroom and grabbed the spackle and knife that she kept under her side of the bed to patch it up.

"We get the house inspected every year," Aaron said a month ago, when she'd decided to finally confront him about her fear the whole house would just cave in on them. She'd catalogued the cracks in the floor, the ceilings, the walls.

"These are just old houses," he'd said. "Prewar. Virtually indestructible."

"You guys are professionally worried about everything. The state of the house doesn't bug you?" she said.

"One word, darlin'. *Prewar.*"

Aretha pressed the last bit of spackle into a stretch of wall next to the staircase between the kitchen and the bedrooms, and sniffed it in all its wet chemical glory. She could keep the house up all by her damn self if she had to. A loud car drove by outside, and she felt a wobble that went from real to existential in a swift-enough second that she questioned whether she'd really felt it at all.

There are no wobbles, she told herself the next morning when she woke up with a start, next to a snoring Aaron, convinced she'd felt another one. If a real wobble had shaken the house, Aaron would have woken up. He woke up for real stuff. Super-loud car honks. Ambulances with their sirens on that take too long to drive down the block. What might or might not have been wobble number three came right when she sat down to breakfast in the kitchen, a trembling her bran flakes reacted to by banging against the side of their bowl. A wobble that reminded her that Brittany and James, both slavishly dedicated to their morning schedules, even if hers was a constellation of business calls and his was the daily ascent to his roof spot, were late to breakfast. But this wobble kept going, as a low-level vibration that sounded more and more familiar the more Aretha listened to it. She crept over to the staircase and climbed up.

From inside any of the bedrooms it was impossible to hear what might be happening in any of the other ones. But from the hallway, Aretha heard the unmistakable thumps of sex, backed up by a squeaky bedframe that was also getting into it.

"Oh my god," she whispered.

She crept back to the bedroom, leaving the door just cracked, to rustle Aaron awake. When he woke up, she pointed to the door.

"What?" he said.

She shushed him. Any second now, Brittany would stomp out of the bedroom and give them a look. She grabbed Aaron's arm. He got it.

"This is somethin'," he said.

"I know."

"I didn't think either one of 'em believed in sex."

Aretha gripped his arm tighter, half from amusement at what he'd said, half to stave off the struck-by-lightning feeling that had set in when he said it. God, she'd fucked up. But if James didn't plan on saying anything, why should she? She'd never tell Aaron about her gun runs, and she sure as hell wouldn't tell him about that. The only problem was that on Monday at noon he would get on a plane to Brazil, and later that day she'd end up in the backyard with Brittany or on the roof with James and she'd feel the relief of not having anything to not tell either of them. She looked over at Aaron, searching for even a flicker of the frustration she felt in his eyes. He had to feel a tiny bit tortured about not telling her why he officially didn't know anything about the guns. But he gave off the same air of calm that he always did. And she hated him for it.

"They're going to change. They're going to be a different kind of weird," Aretha said.

She popped up to shut the door.

"Maybe it would be better if they didn't know we knew," she said.

"It's not that big of a house," Aaron said.

"Yeah, but they might think we're sleeping."

"They'll tell us eventually."

"At one of our big four-way heart-to-hearts at the dinner table?"

"You've been hangin' out with Brittany, so you tell me," Aaron said. "I didn't think she was into hangin' out with people."

"You watch us?"

"Well, sometimes you're right at the kitchen table, talkin' like you've known each other for half your lives. And I sometimes wake up and see that you're gone, and look in the backyard, and see you both out there, sweatin'."

"I don't think she sweats."

"You do."

He watched her swing her arms around in confusion on Saturday mornings instead of doing something more normal with them, like having brunch. Brunch seemed like a faraway dream, a paradise from an era preserved in amber, when she thought spending sixteen dollars on eggs would enrich her life. It did enrich her life. Not the bill for that food in all its money-sucking prime, but the chance to sit across the table from Nia, a person she'd actually known for almost half her life, and figure out what had been up in her world for a week or two. Sometimes, late at night, when Aretha was busy not going to sleep, she'd pick up her phone from the floor at the side of the bed, think about texting Nia, and decide not to. Nia wanted her to leave the house before she got back in touch, but she was having trouble letting go of a lifestyle that gave her a boyfriend and two friends instead of one.

"I've been spackling walls again," Aretha said.

"Don't worry about the walls," Aaron said.

"But I do! They have cracks!"

"They don't, hun. Anyways, you want to do somethin' other than listen to 'em fuck today?"

"Oh god, yeah."

"Let's go walk the bridge."

Aretha's head raced through the possibilities of having vaguely antisocial roommates who fucked. Would the two of them, if they kept putting themselves together, fuck themselves into a whole human being instead of two sets of damaged parts? Fucking: a self-improvement program for people who didn't want to leave their bedrooms. She should have known something was up when they'd both started talking to her in places other than the inside of her head.

But she was thrilled to walk with Aaron. Forgetting came easier on walks. Once a week she walked an extra twenty blocks down from the office instead of immediately taking the train home, thinking about nothing, instead of the failure to get a job that always shot into her head whenever she stopped. And Tonya came through by texting her, so every couple of weeks she went by the garden to forget by helping out.

"We'll start you out on something easy," Tonya had said when Aretha mentioned that the only experience she'd ever had with plants was smoking weed in college.

So Aretha wandered the garden in sneakers, with a watering can in her hand and a scarf tied around her head, and diligently tried to remember how much water each plant got, while Tonya tended to things like fertilizer and restaking the tomatoes, since they'd grown up their vine. Tonya was a lawyer too, but she hated talking about it, so they had awkward conversations about plants, since Aretha was just learning to talk about them. She could handle discussing water and some weeds and what they'd look like at the end of their growing season, and then she'd wave goodbye and walk another four or five miles until she felt sufficiently saturated in the blankness she associated with a decent amount of exercise to go home.

Sometimes a couple of other Black female volunteers would show up. They'd tell Aretha about the invention of their community garden, back in the '70s, when enough people avoided the neighborhood to leave it with vacant lots that could be turned into gardens, and how they'd been feeding the community as best they could for more than forty years. Every so often, on a gun run, she'd blink and picture herself in the garden, surrounded by other Black women in bandannas tending to the dirt. A practically anonymous part of the whole, unlike the flashiness inherent in entering someone's house while heavily armed. Being more than what she did for money, like Tonya had said when Aretha asked her why she got into gardening in the first place.

She and Aaron walked down Flatbush into the Black heart of Downtown Brooklyn before it rose in front of them as a shiny new series of sets of mostly glass condos for the rich white crowds that had descended into Brooklyn mostly, it seemed, to pay fifteen bucks for dessert. They passed artisanal cookie shops and artisanal pudding shops and hand-made, small-batch ice cream and a store that bragged about selling luxury marshmallows, all served in a near silence she felt allergic to, as opposed to the comforting rumble of bars.

But at least this was the weekend, she concluded right when they stepped onto the bridge, with its tourist crowds dutifully wearing sweatshirts with schools on them because nothing in life could ever stop them from cheering loudly for the college football teams slapped across their chests, even if they'd left those teams thousands of miles behind. Hooray for the two days per week she didn't have to enter an office and pretend she still had a purpose there. She was amazed that James didn't do constant weekend gun runs, because wasn't that when people were home? But he preferred night, he'd said to her back when they were talking, when a black bag could hide under a black sky, and she'd grown to love it too, those hours that matched her skin and let her hide from the obligations of day.

She looked over at Aaron, who waved to the cops sitting on the bridge as if it were some imagined '50s neighborly paradise. What kind of Black guy waved hello to cops? He'd given her that whole speech about not being able to call them, so what was the point of saying hello? When she saw cops she did what she imagined most Black people did: shifted her eyes in such a way that it would become instantly clear to the cops that she'd never walked by them. That she didn't even exist. He moved from waving hi to cops to happily agreeing to take pictures for tourists who hadn't had the sense to bring selfie sticks with them on their way over, photographing what looked like ham-handed smiles to her because no one could possibly be that happy without chemical assistance. She looked at the vape in his shirt pocket for the eighty thousandth time. It was not yet time for chemical assistance, even though a good hit of chemicals would really block out the waving-to-cops-and-bothering-to-talk-to-tourists part of this walk.

Aretha waited out the day by erasing her mind whenever it latched on to her upcoming unemployment, until night dropped down over them in streaks of orange and darker blue. She and Aaron had made it to the Eighties in Manhattan, after a long walk up the west side on the water, past the empty docks and the fat white cruise ships all the way to Riverside Park, leaving them mostly surrounded by trees. She felt calm with her hand glued to Aaron's. But across the Hudson, a wooded strip of New Jersey winked at Aretha, reminding her of the possibility of escape.

·

**SUNDAY WAS THE QUIETEST DAY OF THE WEEK. THE DAY WHEN** the streets in their neighborhood didn't really get going until noon, when families left their apartments to walk Vanderbilt Avenue in their finest athleisure. Black stretch pants, short-sleeved tops meant to wick away more sweat than they accumulated, $150 running shoes that could handle so much more pounding than a gentle stroll. The last set of yesterday's coffee beans had roasted overnight, leaving the Vanderbilt house almost silent, since all its residents had slept in. They slept in pairs, with Aretha's legs thrown over Aaron's like a sweater over shoulders, and Brittany's head tucked into James's rib cage on top of her bed.

The only noise in the house belonged to the termites, who had a mission.

They never slept.

They'd lived quite happily in the house's walls for weeks, feasting on them.

A 24/7 all-you-can-eat buffet of wood.

They'd started out in the relatively cool, damp basement, where they'd eaten day and night, from the basement up to the kitchen, to the kitchen and a stretch of wall below James's empty room, on the backyard side of the house. They'd sustained themselves for a month on the wooden beams, which tasted rich and moist, thanks to the neighborhood's summer humidity. The termites munched behind walls through air that mimicked a steam room. Aretha, who'd been so focused on cracks, had never thought to tap the cracked walls. If she had tapped her knuckles on the wall she'd just spackled between the kitchen and the staircase that led to the bedrooms, the wall would have thumped back hollowly with the echo of the last second of a guitar note. If she'd put her ear up to it, she'd have heard the tap-tap-tap of their munching, loud and full of clicks like they were individually writing manifestos on typewriters. If she had X-ray vision strong enough to pass through the walls she'd have seen the result of all the termites' handiwork. All those boards with holes in them like cavities in teeth.

When would the termites finish? They didn't know. The wooden boards that held up the house could sense the sickness that had descended upon them. The flu that ate away at their bones, leaving them untouched on the outside and ready to buckle within. But wood doesn't tell the people who live on the other side of it that a bunch of termites turned it into their Cheesecake Factory. As the people who lived in the house got up and had sex and ate on that sleepy Sunday afternoon, the frame of their house remained helpless against the termites that chomped down noisily on it, a noise loud enough to hear had they not been preoccupied with listening to the sounds inside their own heads.

The four of them made it down to the lunch table, where Brittany told them excitedly about the new tracksuit she'd bought in what she called "visible camouflage," a hunter-orange catastrophe that reminded Aretha of a childhood of watching deer hunters drive back and forth on Wisconsin highways every November. Brittany moved on to the solid-colored hunters' orange tracksuits that Aretha approved of a little more, since they sort of looked like clubwear.

"So I can actively scare predators by looking tough," she said over the first real food Aretha had ever seen her eat, even if it was just two pieces of whole-wheat toast with butter, "because we should probably save the soy. Right, James?" she said to the slightly less fastidiously silent presence in their house, who dug into real food too, a bowl of stir-fried tofu and scallions.

"Mmmm. Protein," he said.

"Right," Aretha said, wondering if sex had brought on their hunger in the way she remembered getting hungry at the beginning of all the rounds of sex she'd had with new people, a craving she'd smothered with spaghetti in college and a second bowl of breakfast bran flakes when she started hooking up with Aaron, who sat to her right, not quite inspiring bouts of love-related binge eating anymore. Since his trip to Brazil had fallen through, he gushed over being home, a place he'd stay for almost three full weeks for the first time that year. "No trips planned until after the fourth, because the vacations have started," he said, meaning his suppliers and coffee shop owners, all of whom spread their vacations out like a fan from Memorial Day to Labor Day, and again from Thanksgiving to New Year's. Three full weeks! Aretha said to herself, since she'd gone over her months in the house and figured out that they'd never quite swung three full weeks hanging out together without him getting on a plane to buy coffee or her to do depositions.

He and Aretha were even going to go on vacation for part of those three weeks. It would be their first vacation together and her first vacation, period. Four days in Maine, on the coast, where they'd go to the beach and eat lobster. She would drink, pretend she was capable of relaxing, and figure out if ninety-six straight hours with him would fix the part of her that felt closer to Brittany's workouts and the house itself these days than him. She'd gotten used to a world that didn't have that much of him in it, because she'd claimed the backyard to kick and punch, the living room to lounge in, and the roasting room to inhale the smell of coffee for a couple of hours straight. She'd even made an uneasy peace with the roof, which felt like her real vacation, the time she spent away from the main sections of the house, up near the tent with James, silently drinking coffee and looking deeper into Brooklyn. Aaron popped in like an appetizer on the pre-lawyer days when she couldn't afford the meal.

She didn't quite see the point of spending vacation money, because she, in the countdown to unemployment, thought every act that required spending money seemed unnecessary. But Aaron had offered to pay for everything, so she'd reluctantly agreed to take a break from anguished job hunting and titillating gun runs to lie out in a lawn chair or whatever the hell else people sat out on when they hit the beach and not think about her pending unemployment. Aretha pictured Aaron, her already always relaxed man, hitting a nexus of relaxation on the beach in Maine, which seemed like the kind of place where all she would notice was the eyes on their Blackness. Or at least that's why she'd officially think people might stare at them. Lately, she'd gotten obsessed with the idea that people could look at them walking in the street and see the inside of their house to judge its coffee and soy and guns.

It was three p.m., and all of them, for the first time since they'd lived together, lingered at the kitchen table after lunch. The kitchen smelled like the butter from Brittany's toast and the eggs Aaron had fried up for himself in olive oil and salt. Summer afternoon sunlight swept across the room as an extension of Aaron's default mood, gently simmering everything in its path and turning the tip of Brittany's chemically straightened ponytail from dark brown to dark red. The sun bleached James's dingy white T-shirt three shades cleaner and shot Aretha through with an energy she hadn't felt since the shock of her first gun run, just from sitting at a kitchen table with three people she liked.

But the bulk of the energy in the house belonged to the termites. They chewed and swallowed and chewed again. When a second colony of termites showed up, the soldier termites and the worker termites fought. The winners killed the losers. Slit them up from end to end just a few feet from where a handful of people ate and slept and fucked and insisted they were prepared for disasters of unimaginable size and scope far beyond what, if anyone had asked, they'd have said termites could do to them.

•

THE NEXT SATURDAY DAWNED, SUMMER COOL, WITH A LAYER OF early-morning sweat draped over the backyard. Aretha left the bed to peek out her window and saw Brittany out back, as usual, tracksuited and well into her exercise set, a sight that called Aretha to action. She walked across the room with purpose, over to her dresser, where she pulled out the only pair of shorts that wouldn't ride up her thighs and cursed the heat for smoking her out of workout pants. Her thick thighs should have turned her into a warrior. A shot put queen or a high jumper or someone who was physically tough in a way that thick thighs said she should be. Instead, she'd gotten the body of a lawyer, physically ready for battles of the mind.

Brittany, who'd somehow dodged the thick-Black-girl-thighs gene, remained physically up for war, even though doing battle with her would be like fighting a very tall blade of grass that liked to round-house kick. Aretha joined Brittany in the backyard right in time for the roundhouse kicks, which Aretha didn't understand, up, around, out, and down, like their legs had turned to yo-yos that wouldn't give up on attempting tricks.

"If we did these in real life," Aretha said, "wouldn't the other person just grab our legs?"

"You're not doing them fast enough," Brittany said.

Aretha whipped her legs in tighter circles, getting up to her max level of roundhouse kick competence, which was about half as fast as Brittany's.

"There you go," Brittany said, in a tone that sounded less patronizing than usual.

More kicks, a few five-finger punches, a set of downward dogs that lasted so long Aretha felt like her thighs would go vibrating clean off her body with pain. Some planking. "You should want good abs as much as you want a glass of water first thing in the morning," Brittany said. Thunderbolt pose, "which helps give you the flexibility to spring up, like a thunderbolt, because there are times in your life when you're going to need that thunderbolt level of energy."

"Riiiiiight," Aretha said under her breath. But she put her whole self into thunderbolting anyway. Fists up, knees shoulder-width apart and bent until she felt what Brittany might have been talking about. A tingle that ran from her feet up to her waist and told her she could suddenly spring forward, even if she didn't need to.

Her load at the office had descended into busywork. In the gaps between meaningless phone calls and boring filings, she had all the time in the world to ponder the thing she she could still control: her physical strength. At work, fifteen neighborhoods away from Brittany, she remembered and executed Brittany's rules, remembering to close her office door to stretch her feet out against the wall, with one heel dug into the carpet while its toes arced away from the wall and its knee aimed forward until she felt a pull in her lower leg, to get her calf ready for whatever might come slicing through the dry office air. If her door had to be open, she could still draw the letters of the alphabet underneath her desk, pointing one foot in the air at a time, and sit with both sets of toes on the ground, pushing just her heels up. As a lawyer she'd grown weaker, but as a body stronger, delighted to find new muscles in her arms and legs. She had a couple more interviews this week, and felt sure her stronger body would ace them as much as her head would. The next interviewer would get done with the experience part of asking her questions, look at her, understand, and calmly ask her to arm-wrestle to seal the deal.

To complement the survivalist part of her training, she'd signed up for a triathlon. On bright summer mornings, she ran an hour and dutifully ended up at the local Y to do laps in the pool at a pace that grew less recreational with every turn, and on days when she didn't swim she ended her runs with a recumbent bike ride in the Y's gym, where she pushed the resistance high enough to feel like she was cycling through mud. In applying for jobs she'd tinkered with her résumé often enough to feel physically ill about its existence and to imagine it when it wasn't physically there, opened up on her home laptop, making her feel shitty with its lack of world-conquering accomplishments.

But in her better moments, instead of mentally rewriting the job entries to read "reinvented the way mid-level associates instruct junior associates" or "ruled a small empire through spreadsheets," she'd picture redoing the hobbies section instead to read "becoming a more physically optimal person," and watching interviewer after interviewer express straight-up glee at their mental picture of her triathlon training, able to surmise just from the way she sat in a chair that she'd achieved the holy grail of seeming tougher than other lawyers. In the backyard, ten kicks later, she looked up at the house, imagining its unknown-to-her termite-infested self as an equally tough force, upright since 1907, according to the internet. Due to remain perched on its wooden legs for another hundred years.

On the next Saturday she and Brittany ran through another forty-five minutes of workout. Punches and stretches and squats that made Aretha feel as tough as the neighborhood garden's tomato plants. Staked to herself, ready to rise. But Brittany called it quits for the day.

"I thought we'd go another hour, at least," Aretha said.

"Didn't think another hour was your style."

"I'm changing. I'm landing more of the moves. I feel better."

"Now all you have to do is eat something other than soy."

"Never," Aretha said.

She followed Brittany inside, past two stories of hidden, ravenous termites, past the roasting room, where she waved to Aaron, who sat reading a book about music instead of coffee, honoring his break in a way she hadn't thought he would, as a workaholic who seemed more dedicated to the workaholic lifestyle than even the lawyers she knew. She and Brittany went up to the bedrooms, where Brittany shut her door, and Aretha shut hers, too. She'd just grabbed fresh clothes and wrapped a towel around herself and made it into the hallway, en route to her and Aaron's bathroom, when she heard a clatter and a set of clangs behind Brittany's door.

She knocked on the door to see if Brittany needed help, and when she didn't answer, gently pushed it open, where Brittany struggled with a stack of fallen guns at least ten times as big as the stack Aretha remembered from the time she searched the house. Aretha stood stuck in the doorway, with her jaw slack and her feet twice as rooted to the ground as she'd felt they were in the backyard until her towel complicated things by falling off, forcing her to reach down and grab it in shame before she could turn her attention to the guns, all over the floor in their abundance. Brittany looked up at her from a crouch, but instead of the anger Aretha had expected from a woman who seemed to run on it, or the embarrassment that would seem natural if your gun stash hit the floor, Brittany had a calm in her face that looked completely alien.

"Do you need help?" Aretha said, surprising herself, a person who'd always figured she'd be out the door running if life ever brought that many guns to her feet. There were oodles of guns she didn't remember seeing the first time, from rifles to handguns to the kind of assault rifles she associated with war documentaries, slung over a soldier's fatigues while he ran into the desert. Apparently the desert was their house.

"Sure," Brittany said, "you can help me pick these up."

They knelt in front of the pile, and at Brittany's instruction, Aretha gently piled the guns on top of one another back inside the closet, on its floor. She took deep breaths until she felt kind of normal again. She'd thought she was over her gun fear phase. She understood why they kept them in the house, and since they'd been robbed at gunpoint, why guns were the particular way they'd chosen to deal with an unknown future that might involve other break-ins. She and James regularly carried a duffel bag's worth of guns on their runs: ten or fifteen all stacked up on the floor of the car's backseat. But watching Brittany struggle with at least fifty assault rifles sent the old ice up Aretha's arms. Did Brittany have a war on her calendar? An attack that she had to carry out right there on Vanderbilt? Aretha was a thinker, happy to google and analyze her way out of so many problems. But the sheer number of guns on Brittany's floor turned her into the kind of animal more into flight than fight.

"What are all these for?" she said for the thousandth time, hoping for more than "just in case."

"You really want me to tell you?" Brittany said, with her face torqued into an amusement Aretha had never seen before.

"I do."

"OK. Look. So you know we're all a little worried about something big going wrong out there, right?" she said, hooking a thumb towards her bedroom window.

"Yeah, you've gone over that."

"Well, have you ever thought about the absolute worst-case scenario?"

"Which is what?"

"We're all sitting around after something terrible has happened, thinking about eating each other, and everyone else is white."

"Yeah, but most people are white in this country."

"I've read W. E. B. Du Bois. I've read Marcus Garvey."

"You're going back to Africa by living in a house in Brooklyn?"

"In Africa we were prepared."

"Prepared enough to be taken as slaves?"

"Prepared enough that many of us fought it."

"Yeah, that's why you and I live here."

"We're part of a long tradition. A Black tradition. Four hundred plus years of packing up in the middle of the night and hopping a train or walking miles under cover of darkness to get somewhere safer. Moving back to the south after the economy crashed in '08. The Great Migration north eighty years before that. You think Harriet Tubman didn't have a go-bag?"

"Do you think she put fifty guns in it?"

Why had she ever thought they might be friends? Brittany didn't have friends. She had soy, and tracksuits, and fucked-up theories about Harriet Tubman.

"Look. I know you think I'm afraid of a bunch of stuff that doesn't make sense. But you're wrong. I'm afraid of something that it makes an absolute ton of sense to be afraid of. Other people," Brittany said.

"Right," Aretha said.

"After something awful happens, the normal white people aren't going to be around anymore, probably, and we'll be left with a bunch of white people with guns. So we better have guns, right?" Brittany said. "A lot of guns. I mean, there's already a bunch of white people with guns, and they like to walk into our churches and kill us for kicks. When the shit goes down, I imagine they're going to shoot up a few more malls, if you know what I mean."

"You're with a white guy who owns guns," Aretha said.

"I wouldn't say I'm with him, exactly. Sometimes I have free time and get bored."

"You're not worried that he's selling them to all his white friends?"

"How many drunk masterminds have you met?"

"OK," Aretha said.

So Brittany knew that James sold dozens of guns a month, and she didn't care. Just like Aaron. Aretha felt a tongue-tied-ness that was alien and horrific to have to suffer through, like what she imagined happened to people during heart attacks. How the fuck could they not care?

"You're not worried that if the shit goes down, he's going to want to find the other armed white guys, join their crew, and tell them about you?" she said, working another angle.

"I think if the shit goes down he'll drink himself to death."

Brittany was talking about James's nihilist self, the guy Aretha had done gun runs with, who seemed only halfheartedly dedicated to living through any particular minute. Aretha stood still for a moment, picturing the newest, post-fucking-Brittany version of James. Skinnier and sober, or at least less drunk. Sometimes he'd sweep into the house with an energy she'd never seen, wearing workout shorts and an only slightly dingy white T-shirt, like he'd discovered thimble-sized amounts of bleach. He'd been replacing the booze in his coffee mugs with actual coffee and sometimes herbal tea. At meals, he'd look at everyone with a softened-up expression that almost resembled a smile. She'd caught him typing in his bedroom, next to a lit candle, with some of his metal music playing softly. He seemed nothing like the drunken mute she'd slept with. If she only saw his new self, she could convince herself that they'd never done it.

The termites launched a new offensive on the inside of the downstairs kitchen walls. James shifted above them in his lookout position on the roof. He wasn't standing down here in front of the largest stash of guns she'd ever seen. Why was Brittany talking about him instead of herself? What was she willing to do with her stash of guns?

"I don't think he'd kill himself anymore," Aretha said.

"Well," Brittany said. "Let's just say I'm not that worried about him, either way."

"OK," Aretha said, "let me shower."

She shut the door behind her and went to the bathroom down the hall, where she turned on the shower and sat on the toilet seat with her chin in her hands before she remembered that there was no problem whatsoever. She'd nail the job interviews, find a new apartment, and tell Aaron the truth: that the thrill of living with an arsenal of guns had worn off now that they'd multiplied like cockroaches. Them or me, she'd say, and then he'd choose her and they could live in a quiet and clean and safe apartment, free from armed people and their stupid, dangerous vendettas against other people who hadn't done shit.

She could picture this apartment, big and full of light, thanks to Aaron's coffee money and the absolutely fabulous job she was going to land by the end of the week. Sure, their new place probably wouldn't have the expansive old-school beauty of the Vanderbilt house, but maybe they could live on top of something cool in true New York style. A restaurant with addictive jerk chicken or a boutique where she'd buy all her clothes or a club where she could get back into dancing or a bar that made the absolute right limeade and would accept their packages when they weren't home. And then she remembered that she really didn't drink limeades anymore, thanks to her newfound love of exercising too much to avoid getting hangovers when she drank them. And Aaron had talked to James, sure, but that didn't mean he'd move out for her. And if she moved out, she'd see him only between bean-sourcing trips and roasting nights, so never.

Or she could admit the truth: that somewhere between her cheating, his endless trips, and the infinite growth of the household's arsenal, something had taken the shine off the car. If she closed her eyes she could feel the good parts: the chunks of spice in her nonalcoholic Christmas mulled wine, her body hooked into his while they floated along with every wave on their ferry rides. And then she'd open them and admit she didn't quite feel close enough to him to override her growing fear of living in the house with all of Brittany's guns.

A few days later, she delivered two job interview performances that she found absolutely flawless. But her phone didn't give a shit. It failed to light up with a phone call of victory or even a text of victory or an email of defeat, just Aaron's loving texts, which left her hungry, like when restaurants turned regular old entrees into plates small enough to leave her seriously entertaining spending thirty-six dollars on dinner, like some kind of psycho. She missed winning. She wasn't ready to replace ambition with love.

Where were the jobs? she howled to her empty bedroom on the day before she and Aaron were due to take their plane to Maine, for the vacation that would fix how she felt about him, if she wanted that.

Were the jobs in Maine? When she'd googled Maine, all she saw was water and the interiors of dark wooden bars that reminded her of Wisconsin. They held sullen-looking people who reminded her of the Wisconsinites she'd known who could survive eight solid months of winter only by drinking nonstop through them. But she could work in a bar. She could pour drinks like a machine. She could teach herself to fish. And most importantly she could start a new life a flight away from anyone who might remember her old, unsuccessful one. On the day after they got back from vacation she'd go in for her last day of work, which she felt as a ticking time bomb inside her chest since her heartbeat had weaponized itself. So if Maine wanted to hurl a job in her general direction, she swore she'd catch it.

The termites ate sympathetically while she imagined herself as a Mainer and Aaron hunted down a new set of the plastic three-ounce bottles he was obsessed with, as an expert traveler. Otherwise his suitcase was as immaculately packed as his go-bag, which stood at the ready, with its emergency blanket and nonperishable food supplies, waiting for another vacation entirely. She'd spent the half hour since he left staring at her work trip suitcase as if she looked at it hard enough it might pack itself between rounds of filling and unfilling it with dresses and makeup that seemed suitable one minute and awful the next. As a person who hadn't gone on vacations and looked at the one coming up as an opportunity to figure out whether she believed in them or not, she had no idea what to stuff in a suitcase for a trip that didn't involve asking questions to someone under oath. "Whatever makes ya feel good," Aaron said, when she'd asked him, the expert, with his pile of retro band T-shirts and skinny jeans neatly folded inside his bag, and a toothbrush tucked into a side pocket. "That's it?" she asked him. "I'm a minimalist," he said, which was when, staring at the unformed mess that lay on top of and over and alongside her bag, she realized she was not.

He came back with the travel bottles in tow and put his face cream in one of them, a fancier brand than hers, which promised to keep his face smooth thanks to seaweed the company had gathered from the deepest of seas and minerals from the highest of mountains, and his shampoo in the other, which promised follicular rebirth. He handed her two travel bottles, so she could decide among her small army of drugstore products while he sat on their bed, triumphantly done. She had just one request for whatever she put into her suitcase: that it make her look like she was employed the rest of the time. So she put in her best casual dresses in burnt orange and teal, and her sneaker-loafers as a concession to what she thought rich New Englanders might wear on their feet, and her thickest face cream, because if moisturizing didn't get her closer to God, exactly, it could at least shake a job down from the heavens into her lap.

Did it fucking matter what she brought to Maine? Why agonize over bringing anything for a trip that, because it wouldn't include landing a job, couldn't possibly be important? Aretha took everything out of her suitcase and threw in three dresses that looked even less formal than the first casual set, added sandals and walking loafers, her way-cheaper-than-Aaron's face cream, and a toothbrush, and triumphantly zipped it shut. If relaxing were a competition, she'd finally won it. Sort of. Aaron maintained his usual calm all the way through the traffic-hindered ride to the airport, the snail-speed security line, and the forty-five minutes it took their tiny plane to board. But Aretha, sure that putting the right suitcase together would magically stick her in the right vacation headspace, couldn't shake off the part of herself that watched all the airport workers scurry from security checkpoint to food court in their plastic name tags, just rubbing in how fucking employed they all were. On the plane the flight attendants gave off that same air of knowing what they'd be doing for the next portion of their life: serving drinks for pay, while Aretha shifted between six unsatisfying seat positions and identified fully with the wailing baby who sat four rows behind her, just as furiously unemployed as she was.

And the worst part of it all was that she couldn't tell anyone she'd been fired. Entering the law had vaulted her into a social class that didn't talk about money, religion, or unemployment. If you'd lost your job, it was your fault, no matter how much bee pollen was to blame, and behind you stood hundreds of lawyers who weren't losers for being fired like you were, ready to take the lawyer jobs they needed so much less than you. There were only two options for the fired: disappear, usually by leaving New York because you'd suddenly discovered it was the right time in your life to move back home to be closer to family, or lie and say that you'd taken a leave but now felt refreshed enough to grind yourself to death for sixty hours a week for another firm. To her left, Aaron slept peacefully, with no idea that she'd added yet another thing to the list of stuff she couldn't tell him.

Aretha cracked open one of the fashion magazines she only bought at airports, which historically had been the only places where she felt like she had time to kill, and dove deep into a fresh round of worry that she knew was unnecessary, but couldn't avoid anyway. Her face looked fine, no matter how many articles argued she should try to drastically change it with makeup. Her hair looked fine, no matter how many articles called it wrong for not growing out of her head straight. Her thick thighs and solid arms represented a classic version of Black girl chic, even though every single article she flipped to informed her that she should weigh one hundred pounds. But plane trips were for worrying, and she was sick of worrying about all the shit she couldn't tell Aaron, so she enjoyed the opportunity to worry about other shit to pass the time.

The flight wasn't long enough for everyone on it to have individual movies on the backs of the seats in front of them, so there was a communal movie, which, since she'd forgotten to ask for headphones, was just a bunch of people making increasingly anguished hand gestures on a beach. She worried about not being able to understand what was going on. She worried about asking for headphones only to, the second she understood what was going on, decide the movie was terrible. The pilot announced their initial descent, which kicked off the period she reserved for every flight to worry about their landing, which was bumpy enough to shift her immediately from worrying in anticipation of landing to worrying about the landing itself. Except the pilot taxied them down the runway to their gate, and a flight attendant opened the door, and her fever broke.

Outside, the Maine sun felt cooler. Aaron grabbed her hand and took her down to the car he'd rented, a seafoam-green sedan that looked like a lighthearted version of the sea that spun out in front of them after they drove through town to the coast. He parked the car, and they walked, hand in hand, to the water. A handful of families relaxed on towels in front of them. Wind kicked salt up Aretha's nose. She reached up and undid her afro French braids, to let her hair flap in the salt air.

"This is fucking incredible," she said.

"Yeah," he said. "You've seemed stressed lately, so I thought it might be cool if we took a couple of days to do nothin' in a place that's kinda nowhere."

She couldn't deal with how sweet he was. She started to cry.

"I got fired," she said, relieved to tell him the part of the truth that didn't involve cheating or gun selling.

She scanned his face for any unacceptable emotions, like the glee she knew everyone who'd previously been competing with her at work had all over their faces. They were lawyers, sure, but they were also brand-new spring flowers, thrust into bloom by the elimination of her as a competitive force. But he looked all right. No glee. No celebration. An uncharacteristic amount of worry creeping across his eyebrows.

"I don't know what the hell I'm going to do," she said.

"Well, first we're gonna check into the hotel. And then we're gonna chill. You'll find somethin' else."

Thank you, Aaron, ambassador of chill. Aretha closed her eyes and took in a salty breath. Maine would will her a job. Just send it to her, right on over the water to her phone. And until it did that, she wouldn't think about it. They drove back through town to their hotel, checked in to a top-floor room overlooking the beach that raised them exactly three stories in the air, and had sunset vacation sex, where Aretha's arms and legs felt lighter and her head clearer just because they didn't have to be anywhere for a while. Afterwards they stared at the ceiling, and Aaron, the vacation expert, told her stories about his other vacations.

"You've really never taken one of these before?" he said.

"Nope."

"It's just hard to believe."

"My family didn't have vacation money or relatives they felt like visiting for a couple of days. In college, I visited my parents until they died, and then during breaks I stayed tucked up in my apartments. In law school I didn't have any money to go anywhere, and after law school, at the firm, we really weren't encouraged to take vacations. So here I am, trying this out."

"We were broke too growin' up, but my mama always wanted to go somewhere a couple times of year, so we'd drive to a rodeo or a

museum or somethin' and she'd get us a couple days in a cheap mo-
tel. I mean, we-could-hear-everyone-thumpin'-on-the-bed-in-all-the-
rooms-next-to-us cheap."

Aretha laughed.

"Later," he said, "in college, I'd drive off with my friends wherever
they were goin' for a week. The casino. The college town with more
bars than ours. Some house party that sounded excitin' enough that
we'd pin three weeks' worth of hope on getting there and findin' the
king of all kegs and some mindblowin' red plastic cups."

"Well, if that's all it takes, I used to drive down to Chicago with
Nia on the weekends in college."

"There you go."

"But those trips weren't relaxing. We'd drive down there in a rush,
and move from eating to going out, to still being awake at six a.m., to
driving back going ninety miles an hour, looking for the cops over our
shoulder, and vibrating from drinking too much of those jumbo cups
of gas station coffee that taste like gasoline."

"Well, look at us, not havin' to rush back. Wanna spend the next
four days lookin' at the wall?"

Aretha slid her eyes from the ceiling to the wall in front of them,
a solid white wall with no distinguishing features. The kind of wall to
get high and stare at for two days.

"Do you have your vape?" she said.

He opened the window and handed her his vape pen. She sat up
to take a hit and held it in until her lungs threatened to burst. The
last time she'd smoked up was a bad college night where she'd drunk
a bunch and smoked a bunch and ended up convinced the trees outside her window planned to kill her. But his stuff was smoother, less
prone to sending her on flights of paranoia. She wondered why she'd
insisted on staying pure in mind for her job, convinced that one dose

of weed would leave her a drooling idiot, unable to even think about making partner, when she could have spent all of those useless hours of sucking up high. She looked at Aaron, fully expecting to think relaxed, weed-enhanced thoughts about him, but the hit of calm she felt next sent her back to the house's living room couch, where she'd taken to sitting three or four times a week after she came home early from faking it at work, its green velvet soft under her heels.

"I guess I can't take any of those jobs where you have to pee in a cup," she said on the exhale.

"Shhhh . . ." Aaron said, pointing at the wall.

She stuck her head back down on his shoulder, and for kicks, decided to see how long she could stare at the wall. A couple minutes later it wobbled twice, then settled back down into being a wall again. After a while it gently swayed on a rhythm that only made sense inside her head.

"This wall's absolutely fucking great," she said.

"I'm more of a fan of the ceilin', but I feel you," Aaron said.

"You're really OK if we just sit here?"

"It's vacation. We can do whatever we want."

"I don't want to do anything," she said, feeling the force of her tightly scheduled law firm years fall away as she said it, right on out the opened window, through the black Maine night and down to the bottom of the sea. She closed her eyes. These were going to be the best four days of her life. And then they'd get back home and she'd stop being a lawyer and tell him about fucking some uncooked pizza dough and hope everything worked out.

She woke up to find Aaron pacing the room in the dark, talking on the phone, which he never did, because no one talked on the phone anymore. What the hell happened that couldn't be handled via text?

"Oh my god," he kept saying.

What was up? Had James drunkenly tripped down some stairs? Had people, en masse, given up on coffee thanks to some weird-ass British colonialism revival and switched to tea, leaving him bankrupt?

"How much of the walls?" he said.

She looked at the wall in front of her for a second, and even though she couldn't completely make it out without light, it didn't look like it had changed. But the answer hit her like hot pan grease to the face. She pictured the walls at home, upright from 1907 until now, no thanks to all her attempts to spackle them. Oh, the house. She saw it falling in like a snowman giving in to a forty-five-degree warm front.

"Wow," he said. "Look, I can be there . . . just a minute"—he said, so he could map the drive home—"in seven hours."

He hung up, turned the room light on, and shook his fist at the window. Aretha pushed the bedsheet down to her ankles and stood up.

"We still have this room for another three nights," he said.

"So what?"

"You could stay here. Have a real vacation. Not worry about the house."

"But it's my house too."

"Yeah, but not in the same way."

"What's that supposed to mean?"

"You haven't lived there that long. And you don't run your business out of it."

"I love the house. I believe in it. I tried to patch it back up with spackle, OK?"

"Maybe the walls don't like spackle," he yelled.

He'd never yelled at her before.

"What kind of fucking walls don't like spackle?" she yelled back. "Besides, Brittany spackles the walls too."

"Yeah," he said, "but Brittany knows what she's doing."

"You really trust somebody who built a bunker off of watching YouTube videos."

"She would never let us all drown," he said.

Aretha looked at him, still stuck in those three inches of dirty hurricane water he'd left years ago. There should be a warning system for guys who seemed like guys but were really broken eggs put back together with Scotch tape. When you sat down across from them at your favorite bar for the first time, something should beep. She could redo one of those carbon monoxide alarms so it had a fragile-guy setting. Jesus fucking Christ. Who the fuck gave this much of a shit about one fucking hurricane? Aaron yelled some more stuff about spackle, but to her his mouth was just flapping in air.

A few hours ago she'd been pleasantly high in a dark hotel room with her boyfriend, and now she wondered who the hell stood across from her. A yeller, apparently. An anti-spackle activist. A guy whose personality could flip faster than a pancake if something threatened his beloved house.

"Just because you're angry doesn't mean it's not my house too," Aretha said.

But was it? She didn't have a hurricane living in her head. She didn't plan on stepping into the backyard and adding to the bunker.

"I have to drive back down there. You comin' or not?" Aaron said, like he hadn't heard her.

Aretha stuffed her dresses, face cream, and toothbrush back into her suitcase. The two of them left in a rush. The part of her that was pissed that all she'd gotten out of a plane ride was a couple of hours, tops, of staring at a hotel room wall while high had duked it out with the part of her that absolutely did not back down over anything and lost. Fuck vacations. And her stuff was in the house too, even if it was covered in dust. Her beloved athleisure pants, for the flexibility they allowed her in getting away from people she didn't like. One or two framed pictures of her parents, before their fateful goring by deer, that she kept on top of her sweaters instead of putting up on the wall, so they could be subtly dead, out of sight. The antlers popped up in her head with their usual threat. She shoved them away and pictured the house, with its newly destroyed walls. The antlers, who hated being left out, attached themselves to the wrecked version of the house in her head. This was it, the end of the four-day stretch in which she'd promised herself she'd think fond thoughts about Aaron. But all she could see was the house caving in.

"OK then," Aaron said.

He pulled his suitcase out of the corner by the window, put it on the bed, and repacked it.

"Let's just drive the rental car down there," he said.

"You want to pay the one-way fee? Those are the worst."

"One of the house walls collapsed and you wanna talk about one-way car rental fees?"

"You're going to end up paying for enough disaster costs already, don't you think?"

"We have insurance."

As a person who'd gotten paid to find the holes in insurance policies for the last six years, Aretha was not impressed. And as a recently fired person who'd gone back to counting every cent, she was probably the wrong woman to talk to about justifying surprise expenses. You could lay down an iron fist on costs if you had to. If it was up to her, they would have taken a bus and grabbed some bran flakes and milk from the grocery store to eat en route. What was another couple hours' delay if part of the house wasn't there anymore?

"Right, insurance," she said on their walk down the stairs to the hotel lobby, not wanting to bring up its pitfalls. Besides, she hadn't read his policy, and she had a sinking feeling they'd find enough stuff to argue about in the next twenty-four hours.

On the drive back Aaron spent a solid hour and a half questioning her about what kind of spackle she'd used, how she'd applied it, and what kind of sandpaper she'd used on it. Like most lawyers, she loved a ferocious round of questioning, so long as she wasn't on the other side of it, especially because in this case the normally airtight answers she knew in her head she'd always give when faced with questions were replaced with stuff like "I bought the spackle that the spackle store had on the spackle shelf and then I did some spackling."

But after the spackle bit, they turned to all the things that in retrospect she thought they probably could have argued about before, because arguments were healthy, right? She kicked him in her sleep, which she figured she did because she was an active sleeper, the kind who sometimes confused sleeping with being the starting forward in a soccer game. But really, who was he to criticize her for her sleeping style when he was practically never there anymore, she said. And he went into the longest explanation anyone had ever offered about sourcing coffee beans during coffee season. Was there a coffee season? she shot back. When was fucking coffee season? The first eight days of November in a year with a solar eclipse? She refused to let him argue her down on coffee season, whenever the hell it was, and before she knew it they'd switched to the radio, mainly that she had terrible taste in music, and really, when she thought about it, he did, too. He listened to shitty hipster-ass music to go with all his hipster-ass coffee and his hipster-ass taste in everything.

But four hours into their drive, she had an idea. They passed a sign for an exit that had its food offerings displayed on six identical-sized squares, and she told him to get off the highway and take them to square number three. He looked at her funny, but did it, and ten minutes later she bit into the first food she'd eaten in months that didn't contain a single lick of optimized soy. A sausage biscuit that she'd plastered with strawberry jelly. Not jam, because her fired ass didn't feel the slightest bit fucking upscale anymore. Jelly. She took a second bite and gave thanks to the animal that had lost its battle to not be a sausage patty that tasted like meat and grease and life itself. Aaron pulled back onto the highway and continued defending his taste in music like she gave a shit. She was busy becoming one with a slab of processed pig.

But by the time they landed on the Brooklyn-Queens Expressway, seven hours of argument had left Aretha with the energy of a limp dishtowel. Her chest ached. She looked over at Aaron, who gripped the steering wheel like having feeling in his hands was overrated. Had she gone too far when she'd called him a useless hipster? But he'd gone at least as far when, to end their spackle argument, he'd looked at her with a dead face she'd never seen on him before and called her a Property Sister. She looked away, into gray stretches of Williamsburg that matched her mood. Aaron left the highway, and the two of them moved silently through Downtown Brooklyn and Fort Greene. Aretha looked out her window and imagined everyone outside the car moving through the perfection of existing another day in the city without their house falling in. In reality they all had on the kind of commute faces that would never convince anyone they enjoyed anything, but through the heavy air inside the car Aretha couldn't picture a world in which everyone in it other than the guy who sat to her left wasn't at least four hundred times happier than she was. Aaron took a left. As usual, the trees framed two perfect rows of brownstones separated by a slim walking path dotted with benches. Except one of the brownstones had lost its perfection. Aretha felt her stomach drop to her feet.

"It looks like someone took a hammer to it," Aretha said.

Aaron said nothing. He found a parking spot right in front of the house and eased in. Aretha stepped out of the car, walked over to the sidewalk, and took a good look up at the house. A couple of years ago, during her last hard-core running phase, she'd gone two or three miles on her daily run when her left knee yelped with the same kind of pain she would have felt if someone had snuck up behind her and hit that knee with a hammer. The house looked like her knee had felt. Maybe a quarter of the roof had crumbled into itself like a shortbread cookie drowned in milk. She laughed at how sure she'd been that she could stop this crumbling with six-dollar jars of spackle.

She followed Aaron out of the car and into the backyard, where Brittany crawled out of the bunker, her usually pristine ponytail matted with dust. She and Aaron hugged, which made Aretha suspicious, since she'd never seen them hug before. So far as she knew, Brittany didn't even believe in hugs, just a well-honed brittleness that kept people a couple feet away from her on the sidewalk in a city where everyone was happy to occupy any available space.

Behind her, James crawled out of the bunker too, with equally dusty hair and a rifle slung over his right shoulder. Aretha froze. Why had he gone back to carrying a rifle?

"Could you put that thing away?" Aaron said. "We're outside, you know."

"Someone attacked our house," James said, his eyes liquid and unable to remain still.

The smell of peach liquor rose off him, deflating Aretha, who really thought he'd kicked it.

"Until we figure everything out, it's probably best to assume our house attacked our house," Brittany said, with her hands on her hips in her best laying-down-the-rules posture.

Aretha watched James fidget from hand to gun to shifting,

toe-tapping feet. Not even twelve hours ago she'd been looking at the sparkling expanse of a beach in a state far enough away from here to temporarily turn her problems invisible, and now she was back here again, behind a crumbling house, standing with three other angry people, in a city she was sick of for its insistence on throwing firings and guns and household drama at her, in open defiance of all the years she'd spent striving to be boring.

Yeah, people weren't supposed to move to New York to chase their dreams of becoming a dull rich person, but she had, dreamily picturing her lockstep future of quietly acquiring money and power, a husband who wouldn't get in the way of her earning money or accumulating power, the 2.5 kids she'd make who would secretly be awed by her money-earning and power-gathering prowess, and the house she'd buy with a private back porch that wouldn't be visible from other buildings. She'd deck the porch in gold to celebrate her accomplishments. She'd come to New York to shuck her memories of growing up working class and blend in seamlessly among the moneyed. To argue and win and have twenty-dollar drinks in bars amid boring, rich-people conversations like the ones the Wall Street guys and the Murray Hill guys and the Westchester guys had, with their big houses and their country club memberships all acquired copiously and, above all, quietly. Unacceptable topics of discussion among the rich, like money and politics, were subtly dismissed whenever she dared to bring them up in the company of people who managed to rule over everything without ever talking about any of it.

"C'mon, James," Brittany said.

His eyes flashed. He bounded obediently back down into the bunker for her. When he came back up he looked a good 25 percent less twisted, which, in Aretha's view, was still a good 20 or 30 percent too much. Had he always looked this off? Or maybe she'd found his earlier drunken depression more controllable, since he mostly kept it in his room or in cars on their way to gun sales. But now he was out here, drunk as shit, out in the open, with armed plans. She felt the deepest sense yet that by coming to live with them she'd discovered that quicksand was real.

"OK, y'all. I'll guard the house," James said.

Three heads slowly turned to face his.

"You're protectin' the business, not the house," Aaron said. "You're not a guard dog."

"The house isn't even safe to go in," Brittany said. "That's why I spent that year out here prepping a backup."

"I don't want to live in a bunker," James said. "I want to live in my bedroom and sleep in my bed, with my fucking peach liquor, just like I did yesterday."

"But c'mon," Brittany said. "We all trained ourselves in what to do if disaster struck, and disaster is here! And we have a bunker for it, because we're good and prepared people! We did it! This moment has been waiting for us to get to it for years, and we know exactly what to do!"

"I thought we were waitin' for another hurricane," Aaron said.

"You think this is over," James said to Brittany. "Now we have to defend a fallen house. It's only just begun."

"A fallen house?" Aretha said. "What do you think this is, the fucking Civil War?"

"Look," Brittany said, ignoring Aretha. "If you're not up to it, I'll defend the house."

"You're not up to it either," Aaron said. "I'll do it."

"I thought you weren't like that," Aretha said.

"I wasn't. But then our roof fell in."

"You don't have to be like that."

"I do."

Until Aaron decided to guard the house, Aretha had been prepared to watch them fight with amusement, since it wasn't her place to make decisions about the house. Except this was it. Their grandstand against the world. Aretha figured they'd been waiting for the moment the entire earth lit on fire or the mountains dropped into the sea or the government blew itself up or everyone ran out of food. But now she saw them, in the yard, rearranging themselves into the people they'd spent so much time preparing to be, in this end of the world of a house with four walls. And Aaron had promised to take up the craziest spot in this new world order. The guarding-the-house spot. How had she ever thought she would yank him away from these people? He was these people.

Aretha would have accepted so many grand theories on how they saw the world falling apart, but not this minor issue with the roof. What was survivalism if its deepest fears were the kind of thing people without money would just buck up and live with? If the ceiling of her parents' apartment had ever fallen in, she could have seen her dad, faced with all their landlords who didn't give a shit about fixing anything, stapling some new temporary ceiling up with one of those hardware store staple guns, and her mom sweeping up any parts of the ceiling that had hit the floor. And now all the rest of them had to do was call someone to fix the roof, since they could afford it. But instead they argued circles around one another about so many things other than roof fixing.

While the three of them went in rounds about who did what chores and how incompetently cleaning a bathroom mirror might have taken down the house walls, Aretha went back to the front porch with the vape pen Aaron had forgotten to take back from her, ready for chemical assistance in dealing with the fuckups she'd impulsively decided to live with until she came up with a backup plan.

It was time to leave New York for someplace cheaper, where she wouldn't have to take the bar, to start a new life at a smaller firm, someplace lawyers could survive as lawyers long enough to buy houses with green yards near good schools that she could send her imaginary children to and she could wean herself off guns and her need to fuck relationships up. All she had to do was get to this new, fabulous, imaginary destination soon, while she was still young enough to have kids. Sometimes she'd run into people she remembered from law school who'd failed to escape the city, walking around alone on the street at insanely early hours like six p.m., or in coffee shops on weekends reading books instead of bent over desks reading documents and perfecting the hunchbacks that were a sign of high achievement or mysteriously not getting fired yet or both. In their discussions an entire generation of the fired would crawl out of a sewer to walk around with the permanently shocked expressions of ghosts.

"No one's really finding anything else," her fellow ghosts would say to her. "It's like everyone simultaneously decided that no one ever needed this many lawyers in the first place."

It might take more laps around the country than she'd originally imagined, or a couple of rounds of adjusting the list of places she was willing to live, but she could do it. The other ghosts showed their hand by being unwilling to move. They were too weak to sacrifice themselves on the altar of employment in the name of finding other employment. Other states' bar exams sounded hard, other cities' nightlife boring, other apartments too spacious.

"I can't leave New York," a ghost said to her, "because I wouldn't know what to do with all that room they give you."

"How can you live in a place without rats?" another worried. "Who the fuck eats your garbage out there?"

"Raccoons," Aretha said to blank face after blank face, remembering Wisconsin, a place none of them could probably find on a map because there were no law firms that paid New-York-large-law-firm salaries there.

But putting on the stiff upper lip necessary to survive conversations about leaving New York wasn't the same thing as actually packing what remained of her stuff after she'd moved in with them, assuming it wasn't covered in dust from the roof collapse. Oh, right, the roof collapse. She took another look up at the house as the argument in front of her shifted between whether, in Brittany's opinion, the whole disaster happened because no one other than her was willing to sweep the floors, or whether James was right that this was a sign they had enemies, right there on the block, looking to take them down, one ceiling at a time.

"Stop," Aretha said, holding her hand up like the road sign. "So we don't know why it happened?"

"No," the three of them said. Brittany's face shifted into defiance, Aaron's confusion, James's pure anger.

"Then the answer is to file an insurance claim and find somewhere else to live until we can get it fixed," she said, startled that she'd said "we."

"It's a big bunker," Brittany said.

"Really . . . ," Aretha said.

"I built it to comfortably house four, just in case."

"Huh," Aretha said, stuck on how to move this sudden turn to living in the bunker into an argument for getting a backup apartment.

"When it gets cold, we have space heaters and blankets. Since it's hot, we have a fan. There's a full-size bed already down there, platform and all, and an air mattress folded up in the corner. We have two years' worth of optimized soy protein stored in bins. And three years' worth of canned food. Last week, as if I knew this might happen, I brought down a hot plate in case we feel like doing any cooking. Oh, and everyone can have a gun."

Sweet, a gun, Aretha thought. Life is just one big party with you fuckers and at the end of the night everyone gets a goody bag with a gun in it.

"I'll guard the backyard," James said.

"There's nothin' to guard," Aaron said. "Unless you mean the roaster, which we probably can't use."

"Why not?" Brittany said. "It's not like it's on that side of the house."

"There's no dust on it?"

"No. I took a walk around the unaffected sections of the house to check, and no, it doesn't look like it was touched."

"Phew. So we don't have to shut down the business."

"No, we don't."

Aretha started to roll her eyes at their devotion to their survivalist coffee dream, but stopped herself just in time when she remembered it had kept a roof over her head for months. If anything, it seemed like the business was growing. When he wasn't taking sixteen-hour-long vacations with her, Aaron spent more time roasting and packing beans in the roasting room than ever.

"So we're going to do it," Brittany said.

"Do what?" Aretha said.

"Live in the bunker together until the house gets fixed."

"Right."

Aaron gave Brittany a completely unnecessary high-five. Aretha's feet felt glued to the grass. Maybe she could sleep in the hammock instead? There had to be some way to survive living in the backyard without ever going into a bunker. If it rained over her hammock home she could tie her two raincoats together like a curtain. Anything to avoid being trapped underground in a small room with three other people, one of whom seemed ready to kill.

She thought about her alternate plan a minute too long. Summer rainstorms sometimes dripped like a broken sprinkler and sometimes almost worked their way up into monsoons. If she slept outside, every fourth night she'd wake up as a human kiddie pool. And the fucking bugs. The roaches everyone called water bugs, like that name made them exotic beachside vacationers instead of reddish-brown pieces of shit with an undying need to eat your cereal. The mosquitoes that bit holes in her legs and arms like they were trying to tunnel their way through from one side of her limbs to the other and flew into her ears to wake her up at night with the low buzzing of drones.

"Where would we shower?" Aretha asked.

"We'd sneak back inside to the first-floor bathroom, which has nothing to do with the broken-down part of the house," Brittany said.

"OK," Aretha said, because anything else would sound too skeptical. And she was probably the only one of them worried that the rest of the house might fall in on her like a row of dominoes while she scrubbed an armpit. How bad could sleeping in a bunker be?

The thing about insomnia, she discovered that night, was that it gave its sufferers so much extra time to think about how creepy bunkers are. Brittany closed the metal door that led into the metal square that she called the room. Aretha shut her eyes and tried to give the bunker trendy architectural vibes. Here we are, living in a minimalist metal masterpiece, where everything this household needs is contained in just one room. Aretha tried to hug Aaron, thinking that even though they'd spent seven hours arguing that day she'd sleep better if she touched him, but he rolled away. So she focused on the rain that tapped on the Astroturf from above, the echo of everyone's breathing, which clanked against the metal walls, and a dripping noise that she hoped wasn't water leaking into the bunker. She looked at the constellation of turned-off flashlights Brittany attached to a metal coatrack. "We have light," Brittany had said after climbing down the ladder that led to the bunker floor, flicking on eight separate flashlight switches and then turning them off. "And a few years' worth of batteries," she said, pointing to a duffel bag at the base of the flashlight tree.

And maybe four hundred square feet, Aretha mentally grumbled. Enough for the bed Brittany mentioned, the air mattress she and Aaron would sleep on, and food and supplies to help them get through a bombing, or a ground war, or a nuclear attack, or the epic tragedy of not living inside their house. Before Brittany turned out the light Aretha memorized what lay on her side of the bed: a water purifier, a hand grinder, beans with their signature armed coffee drinker running across the front of the bag, a French press, a flashlight, and her gun. Brittany had given her a Glock, but she sure as hell was never going to use it.

Everyone's sleeping sounds clanked around the room and gave it that lovely stuck-in-an-elevator feeling. Aretha turned over. She turned over again, slowly, careful not to wake Aaron. She listened to the dripping again. She grabbed one of her flashlights and walked around, trying to find the leak. She saw nothing, and returned to bed. She grabbed her phone, ready for a hit of news since she hated pretending she might sleep when she knew she was just going to kill time for an hour.

But the news reminded her of all the ways in which she'd failed. She slept down in a bunker that might have a hidden hole in its side because she'd forgotten to become a member of one of the stylish couples renovating million-dollar Brooklyn apartments in a way that highlighted the six expensive items they owned, or the twenty-year-old

who'd founded a magazine, or even Mum, grinning at her from a profile that called her a new young legal hotshot for winning the Sandy
case with Aretha's brief. Yet the other side of the news reminded her
of how far she could still fall: going bankrupt from cancer, or sizzling
to death on a sidewalk in the middle of the imminent hundred-degree
January days that climate change promised to give everyone, or every
Brooklynite's dream of getting stressed enough to pass out from high
blood pressure on the floor of the Atlantic Terminal Target. And her
phone's light had the same unwanted electrifying effect as all the low-
level snoring going on around her, which made them twin enemies in
her quest to get bored enough to go back to sleep.

But she had to hit boredom again. She thought of the contents of
the bunker, determined to focus on the most boring thing in it. Not
the guns. Nope to the coffee, which reminded her of the hyper section
of the day right after she'd had some when she thought she might be
able to arm-wrestle a bear. Canned food had a promising dullness, as
did water purification tablets, especially when she imagined Brittany
taking ten minutes to give a speech about them that amounted to
telling her to put one of them in a gallon of water. But she shocked
herself by being most bored with *The Thinking Woman's Guide to Self-
Defense*. She remembered cracking it open for the first time and patiently waiting for it to tell her something useful instead of sounding
like the speech her dad gave her when she was about to go off to college, since the ways women should deal with all the things to be afraid
of in the world had seemed pretty clear to her for a while now. Her
mom had gone for warm platitudes about studying hard and making
friends. But her dad had used his last minutes before dropping her off
at her college dorm to remind her of the dangers of the world.

"Avoid dark places," the book said.

"Like alleys," her dad said, while Aretha wondered if the alleys at her Wisconsin college were between the lake and the beer halls before she remembered that the alleys he meant were located in Chicago, in the 1970s, outside the pool halls where he swore badass him had almost gotten into fights.

"Don't go home with shady people," the book said.

"Like those guys who only want one thing," her dad said.

"OK," Aretha had said in the car, "I'll be sure to only hang out with the guys who want two things."

"This isn't funny," he said.

"Right," she said.

"If you ever get into a fight," the book said.

"Running away is your best defense," her dad said.

That's right. The book and her dad had both kicked out one useful rule. She looked around the bunker. In the dark, all the sleeping people in it looked like a fight. She pictured herself running away from the person she'd become by living with them, in one of the outfits she'd bought to run in. Up and out of their neighborhood into Fort Greene, swinging a right to wind up in Bed-Stuy and a left to end up in Williamsburg, by the water, on the dock of a ferry that could take her to a train, where she could find another train, and then after that a bus. She watched the traveling version of herself take steps, buy tickets, propel herself to safety, and, right after getting on the bus, fall asleep.

In the morning she climbed the ladder, opened the bunker door, and let herself into the backyard, which looked perfect because clouds were light, and light was something they didn't have underground. She remembered this from years spent in Wisconsin basements: cold, damp little holes during the eight months of winter, and lightless boxes perfect for developing claustrophobia during the summer. She walked into the house to make herself breakfast, and it was almost a normal morning, but for the new skylight above the top flight of stairs. She couldn't resist the overwhelming urge to go look at the damage, and so she climbed up to the second-floor landing and halfway up to the third, leaving herself far enough away to judge the new roof hole from the inside.

Up close, the hole was almost beautiful, in its way. The cloudy sky slung a cone of light onto the floor, giving the third floor a backyard-like airiness. The plaster and wood lay in piles Aretha associated with the pictures of archaeological digs she'd seen, like whatever had collapsed the ceiling really meant to unearth evidence of a new civilization. She reluctantly concluded that her parents probably couldn't have stapled what was left of the roof into working order. The only unsettling thing about the collapse was the loud, busy sound coming from the broken zone, like if bees had taken a lot of drugs and started a twelve-hour shift of dancing to the Chemical Brothers between the walls. Aretha took another look at the floor, where among the dust and the broken sections of wall lay hundreds of dead bugs. Right side up and upside down with their bug feet pointing uselessly into the air. She marched back down the stairs, into the backyard, and back down to the bunker, where Brittany stood in the grass.

"How do you feel about termites?" Aretha said.

She remembered, if not termites themselves, the threat of them from growing up in a place where nature attacked. Deer ran through glass doors. Dead deer rushed into your parents' already dead heads. Earwigs with their many crawling insect feet ambled into your sinks. Thunderstorms lost their shit above you. If she wasn't remembering termites from some friend's infestation, she was remembering the termite extermination commercials she'd seen back in the day, with their too-bright, too-neon '90s lighting and the same unmistakable noise she'd heard upstairs, like bugs had found the highest keys on the world's tiniest piano and laid themselves down on them, in shifts, belly and all, composing the most destructive symphony a house could hear.

"Why do you ask?" Brittany said.

Aretha led her upstairs.

The first three exterminators they called went with dismay. "I don't know that we can get all of these out of here," the first one said. "They might have already eaten the living shit . . ." the second one started, looked at Aretha, paused, and started again, with a "sorry, ma'am," tacked on for no reason, since Aretha was in no way old enough to be a ma'am ". . . out of your walls."

"Look, y'all, we're just going to put dish soap down the walls ourselves, mixed with water," James said. "That kills everything."

"The inside of our walls isn't a fuckin' dinner plate," Aaron said.

Aretha jumped back a little. Aaron never swore. And he hadn't told her a coffee story in two days. He'd spent all that time doing the same shit he told James not to do: sitting in a corner of the yard in James's tent, drinking coffee, reading *The Thinking Man's Guide to Self-Defense*, and letting a gun sit on his left, just in case. The air smelled like booze, so she sniffed, but either James had multiplied or forever-sober Aaron had taken up drinking again. He wouldn't. He'd been too drunk to escape that hurricane. He had two religions: coffee and never getting drunkenly caught in a hurricane again. In an hour she would search the tent during one of his bathroom runs and find a half-empty bottle of tequila. When she found the tequila her mind blacked out. This was the guy she used to think was killing off all the darkness in her life? She would say that she and Aaron were over, but truly, Aaron seemed so much more over than that.

The four of them stood in the backyard under a drizzle light enough to host an outside argument. Aretha tilted her head up towards the roof hole, which she did automatically now, like looking for the stars on a drive out in the countryside.

"I called a third one," Brittany said. "Rule of threes. The third exterminator always pays off."

The third exterminator showed up, short and round and darker in his Blackness than Aretha and Brittany, who were plenty dark themselves. Aretha flashed back to her dad, regally dark and possessing an all-knowing face until the end. The exterminator had a shaved head and a '70s porn star mustache. He marched right on up the stairs to look at the space that had perplexed the first two exterminators with his all-knowing eye. Aretha felt better immediately upon seeing him, but since she, as a person who was leaving the house forever soon, didn't have to care if they got rid of the termites or not, she sat back to watch the rest of them react to whatever he said.

"We'd have to clean your house right on out," the exterminator said, stepping back from the top step before the third-floor landing to stand with the rest of them on the stairs. He rolled his sleeves up for what had to be dramatic effect, and crossed his arms, like he was ready to go to work on their house that second. Brittany looked frustrated, and Aaron skeptical, and James half-asleep.

"How?" Aaron said.

"Dig up a section of the dirt close to your foundation and put down a liquid barrier. Then I'd have to come upstairs and put some foam in the walls to kill the mites that are already living inside all the way up here. Let them work for a little bit, then I can come back and see how they're doing. Thing is, and you probably already know this, you're going to need a wall guy."

"I just figured I could nail up some boards and . . . ," Aaron said.

"You like having a house, right?"

"I love it."

"Then you need a wall guy to figure out how much of your walls the termites ate."

Aaron looked at Brittany. Brittany looked at Aaron. James stared at nothing. Aaron's look had a concession in it. Brittany put on the look that meant she was running numbers in her head and getting horrified at them.

"How much do you cost?" she said to the exterminator.

"Let me look around downstairs and take one more peek up here, and I'll get back to you with an estimate."

The exterminator sent an estimate. They called a wall guy, who sent an estimate and told them to get a ceiling guy, who also sent an estimate. From what Aretha could tell, the word *estimate* was only hurled around every twenty seconds in the fights Aaron and Brittany had in the first-floor bathroom, since the bedroom floor was off limits thanks to crumbling walls, and the roasting room didn't have a lock on its door, and they needed privacy to scream about money. Yuck, money. Because Aaron never got around to charging her rent, she'd always had the dream of walking out of the house with a decent pile of money to cushion her descent into the next part of her life. But just because she was done with Aaron didn't mean she had to write off this part of her life as a loss. Before she went to bed on what would have been the day she got back from vacation she waited for the other three of them to go to sleep, and then she quietly lifted all the contacts off James's phone and sent the texts that would get her the rest of her cash and revenge.

After she completed her last day of work, she would win. But for now she had to kick off the longest day of the year by knocking on the door of the first-floor bathroom to hustle Aaron and Brittany out, so they could migrate elsewhere to be angry and make weird sucking noises that she didn't understand and leave her room to shower and dress for her last day at work. It took them a couple minutes, but they finally left, looking sheepish, with their hair and clothes rumpled, like they'd . . . oh, fucking wow. Fuck them. Whatever. For the first time since she'd lived by herself, she sang in the shower, "Always on Time," by Ja Rule and Ashanti, a song she hadn't really given a shit about when she first heard it back in college, on the road trips she and Nia took to Chicago. His voice was too scratchy, she told Nia, and hers too generic. Aretha would whip out her handy-dandy history of decidedly ungeneric Black female singers.

"Diana Ross! Patti LaBelle! Mariah Carey! Whitney Houston! Aretha Franklin, who's also got the right first name!" she'd say, with her feet tucked up directly under the heating vent for their drive past frozen cornfields. Nia, instead of answering her directly, would turn up the car volume and start singing along. Aretha put on a skirt and jacket and pointy-toed flats, which she felt helped her carry on a pointed lifestyle: direct, sharp, winning. And then she remembered her plan, took the shoes off, and crept upstairs to take a couple of pictures of what was still up there in Brittany's room.

She left the house, taking one look back at it to memorize what it looked like on the morning of the last day she would ever live there. She heard Aaron and Brittany arguing in the bathroom again.

"It's cheaper for me to spray the termites away," Brittany said.

"We need a professional. You don't know nothin' about houses," Aaron said.

"I know a lot about houses. I even built one in the backyard."

"It has a leak."

So Aretha hadn't imagined it. She took a few seconds to think of all their underground stuff getting soaked, with pleasure.

"There's an emergency here, and I'm prepar—"

Aretha walked away to avoid hearing Brittany say the end of that fucking word. Through a slat in the fence that blocked their yard from the street, she saw James, with his back up against a tree that didn't quite stop him from swaying. He was leaning on what looked like a black stick from where she stood and she desperately hoped wasn't a gun, because he should really give it up with that bringing-guns-outside shit before somebody saw him, for his sake. Now that he lived down on the ground, he didn't have to worry about his mortal enemy who lived on the roof next door, who he insisted still had a staring problem.

She turned south, to walk up the mild Vanderbilt hill towards the subway. She took her last train ride to Rockefeller Center. "It's the longest day of the year," blasted the radio the nearest halal guy to her office kept turned on at his feet, informing everyone within earshot that the sun wouldn't set until almost nine p.m.

Aretha took off her jacket and slipped it over her arm for the trip to her office on the last Tuesday she would ever enter it. It was eighty-two degrees out and destined to reach ninety, a temperature that made walking outside feel just as pleasant as lowering yourself into a bowl of soup. Too hot for everything she'd put on. Not that she had any idea what to wear to work anymore. Most guidelines on what to wear to work were based on the idea that you went to your job to maximize your achievements and dream of promotion, not drag yourself in every day because they kept paying your failed ass. Her solution to this: old suits. A navy suit an inch away from coming unglued at the shoulder. Tights with mild pulls. Dinged-up shoes she hadn't gotten around to replacing yet. A wardrobe that quietly said, "I don't give a shit about being here because you told me it wouldn't last."

The days when she went to lunch with Mum or talked to the

juniors were long past, and they'd whittled down her workload, making it obvious she was doomed. So she sat in her office, doing her last round of busywork like a robot, taking plenty of breaks to memorize her view. She pressed her fingers against the double-paneled window glass, reinforced for building stability and, she imagined, suicides. You never knew who might be tempted to solve their problems by hurling themselves through fifty-eight stories' worth of air.

In a way she was dying too. An office death. The ending of a term of employment and the disappearing from this building had that finality to it. They would never talk about her after she was gone, because that would only distract them from the hard everyday work of winning, but her DNA would hang out for a while, in arguments from briefs and her contact with the office doorknobs and coffee makers and printers, a ghostly sign that she'd once tried to work herself to the bone here. Offices everywhere were lightly filled with the office dead, the people who quit or got fired or hung out in performance limbo until it occurred to them to slip out and not go back and not tell anyone. She took a two-hour lunch to ponder office death over ramen, convinced that drinking hot liquids on hot days kept a person cooler, and burned out with soy protein, which she'd eaten three meals a day for months other than that one sausage biscuit, and as of tomorrow would never eat again.

Four o'clock arrived. If she was leaving under more favorable circumstances this would be the hour when someone would knock on her door. The other members of the litigation department and lawyers from other sections of the office who liked her would drift down to their favorite of the nondescript happy hour bars for expensive wine and conversation that revolved around sports teams who won and people who'd won something instead of cases they'd won in between toasts to Aretha and her new job, where she'd no doubt go on to find a slightly different but equally socially acceptable way to win. Behind her closed door she heard the rustling noises of other lawyers adjusting themselves in their chairs and the modulated tones of people trying to adjust client expectations for cases that weren't moving as swiftly to victory as anticipated. She closed her eyes and took it in like a breath, a final inhale and exhale of office noise that left her calm, like a paper clip.

She took one last look around her office and left everything there but the suit jacket she kept on the back of her chair, since the partners had told her to always keep one there in case they were suddenly called into court. She left her office and went outside to be fried, which always ruled. The feeling of real honest-to-god hot weather on her skin instead of mummifying office chill. The subway was almost as cold as the office she hated. She and her icebox of a train car hustled to compensate for that morning's crawl. She said a silent goodbye to her commute. See ya, Rock Center. Adios, Koreatown. Catch you later, Downtown. Her train car took flight over the Manhattan Bridge, where she eyed the runners hungrily, ready to run alongside them. But her run would have to wait.

She turned onto Vanderbilt. There was a police car parked up the street, more or less in front of the house, but not right there, obviously, because none of them would call the cops, right? But she kept walking up the street, and the police car didn't move. From a few buildings away she spotted two cops dragging a handcuffed James into the back and a third cop carrying the rifle she'd seen him hold that morning when she went off to work. She stopped, out of a long-standing Black girl habit of not wanting to get too close to the cops, and watched them drive off with him, their red taillights ambling up the street, a little weirded out, since the cops taking James made her plan easier, unless, of course, the cops had searched the house well enough to sink her plan.

When she got to the house, she went down to the bunker and grabbed a couple of damp things from her side of the bed to put in her go-bag, including the Glock, which was miraculously still there. It was her Glock, and she was finally going to use it. When she came back up, she saw Brittany, shaken, sitting in the grass with her head pressed down to her knees, and Aaron, up and pacing, making hand gestures to no one in particular. The adrenaline from watching the cops take James away bled into the adrenaline from the dread of whatever it was that they were going to have to tell her.

"They think he shot somebody," Brittany said.

"Look, maybe he didn't," Aaron said. "Maybe he just went up there and was shootin' across people's roofs and didn't actually hit anythin'."

"Are you stupid? He hit someone. There was a fucking ambulance," Brittany said.

Aaron grabbed Brittany's hand. Oh, so they're openly grabbing hands now? Aretha thought, before reminding herself that she was leaving soon.

"He hated this guy on one of the other roofs," Aretha said. "Shit."

"Shit is right," Brittany said.

"You . . . swear?"

"I'm a person, Aretha. A set of bones and blood and brains who's feeling pretty good that she has a bunker to hide out in when cops show up but who wants to get rid of some stuff she's been keeping around before the cops inevitably come back tonight or tomorrow."

How had the cops not found all her guns, all over her bedroom floor? Didn't cops fucking do anything? Or did they spend all their time eating donuts, not solving rapes, and accidentally forgetting to look for more guns in a house where they'd already found one?

"Well, maybe you should go do that, like right now," Aretha said.

"What the hell do you mean?" Brittany said.

She stood up.

Aaron gave Aretha a look, but she was beyond his looks.

She pulled her Glock out of her suit pocket and held it up to them.

Hello to the sunlight slanting across the backyard, highlighting its summer-green grass and its fake green Astroturf bunker door and Aaron's and Brittany's black-and-pink mouths, open like fish gasping for air.

"You're not up to this, Aretha," Brittany said. "You don't even like guns."

"Go in the house, pack up all your guns into the duffel bags in your closet, and give me the keys to the backup car."

She waited for Brittany to pull out her own gun, but she didn't. Whatever happened to being prepared?

Aaron got up and took a step towards her. She pointed her gun at him.

"You, too. You help her."

He wasn't armed either? What the fuck were all the guns for, then?

Aaron and Brittany looked at each other.

"You're getting rid of them anyway," Aretha said. "You can give them to me. I'm solving a problem for you."

Aaron looked squarely at Aretha.

Their entire relationship went through her head in frames. Their first meeting at the bar, and the warmth that had settled over her when he mentioned his grandma. All the nights they'd sat up talking after he came back from coffee runs. Her head on his lap on so many park benches, and the house's living room, and their bed. Them drinking nonalcoholic mulled wine. Next time she mulled something it would have booze in it. His smell, warm and woodsy, which made him a pine tree of a man. That half-drunk bottle of tequila she'd found in his tent. Nia was right. He wasn't worth it. And fuck memories, Aretha said to herself. Fuck his hurricane. Fuck the antlers. Fuck being haunted by the past.

"Aretha," Aaron said.

"Let's go," Aretha said.

She marched them both into the house and upstairs, where Brittany unlocked all her safes and put all the guns in them in the duffel bags as Aretha had asked them to.

"This is all you want?" Aaron said, after they'd loaded the guns and Aretha's clothes into their backup car.

"Yeah."

"Aren't you worried about doing something illegal?" Brittany said.

"What are you going to do," Aretha said. "Call the cops?"

Brittany just looked at her, open-mouthed.

Aaron threw her the car keys.

"Goodbye, Aretha," he said.

Aretha said nothing.

She walked to the car, dumped the last duffel bags on the floor, pulled up James's contact list, and drove off to her first destination, a house in Hicksville that wanted ten of the rifles. After that, Aretha drove herself to Mineola, to Bayside, to Throggs Neck, to Kew Gardens, to Flushing, to Corona, to Forest Hills, to Washington Heights, to the Lower East Side, to Chinatown, to Cobble Hill, to Crown Heights, to Flatbush, to Canarsie, to Bensonhurst. Down to Bay Ridge. Across the Verrazzano to Staten Island, watching the water glitter in the dark at sixty miles an hour.

She counted her hundreds. She stashed them in the first duffel bag she emptied. She watched them grow, like the tomato plants that Tonya would harvest in a month. Aretha had promised Tonya that she'd be there, handing out some of the tomatoes and feeling like a part of something that wasn't running guns around for crazed loners. And being more than what she did for money. But she still wanted to enjoy the rush of her last trip to make money off guns, even if she spent a hair of it mourning her lost chance to knock James out. Her right hand wistfully mourned her plan to punch his drunken ass into unconsciousness. Asbury Park. South Orange. Fort Lee. Nyack. Peekskill. Danbury. She finished her northern loop and drove back down, amazed and horrified that so many people wanted to buy guns on short notice and ready to strike them from her mind once she was down to the last gun, her Glock. Earlier she'd spent a good fifteen minutes with her finger poised over her phone, waiting to type the sentence that would officially put it up for sale, but instead she did the entire trip back from Connecticut with it in the glove box, just in case Aaron and Brittany ever came after her for stealing their car. She was not like them, and she would never, ever be like them, but if they ever came up on her, she didn't intend to lose. She texted Nia while she waited to enter the Holland Tunnel.

"Things went really wrong over here, and I'm sorry I was such a shitty friend. Can I stay at your place?"

"Of course, girl," Nia texted back.

Aretha pumped her fist.

She drove east, towards Nia's place, on the opposite side of the park, in the beating Black heart of Prospect Lefferts Gardens. She turned off Flatbush and parked at the end of Nia's block. She found Nia sitting on her porch, waving hello. Aretha sat down next to her, gestured for her vape, took an enormous hit, and exhaled it into the dark.

# ACKNOWLEDGMENTS

Thank you, Mensah Demary, for editing this book and a slew of my other published writing with verve, discernment, and panache since 2015. Thank you, Ellen Levine and Martha Wydysh, agents extraordinaire, for your insight, tenacity, and support. A hearty thanks to Megan Fishmann, Selihah White, Rachel Fershleiser, Cecilia Flores, tracy danes, Nicole Caputo, Wah-Ming Chang, John McGhee, and Chandra Wohleber for understanding this book, helping me put it into the world in its best possible form, and letting people know it exists.

A shout-out to some friends, fellow writers, editors, and people who gave me a chance: Shveta Kulkarni, Hani Omar Khalil, Ryan Carter, Doug Brooks, Rohit Sachdev, Darpun Sachdev, Nona Mei, Bill Rodriguez, Anna Hezel, Gabriella Paiella, Christian Hoard, Penina Roth, Michelle Dean, Gary Shteyngart, Maris Kreizman, Brook Stephenson, Benjamin Dreyer, Percival Everett, Ester Bloom, Lauren Szurgot, Sylvie Rabineau, Natalia Williams, Natalie Guerrero, Morgan Jerkins, Trevor Noah, Zhubin Parang, Roy Wood Jr., Samantha Irby, Kelly Link, Jade Chang, Deesha Philyaw, Tammie Teclemariam, Jenée Desmond-Harris, Jennifer Parker, Mateo Askaripour, Jin Auh, Syreeta McFadden, Rob Spillman, Nona Willis Aronowitz, Camille Bromley, Rahawa Haile, Danielle Henderson, Kat Stoeffel, Colin Dickey, Cari

Luna, Lydia Kiesling, Jennifer Acker, David Granger, Tyler Cabot, Alex Chee, Jake Swearingen, Julie Beck, Michaelangelo Matos, Harry Siegel, Andy Hunter, Jill Mapes, Yuka Igarashi, Sandy Allen, Ryu Spaeth, Mari Uyehara, J. Robert Lennon, Nate and Nico.

Other shout-outs: To the gun and food stockpilers of my youth. To all the Matador Records employees who didn't kick me off your building's front steps, where this book was written, unless it was raining.

**KASHANA CAULEY** is a former Midtown anti-trust lawyer and Brooklyn resident. She is a writer for the Fox comedy *The Great North*, a former contributing opinion writer for *The New York Times*, and a former contributor for *GQ*. She has written for *The Daily Show* with Trevor Noah and *Pod Save America* on HBO, as well as for *The Atlantic*, *The New Yorker*, *Pitchfork*, and *Rolling Stone*, and has published fiction in *Esquire*, *Slate*, *Tin House*, and *The Chronicles of Now*. Cauley now lives in Los Angeles.